Sink Rate

Sam Deland Crime Novel Book One

Mike Fuller

Credits
Cover Artist: Designs by Cherith Vaughn
Editor: Kitty Carlisle

Printed in the United States of America

Dedication

To Vergie Fuller Walker, my Aunt Vergie. She taught me what I needed to know about beagles and rabbit hunting, how to sing harmony, and table manners.

36 Hours Before...

It must be thunder and she opened her eyes to the near darkness for a full minute before closing them again. It always frightened her, even now. She waited for a flash of lightning, but it did not come. The dimly lit bedroom was familiar to her after so many years, but the house was empty, except for her. Empty of fun and sadness, of love and success and failure. The rumble came to her ears again, but she did not trust them anymore. The hearing aid was on the dresser and she would have to get out into the chilly air to find it. It was raining and cold outside, but she could only hear it when the wind blew hard against the window. The heavy comforter held her in, keeping her warm and the thunder never came again. Only the muted sounds of the ancient clock in the hallway to her aging ears and the rain. A quiet, empty house. She turned the other way and thought of what she would wear to church tomorrow. *Maybe the green one or the gray with the lace collar...*

Monday

That sound, it just seems to go right to the center of his insides. He couldn't think of anything else like it. Molly ripped over the ledge and tumbled head first into the stubble of the cornfield, all legs and white tipped tail. Her song just rippling out of her gullet as hard as she could push it; rabbit in her nose and joy, if a beagle can have that emotion, mixed in with instincts and excitement and pure energy. Like a twelve pound freight train on a downgrade with no brakes and Casey at the throttle. Her yelp helped him track her left and back up the rise into the woodlot and briars above the field. She had that rabbit now, and once she got her nose that close, well. Sam knew he better pick his spot and hold tight. She would work out that bunny and turn it back to Sam for the shot sooner than later. Sam eased into the edge of the tree line and picked a big maple to lean against and listen to Molly sing. She hollered and yodeled and talked up a storm and if that rabbit had any chance to hole, it better drop now or sprout claws and tree climb.

November can be one of those odd months of the year in this part of America. Miserable, wet and cold for days at a time and then Canada sends down enough moving air to push out the moisture, clear the clouds and, when the sun comes out, wow! The air gets so clean and crisp you wish you could bottle it and save it for next July. Sam kept a few "Personal Days" to use, choosing his time with Molly in the woods and being rewarded today with a wondrous display of God's best. It was breezy but, in the windbreak of the big maple, warm enough for Sam to feel the sweat down his back from chasing his young beagle up and down the ridges after cotton tails. Sam thought that with no amount of money could a man buy this combination of bright sun, clear sky, open space and the ... *Lord, here she comes.* Sam felt the rabbit even before he could see it. Molly was no more than sixty yards out and coming right at him.

Sam's listening skills were probably at their best now. Years of straining, trying to tell if the dog was going left or right, out or in. Trial and error and several dogs taught him how to put together the land and the two animals running over it like a computer soaks up electrons to figure how and what to add. Sam was seldom wrong and today was no exception. She was nearly roaring a steady stream of raw dog noise now, like only beagles can. Her nose had to be just busting with scent and her little legs pushing her on as fast as her nose would let her without losing the track. That tail pounding back and forth marking her path with its pure white tip. Sam knew he would see the rabbit first, but always watched for Molly just in case she was too close. He tensed and the world around closed in tighter, more focused now on just that piece of woods in front of him. He no longer took notice of the sky or the birds or anything else. Molly's song was all he could really hear and he braced for the shot.

There, there it was. A big one, too; fat from autumn and feeding on plenty to survive the winter. It stopped as if it had not a care, not a worry. It looked back at the noise that dog was making. The rabbit turned around to face forward after a moment and shook itself. It even bent down and licked its front paw. The silly critter was sitting there not but a few yards in front of the noisiest thing in those woods bent on catching it and doing whatever dogs do naturally to rabbits, given the chance, and that rabbit was cleaning itself. Sam lost his concentration and nearly laughed out loud. He couldn't believe it. *Why isn't that bunny running for the hills? Stupid rabbit.*

Well, he figured now was the time. Molly would be on top of them in seconds anyway and the rabbit isn't going to sit there much longer. Sam set up for the shot, sight picture, breath control, trigger squeeze, lessons learned from generations before him and from years of his profession. He acquired his target, aimed, exhaled half a lung full of breath and squeezed. Click clack! The rabbit froze and looked right at him. But it didn't sit long. Molly was right there only steps away. The rabbit streaked out of the tree line and ran, white cotton bouncing high and disappeared ninety degrees to the right back into the woods.

Sam laughed; he couldn't believe it. He knew that if rabbits could speak, that rabbit would have said, "Oh, shit!", looking up to see Sam not ten feet from it pointing some long nosed contraption and that yelping dog only steps away. Molly exploded out of the brush and ran right into Sam. He picked her up and her legs kept running and she yowled the most miserable sounding noise, as if to say, "What the heck are you doing, let me at that rabbit!" she kept barking and twisted herself sideways trying to get her feet back on the ground.

Sam spun her around and walked a few steps out into the corn, talking to her real easy like, "It's okay, baby girl. You did just fine. That old rabbit didn't have a chance with my little Molly girl," she yipped and panted and slowly started to settle down, "We got him good. He sat still and I got a real nice shot of him. One of these days we'll bring the old twelve gauge out and take one for dinner."

Sam and Molly eased down the slope toward the narrow dirt road that cut through this part of the forest where a few fields still took the plow and produced at least some corn for the farmer who leased the land from the state. As Molly quieted down, Sam slipped a short leash onto the ring of her collar and let her walk out the muscles in her legs. Molly seemed to forget about the last rabbit and pulled on the leash trying to sniff every inch of ground to find the next strike. Sam kept talking to her as if she understood every word he said. He'd changed a lot over the past few years. He still loved the woods and getting out with Molly to run a bunny was just about as much fun as any good Pennsylvania country boy turned forty some could have, that was still legal. He checked the lens cover on his worn and scarred Pentax and thought about the look on that rabbit when he snapped the shutter. He hoped he hadn't jiggled the camera too much trying to hold back his laugh, but he knew he had plenty of light and with 400 speed film, a little movement didn't matter too much anyway.

He used to hunt with his grandfather's Model 12 for rabbits and birds, but time has a way of making a lot of changes in people. Nowadays, Sam shot more game, but rarely took it home. His pictures tell the story now. Deer caught mid step and squirrels head to tail chasing one another around an old pine like a furry gray rope. Sam discovered hunting season lasted all year and even on Sundays when he hunted with a camera. He found what he really wanted was to just be there. Out, out and trying to be part of the field, part of the woods, to see and hear and smell and sense. He didn't have any fancy equipment, just a manual 35mm and a 200mm zoom lens and he loved it. He didn't really care. He took pictures when he could, but often forgot he even had the camera with him. He would sit and watch turkeys yak with each other off at the edge of a clearing, but not lift the camera to his eye for fear of them seeing him move. He just wanted to look at them for as long as he could. Just as good anyway. A photograph could come another day. The picture in his head would last forever.

Sam still took his Remington 30.06 out on the first day of buck season every year, but it had been six years since he'd even taken a shot at a buck. He passed up a few and a couple of years he didn't have much time to hunt, with work and all. *And all, yeah, and all.*

Molly spun around in tight circles at the edge of the parking area as they came to Sam's truck. She squatted to pee and then dug at the dirt. Dogs will be dogs. Sam sat on the tail of his Nissan and peeled off bits of a ham sandwich to flip to Molly. She danced and walked on her hind legs begging for every scrap. She was just about the happiest dog alive. Good hunting, lots of room to run, and this big jerk feeding her his breakfast. Yowee! Sam was just picturing that old beer commercial "It don't get any...," when he jumped straight up an inch off the back of that Pathfinder. He felt stupid when he realized that what felt like a rip roaring rumbling gas bubble in his left side was really his phone, set on vibrate so it wouldn't chirp while he was at his fun with Molly, going off.

"Damn," he snorted, "Who the hell is this callin' me on the best day in a week, and my day off?" Molly had no idea why Sam was ignoring her and fiddling with his belt, but watch out, he put down the sandwich and turned his head. Zap, she was up on that truck in a flash and in two gulps had ham, bread and spicy mustard down and swallowed.

"Molly!" Sam shouted, "You little witch!" Sam soon forgot his irritation with Molly when he saw the number appear on the phone. He knew that when the barrack's inside line number came up, either he was in deep horse crap for some disregard of the time honored, well documented, convoluted, and nearly religious, rules and regulations of the Pennsylvania State Police. Or, some citizen had met with an event involving loss or pain and suffering and Sam had been chosen, by the officers appointed over him, to resolve it for the good of all and the Commonwealth.

"Corporal Deland," Sam answered.

"You out and about?" Trooper Walter Stanislaus "Ozzie" Ozliewski was undoubtedly standing in the squad room in shirt sleeves surrounded by a can of Pepsi, a box of Entenmann's chocolate doughnuts, and a copy of the latest Outdoor Life. It was 9:30 on a Monday morning and Ozzie had priorities. Number one was his morning caffeine and caloric intake followed by his 9:45 trip to the locker room head. That was, unless some unknowing individual unwisely interrupted the natural flow of Ozzie's day which, to their regret, set into play forces that even Mother Nature did not fool with. Ozzie stood 6' 3 1/2" and weighed every bit of 255 pounds. When Ozzie went into motion, you got out of the way and until 10:00 AM, no one messed with him. Except Sam that is, and every chance he had. Sam was a good sized man himself but two inches shorter and fifty pounds lighter. It didn't matter though, Ozzie would do anything for Sam; Sam was his friend. That meant a lot to Ozzie.

"Ozzie, what's up?" Sam asked.

"Yeah, got a bad one. Patrol took a call from over in Porter. Neighbor hadn't been able to get an answer at the back door of the house across the alley and called in. Adams, the new kid, took his time getting there, stopped to write a speeder on the way. Complainant was pissed..."

"Ozzie, just tell me for Christ's sake. I'm out at the game lands on the mountain runnin' Molly, I'm on a personal. It hasn't stopped raining for four days and I got a beauty today, sun's out and all. So tell me what's so damn important about some beef with a rookie trooper in patrol?" Sam sounded bored and just a little pissed.

"They're dead. Shot up real bad, blood and brains everywhere. Adams puked his guts on the step, called in screamin' like a twelve year old girl, says he didn't sign up for this shit..."

"Oz, who's dead? What the fuck are you talkin' about, man?" Ozzie had Sam's full attention now.

"Corp, the guy McFadden and his old lady, you know, over in Porter, the gun shop guy from Philly. He and his wife are dead, shot. Probably robbery, don't know yet. Been dead a day or so. I got Dickson, lights and siren, on his way over to diaper Adams and hold down the fort. This is bad, real bad, Sam. You better come in or head over there. 'Oh, Jesus' will be havin' a shit fit as soon as I can find him to tell him."

Ozzie knew what he was talking about. "Oh, Jesus" was Sergeant William T. Dawes, the station commander at Straus Valley and the single most nervous man on the face of the earth. "Oh, Jesus" got his nickname because no matter what happened "Oh, Jesus" was usually the first thing out of his mouth. "Hey Sarge, I'm going out to handle an accident on the interstate,"..."Oh, Jesus." "Hey, Sarge, I need a day off to go get school clothes for the kids,"... "Oh, Jesus." "Sergeant, call the captain at Bethlehem, right away,"... "Oh, Jesus!"

Sgt. Dawes meant well, he really did, he just couldn't handle the pressure. It only made it worse that his job, a sergeant in charge of a whole barracks, was about the most demanding for attention to detail in the whole state police. Even the colonel had tons of staff people to keep him out of trouble. But poor "Oh, Jesus" was alone with his misery. Sam, the corporal running the crime room, had no time for administrative bullshit. Brad Dickson was the patrol corporal, a truly nice guy who tried to avoid "Oh,

Jesus" at all times. Dickson had enough problems of his own ramrodding the patrol troopers, most of them fresh faced jocks recently out of the academy.

Sam didn't know where they got these kids now. Almost every one of them looked like a United States Marine Corps recruiting poster child. They preferred buzz cuts and talked endlessly about gyms and protein supplements. They really made "Oh, Jesus" nervous. Sam, too. A change in the retirement in recent years made it almost impossible to find a trooper with gray hair. They took seventy five percent of their top pay at twenty five years. When the courts finally made the governor agree, after a bitter battle, several hundred troopers went out and recruit classes had been churning out fresh meat at a steady pace since.

Sam thought a moment, "Where's Livingston and Bonner?"

"Monthly criminal investigations meeting in Bethlehem," Ozzie said. "I called the desk, should be hearing from them any minute. I'll send them over, too."

While he talked to Ozzie, he scooted Molly off the tailgate back onto the ground quite unceremoniously and then got her traveling bowl out of the back of the truck and poured her some fresh water. She lapped at it and managed to spread a good bit of it on the ground around her.

"Get crime scene up and out, we'll for sure want them to process. What about the lieutenant?" Sam hated to ask that one.

"Fuck him, the fat bastard, he should rot and die from VD," Ozzie rumbled. "Besides, Sam, don't you remember? He's on vacation in Disney World. Had to get his Mickey Mouse refresher bonus points." Ozzie had good cause to curse Lt. Harman. Harman tried several times to forcibly pry Ozzie from The Job. Ozzie was too smart and too lucky for a weasel like Harman. Ozzie liked to say he had more time on the "fucking john" than Harman had on the state police. Almost true, Harman was one of the "Whiz Kids" who studied every moment of the day, while everyone else did their work for them, and got promotions so quick the cleaners couldn't change the stripes fast enough. Harman ran the criminal investigations unit in the troop and effectively made life miserable for all the crime guys. Sam stayed one step ahead of him, but just barely. Harman's philosophy was that he was the only person fit to be on the state police, everyone else was subject to immediate and summary dismissal. Nothing anyone did satisfied him and he knew how to do anything and everything and was not shy about telling anyone within earshot. Harman was a pudgy, balding terrorist who had rarely, if ever, said the four magic words: "You are under arrest." And he was in charge. But not today. Sam knew the captain would stay out of the way and let Sam and Ozzie handle the case.

Sam told Ozzie, "Be sure Sgt. Dawes notifies the captain. If you can't find Dawes in the next half hour, call me and I'll call it in to her. I'm going to stop by the farm and drop Molly off and then head to Porter. Oh, and keep that stupid fuck of a coroner out of the way until crime scene is finished. That ham handed dick will screw it up given half the chance. Oz, get Brad on the radio and have him find a phone and call me when he gets there."

"10-4, Corp. I'll be *en route* as soon as I'm done here. Meet you there. Kiss Molly for me," Ozzie chuckled.

"Hey, by the way, can you drop off the rest of those PVC fittings for the loft bathroom? I'd like to get that finished up by the weekend," Sam just did hear Ozzie say something about ladies and toilet seats before Sam hit the end button on the cell phone and tossed it on the front seat. He turned back to the rear of the Pathfinder just as Molly was nose to the ground and circling for another track. Sam grabbed her up and put her in her dog box in the back and snapped shut the cage door. Molly seemed to know the game was up, dropped her head and looked up with just her big watery brown eyes. Man, was that a look. Melt candle wax and your heart.

"Sorry, baby, all done for today, gotta go get the bad guys," Sam jumped in the driver's seat and fired up the V-6. He took the .22 magnum High Standard out of his hip pocket, reached around and opened the gun safe mounted behind the driver's seat. While the engine warmed up, he took out his issue .45 state police Glock semi-auto and slipped it into his waistband. He picked up a spare magazine and put that in his left back pocket. His cuffs went over the back of his belt and he dropped the 4x4 into gear and moved down the dirt road as fast as he could without finding out how the truck handled in the ditch.

The state police don't have detectives like most police agencies. The troopers who do the follow up criminal investigations from the initial crime reports taken by the uniformed patrol officers are still referred to as trooper. They wear civilian clothes and work better hours, but remain a trooper, subject to return to the gray bag at any time it so pleases the bosses. The troopers who work crime try real hard to keep everyone happy, within reason. Shift work in uniform is a grind.

~ * ~

Trooper Calvin Livingston had just started to get a smile out of little Jennifer Santiago when the radio console in front of her came to life with what, to Calvin, sounded like a car wheel with no tire at sixty miles an hour on a gravel road. It continued on and Calvin was able to hear a very exited and broken voice screaming about help and bodies and dead. Now Calvin was a good cop, no, Calvin was a great cop, but Calvin was looking into the most beautiful brown eyes he'd seen this week and he was seeing something in those eyes that gave him hope for mankind. The world could go to heck; he had to concentrate on the matter at hand. He was working hard on Jennifer.

He'd briefly met her two weeks ago when he dropped off some evidence at the lab and knew when he came into headquarters for the monthly meeting of state and local officers to trade intelligence and crime reports, he would have time to work his magic on sweet little Jennifer. Calvin was a master at the move. He knew just how to do it. He tried to explain it once to his partner, but realized he couldn't. He just did it and it worked. Calvin got laid regular. He didn't brag, it wasn't in his nature. He just loved being around women, he took honest joy in it. Calvin also spent a lot of his paycheck at a special clothing store on the east side of Allentown. He liked nice clothes. He didn't have nice clothes when he was a kid. The owner of the clothing store had come down from New York City and brought his talent for cutting and fitting with him. Calvin discovered how to choose fabric and color for suits that made them look like suits that cost several times as much. Today he'd chosen a brown, single breasted and his Bogart trench coat. His shirt was starched and his tie was silk and brilliant with just the right matching tones and flashes of color. Not every man can carry off wearing a brown suit. Calvin could.

He was looking and feeling like a million bucks and he was losing the radio operator. He could see her eyes trying to look at the speaker, blaring a stream of urgent trooper stuff instead of into Calvin's. Always look into their eyes. He leaned over, cocked his head toward the radio panel and gently whispered to her, "It's okay, let's just see what this fella' is so excited about," she smiled and sighed. He could see her chest rise and fall. He had her.

"Straus Valley 4, 10-9, you're breaking up, slow down, 4 and say it one word at a time," Calvin could tell that Trooper Miles, working the desk at Straus Valley, was trying to be patient, but it didn't work. Whoever was calling in wasn't listening. Several people milling nearby Calvin at the front desk in Bethlehem froze at the next transmission.

"Dead, I advised you that I have two...they're, they're...I, I don't know what to do, they're just all shot up. The gun shop in Porter...," it was Adams, the rookie. Just cut loose from his coach last week. Another hotshot kid. Spit and polish, eager. He sounded hollow, like he radio room of Troop Headquarters. Everyone was holding their breath.

"Valley 4, are you 10-4? Any suspects on scene?" there was no response. "Valley 4, are you okay?" Silence. "Valley 4? Valley 4? Adams you've got to answer, you've got to tell us what's going on. Adams? Adams! Report!"

"I had to sit down, it's spinning, I threw up...I, er ahh, no suspects, just the man and a woman down, blood."

A new voice came over the monitor, "Valley 4, this is Ozliewski. Now, you get yourself back up and act like a trooper. We've got an ambulance started toward you and Corporal Dickson is in car 2 heading your way. Adams, you have to do this right. Secure that scene. Give us a chance to catch the shooters, okay?"

"Okay, I'll keep everybody out. I'll see if anyone saw this. I'll, I'll..."

Ozzie jumped in as soon as Adams released the mic button, "That's right, get us a perimeter, give us a chance with this one. Now I want you to stay off the radio unless you absolutely have to. I want you to think. Use your head, take charge there, take charge."

Johnny Bonner flew through the door from the back office area and grabbed Calvin by the arm and dragged him toward the door. "Let's move, partner!" Calvin gave radio operator Santiago his best puppy dog eye shot and mouthed "I love you" silently toward her as he spun in Johnny's grip and broke into a run to the parking lot. Calvin was figuring the angle to his next meeting with her and trying to remember where Bonner parked the car at the same time. He kept moving with Johnny and they split side to side when they came to the unmarked burgundy Crown Vic. Straus Valley barracks was about fifteen miles from the Bethlehem barracks and Porter was another twelve or thirteen beyond that, depending on which narrow back road you took. No matter how you looked at it, Calvin was in for an ass pucker ride.

Johnny Bonner had been a cop in Georgia for a couple of years before moving to Pennsylvania to drive tractor trailers and wait for an opening on the state police. When Calvin arrived his first day at the state police academy in Hershey, he thought he'd really fucked up good. In the middle of nowhere, trees, grass, and not another black face to be seen. Calvin lived in a ten block area in Norristown all of his twenty-one years with the exception of a rare trip to Philadelphia to visit some aunts and cousins, and recently, college classes two nights a week up the road in Gwynned.

Norristown looks and smells like dirty work clothes. Calvin lived under the grip of a grandmother, two older sisters, and his mom, who had a heart as big as a mountain, but high expectations of Calvin and fists of iron. Calvin needed a break, and when he was approached by a trooper taking classes with him at Montgomery County Community College, he was easily convinced. Join the state police and see the...well, see something besides Norristown. He and Johnny were roommates at the academy and they both thrived. They watched each other's back. Johnny's slow drawl singled him out for special attention by some of the instructors, but it slowly went away and Calvin learned that even southern white guys have a sense of humor.

Calvin also learned he wasn't going to get any free ride there. The barracks life seemed like a vacation after living at home, but the class work and study took its toll. He worked hard and Calvin graduated number one in his class. No one was prouder of him than Johnny. Johnny had no family to speak of. His brother was a drug addict in Atlanta and both parents were dead. Calvin's grandmother, mother, and sisters all came to Hershey for graduation. They'd unofficially adopted Johnny. Johnny had a beat up pickup truck and drove Calvin home on the few weekends they were allowed to leave Hershey. Grandma fed him greens and cornbread and Johnny kissed her on the cheek each visit. After graduation they were split up, but somehow both ended up at Troop M in Bethlehem years later and now were working for Sam at Straus Valley.

"God damn you, cracker peckerhead, motherfucker!" Calvin screamed as Johnny horsed the big Ford out onto Route 22, just missing the biggest Peterbuilt Calvin had ever seen. "You are the worst driver I have ever...Shit!" Calvin prayed. Johnny wound up every drop of power he could force into that engine and hurtled through both packed lanes of traffic on the narrow four lane. He ran the shoulder and squeezed and swerved through six minutes of nightmare. Just as they finally broke free in the left lane, Calvin's cell phone sang out. Calvin almost pissed himself. If he hadn't been holding the armrest so tight with his hand he would have, but the muscles in his arms, legs, and ass had locked up. Calvin knew who was calling him when Johnny's phone went off not fifteen seconds later. Just long enough for Ozzie to punch in the second set of numbers. Johnny reached over and grabbed the microphone to call in on the radio. Calvin was dumbfounded.

"Drive the fucking car, JB, I'll talk on the radio," Johnny shot him a "suit yourself" look and turned his head back forward just in time to slam the anti-lock brakes to the floor to keep from hitting a minivan in front of him. "That's it, I'm resigning as of now, stop the motherfucking car, I want out!"

Johnny tried flattery, "Calvin Livingston, you are the most beautiful brown man I know and it would be a terrible, terrible loss to the citizens of this here commonwealth for you to do something like that. Especially with all those women out there who depend on your health benefits to keep your many children in cough syrup and tetanus shots," Johnny grinned.

"Racist shithead. Straus Valley 17, Straus Valley."

"Go 17," it was Ozzie.

"We copied the situation in Porter, en route. ETA thirty," Calvin glanced over at the speedometer in front of Johnny, who now had his window down and his arm draped over the rear view mirror like he was taking Betty Ann to the hoedown.

"A hundred five! Jesus H. Christ slow down!" with that, Johnny grinned again and drove even faster. Calvin almost keyed the mic to revise their ETA but then thought he would probably die before they got there anyway, so what the fuck, over?

~ * ~

Ozzie found "Oh, Jesus" coming out of the locker room adjusting his zipper. It had been a very quiet Monday morning and Sgt. Dawes' blood pressure was beginning to come back down into two digits. Then he looked in Ozzie's face. "Hey, Ozliewski, how are ya? Beautiful day."

Ozzie let him have it straight out, "Sarge we got a double murder out in Porter, you need to call the captain."

Dawes just looked at him and began to smile, "Yeah, right. You guys are always screwin' around. Is there any coffee left?" Bill Dawes should have taken up a trade or sold shoes, he was just not cut out to be a cop. He'd survived his twenty-four years on The Job so far without any distinction at all. He had no enemies and fewer friends. He was married to the same wife, had no kids or dogs and drove a twelve year old car with plastic seat covers. If you blinked you might miss him. He'd somehow gotten promoted and was only months from retirement. He didn't want to get involved in anything he didn't have to. Deciding which black clip-on uniform tie to put on in the morning caused him severe nervous pains. He saw the look in Ozzie's eyes now and it began to sink in. Ozzie wasn't screwing around. Ozzie had to reach out and grab his shoulder. Dawes was about to faint.

"Sarge, I wish it was a joke, but it ain't," Ozzie tried to sound reassuring.

"Oh, Jes...," Dawes' eyes sort of rolled up and out. He stopped breathing and turned the color of skim milk. "Oh, Jesus. Okay, okay, okay, ahhhhhhh. Okay, no you call, tell them, tell them that I, I..."

"Hey, Sarge. That's why they pay you the big bucks. Come on, I'll help you. Dickson and Deland are both going to the scene. They'll take care of everything. Miles is on the desk, he'll handle the phone. Just tell the captain where it is, that everyone else has been notified, and that she should call Sam if she needs any updated stuff. Two dead people at the gun shop in Porter, man and a woman, gunshot wounds, no arrest, no suspects yet. Got it?" Ozzie was leading him into Dawes' office and sat him down behind his desk. Ozzie punched in the Bethlehem number and when he got an answer he handed the phone to "Oh, Jesus."

Ozzie almost felt sorry for the sergeant as he heard Dawes stumbling through his report to the captain. But Ozzie didn't have time now to putz around. Once he was sure the captain had gotten the word, he booked. He grabbed his sport coat and his topcoat and looked like a bear in a wrestling match with a blanket trying to get them on and get out the door. He yelled back over his shoulder to Trooper Miles that he would be in car 16 and was gone.

~ * ~

This time when the cell phone rang, Sam was even less ready for it. He'd made the twisting descent down the north side of the ridge and got a good head of steam up on the hard road. He slowed at the intersection where a worn out building that once was a service station now stood weathered and peeling. The Pathfinder slid in the gravel coming into the lot and Sam got it stopped before he ran over the concrete island now empty of gas pumps and sprouting a healthy stand of thistle. The image of a goldfinch flashed in Sam's head when he saw the weeds. He'd watched the goldfinches feed on thistle in his back yard when he was a kid. He remembered his dad complaining about the weeds spreading, but his mom stood firm. No, she liked watching the little yellow and black rockets dart around and she didn't care about how hard it was to get rid of thistle once it took hold. He grabbed the phone from the truck seat and looked at the unfamiliar number. Before he answered, he was back on the blacktop heading north and west. He was going out of his way to take Molly home, but he figured this to be a long day and he didn't want to be worrying about her. The victims were dead, only the living can afford to be impatient.

Brad Dickson had a rough voice and a rough exterior. He demanded respect and total truth from the patrol troopers. He also was their buffer with the bosses. No one messed with his boys and girls.

"Hey, Brad. I'm still a ways away, what's the story?" Sam squealed around a bend too fast and the road turned and dropped like a bobsled run.

Corporal Dickson was standing in the tiny immaculate kitchen of Mrs. Freda Bern directly across a small alley from the rear of Patrick and Ginny McFadden's apartment, which was also at the rear of the Pro

Sportsman Guns shop. Freda Bern was sitting at the metal table where she'd fed a husband and three sons for over forty-five years. Freda looked awful. She was mumbling, what to Brad sounded like a prayer and shaking from head to toe. Freda Bern had wrung the neck of many a chicken and pulled the guts from her husband's fish he caught, but she'd never seen, in her sixty-eight years, what she'd seen this morning.

Freda had taken quite some time to befriend The Irish, who moved in across the alley several years before and renovated the old bakery into a small sports and gun shop. Not because of any ethnic or religious prejudice, but because they were from that awful city, Philadelphia, where Freda knew all sorts of evil and wicked things happened. People out here are afraid of the city and don't want to understand it. They are afraid of the people from the city, too. But Ginny McFadden paid her respects to Freda and was only a few years younger and they became very good friends. They shared the green tea Freda made fresh every morning at 8:30 and Ginny made her soda bread and little butter biscuits that melted in Freda's mouth. Now that Freda's husband was dead and her sons busy with their own sons, she liked the company. She'd seen Ginny when that young state policeman pushed open the door. Freda couldn't get the picture of Ginny's open eyes and mouth out of her mind. All that blood.

"Sam take your time, they may have been dead a while. The neighbor last saw them Saturday afternoon. No witnesses so far, when Livingston gets here I'll break loose and start a canvass," Dickson said.

"What's your guess, robbery, family, or what?" Sam asked.

Dickson looked down at Freda sitting there visibly shrinking. "Better not go into it on the phone, I'll keep it tight and call you if anything breaks. How long before you get here?"

"Probably forty-five minutes, maybe less. How's Adams doing?" Sam was on the main road now and pushing his truck hard.

"Well, he bought the ticket to the fair, now he has to ride on the roller coaster. He'll be okay. He's guarding the door, looks like he'd shoot his mother if she tried to get past him. Sam, this is...well, this is serious.

This stuff just doesn't happen out here that often. Kinda scary," Freda looked up at Brad, tears running down her cheeks.

"Okay, brother. I'm almost at the house, I'll be turned around shortly," Sam hit the end button and dropped the phone again. He made the right turn onto a narrower blacktop and drove the four miles to his lane in silence and dark thought. The entrance to his place was almost invisible if you didn't pay attention. Sam was glad he didn't have to give directions here very often. An opening, between two old maples at a sharp bend in the road, led to a single width drive, grass growing between tire paths. The drive curved right then left past an aging apple orchard and through a magnificent oak stand, ground darkened from the sun, but not too dark that at least some undergrowth was able to survive.

It turned again hard and up a slight grade to a clearing on the left where the outline of a charred foundation could still be seen. Past that and up the hill a bit more was Sam's house. It looked like a barn because that's exactly what it was. "Was," Sam would tell folks, "is a word earned with a hell of a lot of work and even more money." Sam found the place while he was still a trooper working the Violent Repeat Offenders Task Force in Philadelphia. The farm had not been active for many years and the family moved to towns where they could get work. They were descended from the original German immigrants to the area and this family had forged beyond Blue Mountain and settled north of the ridge. The stone house and big barn were very typical during the 1800s. Renters lived there last and the house burned to a shell.

Sam guessed either the owners were too far away or didn't have the desire or the insurance to rebuild the house and tried to sell the property. He was making a ton of money in overtime and, with his other interests, was getting killed in taxes. Besides, when he came to look at the place and kicked out three rabbits, a grouse, and an old doe and her triplets, he sat right down in the barn yard and did the addition in the dirt with a stick. The real estate lady thought he was nuts. Sam wrote a deposit to her that day. He'd written a lot of checks for this place since, too. He loved it here, he'd never leave.

He stopped and jumped out, moving quickly to get Molly down and clipped her to her outside run. She had an old whiskey barrel on its side filled with fresh straw to keep her warm and an overhead wire that she was hooked to by a light chain, so she could scoot around the side yard. Sam liked to leave her out as much as he could, but he brought her inside with him at night and when it got too cold. Real die hard beagle trainers would never agree with Sam about keeping a beagle inside. "Ruin their nose," they would say. He got her food from the old milk house that served as his lawn equipment shed and gave her two bowls of water.

"See ya when I see ya," he told her. She paid him no attention, she was trying to eat the dish along with her food. She would be asleep not long after she ate and have the rest of the day to figure out where that rabbit had gone when Sam cut her off.

Going in through the side door, he switched off the primary and the secondary alarm systems. The original owners and their later families probably slept with their doors open or at least unlocked and could go to town or to church and leave all their worldly goods on the front lawn and no one would have touched a thing. But not now. A good part of Sam's case load was residential burglary, especially rural homes and cabins. He didn't take any chances. Sam knew a retired cop from Reading who was a first class alarm guy and had him fix up the place with a good package. He felt a lot better about it since he had to be away so much of the time anyway.

As he came into the mudroom, he kicked off his heavy trail boots and threw his camo coat over a hook. Off the mudroom was a laundry room and that led into the kitchen. Sam turned left and charged down the stairs into the lower level and his workshop, such that it was. Ozzie used it more than Sam did, but he still liked to butcher wood now and then and found the radial arm saw and drill press helped him make a lot fewer mistakes on his projects. Sam dumped the old Pentax and grabbed his Nikon digital camera and ran back up the stairs.

He picked up the house phone and put it on speaker as he moved. He had voicemail and played the messages as he changed shoes. "Hey,

Dad, I've just got a minute before class. We still on for this weekend? I don't have duty. Can you pick me up Friday night at six? Send money or girls!"

Sam felt real good inside. His son, Ken, turned out to be his best friend. He missed him a lot, but they worked real hard at making time for each other. Both were real busy men. Ken was a senior at General Varnum Military Academy just outside Philadelphia on the Main Line. He was on the fast track and had just about everything but the actual acceptance letter to the Air Force Academy for next fall. VMA had a pre-academy prep course that included flight training and some tough academics. It was unusual for Ken to have a free weekend. Ken also was a football fan and Sam had tickets for Saturday's Penn State game in Illinois. He would have to hope this mess in Porter didn't screw that up.

"Sam, this is Peggy," Sam felt good at hearing that voice, too, but in quite different way. Peggy was thirty-seven, divorced, smart, drop dead gorgeous, and, on occasion, very personal with Sam. She also could be very businesslike. "Just reminding you that you're up for departure Friday night at eight-thirty. Six, plus light luggage. Return on Saturday night, time dependent upon weather. Prelim reports for Friday say an approaching front and good chance of rain, Saturday clear, but gusty. Give Ken and Ozzie a hug for me. Bye, bye," Ken maybe, Ozzie can do without.

Ozzie's voice came on next, "Sam, if you're there, call me, real important...Sam?" *Must have tried here first.* That was it. Sam looked at his watch. He would have to wait a little bit before he could call Ken. Peggy could wait a bit, too. He jogged into the living room. It was more than a room. When Sam bought this place, he was just going to use it for hunting and getting away. He looked at the barn, but the idea hadn't come to him until about a week before he closed on the sale. He was tired of living in a rented townhouse, Ken was going into VMA, and he needed a change anyway. He checked with some troopers he knew upstate who also did construction work on the side and after describing the barn and its relatively good condition, they told him it could be done. It would cost him, more time than money, but if the timbers and foundation were solid, the rest could be fixed. They were wrong about the money.

He looked up as he trotted into the open area that made up the living and dining room. Large, sturdy beams of solid wood crisscrossed each other in geometric patterns, forming two columns of support for the second floor and roof. The room opened to a loft upstairs and all the way up to the roof. It was beautiful. The walls were tongue and groove oak, finished with clear urethane. A massive stone fireplace, made from the remains of the burned out house walls, cornered at one end of the room and a wood pellet stove was tucked into the opposite corner, just under the loft. Sam preferred real wood heat and had a regular wood burner in the stable below that usually warmed the whole place. His room was upstairs, off the loft that served as an office and sitting lounge. Windows along the south side provided a breathtaking view of the valley, below the farm, that led out to the mountain.

That mountain separated southeastern Pennsylvania from the Pocono region and kept Sam peaceful in the thought that this was still too far upstate for most of the busyness associated with the flatlands beyond. Sam hadn't waited to finish the remodeling of the barn to move to the property. He bought a used thirty-two foot travel trailer that was pretty much self-contained and towed it to the property so he could work there in his spare time. Trouble was, Sam didn't have any spare time. He piddled at it while trying to work a zillion hours a week chasing triple ax murderers in Philadelphia with the task force.

When he got promoted to corporal, he was transferred to Bucks County to run a patrol squad. He worked fewer hours, but hated the scheduling and the problems of all his troopers in meeting that schedule. The transfer to the crime unit in Straus Valley put him a lot closer to the farm and put his police talents into high gear. He'd found the job he was meant for. He had good people working for him that he didn't have to worry about. He worked the cases with them and they formed a team that was hard to beat. Even Lt. Harman usually didn't take Sam on. Sam knew how to do investigations and had the patience needed to see the case through. Step by step, one thing at a time. The military taught him that, along with some other very valuable things, too.

The big wood stove had probably burned down by now. It wasn't real cold out, just a nip in the air, so Sam hadn't made it too hot this morning before he left with Molly at daylight. It was going to be cold tonight, though. The sun was streaming into the barn through the windows and the place had real character in the light. The sun provided a lot of free heat, too. Sam lit the little pellet stove and set it on low. He didn't use it much; the fan noise bothered him. But it helped out on real cold windy days or when Sam needed just a little heat. It also didn't need any attention. The pellets fed automatically into the burner from a hopper in the back and it would run for quite some time. Sam didn't know what time he would be back and didn't want to come home to a cold place.

He remembered his lined denim coat was in the Pathfinder so he grabbed his bomber jacket and retraced his steps back through the kitchen, stopping for a jar of sport drink out of the fridge and resetting the alarms. He fired up the truck and tore down the lane heading back over the mountain to find out why someone would find it necessary to kill two people.

~ * ~

Johnny gave into Calvin's begging and rolled up the window. He thought he saw Calvin's perfect white teeth chattering. He could tell his partner was not happy. Johnny was making good time. He had to slow down a few times, but blew through Allentown and out past the brewery onto the interstate. He passed the cutoff to the barracks and accelerated on the open road. The radio chattered with Miles and Dickson setting up notifications and checking on the ETA of the ambulance. They also heard the crime sergeant, Sgt. Yakavich, sign on from Bethlehem and head for the scene. He wouldn't stay long, thought Johnny. Keep him away from his bookie too long. A lot of college games over the weekend to worry about. Captain probably made him go. Calvin started to stare out the window and stopped jamming his foot into the floorboard to help Johnny brake at every approaching car.

Calvin had this way about him. He got something in his head and he would turn it around every which a way, over and over until he came up with an answer. Calvin tried to fit puzzles together, people puzzles mostly. Why this happened, why that happened, what if we do this, how will they react to that. Calvin was a thinker, among other things. If you were a crook and Calvin got to thinking about you, you might as well report to the county jail, you're had. Calvin was thinking now, but it wasn't going well at all. His forehead was all washboarded up. Johnny jumped the Crown Vic off the interstate and down the ramp way too fast. Calvin snapped out of it. "Gonna make this turn, Mario?"

"Yeah, I think so," Johnny didn't sound so sure. But Johnny was the best. He knew just how much to brake and where in the road to set up the car for the turn. He didn't factor in the stop sign at the end of the ramp and went through it at just over sixty. "No problem, my man. Not much traffic today." Johnny could drive anything.

He started driving at twelve. He and a buddy found an old Plymouth at a sawmill just sitting in the back lot. Johnny worked sorting slab wood for the whole summer to get the sawmill owner to give him that car. It ran, but needed oil and plugs and a battery. He got the oil from a neighbor who'd just drained it out of his Ford, the plugs from the John Deere dealer's trash can, and the battery, well, he never did say where he got that.

They fussed and cursed and spit tobacco juice on the ground and in a week they had that car running laps around Mrs. Johnson's pasture. Nobody ever said they couldn't, so they drove it to the next county and got a gas station pump jockey to buy them some beer. Johnny's teen age years got a jump start with that car. It was going real good, selling rides for gas money, beer runs across the county line, until about two months later. The Georgia Highway Patrol, in the form of the biggest man in uniform Johnny had ever seen, decided that Johnny and his pal committed at least a dozen traffic offenses and several criminal ones, too. The trooper could have towed his car away and hauled Johnny off to the Justice of the Peace, but instead parked Johnny's Plymouth on the side of the road and took him home.

The trooper came for him the next day and took him to the biggest service station in the county. It was out on the main highway and had three service bays, a real car wash, and two cold drink machines. The man who ran it was as big as the trooper and looked just like him. Probably because it was his younger brother. The brother hired Johnny to help out at the station, Johnny was sure the trooper had something to do with it, and taught Johnny how to really work on cars. He never forgot that trooper, he couldn't believe he'd been that kind to him. The Plymouth ended up stripped, painted with flames coming out the sides, and with a newer and stronger engine. The brother sponsored it at the racetrack nearby and when Johnny turned sixteen, he raced it and won more often than he lost.

Johnny went into the Army after high school. He just didn't seem the college boy type. He saw and did a lot of things he wished he could forget. He met a kid from Meadville, Pennsylvania there and the kid saved Johnny's life one cold night at ranger school in the swamps of north Florida. Johnny discovered he couldn't swim in fifty-five degree water with boots and pack on as well as he thought he could.

That kid went on the state police when he got back to Pennsylvania and Johnny got a job on the police department in the county seat. The kid from Pennsylvania wrote to Johnny once in a while and talked about Pennsylvania and how he really liked being on the state police and all. Things didn't work out for Johnny on the police department. He found out the Deputy Chief was protecting an after hours club that sold a lot of dope and had to testify to the Grand Jury about it. Johnny enjoyed living a lot, so he decided he would check out this deal in Pennsylvania and packed up for the north country. Eighteen months later, he walked into the lobby of the State Police Training Academy and shook hands with Calvin Livingston.

"Johnny, I've been pondering something. That guy McFadden was from Philly, right? Had a gun shop down there, too, I think," Calvin didn't let Johnny answer. "That's the big city, Johnny boy, they don't play around in the big city. If this McFadden was some kind of a boob, how would he last this long in the gun business? And to let them get his wife, too? Doesn't make a lot of sense."

"Well you know it's always the family or friends until proven otherwise," Johnny heard that somewhere. It usually was someone who the victim knows. Murders committed by total strangers are greatly outnumbered by acquaintance murders. "Everything changes, though, when guns and dope are involved," Johnny had been studying for the corporal's exam, again. "Better let Dickson know we're about there, see where he wants us."

"Straus Valley 17, Straus Valley, 10-23 in three," Calvin didn't wait for a response. He reached over to the radio control head mounted under the dash just over the console and switched to car to car. It was easier to talk car to car without having to relay through the station. "17 to 2," Calvin didn't know if Dickson had a portable radio or not. Calvin waited in case Dickson had to get back to his car to respond.

"2 to 17, go ahead," Dickson replied.

"We're two minutes out, where do you want us?" Calvin always treated Brad Dickson quite formally. He didn't really like Dickson, although he didn't know why.

"Park at the end of the alley that runs by the rear of the shop at the west side. I want to keep all vehicles out. Block the alley with your car. Mine's at the east end. I'll let the ambulance park outside, won't need them anyway. They haven't even left their station yet, they can't find a driver," Dickson would have been really pissed if this had been a situation where someone needed immediate medical treatment.

Out here in the country, all the ambulance and firefighting work is done by unpaid volunteers. They usually are real quick to respond, often overanxious, too. But today they couldn't get their act together. The local fire company doesn't have an ambulance; they rely on the next town, which is eight miles away. That crew must be all working their regular jobs or sick or something. These local volunteers run to fires with blue flashing lights in their personal cars. Drivers are not required by law to pull over for them and though the blue light doesn't allow the volunteers to ignore traffic rules, they ignore them anyway. Johnny remembered seeing a county sheriff's deputy in Georgia pull over a car, probably from Pennsylvania, that had twin blue lights mounted on a roof rack. Down south the police use blue lights or a combination of red and blue. The deputy made the driver remove the light bar right there and gave him an equipment citation to boot. Guy was real mad. He was lucky the deputy didn't shoot the bubbles out.

Johnny rounded the last curve before the road dropped into Porter. The village had about three hundred fifty people living within a five minute drive from its center. A couple of gas stations, a mini mart, a beauty parlor, and Pro Sportsman's Guns. Eighty-seven octane, a Slurpee, a little trim, and a .357, the American dream. The gun shop was in a building that had served many businesses in the past. It was right in the middle of the village and several other empty stores stood on either side. The beauty parlor was across the road and down about fifty feet. The only other store nearby was a two pump, candy bars, and cigarettes station in the next building to the east. Johnny pulled past and turned at the end of the block stopping cross ways to the alley entrance that ran behind the store. Calvin could see Adams' marked cruiser midway down the alley and Dickson's at the other end. Several people were standing around looking grim.

~ * ~

Afif was beginning to wake up. The traffic outside never seemed to stop. Day and night it pounded by on the Schuylkill Expressway. He couldn't get used to it when he first moved in. He thought the trucks were going to come right through the wall. It was only one of the things that scared him about being in Philadelphia. What scared him the most was not being able to finish what was expected of him. He shook from the thought. How they used him and pulled him into this mess. He could smell something cooking in the kitchen. He wasn't at all hungry, but he had to pee, bad.

He started out from under the covers and discovered how cold it was. The rain stopped last night, he remembered that, now the air must have turned cold. The filthy fools who lived here must not have the heat on. He wished he was back at his home. He wished it was the month before this, he might change what had happened and he would not be here. He summoned his courage with a prayer for the morning and for his bravery to return to serve the good he must do. His stocking feet went down on the hard tile floor in the tiny bedroom.

When he went to bed, the room had six other bodies in it. All sizes and ages. One did not question these things. Now the room was empty except for the piles of dirty bedding and discarded clothes of all sorts. *Filthy fools*, he thought again, *no pride*. He must not let his feelings show, though. His host would not understand. The bathroom was thankfully empty, a small miracle this day. Afif took it as a sign.

His luck was short. The toilet was disgusting. It was stopped up and several had used it before him and left it full for him. He added what he could not withhold any longer, closed his eyes and tried to breathe through his mouth. The small cement block house that he was in was really an attached one story apartment in the projects of South Philadelphia. He didn't know much about Philadelphia, but he'd always heard of the wonderful markets and the food displayed on the walks for all to inspect at their pleasure. Rows of shops and vendors like he'd seen as a child far away. But the markets of South Philadelphia were many blocks away and he was allowed no time to visit them.

He looked at his hands. They were crusted with black grease around the folds of his knuckles and his fingernails. He had nothing with which to clean them. It would probably be a waste of time anyway; he had more work to do today. He managed to get cold water to run from one of the faucets over the brown stained sink. A splash to his face and over his upper body was all he could do for cleaning. He wondered if anyone would notice anyway.

He nearly jumped out of his skin when someone pounded hard and long on the bathroom door. The sound bounced off the walls of the tiny room, there wasn't even a shower or window curtain to baffle it. "My little brother, get your ass out of there, we got to go!" the deep voice was not that of Afif's brother. He was not related, except by purpose, to its owner. He knew he must instantly obey and moved quickly to the door.

"I am sorry, my brother, I have rested far too long. Please forgive my behavior," Afif was not at all sorry and felt he still needed more sleep. He'd worked late into the night, his special skills were needed. He opened the door to see his host standing in the hall looking straight through him.

"Just move out the door, now. We goin' to the auction. Leavin' in two minutes," Jerome Yancey wasn't called that anymore, he preferred something else. He liked to change things, like what people knew him as, quite often. For the last six months he'd been called Jamal. He said that was who he was and nobody argued with him. All this changing required a lot of paperwork. Sometimes Jerome didn't bother. He preferred the big Colt .45 in the small of his back to identify himself if anyone was stupid enough to ask. Jerome knew most folks didn't require much explanation from an angry black man with a gun.

The living room was filled with black children and three women. One of the women wore the veil and long clothes expected of her. Afif didn't know why the others did not. He took his shoes and his coat and went straight for the door. The two other women glared at him with dark piercing eyes and scowls on their faces. They turned back to the talk show on the television as Afif stepped quickly out the door. To the right was a 2x6 set across two plastic crates. A make do bench. Crack vials and needle protective covers were everywhere on the dirt. Afif sat down and put on his shoes and coat. It wasn't as cold as he'd thought, but it was windy. Usually the he ground was nearly dry and Afif could smell the fresh air washing over them fro the north. The air smelled terrible, coming from the south and west over the open pits of sewage sludge between the project and the airport.

He had little time to sit, though, Jamal burst through the door and scanned the area with care. No threats or even any police. Jamal looked at Afif and flipped his head toward a big, dark blue Ford van at the curb. Another man Afif did not know well was sitting in the driver's seat and the van was running. The side door slid open as Jamal and Afif approached and Afif saw his cousin, Yusef, hold open the door so they could just step right in. Jamal did not like being outside in the daylight, but money was involved today and he always watched the money.

Afif and Yusef did not speak. A look exchanged between them, as they sat beside each other in the back seat, was all that they allowed themselves. Yusef seemed much more relaxed and at ease than did Afif. Afif knew his younger cousin was more like these other men and was part of their circle. Yusef told them about Afif and now Afif was far from home and working very hard trying to please those he feared. The van had only two rear windows and they had rough curtains drawn over them. Afif thought how strange that the bathroom had none, only opaque glass, but here were curtains. Jamal sat low in the middle seat. From the outside, the world would only see a well dressed black man driving alone in a plain blue van. They merged into the westbound expressway and the driver stayed just under the speed limit as they began their trip north out of the city.

~ * ~

Corporal Dickson met them halfway. Calvin said nothing. Johnny asked, "Anyone gonna be a witness?"

"Not so far. The caller is the lady across the alley, Freda B-e-r-n. She last saw the victims on Saturday afternoon. Thinks they came home

30

from getting groceries. I think she saw the body before she called, but didn't tell Miles that, just that her neighbor should be home and wasn't answering the door. Said she saw the kitchen was all messed up. Kitchen is just inside the alley door. Store's in the front. Male and female, both about sixty something, she's shot multiple times. Adams just looked in, I went in and checked for a pulse, cold. Tried not to step in anything. Mrs. Bern says it's just the two of them. You guys want, I'll start knocking on doors," Brad stopped to catch his breath.

God, thought Calvin, *he's like a fucking tape recorder*. "Yeah, yeah a canvass would be good, Bern you said?" Calvin tried to be polite. Brad just nodded. Johnny was two steps in front and walked right up to Adams.

"Hey, Adams. We got some left over poached eggs and scrapple in the car, they're a little runny...," Johnny never let up. Adams was pretty green around the gills when Johnny came up to him and now his knees wobbled and he stepped over to lean against his car. He was not doing well at all. He'd been busy after Ozzie gave him the pep talk, but things slowed down and he took time to think about what he'd just seen. He wanted to go home.

Johnny slipped through the door and stepped over Ginny McFadden lying feet first into the kitchen from the little hall that led into the living room. She had twenty or thirty bullet holes in the front that Johnny could see. In the living room, furniture and papers were lying everywhere. Patrick was half in and half out of the doorway at the other end of the room that opened into the shop with his head toward the living room. He was face down and a dark stain covered the carpet around his head. Johnny couldn't see any wounds, but he didn't have to to know they were there.

Calvin was right behind Johnny, "Dead, dead, dead, dead, dead," Calvin checked his watch, 10:23 am. They slowly searched each room and found no other victims.

Adams could hear it coming. The sound the big Ford engine in the police package Crown Vic makes when the driver is in a hurry. He looked up and saw Ozzie arrive in the unmarked, black, car 16. Ozzie pulled up behind Dickson's Crown Vic and unleashed himself on the scene. He almost ran up to Adams. Ozzie looked like a defensive end charging the quarterback in a topcoat. A few years and a few pounds ago, he'd actually been an offensive end and caught little pigskin balls for touchdowns at Kutztown State University. That is, until Walter Stanislaus, Jr. started needing bigger diapers and more than just breast milk. Ozzie made due with two years and a football season before he gave up academics and playbooks for midnight shifts and ticket books.

"You look like shit, kid. Go sit down in your car, I'll watch the door," Ozzie was actually the junior man in the crime unit, but everyone did whatever Ozzie said, he was usually right anyway and too big to argue with. He looked in the door and could see Calvin and Johnny moving around inside. Brad was knocking on doors at the alley corner and the cross street.

Ozzie felt her looking at him from behind and turned around to see Freda at her door. He stepped across the little alley to her. "Are you Mrs. Bern, the lady who called us?" she nodded her head.

Ozzie pulled himself straight up and then leaned slowly down to her and said real low, "I'm Trooper Ozliewski from the barracks down there. You must feel terrible right now, is there someone I can call to come and be with you, can I fix you some coffee or something?"

"Tea, I got the green tea, it's on now, ready, too it is, have some?" she smiled at Ozzie and then thought better of it and straightened her face back out.

"Mrs. Bern, green tea, my ma made that. I would like some if it's not too much trouble," Ozzie stepped right into the kitchen and took off his coat and hung it on the hook on the back of the door. Freda stopped still for just a moment. Her late husband used to do just exactly the same thing. Adams watched Ozzie step into the back door of that nutty old lady's house and got right back out of his car and again took up his post in the alley.

"He's got a gun," Johnny was looking down on Patrick. They'd been upstairs and back down, no one else in the place. "Looks like a .38 in a little holster on his right side. Still snapped in," Calvin looked over from the pile of invoices he was kneeling next to on the living room floor.

"This all looks like business records, purchases, licenses, checkbook," Calvin didn't touch anything, left it as it lay. "He had a little filing cabinet behind the big chair, someone pulled it over and dumped this stuff out."

"Had a computer in the shop. They smashed it with a hammer or something. Cash drawer just had some coins in it, they could have taken his money," Johnny was over Ginny now. He looked at her and at the frame around the doorway into the kitchen. "They put some into the trim work on this door. Might have been a full auto," 9mm shell casings littered every part of the floor. Calvin and Johnny had to walk on tip toes some of the time to avoid stepping on them. Calvin stopped counting at twenty six. "Federal Hydra Shock, same stuff we use," A nasty round with a low velocity and the ability to expand in flesh so that all the force of the bullet was spent on tearing up meat, not coming out the other side. Calvin was staring at the couch. Johnny was trying to look past Ginny into the kitchen to see if any bullets went that way.

Calvin stood straight up and walked back toward the shop, "JB come here a minute."

Johnny was twisting and leaning trying to get a better view of the floor below Ginny's back. Calvin said it again, "Johnny come here and look at this," Calvin was standing over Patrick and looking into the shop. Johnny stepped carefully over and around the shell casings and came up next to Calvin. "Johnny, what do you see?"

Johnny didn't get it, "It's the shop, the cash drawer is under the counter, it's not locked, just some coins in it, the computer is whacked up, I don't know, what do you want me to see?"

Calvin took a deep breath, "The guns, Johnny. The guns. Look at them. Hunting rifles worth a few hundred apiece and shotguns. Must be two, four, six, maybe fifteen or twenty long guns. And the handgun case isn't touched. Some nice stuff in there, couple of 9mms, a .22 target that's worth four or five hundred."

Johnny shrugged, "Maybe they got scared off."

"They shot the shit outta' these people and they're gonna get scared off? Man, this old dude had a gun on him and they fucked him right up. No, they weren't scared off, they got what they came for and left no witnesses. They didn't want the sporting stuff, they wanted something else. Maybe it was just a hit, but I don't think so. Let's get the crime scene guys in here. I want to dig through this paper and look for a phone message pad or something like that. We need to find out who Patrick has been talking to lately."

About ten minutes out from Porter, Sam noticed the time on the digital clock on the dash and figured he might be able to catch Ken on the phone. Cadets at VMA aren't usually allowed phone calls except at lunch or after the evening meal. Sam knew Kenny had a computer lab three days a week and the instructor had a phone in his small office next to the lab. The instructor also owed Sam. They met during orientation and when Sam told him where he worked, the instructor pulled him aside and told Sam about a neighbor who was bullying the decent people on the block, throwing trash around, racing cars up and down the street, and probably selling drugs. Sam tried to tell the guy to work with his local police, but apparently they wouldn't touch the bum because he was related to some county commissioner.

The instructor was returning from his early morning run two months later and witnessed the State Police Tactical Narcotics Force dragging neighborus jerkus out in handcuffs and towing away his vehicles. Not a peep out of that house since. Sam never told the guy how it was done, but it tickled Sam how tough, savvy, dopers always fell for the pretty female narc and sold her a bunch of dope.

"VMA Computer Center, Cadet Winters," the young voice said.

Sam tried to sound official, "Cadet Deland, please," Ken got right on the phone and Sam said, "Hey, bud, sorry I missed you this morning, I took the day off and ran Molly up at the Game Lands, but I'm back working now, double murder down in Porter."

Ken paused, his dad didn't usually talk about work unless he was trying to make a point. "This going to mess up this weekend?" he asked.

Sam made him work for it, "No I don't think so, but we're departing ABE at 2030. It's going to be too tight if I wait until 1800 to get you on Friday and still be able to do the weather and preflight. What are our options?" the academy ran on military time.

"I can get out at 1530 if I get extra credit in biology. Major Whiteside gave us a list of research essays that will excuse us from last period on Friday. I was planning on using my extra time prepping for my calculus final in two weeks, but if I can catch some time for that on the flight out and back, maybe I can use the library tonight and tomorrow for the essays," *This kid is going to be a general someday*, Sam thought. "I'll catch a ride to the train station and hop the R-5 to Lansdale. Pick me up there at about 1700?"

"Roger that. We're really going to miss it tomorrow. Winds are going to be about three ten at twenty-five. What a day to run the ridge. Maybe we can catch a front at Thanksgiving. 1700 Friday, call me if that changes, get back to work," Sam hadn't seen Ken for over two weeks. Ken took his school work very seriously and with Officer of the Day duties and his flying, had limited spare time even on weekends.

Sam shut down the cell phone and drove on toward Porter. As he came to the mini-mart, he quickly braked and pulled up into the parking lot. He bounded up the steps into the small country store and pulled open the door. Convenience stores in the city usually look a lot alike, but country stores each have their own flavor. They have to serve a lot of different uses. This little store sold candy, cigarettes, bread, and milk, but in the back were bags of animal feed, rolls of fence wire, and various bins of tractor parts and lubricants. Spread out on a cutting board behind the counter were rolls and several types of lunch meats and cheese.

He spotted her bending over to pull a head of lettuce out of a cooler at the back end of the counter. The view she offered to Sam included the label on the back of her very snug blue jeans. She had on a forest green knit sweater and soft, brown leather cowgirl boots. As she stood and turned, the sweater came to life and she looked right at Sam, brushing a lock of long brown hair out of her eyes. She was about thirty, not thin but almost, and there was no ring on her left hand. And that made Sam very interested in finding out just a little more about her. She gave him a bit of a smile and Sam felt himself flush just a little.

"Which one were you on?" she asked in a small quiet voice.

"Wha...wha...I don't understand?" Sam felt like he couldn't get the words out. *Careful with this*, he thought. "What do you mean, which one?"

"Carrier. Which one were you on? Your jacket, naval air. You weren't land based anti-sub were you?" she walked toward him inspecting his flight jacket. He didn't quite know what to do. Now, she was very interesting.

"Long time ago, the Kennedy. I was young and foolish. I know better now," *That's it Sam, get your feet back under you.* "You Navy, too?"

"Only by former marriage, sort of, a jarhead. Talk about young and foolish," she started it, but it took hold of both of them and they laughed out loud like kids. She put down the lettuce, wiped her hands on a wad of paper towel, and stuck it out toward his to shake. "Eileen Matthews, I run this magnificent establishment. And who might you be, sailor?"

He could feel his pulse jammering up his chest and back. It was like he was in a movie or something. He'd forgotten why he'd come in here, but he was sure as hell glad he did. "I'm Sam Deland. Looks like you have some excitement going on down the road."

She turned rock solid, "I can't believe it happened, they were real nice people, not like they were from the city at all. She used to come in here and get pies when I'd make them up fresh. Her husband liked pumpkin. Didn't see him too much, but he always said hi and how ya doing and talked about the weather," she took a half a step back and looked him up then down, "You're here about that, aren't you?" *Oh, oh. She can read minds.*

Sam nodded, "State Police, ma'am, do you still love me even with my warts?" she shook her head no, but her eyes said yes and she smiled again. He added, "Listen, do you deliver?"

She gave him a look of surprise, then thought about it, "Oh, food you mean? Yeah, I can, sure."

"If it's not too much trouble, I got a bunch of guys over at the gun shop earning their pay and then some. How about a case of Snapple tea and a dozen sandwiches on those good rolls so they don't pass out from hunger. I think we're going to be here a while," Sam took out several twenties and dropped them on the counter. "Throw in some chips and, oh good, a couple boxes of those chocolate doughnuts," Ozzie came to mind when he spotted the doughnuts. "I've got to get over there. It's been a pleasure meeting you," *indeed it had.* He gave her a quick nod, a smile, and spun back out the door. She was asking about mustard and mayo as he jumped off the top step. He gave her a thumbs up, slid into the Nissan and backed out.

~ * ~

Ricky was up in the mirror of the big rollback trying to get the last of the goop out of the zits on his chin when the blue van pulled in behind him just outside the tollbooth at the Quakertown exit of the turnpike. He didn't see it at first until the driver tapped the horn. Ricky was wired from the hit of meth he'd snorted and the horn startled him big time. He jumped up high enough to bash his head against the top of the cab and came down with his teeth on the mirror. The one good tooth he had in the bottom front of his mouth easily sliced right through his lower lip and blood began to run down his chin and onto his shirt. It wouldn't hurt the shirt, but Ricky's eyes watered and he felt like he was going to cry. He bailed out of the cab and stormed back to the van. He was going to give that stupid asshole a smack for that. *Jerk him right out and...*

Afif was almost asleep when the driver tapped the horn. He sat up straight and saw the big black truck parked in front of the van. He could see he was at the exit. So close to home. He wished he could taste his mother's fine pastry and vegetables cooked in the pot she'd brought with them from the West Bank on their long journey to America. His mother and his father would be sharing their meal soon at midday. He missed them. He knew his duty would keep him away from them and he did not know when he would return. They did not know where he was, but were honored that he had been chosen. They would be proud of him.

He saw the door to the truck open and a tall, thin boy with clumps of stringy blond hair stumble out. He looked crazed. He had blood all over his face. It was Ricky. The blood was running down onto his black shirt with the picture of a big motorcycle driven by a flaming devil with a skull head. Ricky walked like he could barely pick up his heavy boots one in front of the other. He was yelling and gesturing at the van screaming foul words. As he came up to the door, it opened and Ricky was pulled inside by Harold, the driver, a big man who rarely spoke. Harold had Ricky by the hair and handled him like a doll. Harold pulled Ricky right over his lap and dropped him on the floor at the base of the engine hump in the middle of the van. Jamal was moving now and pounced upon Ricky, hitting him rapidly and hard on the chest and stomach with a short piece of baseball bat. Afif was so scared a dribble of urine stained the front of his pants. Only by grabbing his privates could he stop the flow.

Jamal suddenly stopped and leaned down to Ricky's face. "You fucked up, little shit. Never, ever come at me again without permission. Get out!" Jamal sounded like a leopard growling. Yusef unlocked and slid open the side door only a few inches. Ricky tried to go out head first, but stopped and with what looked like great effort, pulled his feet around and left the van.

Yusef opened his coat and handed a thick business size brown envelope to Jamal and sat back. Jamal rubbed his fingers over the outside of the envelope and passed it back to Afif. "The list is in there with the money. Report back to me immediately if there are any problems. Call Yusef when you make the delivery. May God be with you, my little brother," Jamal never looked at Afif, he stared out the front window at Ricky limping back to the tow truck in obvious pain. Afif stepped out of the van and walked ahead to the truck and got in beside Ricky.

Ricky looked over and said, "You're nuts for riding around with them shitheads." Advice given, Ricky started the truck and pulled out turning at the corner and heading west. Afif took out a perfectly clean white handkerchief from his pants and handed it to Ricky. Ricky just nodded and wiped the blood off his chin.

The blue van made a U-turn and went back through the toll and onto the turnpike.

Trooper Damon wasn't sure about the last digit of the tag number, either a six or an eight, maybe a three, but he jotted the rest of it down and noted on his sheet, "Susp veh @ Qtwn 11:15 bl van B/NM poss. 64? 2 W/M blk rollback w/b." Damon had worked uniform patrol for six years. He got a transfer to the Pike at Ft. Washington to get closer to home, Philadelphia. He also wanted to be closer to the Regional Drug Strike Force office to make friends there. Damon wanted to be a narc. He figured this was some sort of meet or something, but didn't have enough to make a stop. He'd maybe earn some notice by doing an intelligence card on this later. He might have done more, but he had court at 11:30 in Quakertown at the magistrate's office. A radar pinch wanted a hearing. Lunch at Giovanni's.

"Trooper," Harold actually spoke. "Unmarked job over in the maintenance yard, a brother."

"He's just a turnpike trooper, only traffic, not a problem," Jamal sounded confident. He learned much about the police he'd never known before, during his last prison term.

~ * ~

Brad Dickson was not having any luck at all. He'd interviewed nearly a dozen residents on all sides of the scene and nothing, except a near dog bite. The black Lab-something mix had a gray muzzle and could hardly get around. When Brad was invited in by the old couple, the dog started up growling and barking hoarsely. "It's okay," the lady said, "she doesn't bite," bullshit! That dog hobbled across the worn area rug in the parlor right at Dickson who had to feed it his Smokey hat to keep it off his leg. Dogs get nuts when they see all the buckles and dangles and stuff a uniform cop has to drag around.

Brad backed out the door and examined the dog spit on his hat. He tried to wipe it off, but it was on good. "Lady would a shit if I shot her senile dog right on the hook weave," he sputtered to himself.

The Pathfinder eased up behind car 16 and parked at the corner. Sam just sat a minute and looked all around. A few people were out in front of the shop on a sorry bit of sidewalk that ran the length of the green shingle sided building. The front door to the shop was closed and the people looked curious and were trying to see in the windows. Several signs in those windows proclaimed that now, during hunting season, was the time to buy ammo, licenses, and various other sale items sure to make your outdoor fun even more enjoyable. Sam started taking his own pictures several years ago at crime scenes. The crime scene troopers didn't take offense anymore. He picked up his Nikon, took off the telephoto lens and put on the 55 mm. The long lens went in his pocket.

When he got out, he stepped around the truck and looked down the alley behind the building. Several old metal garbage cans sat at Sam's end of the building. A small overhang protected them and a coil of garden hose that probably should have been taken inside for the winter before it cracked in the cold. Narrow stairs ran up to a wooden door on the second floor. It didn't look like it was used very often and the railing was coming loose near the bottom. Adams was standing at the back door to the first floor writing in his pocket notebook. Calvin stepped out the door and looked left and then right toward Sam. He flipped his hand up to wave hello, said something to Adams, and started toward Sam. Johnny came out right behind him, waved to Sam and went the other way toward his car.

Calvin looked worried, but still had enough spirit to say, "Nice outfit. The country fighter pilot?"

Sam hadn't really thought about it until now but he was wearing loafers, jeans, mud splattered from chasing Molly, his favorite Villanova sweatshirt, rips and all, and his old flight jacket. All that was missing was his scarf and pipe. "Attack pilot, get it right, how's it going so far?" Sam thought Calvin should be a captain or a major by now he was that smart and a natural leader. Calvin had never taken a promotional exam and was happy to let Ozzie and Sam run things. Calvin didn't like telling people what to do, he knew what the other side of that was like.

Calvin let it out, "We need to get crime scene in here to photo and process. I want to dig into some paper in there. This stinks like maybe a family or business spite hit. Real anger, lots of bullets, lot of good stuff left behind, can't figure the angle yet."

Oh, but you will, thought Sam. Sam asked, "Where's Ozzie?"

Calvin turned and pointed at the rear door of the house directly behind Adams' cruiser, "Adams says he's in with the caller in there. Bethlehem sending anyone out besides the crime scene folks?"

Sam thought a moment, "Yeah, probably, I don't think any court is scheduled today except maybe a preliminary hearing, should be some manpower available. If they do, I'll have a couple stand by at the Valley to do statements. We can get Adams and Brad to shuttle for us."

Calvin nodded, "We'll need the lady who called in for sure, if Ozzie hasn't already done it and anyone Brad turns up on the first round of door to doors. Oh, and if they send out Hamilton, don't put him on statements, stupid fuck hands the witness a tablet and says, 'Here write down everything you know about the case.' You should see those beauties, useless. I've got to make some notes, give me a minute, Corp?"

Sam moved into the alley and stepped over to Adams. He took a quick look inside at Ginny's lifeless body and the death mask she wore on her face. Sam knew he would see that again, probably late at night when he didn't want to. Sam nodded to Adams and stepped into Ginny's kitchen. The

41

cruelty of human beings never ceased to amaze Sam. These two ordinary people ran into someone very not at all ordinary. Someone who was willing to look into another person's eyes and kill them. Cold, cold heart. He couldn't tell where Patrick had been hit, or with what, but Ginny was obvious. Their earthly remains would tell a story to the medical examiner, who, if Calvin was as good as Sam thought he was, would tell that story to a jury of twelve citizens of this county.

He photographed the bodies and the areas all around them to give perspective to where they ended up. He was curious about the shop. The front door was dead bolted and Sam tried to think of any reason for that, other than it had been all along, and whoever did this to the McFaddens came in another way. Like through the kitchen, and that door didn't appear to have been forced in any way. He was also puzzled about the personal computer he found in several broken pieces on a desk behind the sales counter.

Sam learned a lot from his son. Ken was into very difficult academics and learned how to use computers to help him cut through the volume of school work he took on. Sam knew computers not only were very helpful in doing things, but could store huge amounts of information in very small areas. Why this one was smashed and little else was disturbed sent up a large red flag. He made his way carefully upstairs and found the bedrooms and a bathroom. Sam went to a front window and looked down on the street. He had a good view of most of the area in the front of the building. Changing lenses, he zoomed in on the gathering onlookers and shot them in groups and individually. Back down stairs and out through the kitchen, he paused to examine the door and lock before he headed for Mrs. Bern's back door.

When he got just outside her door, Sam stopped and looked across at the back of the gun shop. He soaked it in, trying to get an idea of what Mrs. Bern may have seen. He stepped over to her small kitchen window and looked from that angle, too. Didn't look promising. He saw Adams was making a list of names and times, keeping a log of the scene. At least the Academy still gives them the tools if they remember to use them.

The laughing sound reached Sam in the alley. It had to be Ozzie and it was coming from Mrs. Bern's. He could hear a woman laughing, too. Sam went up to the door and listened. Ozzie and the woman were yakking back and forth in English, bits of German, and Polish. He knocked on the door and opened it to look into the little kitchen. Ozzie was standing at a tiny counter top to the right of the stove with his sleeves rolled up kneading dough on a bed of flour. The woman stood only chest high to Ozzie and was looking up at him with a big smile and listening to him tell the punch line from one of his preacher, priest, rabbi jokes. This was the one about skydiving that Sam really didn't think was funny. Sam missed the last of it when Ozzie slipped into pidgin German again and the lady shook, she laughed so hard. She was at the stove over a sputtering pan making fried cakes. It looked like some Norman Rockwell painting. "Hey, Ozzie. Who's your new girlfriend?"

They both turned to him and Ozzie said, "Mrs. Freda Bern, this is Sam Deland, my boss. Don't let him eat all them cakes, my wife has to hide 'em when he comes to my house," Sam loved the little sugary doughnuts, especially on a nippy day like today. Ozzie wiped his hands and put his arm around Freda. "We decided we needed to cook. Always cook in time of sorrow, makes you think of helping the living, don't it Mrs. Bern? Besides I was hungry, been over two hours since I ate last."

"Pleased I am to meet ya, Mr. Sam. Sit and drink some tea before cold it gets," she was short and round and her wire framed glasses were perched at the end of her nose. She looked like Mrs. Santa Claus. Sam was charmed.

Ozzie said, "Mrs. Bern says the folks over there have a couple of married daughters. Their son was killed in a crash a few years ago. She thinks one of the daughters is in California, the other lives in Pottstown. We need to notify one of them. Probably a phone list in the kitchen over there, maybe we can run down the address. They lived alone and ran the shop,"

Ozzie waited as Mrs. Bern left the room to get something at the front of the house.

He turned to Sam and said quietly, "It happened around 11:30 Saturday night. Freda said she didn't see anything, but heard thunder at 11:30, woke her up. No thunder out of that weak front that came through, was probably the gunshots muffled by the rain. She says most of the customers use the front door to the shop, but every once in a while a van or a truck pulls in the alley and they load or unload boxes that take two men to carry. Right through the kitchen. Doesn't sound right. A yellow rental box van did a delivery like that on Saturday morning about 8:00. Real early. The rain let up a little and Freda saw two guys she says were medium, medium, medium, taking boxes in," Ozzie was on the job, did an interview while making fried cakes.

Ozzie flipped the doughnuts and got down a plate and covered it with a double layer of paper towel. A brown paper bag sat on the counter and Ozzie filled it part way with sugar. He forked out the cakes and dropped them on the paper towel. Before they could cool he dumped a couple at a time in the bag and shook it. The sugar stuck to the fried cakes and he took them out and sat them on another, bigger, serving plate Freda laid out on the kitchen table. Sam thought while Ozzie worked. Ozzie was cutting the holes in a fresh batch as Freda came back into the room.

"Here, Mr. Sam. A Christmas card I kept from Ginny's daughter over to Pottstown. The picture is good of her family and on the back the address is," now tears were coming back into her eyes. Ozzie stepped over to her and gave her a gentle bear hug and kissed her on the top of her head.

"Freda, you sit down a minute, let me finish this up. Me and Sam are going over to Pottstown to tell her daughter in person, it's better that way," Ozzie calmed her and she looked up at him and nodded her head. Ozzie reached over with a paper towel and wiped the tears from her cheeks. "I'm going to have one of these nice young troopers take you over to the office so we can write down everything you told me and anything else you can remember, shouldn't take long, it'll be easier for you to think there.

Should be a little while yet, they'll let you know when, okay?" she nodded, got up and got busy again.

Sam walked back outside with Ozzie and found the troopers from the crime scene unit unloading their equipment and talking to Calvin. Johnny was walking with Cpl. Dickson around the end of the building toward the houses across the street from the shop.

Sam heard a car door slam and locked eyes with Sgt. Yakavich as he got out of his car at the end of the alley. Sam turned to Ozzie, "I better get this over with," he walked to Yakavich grinding his teeth. Yakavich wore the worst toupee. It was jet black and the real Yakavich hair sticking out of the sides was a reddish gray. He had his twenty-five years in, most wondered why he didn't retire. Yakavich had a cigarette hanging out of his mouth and his dark cloth overcoat shoulders were covered with a thick mat of dandruff and other disgusting flakes of dried skin and hair. He was short and thin and smoked constantly. Everyone who wanted to see him gone thought the new smoke free building policy the state police enacted might do the trick, but Yakavich wasn't leaving, not yet.

Yakavich took a long pull on the cigarette, blew the smoke through his nose, and snarled, "Well if ain't the frog prince. Your relatives lose any wars lately?"

"What do you want here?" Sam blocked his path and didn't let him enter the alley.

"What I want here is to supervise my men and see that they provide the commonwealth with proper service, and I also want a little respect from you," his lip curled.

"Oh, you have my respect all right, Sergeant, sir. Now that you've made your appearance, shove off. Willy at the club will be waiting for your 2:00 PM call," Sam went for the throat with that one.

Yakavich coughed and spit a wad of phlegm on the ground. He started to say something, but turned without another word, got in his car and left. Sam knew why he didn't retire, he couldn't. He couldn't live even on the seventy-five percent pay, he was in debt to Willy, the bookie, for nine large. Actually it wasn't to Willy, but to the resources Willy represented in New York. Yakavich had a big problem. Age was catching up with him and he was a lousy gambler. Even if he started winning, he probably wouldn't break even any time soon. He also served as Harman's hatchet man and enjoyed it, in some sick way. Sam felt sorry for him about the gambling, he felt like shooting him for some of the things he did to people just to kiss up to Harman.

The pace began to pick up. The troops were starting to arrive. Two Bethlehem crime troopers and three county detectives from the DA's office. Sam was glad to see that Hamilton wasn't among them. He gave some quick instructions to the new troopers and asked the county guys to check with Calvin for assignments. He spent a few minutes with Calvin to go over a crime scene plan and decided on details about the things to take in for evidence. Sam made sure Calvin knew to unplug the computer and bring it in, broken pieces and all. When they were ready to leave for Pottstown, Sam saw a battered Pinto wagon pull up and an older man get out and start unloading several boxes with the food Sam ordered. Ozzie looked like he was in heaven.

The man picked out Sam and handed him a small brown bag with a receipt stapled to it. "Your change," he said. Freda was watching what was going on and asked Walter to have them put the food on her table and she would make sure everyone got some, along with her fried cakes. Even at times like this, cops still eat, doesn't seem to bother them a bit.

Sam pocketed the change and read the note on the back of the receipt. He knew where he would be stopping the next pass through here. "Come on, Ozzie. I'll drive, you eat," Sam pulled him by the coat away from the food and picked up his phone from the Pathfinder. They got in the black Ford and headed south to Pottstown.

Johnny and the other plain clothes cops spread out and knocked on every door within blocks. At those where no one answered the door, a card was left hanging in plain view or in the mail box, requesting a call to the barracks for an interview. They kept a list so they could check back if the resident never called in. Those with some type of information, either about the weekend, or about their knowledge of the victims, that required a written statement be taken from them for later possible court use, were taken to the barracks. Dickson set up a shuttle service to take them to Straus Valley using Adams and another uniform trooper from the southern end of the county called in to assist.

When they ran out of doors, they converged on the alley and looked and poked into every corner and crevice. They walked from one end to the other and back again. They discussed, argued, and wondered about all different sorts of theories. Anything and everything that looked like it had been dropped or discarded in that alley was logged on a sketch, photographed, and bagged for evidence. Dickson and Calvin ran the show, mostly Calvin. The crime scene men found three .45 shell casings in the living room among the thirty 9mms in the hallway and kitchen. When they could roll Patrick over, they found it probably was the .45 that put a couple of holes in his chest over his heart and one through his nose and into his head.

"Tap, tap, tap," Calvin commented. "Just like the feds teach. Two to the chest, one to the head," Calvin got the computer and the contents of the filing cabinet boxed up and also found several other boxes worth of home and business records he needed to go through back at the barracks. All that work and the mystery of Patrick and Ginny still wasn't at an end.

Death notifications are a bitch. This was a little different, though. It's one thing to have to tell someone their son or sister has been killed in an auto accident. That's bad enough. Murder, being the intimate crime that it is, often involves family. The notification then, is also a time to get information, to get incriminating information. You have to step carefully. Ginny's daughter was home with her three kids. The house was on one of those side streets you would never notice unless you lived on it. It was small and the yard needed a lot of work. It looked tired.

She didn't realize at first who they were. They had to keep their badges and ID cards out and explain again they were state police, not

Pottstown police, and could they come in. Yes, it was important. She cried and sobbed and called her husband at the store where he worked to come home. What was she going to do with Grandma in the nursing home in Allentown? How was she going to tell her? She called her sister in California, but had to leave a voicemail. She didn't know anything about the murders and Sam knew she couldn't have done it. He felt like shit. Ozzie went and got the neighbor to come over and cry, too. The priest was called. Ozzie gave her his card and asked her and her sister to call him about the funeral and such, he would be sure to help with that.

"Get the person who did this to Mommy and Daddy, please, get them, don't let them get away with this," she said when they left.

Riding back north was quiet. Sam told Ozzie they would talk to Grandma's doctor about doing a short interview with her if she was up to it. They would follow up with this daughter the next day when she was twenty-four hours into it and maybe had thought of something else. Then they would call the one in California to make sure she was coming east for the funeral. It was tough, but necessary to get their statements on the record and in writing. Ozzie checked in with Dickson at the scene by radio and found out the coroner had made it there and wasn't being a problem at all, but Sam should get back there right away.

Ricky ate candy bars and tried to flirt with one of the insurance company clerks at the title counter, but he didn't get anywhere. Afif was studying the sales sheet and preparing his bids for the wrecked cars Jamal ordered him to buy. The auction was actually an oversized junkyard that sold only whole pieces and no parts. Insurance companies from all over the area shipped their damaged cars and light trucks here to be sold to dealers and repair shops. The buyers had to be registered with the auction and licensed by the state. Among other things, Afif was a Certified Inspection Mechanic, authorized to issue annual inspection stickers, and the registered representative of Lehigh Valley Rebuildables, his father's shop on the south side of Allentown. Afif had a lot of power and authority granted to him by the Commonwealth of Pennsylvania over vehicles and the paperwork that went with them. That made him very valuable to Jamal.

The list was for five cars, the most Ricky's big flatbed tow truck could haul. Ricky had an overhead rack that would arrange four cars on the bed and he could tow the fifth, as long as it had one functioning axle. Three on the list were burn jobs and could be jammed on top of each other. A BMW that rolled and rammed a bridge, and a new Lexus that killed its teenage drunken driver and looked like a red accordion. Afif made sure the parts he needed from the cars were still on each of them. This was very important on the burned cars. They passed his inspection and he knew he would be awarded them in the auction, his bid would be several hundred dollars above the rest of the bidders for each of them. Profit was not a problem here. Not with what he had planned, or rather what Jamal and the others had planned.

~ * ~

His cell phone vibrated about fifteen minutes before they got back to Porter. Sam checked the number and recognized it. "Hey, Lucky, anyone run a K today?" Sam asked.

"Naw, slower'n molasses here. Got a couple a guys lined up for tomorrow. Wanna crew or do some towin'?" Jack Conner had been a glider pilot on D-Day in Normandy. He was older than heck now, but still loved the business. He ran the gliderport out near State College that nestled right up next to the neatest ridge line going. When the wind hit it just right, especially in the spring and fall, you could run the ridge from Lock Haven down to Tennessee. Sam and Ken kept their Schweizer 1-26 sailplane there this time of year and tried to get a few runs in if their schedules allowed. Sam bought the little glider a few years ago when Ken got old enough to fly solo. They flew out of Kutztown in the summer on thermal lift and trailered their glider up to State College around the first of October each year. The 1-26 was made near where Sam had been born and where he'd seen a sailplane for the first time: Elmira, New York. Sam didn't know how he was going to do it then, but he knew he had to fly. He'd flown a lot since then, but not tomorrow.

"Jeez I'm sorry, Jack. Just started a murder job and I'm all tied up. Hope that doesn't leave you hangin'," Sam would have taken another personal if he could, the ridge would be cooking tomorrow with the wind steadying up out of the northwest and hitting the ridge just right. Even flying the tow plane and watching some kid hook into the sweet spot on the ridge and put his nose down and run was worth it. "A week from Saturday they're at home and I have a charter on for the 182. Be up then, probably rain all day."

"Yeah, well, I'll pencil you in for needing a crew, or is Kenny coming?" Jack tried to set up ground crews for the glider pilots running the ridge and had several local Penn State college kids that did it for air time credit.

"No, he's off with me this weekend to Illinois in the Lear. He'll have to stay in next weekend. We'll both be up at Thanksgiving; arrange a good strong front for us, okay?" Sam hoped that they could get at least one good flight in for Ken over the long holiday weekend.

A few minutes later they were back at the alley. It was a mess. Overhead, a news helicopter from Philadelphia was making camera passes and a lot of noise. On the ground, the news van from the Allentown station was there and the lady reporter with the bad hair was yelling at her cameraman and pointing at the helicopter with her microphone. "Do something, you useless faggot! I've only got ten minutes left to close!"

A crowd of about thirty people, a real throng for this village, was straining to get past poor Adams at the east end of the alley. They were bringing out the bodies to the coroner's van. Everybody wanted a view of the gore. Sam got really irritated when he spotted the First Assistant District Attorney, Janice Briggs, at the rear door of the shop talking to Dickson. Calvin came out after the second body and watched them being loaded.

Briggs was trying to say something to Calvin who ignored her. Sam knew why Dickson wanted him back here now.

Janice graduated from Temple Law School in Philadelphia a few years before. She worked her way up through the Philadelphia District Attorney's Office, at a snail's pace, to handling pleas and continuances. She was doing intern level work and felt it was beneath her stature, being the smartest lawyer she knew. Her bosses sharply disagreed with her intelligence assessment. She left before she was fired and then bounced through a couple of law firms that tried to train her, but couldn't. She got her lucky break at a Bar Association conference in Pittsburgh when she discovered the local DA couldn't hold his vodka. He woke up with his new Assistant District Attorney in bed with him. She passed the entrance exam, orally. His wife met her later and was charmed by her cutting wit. Now she all but ran the office.

"Hello, Janice. How are your cats?" Sam looked straight at her, she couldn't run away.

"Deland, these stupid fucks here have fucked this all up. Where do you find these fucking dopes? I can't get them straightened out, they're just plain, fucking incompetent." She was turning red and her thin, unkempt hair was sticking straight out in several places. It looked like she might be receiving signals from outer space through that straggly stuff. "We have to start all over, they've moved the bodies, the witnesses are being dragged all around. I'm here, I want the witnesses here so I can talk to them and the bodies to stay right here until I can get this clusterfuck fixed."

"Janice, be sure to give that big blond stupid fuck of a trooper over there your home address and your Social Security number, okay?" Sam pointed to Ozzie who tried to look innocent.

"What, what the hell are you talking about?" she was actually foaming at the mouth and spit flew up and out. Sam took a half step back and turned slightly sideways. He wasn't going to take any chances.

"For the subpoena I'm going to serve on you, ma'am, you're now a witness in this case just like the rest of us stupid fucks here at this crime scene. You want phone standby or what?" now he let just the slightest bit of a smirk come onto his face, that would torque her.

"Wit...wit...I'm not a witness in this case, asshole, I'm the DA, I tell you who the witnesses are! Now you listen..," her index finger dotted the i in Villanova on Sam's sweatshirt and guaranteed she wouldn't get a chance to finish. She didn't see Sam's hand until it was too late. Sam grabbed the outstretched finger she bashed into his chest and twisted it up and over and then down and back toward him. Her eyes crossed and she let out a whoosh of air. It must have really hurt. She turned herself into the hold and Sam sidestepped and caught her free hand with his. He had both her wrists in his right hand and backed her up against the coroner's body van where the camera couldn't see them. He pulled out his cuffs and dangled them in front of her nose. The pee running down her leg filled her left shoe where her heel vacated upward with Sam's help. He closed in and almost touched her nose with his.

"Obstructing, Assault on a Police Officer, Disorderly Conduct. I need some legal advice, Miss DA. What else can I charge you with? Oh, don't answer that, you have the right to remain silent." He lifted her a little higher and said, "Now, we can negotiate this deal or I can haul you before the magistrate here. Who is that, oh yeah, you remember, District Justice Robbins. You told the newspapers he made amateur decisions and didn't know anything about the law like you real lawyers do and should be recalled from the bench. You remember him? He'd probably let you have very reasonable bail. Maybe $100,000 or $200,000 if I asked him real nice for you. And if you couldn't post it, why we'd get one of our big, state payrolled dopes here to transport you to a nice double or triple room at the County Jail. Do you begin to understand me now? You are a civilian here, this is my crime scene. I have a job to do, that I do quite well, thank you very much. Your job comes later on, try to remember that. Any questions?" The county detectives were quickly walking the other way. They didn't want to see or hear any of this.

She didn't say anything for a few moments. She knew damn well the magistrate hated her guts and would do what Sam said he would do. Another battle, another day.

She turned on the charm, "Oh, I'm such a jerk, I'm so sorry. This is all a misunderstanding, right?" her eyes looked around for some support from any of them. Stone.

He released her hands and walked to the other end of the alley to cool off. He was starting to have second thoughts, but he had to do it. By the time he got to where Johnny was standing by his car, Janice was around the first bend on her way back to Allentown. "She's a real doll, huh?" he said to Johnny.

They finished up at 8:00 that night. Johnny taped and sealed the doors and windows and everyone stopped in to say goodnight to Mrs. Bern. Sam personally thanked everyone and they set a start time for 7:00 the next morning. One crew back in Porter and the rest working leads out of Straus Valley. Sam invited Ozzie, Calvin, and Johnny out for beers on him, but they all wanted to get some sleep. Calvin needed to stop by the barracks to do a press release and log in some evidence anyway. The excitement over, they got in their vehicles and left. Sam drove by the mini mart on his way out of town and slowed to look, but no lights were on and it was locked up tight. He'd be back tomorrow, that much he knew.

He thought about Molly for the first time since this morning. It was starting to turn cold, but she would still be all right in her barrel. He fed in a generous amount of pedal and pointed the Nissan toward the mountain. He had to slow now and then when his high beams picked out the glowing eyes of deer in the fields near the road. Just in case one would jump out, but they didn't. He was just starting to unwind as he turned carefully into his lane and eased up the slope to his home. He pulled into the lower drive and hit the opener over his visor. The third of four large garage doors, on the outside wall of what used to be the stable in the lower part of the barn, opened to admit the Pathfinder. He shut it down and put his phone in his pocket. He would have to put it on charge tonight. He walked out into the yard, hitting the closer as he went. He turned left and went up the slope to get Molly, realizing now he had not heard her bark as he drove up. That's strange, wonder what's...

He caught it out of the corner of his eye. The shiny white Crown Vic was parked up at the top of the drive by his front door. *Well, looks like Molly got in early tonight.* He took his time going up the wooden steps at the side of the barn to the mud room door. He tried the handle and it was locked. He opened it with his key and could see, once inside, the alarm had been deactivated. He heard footsteps and Molly came around the corner from the kitchen wagging her tail so hard it pulled her back end from side to side. He picked her up and gave her a squeeze and rubbed her ears. She tried real hard to lick his face and squeaked ·with happiness. He got out of his jacket and slipped off his loafers.

Putting Molly down, he walked around the corner and into the kitchen. She was standing right in the middle of the room. She had candles lit and a fire in the big stone fireplace. He could hear the bluesy sound of that old Rita Coolidge CD on the stereo. She was much shorter than Sam and her hair was cut in a blond pixie. She stepped to him and her green eyes flickered in the candlelight. She smiled and showed her beautiful teeth. She was wearing pink fuzzy piggy slippers, one of his old uniform shirts that just covered the top of her full, muscular legs, and nothing else. She reached up and put her arms around his neck and kissed him softly on the lips, pulling him into her until she fit tight against him. Sam was rising to the occasion and kissed her back while he wrapped his arms around her and cupped her soft butt in his hands. He could taste that she'd sampled the wine he put on to chill last night when he received her call. They held the kiss and it became more and more passionate. He released her and looked down into her eyes again and said, "Reporting as ordered, Captain. It's been a long day, I'm real glad you're here."

Tuesday

She was not there when the timer clicked on the television at 5:00 the next morning. He'd gone to bed early, but got to sleep late. He could smell her perfume on him and the bedding around him. That's right, she told him she would call him later in the week when she left in the night. He let the picture of her lying on the bed beneath him float through his head. The pretty redhead on the weather channel was telling him the northeast was going to have a bright sunny day again with temperatures in the fifties. Thinking about Jess and looking at the woman on TV got things stirring down below. Time to get the blood flowing in another direction. Rolling out of bed in the morning was always a challenge for Sam. He went through lazy periods of sleeping until he absolutely had to get up, but for the past few years he'd been trying to hold off middle age by force. This up early stuff was part of that force. That and working all the time.

He thought about the bathroom next. Good thing Ozzie didn't drop off those plumbing parts last night. Ahh, Ozzie probably knew about him and the captain anyway, just didn't say anything about it. He had to go down the staircase to the john just off Ken's room. The one upstairs was never really finished, but was almost done now. If he could get Ozzie over for a half day, they could knock it out except for the floor tile. Molly was awake, but hadn't moved from the big oval rug in front of the fireplace. The coals had died and Sam shut down the vents on the glass doors so the heat from the house wouldn't get sucked up the open chimney. After he and Jess worked off some of their mutual stress overload last night, he built a good fire in the wood burner down in the stove room. That's where he headed next. The steps down were wide and open to allow the heat to flow up into the main part of the barn. The stove was in the second bay of the old cow stables on the lower level and sat below the area between the kitchen and the great room. Sam stirred the embers and tossed in a few shards of kindling and several quartered pieces of oak. He opened the vents to draft some extra air in for a while until the larger pieces took. That would take the slight chill out of the place.

He was still buck naked and stopped in the kitchen to start a half pot of coffee before going back to the loft to put on heavy sweats and lightweight hiking boots. Molly was at the bottom of the steps waiting now, wagging her tail ready to go out. She followed him back down to the stove room and through the next bay past the Pathfinder to the last of the four divided sections. In the end room was a Ford tractor and various pieces of equipment that could be attached to it. The largest being a snowplow rig so Sam could get in and out of the lane in the winter. He'd been at work one day when over ten inches of snow fell in a howling wind. He couldn't get the two wheeled drive pickup truck he owned then into the lane. He parked it on the road and by the time he hiked in and plowed his way back out with the tractor, the Township plow buried his truck and taken the side view mirror and half the driver's side door with them. He owned four wheeled drive vehicles since then.

The stove room held the stove and about a week's worth of wood. Another two weeks' worth was just outside of the garage door of that room under Sam's deck. The rest of the winter's wood supply was up on the hill behind the milk house. Today, Sam needed to finish loading the old manure spreader he'd converted to an all-purpose farm wagon parked up at the wood pile and bring it down to the barn. He lifted the door and the cold early morning air rushed in around him. Molly headed for the yard and Sam got the old Ford started and warmed it up. It came from an auction in the next county Johnny took him to. The next day they rented a trailer and brought it back. It ran rough and was hard to start, but Johnny tinkered with it for half a day and then came back the next week with parts and got it running like new. It was too small for real farm work, but did the job for Sam. Besides plowing and hauling around his spreader, he cut grass and cleared brush with it. It was still very dark out. The yard lights flipped on when the motion detector picked up Sam walking out to hook Molly up to the chain. He would have let her come up to the woodpile with him, but didn't want to chase her down if she struck on a track.

Molly got her food and water dishes filled by Sam from the milk house and he went back down and backed out the tractor. It was a short drive up to the hill behind the milk house. Sam carefully backed up to the spreader and connected the hitch. He shut down the Ford and got the maul out from under the spreader.

Sam didn't lift weights or go to a gym. He got plenty of exercise around this place. He began splitting rounds, pieces of tree trunk too small to bother with when he rented the log splitter over the summer, but too big to catch quickly in the stove. Sam hit them once and they fell in two pieces. The heavy maul was very effective, both on the logs and on Sam. Sweat began to flow in no time. He had just enough light to work now that his eyes adjusted. Working quickly, splitting and loading, the spreader topped off in short order. He did quite a bit on Sunday in the rain and the spreader was almost full. The clear weather today and yesterday would dry the moisture out of the wood. He would take the spreader down to the barn and stack the wood under the deck after he moved some that was there now into the stove room to really dry out. By spring the woodpile would be nearly gone and he would begin his work in his woods to cut for the following year. The stand of oak, maple, and beech on his property had been an added bonus. He took only storm downed trees and those that could be thinned to promote better growth. A retired forester was a friend of Johnny's and came by in the spring each year to help Sam plan the use of the woodlot.

The spreader was filled mostly with the quarters Sam split with the rented machine in July. The wood seasoned nicely over the summer and was ready to burn. By rotating it first to the dry area under the deck and then into the warm, dry stove room, Sam always had dry wood. But it was a lot of work. It was beginning to get light now and Sam finished with a few last swings. He slid the maul into a rack under the spreader to keep it out of the weather and looked out over the fields beyond. The barn sat almost at the highest point in the clearing that was the center of Sam's one hundred eighty-five acres. He could look out the loft window and still be above the level of the woodpile and see from there what he could see now from where he stood. The oak woods followed the steeper hill north and east and mirrored a creek bed flowing down and crossing under the lane to come out to the hard road near the orchard. The ground rose more sharply into the woods. That's what saved them from the settler's axe, too steep to plant on. Wasted ground to the farmer, peaceful cathedral to Sam.

He began to stretch and loosen his leg and back muscles. When he felt the blood flowing evenly, Sam took off at a trot directly into the woods and up the hill. He sprinted when he could find an open space and slowed in the thicker parts. He tried to find a different path each day and covered most of the woods and a lot of the fields beyond. He circled east then north and west until he was straight out from the barn at the edge of the still standing cornfield visible from the loft. He stopped and caught his breath. Somehow he always ended up at this spot so he could look back at his barn and think about how much joy this place gave him.

Over half of the property was woods, but the rest had been farmed for years. When Sam bought the place, the fields were overgrown and hadn't produced crops for a long time. Small dairy farms struggled through the sixties and seventies trying to balance the stable price of milk with the rising price of fuel, feed, parts, and almost everything else. A lot of farms were purchased by farming companies who tried to use modern resources to farm bigger areas to cut costs. Sam was approached by the manager of a company farm nearby about selling his land or leasing the fields. Sam figured crops meant wild game would be attracted to them and that was just fine with him. He made part of the deal that they had to plant corn and alfalfa in the two smaller fields directly visible from the barn and leave some of the crops standing for the deer, pheasant, and other critters to meander around in while Sam sat and watched. He hadn't been disappointed. It was like having a big screen wildlife show. He watched bucks with beautiful racks feeding where he now stood, does and their yearlings fattening on the corn as winter approached, along with you name it, including a black bear. He looked down and could see fresh tracks of several different animals in the mud along the edge of the cornfield. It was time for him to get back to reality, at least for today, and he took off at a quick jog toward the woodpile. He enjoyed these morning explorations. He was getting quite good at surprising unsuspecting grouse and turkey roosting in the pines near the creek. One morning last spring, he came over a rise and dropped into a new stand of young oak and ran right into two twenty pound gobblers parading for a hen. Feathers and wet leaves went everywhere. Sam was as startled as the birds.

The Ford started up and he parked the spreader under the deck until he could unload it tonight or tomorrow morning. The tractor back in the bay, he reset the air intake on the stove as he passed through and went up to shower, shave and get in to work.

~ * ~

The light of the morning sun popped through the broken half-moon shaped piece in the filthy overhead window of the warehouse. Well, it used to be a warehouse. Lately this part of Philadelphia hadn't produced much in the way of goods that would need a warehouse anyway. Now it was abandoned. The records at City Hall reflected that it was titled to The Gibralter Trading Company, the taxes were paid, and it only had thirty or forty warnings from Licenses and Inspections Department about unsafe conditions. Nothing that an occasional letter from a lawyer in New York representing Gibralter couldn't take care of. To Afif, it was cold and frightening.

He worked without complaint, though; he did not wish to experience Jamal's wrath. He finished two of the five cars by 3:00 AM, but was having trouble with the Lexus. The impact had done more damage than he anticipated at the auction. His fear now was that Jamal would come and see him struggling at his work. Jamal would not understand. Jamal only understood power and would see Afif as weak and a danger to him. Afif was worrying about Jamal. The razor he was using to remove the last of the rivet holding the Vehicle Identification Number plate on the Lexus' dash slipped and cut slightly across the surface of the VIN.

Afif could not believe it. He was looking at what would earn him a beating. This mistake would ruin the usefulness of this piece. It would show he was not to be trusted with things of importance. He would...Afif could hear voices outside of the door.

He had been alone since yesterday afternoon. No one was to disturb him. Now Jamal would be coming to inspect his work. Afif quickly took a small can of spray solvent and mixed a bit of it with a spot of engine grease on a rag. He rubbed it lightly with his fingers and spread the mixture over the razor cut on the VIN. The cut disappeared from view. Afif could have laughed out loud but the voices were coming through the old office area and into the main warehouse. He removed the VIN and was getting ready to glue it, rivets and all, onto the waiting dash of a nearly identical Lexus stolen yesterday from the parking lot of Chestnut Hill College and delivered shortly after Ricky left Afif alone with the five junk cars from the auction. The junkers never made it to the south side of Allentown to be inspected for their new titled owners. Instead, they were on the south side of Philadelphia.

Afif was almost an artist. He learned his special craft from his father and uncles who saw it as a perfectly good way of making an extra few dollars that the government didn't need to know about. They were careful to only sell the re-plated stolen cars to buyers in New York or Boston where so much of it went on, the police would not suspect them all the way down in Pennsylvania. The vehicles were rarely discovered anyway.

~ * ~

Johnny was sitting on a folding chair just outside the back door of the barracks smoking a cigarette. He was bundled up against the cold and looking through a stack of papers and folders. Sam wheeled into the lot and parked. It was two minutes before 7:00 AM. Sam tried to be on time, but never too early. "I thought you quit that crap," he hated to see Johnny start back up.

"My completely stress free environment, I need to worry about something, might as well be my lungs," Johnny was reading the statements and interview reports from yesterday. "Boy, did we come up with zip. I think it was space aliens what done it."

"Where's the hog? Too cold to ride it?" Sam often saw Johnny roaring down the road on his Harley Low Rider as late as Christmas, refusing to give in to winter.

Johnny finished reading a sentence and looked up at Sam passing through the door into the barracks, "Naw, wifey and me are gonna go for groceries after work, I can't wait," wife number three, for the second time. Johnny was trying to light another smoke and hold on to the papers in the gusting northwest wind.

Sam almost ran right into Ozzie in the small hallway near the locker room. Ozzie was on a mission and Sam let him pass with a quick "Good morning, dear." Ozzie just waved and lunged ahead, loosening his belt. The squad room served both the patrol and crime units and was the meeting, conference, and work room all in one. Sam's office was past the squad room and in the next door. It was made up of two rooms. The larger outer office had three desks, one for each of the crime troopers, and a prisoner processing station. Sam had a small private office that actually had a door on it that he never closed. Sam didn't spend much time there, he worked on the move.

Calvin had papers scattered all over his and Johnny's desks. Several boxes of documents sat on the floor next to him. Sam could see Calvin had on a different suit, but looked like he hadn't slept all night. He hadn't. "Did you at least get something to eat, or did you work straight through?" Sam asked.

"Oh, I went home about 2:00 and stretched out for a while, but only cat napped. This stuff got me wound up. It's not as bad as it looks, pretty simple record keeping, just disorganized. McFadden has the house and the business stuff all thrown in together, but I got it mostly sorted out. Just can't find much that's recent," Calvin never looked up, just kept on moving papers.

Sam hung up his overcoat and sport coat on the rack in the corner of the outer office. He wore a blue, button down shirt and plain fabric tie with his gray slacks and dark blue sport coat. It was about as dressed up as Sam got. He didn't mind the tie, but didn't like to wear a sport coat. He gave in today. "Where are we?" Sam asked.

Calvin looked over and gathered his thoughts. "Two county detectives, Oh, that reminds me, you're supposed to call the DA first thing, are with the Bethlehem guys in Porter to catch as many of the neighbors we missed yesterday as they can. Johnny's going out as soon as he gets the interviews organized from yesterday. Ozzie has been on the phone with the ME's office about the autopsy and a lot of other calls, I think to the family. I'm gonna piece together this stuff and see who might know something, maybe one of his customers or a supplier, until I go to the post mortem. Figure we'll brief everyone here at 7:30, or so, and brainstorm, okay?"

Sam hadn't heard much after "call the DA". He knew he probably should have called him last night but other things occupied his mind and body when he got home. "I'll have Brad and the sergeant in on it, too."

Dickson was in the patrol supervisor's office trying to straighten out the overtime from yesterday. Harrisburg didn't care how important this case or that case was, but they did care about time sheets and hours worked. "Hey, Sam. Good morning, any luck so far?"

"Too early to tell, but Calvin's getting warmed up, we'll see. 7:30 for a skull session okay with you?" Brad looked puzzled, but it sank in and he nodded. "Where's the sergeant?" Sam asked.

"He's hiding in his office, hasn't said boo to anyone yet today," Brad smiled. "I guess he thought if he tried wishing real hard this would all go away."

"Okay, 7:30," Sam headed out the door and toward the front of the building where the radio desk and the sergeant's office was.

He stuck his head in and found Dawes reading the morning paper. "We make the headlines?" Sam asked.

Sgt. Dawes jumped and the paper rattled in his hands. Sam had startled him. "Oh Jesus, Sam. You scared the shit outta me!"

Sam stepped in and sat down without being asked. "Brad and Adams did a good job yesterday. The kid settled down and really helped out. I'd like to have them available for the next few days to assist, if that's all right with you," Sam took his lack of response as a yes and said, "Good, we're briefing at 7:30 if you want to sit in."

"Ahh, I got to… Ahh, Oh, Jesus. I got to go over to the...the, you know, the...," Dawes' eyes bulged and he just couldn't get out any more words.

Sam let him off the hook, "Yeah, okay. Stop in if you can," with that, Sam left poor "Oh, Jesus" alone to simmer down.

The briefing went quickly. There really wasn't much to key in on. Lots of little bits and pieces that didn't point to an obvious motive or killer. With what they had now, they all thought Patrick and Ginny McFadden should still be alive. It didn't add up. Ozzie said the autopsy was going to be at 10:00. Crime scene troopers would meet Calvin there. Johnny was going to call back some of the people who'd called in about the cards on their doors and go out to Porter to finish up there. The Pottstown daughter would meet Sam and Ozzie at the nursing home to tell Grandma and then come back to the barracks to give her statement. The lab would start having some preliminary stuff on bullets, blood, and prints by this afternoon.

Sam asked Brad to start gathering up the activity from the interstates and the turnpike into the area from Philadelphia and New York. Wrecks, abandoned vehicles, tickets and arrests. He asked Adams to start checking the records computer for any mention of the victims or their family in any crime or incident reports taken in the past two years. Also, Adams was to pull all the incidents from in and around Porter for the same time period. And Ozzie ate the last doughnut.

Sam dialed the number to the DA's office and tried to remember how he was going to describe his side of the story. The DA never mentioned Janice Briggs. He said the 6:00 AM Philadelphia news showed the helicopter shot and got the victims' names wrong and did Sam have anything he could say if the reporters asked him. He offered his county detectives for as long as Sam needed them and help on any court orders or warrants they might need. The DA asked Sam to keep him informed, but Sam knew the county detectives working the case were probably calling in a couple times a day anyway. After he hung up, Sam felt so relieved he told Ozzie he would buy him breakfast.

"Hey, Corp, what do we do with this computer?" Calvin asked. The poor thing sat beaten and in a lump on one of the squad room's long tables. "A lot of this business paperwork looks like it was done on it. Think there's any chance it will still be any good to us?"

"I'll make a call later to the forensics lab. We'll get it down to them once it slows down. Let them pick it apart."

The diner they went to was on the way to Allentown and fed Ozzie many times before. Sam ordered Cheerios and orange juice, Ozzie had three eggs over corned beef hash, home fries, sausage, a short stack of pancakes, milk, and a sticky bun. Sam never ceased to be amazed at how Ozzie could eat like a platoon and keep his waist from spilling over his belt.

Ozzie wiped his face and said, "Junior said if he doesn't have a ball game, he'd be over after school on Friday to feed Molly and put her in the mud room for the night if it's cold. Otherwise, I'll take care of the pup. We'll get her up early and chase a few rabbits up the creek bank on Saturday morning." Sam let Ozzie and his oldest son hunt on his farm anytime they wanted to. Junior was fifteen and almost as big as Ozzie. Sam's place was like a second home to Junior. Sam gave him plenty of odd jobs to do and Junior loved running Molly almost as much as Sam did. "I've got the rest of the parts for the bathroom, thought I'd finish it up after we hunt a while, as long as I got Junior to help. What time will you be back from Champaign?"

Sam depended a lot on Ozzie both at work and at home. Ozzie was the driving force behind the rehab of the barn. His skills with a hammer and a saw balanced Sam's vision of the design. Together they created a special place. Ozzie didn't want to take money from Sam, but Sam knew the hours that Ozzie worked at the farm took him away from the other paying customers he did part time remodeling work for. When the barn was completed enough to move in, Sam signed over the title to the thirty-two foot trailer to Ozzie and had it towed to a small trailer park in Slatington so Ozzie could rent it out. Ozzie built a deck and a porch onto the trailer and got a nice monthly rate out of it. "The game's over about 4:00 central, so we won't be back, even if the weather is good, until after 9:00. There's venison chili in the freezer, why don't you and Junior help yourself while you're there."

Sam remembered the huge smile Junior had on his face the first day of deer season last year. Sam was hunting the forest that ran along the northern property line of the farm. The tract of timber was owned by the University of Pennsylvania and used for summer workshops. He contacted the school shortly after he bought the farm and they were quickly convinced to let Sam have the run of their twenty-five hundred acres for the use of his eyes and ears to protect it from wood thieves and poachers. He treated it like his own. That day was bitter and cold. Sam took the Ford to the fence line at the start of the university property and walked in a few hundred yards from there. Around noon he heard two shots from the direction where Ozzie and Junior were posted back closer to the barn. Sam figured on coming back in for a quick lunch anyway, and by the time he rode the tractor into the barn's clearing, Ozzie was hanging the six point buck up in a tree. Ozzie stood behind Junior and grinned, too, Junior had taken his first buck. The venison chili was compliments of the Ozliewskis. "Let's get going."

The Pottstown husband was with the Pottstown McFadden daughter in the lobby of the private nursing home. They both looked like they'd been up all night. The husband said, "We told her early this morning, she's a tough old woman, but it hit her hard. Can't you fellas do this some other time?"

Ozzie put his arm over the husband's shoulder and led him aside toward the front door. "Look, we know this is a terrible time for your family, but we have to talk to everyone we can. Bad news like this is very hard on older people and the longer we wait the more difficult it can be, health wise for them, you understand, don't you?" Ozzie was doing his priest voice now. "We want to get whoever was responsible for this as much as you do, probably more. Just let us do our job."

She was sitting up in bed and her eyes showed the sadness she felt. She told them she cursed the devil who did this to her son and his wife. No, she didn't know anything about his business and had no idea who would have done this to them. She said her son left the city to get away from the grief and violence. He found the little town and built his business there. She became disabled later and they moved her through several homes until they found this private one in Allentown. They took good care of her here, not like those others. She said it is a terrible thing to bury one of your children.

The husband walked them out to the lobby and said he would bring his wife to the barracks on their way back home to the kids. He told them his wife's sister would be arriving later tonight. He would have her call when she got in. Ozzie told him the bodies would probably be released later today and they should decide on a funeral home to handle the matter.

As they were ready to leave, a man in a suit walked over from the office area to them and asked, "Are you the police?"

Sam said, "Yes, and you are?" the man was well dressed and his hands looked as though they had been required to pick up nothing more than a pen.

"Oh, pardon me, I apologize, I'm Carl Sheldon, the director. Is there anything I can do to help, this is a tragedy for Mrs. McFadden, she's one of our family here," false sincerity dripped out of him. Sam got a chill up his back. "I do hope you can catch them."

"Well, we are going to do what we can. Did the McFaddens come to visit often? When was the last time they were here?"

"Oh, I believe they come every Friday evening and sometimes Sunday afternoons. They were very concerned about their mother here. She had such awful experiences at the other homes," Sheldon said.

"Awful experiences? What do you mean?" asked Sam.

"Ahh, well the other homes were not private, you see. Not privately funded, I mean to say, so they couldn't keep the better staff and facilities. We take great pride here in having the best home for our clients. Assisted living and skilled nursing." It hit Sam now, this place didn't smell like a nursing home, it smelled like a hotel, or an office. The carpet was thick and the walls didn't look like nursing home walls. "Do you know who will be handling the estate, perhaps the family attorney?" Sheldon's left eyebrow rose just a bit.

"The estate? I think the daughter would know, I don't know how much of an estate they had...," Warning bells began to go off in Sam's head now. He paused and then said, "Look, you don't have to tell me how much Mrs. McFadden pays here, but just give me a rough figure, off the record."

Sheldon didn't even hesitate and quoted Sam a monthly figure for a basic plan and what several types of additional services would add on to it. The amount was almost more than he earned from the state in a month. Sheldon added, "Mrs. McFadden has the finest care here, the kind you cannot get with government subsidized funding, I assume she will want to continue to stay here, we hope she does."

Sam knew something wasn't right here, "Mr. Sheldon, can you tell me who writes the check for Mrs. McFadden's stay here?" Sam knew the answer even before he heard it.

"Oh my, no, officer, that is very confidential," now Sheldon began to look worried. "Is there a problem we should know about, about Mrs. McFadden staying here?" Sam could almost hear the cash register ringing in Sheldon's head.

"Thanks for your help, Mr. Sheldon, We'll let you know if we need anything further," Sam thought. *Yeah, with a warrant to search your records.*

Sam walked over to Ozzie and the husband. "Who pays for her staying here?" he asked.

The husband looked puzzled, "My father-in-law did, of course. We can't afford it and my wife's sister is worse off than we are."

~ * ~

Trooper Damon got it on the third try. He typed in the tag number from the blue Ford van and ran it using several different numbers for the last digit. The state computer spit out a Mazda pickup for the three, a Chevrolet for the six and Damon got a Ford with the eight. "That's it," he said. He attached the printout, showing a woman's name with a Philly address as the registered owner, to the Narcotics Intelligence Report form and dropped it in the corporal's basket at the Ft. Washington barracks before he went back out on patrol. Damon hoped these bits of information he kept sending in would get someone to notice he was doing more than just ticketing speeders and working wrecks.

~ * ~

Jamal looked at least not angry. That was the best Afif could hope for. Afif told him of his difficulties during the night and promised to have the others ready by tonight. Jamal told him they had to be delivered by 6:00 PM for loading on to the boat. All except the Lexus. Jamal wanted that. He had a very special lady who would look real good in that. She would be very thankful for her present. Jamal said Ricky would be back at 3:00 to put the others on the tow truck, have them ready. Jamal left some grape juice and bananas for Afif to eat and Yusef to help.

Afif was almost as afraid of Yusef as he was of Jamal. His cousin was very different from Afif. Yusef once lived with a witch of a woman who was his mother only by blood. Yusef's father killed her in front of Yusef when he was only eight. She would not beat him and burn him anymore. In America, Yusef found himself without his father's protection and did not adjust to the western ways very well at all. Most of Afif's family were thieves, but they also believed in having a business or a shop to make themselves look respectable. They found America to be a place that such a relationship between the legitimate and the other side flowed quite naturally.

Yusef had been stealing cars and guns in Detroit until he got careless and began to kill people who happened to get in his way. The family sent him east and he eventually had to leave Allentown and made his way to Philadelphia. There he found Jamal. Jamal did not discourage Yusef's violence and Yusef rose among Jamal's group to be trusted. It was Yusef who then brought Afif down to Philadelphia to work for Jamal.

~ * ~

"Let's go, Ozzie," Sam said. They talked in the car on the way to the hospital to meet Calvin and get the autopsy results. Sam was concerned about what Sheldon had said. He wanted Calvin to try to find some answers in the records taken from the murder scene. "We'll see what the numbers add up to, but I'll bet you right now that shop didn't generate enough cash to support Ginny and his mom."

They split up. Calvin took Ozzie back to the barracks where Calvin would dig into the papers and Ozzie would finish the interviews and work the phone. Sam took the black Ford and hit the interstate westbound toward Porter. He had a lunch date that he hadn't made yet. He wasn't too far from the Porter exit now. His mind turned to much more pleasant thoughts.

One exit before the road that led to Porter was a restaurant and gift shop that sold fresh flowers. Sam took the exit and went into the shop and picked out a modest bouquet of daisies and baby's breath. He went to the card rack and bought a thank you card and wrote "Thanks, Sam." He got mad at himself for not being able to think up something clever and almost threw the card away and started over. But he thought *oh, what the heck*, and left for Porter. He didn't get back onto the interstate before he slammed on the brakes, turned around back to the store and bought a second bouquet and card. Now he could go to Porter, he would have a lunch date one way or another.

~ * ~

The windshield fit perfectly back into the Lexus and took the seal just right. *This will not leak*, thought Afif. Yusef was no help except with the windshield. He preferred sitting on a crate and cleaning the gun that he carried whenever he could. The ugly thing looked like a plumber's tool to Afif, but it was deadly and Yusef knew how to use it.

Afif waited until he finished the other cars before going back to the Lexus so that they would be ready when Ricky arrived. He finished much sooner than he thought. Jamal did not want Afif to do any more than necessary to disguise the stolen cars. Afif knew there were hidden serial numbers on all these vehicles and would have preferred to grind them off or even to cut the ones off the wrecked cars and weld them onto the stolen ones. That would be a work to be proud of. But Jamal only wanted the VIN in the dash and most of the stickers transferred over to the stolen cars.

These foolish Americans, thought Afif, *they pass laws to put serial numbers on the parts of cars to prevent thieves from switching them around and only require that they be stick on labels.* "They are easy to switch, Jamal," Afif tried to explain, "it will not take much longer and it will look much more authentic." Jamal relented and Afif used a heat gun or a solvent and anti-freeze to remove the labels from the wrecks and then re-glued them onto the stolen cars. To all but a few trained eyes, they looked like they came that way from the factory. Afif could take time to eat something now before he began the most important job with the stolen cars.

~ * ~

Sam parked on the quiet street in front of Mrs. Bern's house. When he knocked, on the door he could hear her footsteps thumping through the small house toward the front door. "Good morning, Freda," said Sam as she opened the door.

She looked a little surprised and when she saw the flowers, she smiled and opened the door wider. "Please, come in, won't you?" she took the flowers and stepped back to let Sam in. She told him she hadn't slept well the night before, she was afraid. Sam told her that she was probably safe, that whoever killed the McFaddens wouldn't be coming back. She told him she tried to think of anything Ginny had said that might be important now and remembered her talking about how Philadelphia was getting so bad and they felt much safer here in Porter. "Ginny told me her husband, he wanted to go back to Philadelphia because the pace, it was so slow here. But she didn't want to and a fuss about it she put up," Freda told Sam.

"How were they doing with their business?" asked Sam. "Did Ginny ever say anything to you about that?"

"Only that sold out everything they did when they moved and her husband was hoping they would get enough of the customers here. But he was always busy. He did the notary work and with cars was always fiddling some, too," Freda was putting the flowers in water and sat them on her table in the small dining room.

"He fixed cars? I didn't see any tools to speak of," said Sam.

"Fixed? No, no. He would sell one now and then. Sometimes he would have them parked at the corner or in front of the store. Always had nice cars to sell, shiny and clean, not old ones. I think he must have had a

71

friend in the automobile business and for the extra money helped out. Always busy...," she looked out the front window and wiped her eye with a tissue from her apron. "I can't get used to Ginny being gone, miss her I do."

"Mrs. Bern, you try to rest. We still have some people in town doing interviews that I have to check on. Why don't you try to take a nap. No one will bother you," Sam thanked her for her hospitality yesterday and heard her lock snap as she closed her door behind him.

In the alley, Johnny was sitting in his car writing in his notebook. A cigarette was dangling from his mouth and his left eye was squinted shut trying to keep out the smoke curling up and past it. "Hey, Sam. What's up?" Johnny asked.

"The ME says they died from the gunshots, pending lab work on the tissues. Time of death fits with what Ozzie figures to be late Saturday night. The .45 got him and the 9mm for her. Anything with the interviews today?" Sam said as he looked at the taped rear door to Ginny's kitchen.

"Nope, Mr. and Mrs. Wonderful. Nobody hated 'em, not too many people even knew who they were," Johnny flipped the cigarette out into the alley and got out of the car to stretch. "We should be finished up here by later this afternoon. I figure to cut the county dicks loose and see if Calvin or Brad need any help from the Bethlehem guys."

"Okay, I've got a couple of stops to make, I'll see you back at the Valley later," Sam went back out to his car and left.

There weren't any other cars in the lot when he parked at the mini-mart. He went through the door, but still didn't see her. He walked past the counter and looked around at the back of the store. No one there. He could hear the sound of a truck engine coming from the rear. He went through a storage room and saw an open double door leading out to a loading dock.

Eileen was swinging around behind a hand truck loaded with fifty pound bags she was wheeling from the rear of an enclosed truck that was backed up to the dock. Sam caught movement out of the corner of his eye to his left and turned his head. His eyes locked with the biggest, blackest German shepherd he had ever seen, lying at the end of the dock five feet from him. The dog looked quickly at Eileen and back to Sam. Sam stood very still and thought, *What am I going to do if he comes, hit him with these daisies?* The bouquet was clinched in his gun hand and the little card was in his left. In one fluid motion the shepherd uncurled from his spot and was up facing Sam.

"Dutch, lay down!" Eileen was standing right next to Sam. The black dog dropped like a sack of potatoes. "He won't hurt you, Sam. Really, he's a big baby," Eileen took Sam by the arm and walked him over to where the dog was.

Sam kneeled down and looked right at him. The two tan dots over his eyes bounced up and down as the dog looked at Sam and then Eileen. Sam offered the dog the back of his hand and was rewarded with a wet sniff. Sam gently rolled his hand around and caught the dog's right ear and scratched it at the base. The dog moved into Sam's hand and cocked his head to soak up the attention.

"He's a real beauty. How's that, Dutch, you like to have your ears rubbed?" the hundred pound lug rolled over on his back so Sam could scratch his tummy and wagged his tail so hard it thumped against the wood floor. "Oh, these are for you, to say thanks for helping out yesterday," Sam handed Eileen the flowers and the card and left Dutch wondering what happened to his tummy rub.

The skin around her beautiful brown eyes crinkled just a little as she smiled and took the small bouquet from Sam. She didn't say anything, she didn't have to. She looked at Sam and Sam looked at her and Dutch looked at both of them upside down with all four feet in the air.

Sam barely nibbled at the sandwich she fixed for him. They giggled and talked about the store, the town, the weather. Dutch sat and stared at the food until drool began to run down the side of his mouth. Finally he couldn't stand it any longer and sat up on his hind legs and roared out a bark at Sam that startled him and gave him the hiccups. Sam flipped Dutch a big piece of the sandwich and Dutch swallowed it in one gulp.

"Aren't you even going to taste it, all the trouble she went through and all?" they laughed and Dutch sneezed, wanting more goodies. After lunch they went out back and Sam threw an old tennis ball for Dutch in the field behind the store. Dutch wouldn't give up and kept bringing it back until it got so wet and slimy Sam could hardly hold onto it. Eileen watched from the loading dock and clapped every time the dog found the ball in the high grass.

"I got him a couple of years ago to keep me company. He's a great watch dog, watches me work, watches me fix his food, but I feel better having him around. Old Charlie, one of the bread delivery men, thought he'd play a trick on me one day and tried to sneak up behind me while I was marking some hardware at the back display case. All I heard was Dutch snarl and dig his claws into the floor trying to get at Charlie. I thought old Charlie was going to wet his pants before I caught Dutch coming past me. Charlie leaves the bread on the step out front now and honks his horn for me to come out," Sam could just picture what it must have looked like to Charlie, all those white teeth set in that jet black muzzle.

"I'd like to take you to dinner on Sunday evening. Would you like to go?" Sam gave her his patented "I'm just a simple country boy" look and hoped for the best.

"Sure, sounds like fun. I close up at 3:00 on Sunday," she shot right back.

Sam caught himself and took a deep breath so his voice wouldn't come out all squeaky. He was all a flutter. This woman was something special, and Sam liked her dog, too. "I have to take my son back to school on Sunday afternoon around 4:00, if you don't mind a little ride down toward Philly."

Eileen looked puzzled, "What will his mother think about that?"

Sam took another of those deep breaths, "She passed away a long time ago. Ken and I have raised ourselves for the last fifteen years. We could stop at a real nice Italian restaurant I know after we drop Kenny off. I promise not to keep you out too late."

"Promises were made to be broken," she said and winked at him. *Oh, boy!* She gave him her home number and her address. She lived about five blocks from Mrs. Bern in Porter. Sam was so caught up in thinking about what had just happened he almost fell off the top step coming out to his car.

"Straus Valley 16, Straus Valley," Sam was roaring back out toward the interstate again after easing through Porter just as the school busses were lining up to haul away their cargo from the elementary school.

"Straus Valley to Straus Valley 16, go ahead," it was Mrs. Tuttle, the civilian radio operator who was out sick yesterday.

"Advise Troopers Livingston and Ozliewski I'm en route back to the station from Porter and would like to meet them there," Sam wanted to get everyone briefed before they quit for the day.

"10-4, 16. Also, be advised you have a visitor on station, ADA Briggs," Mrs. Tuttle sounded like she was enjoying this. Sam didn't answer and shut off the radio.

~ * ~

Ricky cursed and slammed his fist against the control handle on the side of the truck. The last of the now renumbered stolen cars was not going up on the rack how he wanted it to. Of course, the fact that he was stoned silly probably had a lot to do with it.

"Freakin' piece of shit! Get the fuck on there, God damn it!" he engaged the winch and backed the BMW down the ramp and reached under the front to reset the chain and hook used to drag it up on the rack. The two Toyota SUVs and the Honda minivan were already loaded and the big Buick was being set up to be towed behind the black flatbed wrecker.

Afif watched and thought about sleep. He wished Ricky would get done so he could ride with him back to the awful house where Jamal let him stay while Afif was in Philadelphia. Afif had been up well over twenty four hours now. Ricky offered some of the methamphetamine he was snorting to Afiif, but Afif never used drugs, alcohol, or tobacco.

Finally the Beemer locked into place and Ricky connected the safety chains. The paperwork on the cars was on a box nearby and Afif was busy signing documents over the notary stamp that was already on them even before they were signed. The paperwork was seldom checked anyway before the cars left the country, but Jamal insisted that it go with the cars. Just one less reason for any nosy authority to get suspicious. To anyone that cared to look, the papers stated that the vehicles were reconstructed by four different people at four different false addresses after they were purchased "as is" from Lehigh Valley Rebuildables. To attest to the honesty of these four enterprising people, the vehicles had been inspected as roadworthy by a certified Pennsylvania licensed inspection mechanic, Afif Ahmed. Jamal made a lot of money on these cars, but made a lot more from the thirty M-16s and twelve LAW rockets hidden under the false trunk liners Afif made from plywood and packing foam.

~ * ~

Trooper Damon's corporal forwarded the morning paperwork to the sergeant who sent it to Harrisburg with a trooper going there for CPR training. The lieutenant was a real stickler for detail and checked over everything real close. He was notorious for sending back reports for even minor things and was considered a royal pain in the ass. Being a pain in the ass was part of the promotion process in the state police. When he saw a copy of Trooper Damon's Narcotics Intelligence Report that afternoon, he thought that silly Damon was trying to kiss up to the strike force again.

The original report was forwarded straight to the strike force, but a copy stayed in the turnpike file. The lieutenant noticed that Damon described the vehicle only as a work van with no side windows, but had not put down the model type in the space provided for it on the form. The lieutenant thought, well, I'll fix this and send a corrected copy to the strike force. This would accomplish two goals; show how smart the lieutenant was and how careless Damon was. The lieutenant cross referenced the VIN of the van with the model year book supplied by the Automobile Theft and

Fraud Bureau. The free books were distributed to police all across the country and paid for by the insurance industry. He located the model number on page 77.

"That can't be right," mumbled the lieutenant to no-one in particular. The model indicated by the VIN was that of a Ford Aerostar, a minivan. Damon described it as a full sized work van. That would have a different model number in the VIN. The lieutenant couldn't stand it when he found a mistake, it really bugged him. Really, really bugged him. He didn't like Damon anyway so he picked up the phone and called Damon's sergeant. Soon afterward, the sergeant called Damon's corporal, who radioed for Damon to call in by phone. By the time Damon got off the phone with his corporal, he wondered why he even bothered. He could just put in his eight hours and go home, but nooooo, he has to play narc, and now he had to fix this stupid intel report when he got in at the end of tour.

~ * ~

Sam almost drove right by the entrance to the interstate. He was caught up in thought about Eileen, the case, the captain... "Shit!" he cursed himself. Now he remembered that he had forgotten to make another call. He picked up his cell phone as he merged into eastbound traffic.

"Corporate Charter, Peggy Newell," she had a melodic, smooth voice.

"Hi, I'm sorry I forgot to call you yesterday," said Sam.

"I heard what happened out in the county, you get anyone yet?" she asked.

"Not yet, it's still early. How's the weather look for Friday?" well, at least she's not mad, thought Sam.

Sam could hear her shuffling papers, "I have the latest right here. Looks like the next front is through here late Thursday night. If the high pressure holds west of here, you should be clear out and back. Is Ken going?"

"Yeah, he picked a good weekend to be off, the game should be great. Why only six? Who are we missing this trip?" Sam asked.

"One of the bankers, I think. Wife's mother is sick. She must be near death for him to miss a game. Scotty is your number two. Are you still coming by tomorrow night?" she sounded hopeful.

"Yeah, if this thing doesn't get any more complicated. I'll call if I can't," Sam didn't like to get too detailed on the cellular phone. You never know who's listening. "Bye for now."

"Bye, bye, see you tomorrow," she hung up.

Sam liked Peggy. Peggy liked Sam. Somehow the chemistry didn't work, though. When they first met, they circled each other like a mental wrestling match was about to happen. A few dinners and movies and one evening of near passion on her couch was as far as it went. Peggy learned about things that happened in the past to Sam and didn't push it too much after that. He came over for dinner a couple of times a month and took her to plays at the community theater each spring and fall. They also made each other a lot of money.

Sam spotted Janice Briggs' BMW in the visitor's space in front of the barracks as he pulled in. Actually it was taking up two of the visitor's slots the way she parked it. *Slob*, Sam thought. Sam had seen her car several times before. It was always filled with papers and food wrappers and cat hair. He found another familiar car in the back lot. The captain's white Crown Vic. He went in through the back door and into the bathroom. Someone was calling for "Ralph" down the porcelain tunnel. Sergeant Dawes was throwing up in the second stall. "You gonna be okay, Sarge?" Sam asked.

"Oh, Jesus. Why do I have to put up with this shit?" Dawes sounded awful.

Sam went back out into the hall laughing to himself and could hear the loud arguing voices from the front of the barracks where Dawes' office was. Briggs was swearing like a sailor and getting it right back from the captain.

Calvin caught him in the hallway and shook his head "no" and pulled Sam into the crime room. "Briggs shows up this afternoon and bullies her way into Dawes' office. He can't handle her and she starts pissin' and moanin' about how everything is going and trying to tell everyone how things should be. Captain eases in the back and saves us from the evil bitch."

"You find anything about McFadden selling cars? Freda Bern mentioned it to me earlier today," Sam asked.

Calvin nodded, "Yeah, a couple of the interviews mentioned that he always had a car for sale. That's part of the mystery. The gun and sporting goods inventory and sales records are pretty good, but he wasn't selling enough to pay his bills and Grandma's, too. Came up a few thousands short. Checkbook shows a cash deposit just before he paid the nursing home each month. I want to find out where that cash came from."

Sam noticed the documents in Calvin's hands, "What's up?"

"I talked to the computer lab geek. He called up wanting some information from McFadden's computer manuals. We talked about the missing stuff and he agreed that the machine looks like a good bet. McFadden had to be into some sneaky stuff. I got a search warrant ready to go for the computer, just in case we turn up something and it hooks back to a shooter. DA approved it over the phone, cut Briggs right out of it. I'm on my way over to the magistrate now to get it signed."

"Okay, sounds good. See you when you get back," Sam watched as Calvin slammed out the back door.

He found Ozzie and Johnny in with Brad in Brad's office with the door closed. "Who's going to go up and rescue Mrs. Tuttle?" asked Sam with a smile.

Brad looked gloomy, "That Briggs is nuts. You can't talk to her. I tried to let her read some of the interviews, but she went batty. Screaming about how stupid everyone is. She needs a shrink."

Ozzie said, "She was on the TV. Gave an interview out at the scene yesterday, before you bounced her, about how she was in control and expected an arrest soon. Guess she's feeling the pressure."

"Sergeant Dawes!" the captain roared, "Get this, this woman out of here, now!"

Sam had to see this. Dawes came by and said timidly, "What is it, Captain, Oh, Jesus, what's wrong?"

Jess had Briggs by the arm and was pulling her out of Dawes' office. Briggs' eyes were wide open and the white was showing a full circle around her pupils. The captain still had her hat on, looking quite official. She was a bit shorter than Briggs, but Briggs didn't have a chance. When they got to the outer door, Sgt. Dawes was ringing his hands and trembling visibly. The little captain looked Briggs in the eye and said, "Now you've had your say. If I need anything from you, I'll let the DA himself know. You stay out of my stations unless I invite you back in," she turned to Dawes and Sam and said, "She has nothing more to do with this case, understand?"

Sam and "Oh, Jesus" both answered, "Yes ma'am," at the same time.

Sam was able to look at Jess as a different person here. They agreed a long time ago not to talk about personal things at work and not to talk about work during their time together. Janice clutched her purse in both hands and went out the door Sergeant Dawes held open for her. The captain said, "Give me a minute" and disappeared back down the hall and into the smaller women's locker room.

She and Sam met when she was the crime sergeant in Philadelphia and he was on the task force. Although she was younger than Sam, she had more time on The Job and rose through the ranks quickly. Her divorce had been final for over a year when they met and Sam was the first man she found she could be friends with since her college days. That friendship changed on a hot summer night after linguini, chicken, and wine. It had matured since, and Sam found her to be one of the most stimulating and interesting women he knew. And now she didn't like Janice Briggs either, that made Captain Jessica Swanson quite all right with Sam.

~ * ~

Yusef drove the Lexus away after Afif completed the paperwork for it. Yusef was in a hurry, he had to meet Jamal for some mysterious reason later. Afif watched earlier as Yusef emptied and refilled the magazines for the gun, checking each bullet. Yusef was an evil man, but Afif was his blood and tried to remember he must honor that bond. Afif had never even been in a fist fight. He chose to work for Jamal because he believed that the cause he supported was what God wanted and what was meant to be. Afif tried not to think about the horrible things that Jamal and Yusef did to people. What must be, must be.

Ricky was ready to go now. Afif carefully removed every trace of his work from the warehouse that he could. His tools and rags were placed on the tow truck and they left behind only the shells of the wrecked cars. Ricky would come back tomorrow to haul them to a scrap yard with a crusher on 2nd Street whose operator didn't ask for any paperwork in consideration of a reduced price for the metal. Thursday they would start over again with four or five new cars. The ride to the project did not take long. Afif got out of the truck and was met with the stares of the full time residents. He was afraid of them, but he knew Jamal's protection was unquestioned here and he was safe. Ricky lurched out of the project and headed for Camden. It was getting dark and he had a boat to catch.

~ * ~

Trooper Damon came in a few minutes before the end of his shift to try and figure out just what that dickhead lieutenant wanted him to do about the intelligence report. The corporal tried to put a positive spin on it and told Damon not to get discouraged. The strike force needed the road troopers' input and just fix the report and forget it. Damon pulled the station copy and sat down in the squad room. He could have just written in "Cargo" or "Econoline" on the form and called the strike force in a couple

81

of days to have them make sure they put that on their copy, but the lieutenant said the VIN book showed it was a minivan. Damon knew he hadn't seen a minivan, it was a full sized half or three quarter ton model. Maybe he got the wrong tag number, but he was sure about all of it except the last digit.

He went to the state computer and ran it again, this time plugging every other possible digit from zero through nine. The only Ford that came up was the one he was looking at on the printout he made that morning. He remembered that a trooper from Philadelphia was an instructor at the academy and taught classes on auto theft and VINs. He didn't remember his name from the refresher class a few years ago, but knew the desk might be able to help him. He called the Philadelphia barracks.

Trooper Don Mitchell was just about to lock up his office on the second floor of the barracks when his phone rang for about the hundredth time today. He almost didn't pick it up, but thought it might be his wife and grabbed it on the fourth ring. "Trooper Mitchell," Don Mitchell was another late comer to the state police after short careers as a Coast Guard machinist and a produce manager for a supermarket. Neither job held his interest for any length of time.

Mitchell didn't look like a trooper. The gray hair in his beard made him appear older than he really was. He wore a plaid flannel shirt, blue jeans, and heavy work boots. He was a solid man and his thick Harley Davidson belt buckle tilted forward from the weight of the cheeseburgers and milkshakes he usually ate at lunch. If you met him in the hallway of the barracks, you would wonder if he was a farmer applying for a driver's license or a biker bailing out a buddy. That's how Don wanted it. He blended right in with the junk yard operators and body shop workers he dealt with. It drove the bosses nuts, but Mitchell was the guy they had to come to get it done when it came to stolen cars.

"Hi, this is Trooper Damon from Troop T up at Ft. Washington," Damon said. "Could I ask you a question about a van? I'm having trouble figuring out the VIN."

Damon apologized for bothering Mitchell with such a bullshit deal as this but, the lieutenant was on him about it. Mitchell said it wasn't any trouble at all and tried to help the young trooper. "What was that VIN again? Let me write it down. You say it met with a rollback?" Mitchell dropped the note on his very cluttered desk and pulled out the VIN cross reference for that year.

"Yeah, a white guy gets out of the rollback and goes back and jumps in the van. A minute later he pops out the side and a dark skinned white guy gets out, too, and follows him back to the rollback and they leave westbound. The van flips a u-ey and goes back toward Philly on the pike," said Damon.

"The book says the number comes back to a minivan, doesn't fit your van. Let me do some checks. You on days tomorrow?" asked Mitchell.

"7:00 to 3:00 tomorrow, can you let me know something so I can get the lieutenant happy again?" Damon sure hoped so.

Don knew the shithead who was Damon's lieutenant and had crossed paths with him before. Even though The Job had over four thousand men and women, it seemed like almost everyone either knew each other or knew of each other in some way. "He's a jerk, been one since he first came on. Nobody would even talk to him. He kissed ass all the time. He'll never be happy so don't worry about it," Mitchell had been on The Job almost twenty five years. He said what he thought. Sometimes it made people mad, but he didn't worry about that. At any rate, Damon agreed with him. "I've got to run now, but I'll give you a call tomorrow as soon as I figure this out."

Damon didn't know it yet, but he'd just made the most important phone call of his short career.

~ * ~

Trooper Adams was trying to make some sense out of the printouts and other papers he had stacked around him. He didn't really know what he was looking for, so he sorted them by date and then by type of incident. He was distracted by all the carrying on in the front of the station, but decided he didn't want to know what was going on and he would let all the brass figure it out. It came as a surprise to him that the quiet farm area around Porter would be responsible for so much attention from the state police. There weren't that many actual crimes reported, but a lot of minor things like vandalism and damage to property. Country kids get restless, too. Many of the hits he got when he began to pull the records from the patrol sectors surrounding Porter were actually traffic tickets and warnings from the interstate nearby. He knew that one spot east of the Porter exit was a favorite for the troopers to set up radar. At the bottom of a long hill were an overpass and a wide flat space for a patrol car to hide. The state speed limit had been raised recently to sixty-five, but that part of the interstate was near enough to Allentown that it was still restricted to fifty-five. Drivers tended to fudge a little on that and would let their speed get away from them running down the long hill.

Adams stacked the traffic reports and thought they wouldn't be much use anyway. He found only one mention of the McFaddens in all of it. About a year and a half ago, Patrick McFadden reported a traffic accident on Main St. in front of his store. A salesman passing through struck a parked car and damaged it slightly. Unfortunately, the salesman only stopped for a moment, long enough to get out and check his fender and then left the scene. Patrick got the license number and Trooper Miles stopped the salesman just outside of Allentown. Adams placed the report on the top of the pile.

Things had just quieted down and Adams was thinking about the gym where he lifted weights and the little redhead who actually talked to him the last time he was there. He would go after work and maybe she would be there. His erotic daydream of the redhead in just the right position vanished when the captain, sergeant, both corporals, Bonner, and Ozliewski walked into the squad room. Adams was uncomfortable around the senior troopers, let alone all these bosses. He felt the tension well up in his stomach when Corporal Deland asked him what he had found.

"I, I, got all the incidents and crime reports from Porter. The traffic stuff is mostly from the interstate. This is the only one I've found so far that mentions McFadden," Adams handed Sam the hit and run accident report.

Sam read the report and the others found seats. Ozzie and Johnny opened their folders and Brad dropped his own stack of reports on a table. The captain looked at Sam and then at Adams.

"How do you like detective work so far, trooper?" she said to Adams.

"Oh, okay, ma'am. All this is still pretty new to me," Adams didn't like talking to officers.

Sam flipped the pages of the report and then went back to the first page again. "Brad, could you check with Miles and Newberry, they worked this accident. See if they remember it. Let's find out what happened to this fella' that got pinched for this just in case he may have held a grudge."

Dickson said, "Miles left at 3:00, but Newberry is out on the road. I'll call him in," Brad got up and went out toward the radio room.

Sam put down the papers and said, "Okay, Calvin may not be back for a while, so let's go over everything and see where we are. As I see it so far, we have two cold bodies and no warm ones. These jobs get harder as time goes by. We need a break and soon. Ozzie?"

Each of them summarized what they knew. Almost every living soul within a several block radius of the murders had been interviewed. No one saw anything of significance. Ozzie still thought it happened at 11:30 Saturday night. No one could do better. The rain over the weekend kept most people inside, not that there was much of anybody out at that hour in a small town anyway. They had two murder weapons which probably meant two murderers.

The McFaddens had not just been murdered, though, they had been brutally killed. Any of the three bullets in Patrick would have killed him and Ginny was hit by eighteen of the thirty-two bullets fired at her. The last seven fired into her body as she lay dead on the floor. The members of the family were not good suspects, not yet, and appeared to be honestly grieving. The mystery now was the money. How did the victims pay their bills? Where did the extra money come from?

They exchanged thoughts and possibilities, but kept coming back to motive. None of the interviews even hinted at the victims having an enemy. They lived quietly in the small town and minded their own business.

Jess said, "You might want to go back to Philly. Find out what they did there, interview old neighbors, check the business, they had a gun shop there, too, didn't they?"

Johnny moved some papers around and said, "Calvin came up with their former address. Looks like an old business address, too. Where are these places?" he handed the paper to Sam.

"The house was in West Philly, the shop was near the stadium, down in South Philly. I agree, we should go down and nose around, see what we come up with. Ozzie, why don't you and Johnny take a road trip tomorrow? I'll call my guy in Major Crimes and let him know what's happening. His name's Frank Dugan," Sam looked at his watch. "Too late today, but I'll call him tomorrow. You guys can reach out to him if you need any juice."

Dugan worked with Sam on the task force. He was the toughest human being Sam knew. He had to be fifty-five years old, but had the energy of a teenager. Dugan was a street kid who grew up and married the police department. He had a fierce reputation and could back it up with his fists. Dugan was always the first man through the door when they went in after a fugitive and Sam had seen him make short work of the foolish ones who didn't give up fast enough. Many nights after their tour at the task force, they sat at the Fraternal Order of Police Lodge bar solving all the problems of the world to be joined by deputy commissioners, inspectors, and one night by the former Mayor, all who knew Frank Dugan and were his friends.

Jess smiled and said, "Better let me call his eminence, Captain Bell at Philadelphia. I wouldn't want him to be upset that we are working in his troop without him knowing it. He won't be a problem,"

"State Police" is sometimes not an accurate description. Territorial sensitivities had to be considered. Each troop is somewhat independent and the commanders can be touchy about outsiders. Bell wasn't usually a prick and Jess knew where the bodies were buried. She saved him from an embarrassing situation once when he was a lieutenant. His wife still didn't know, and neither Jess, nor the hooker, were talking.

"I'll stick here with Calvin tomorrow. We need to start going over their phone and bank records," said Sam.

Brad and Trooper Newberry walked into the squad room. Sam showed Newberry the hit and run accident report. Newberry looked it over and said, "Yeah, I remember this. The salesman didn't think it was a big deal. No one was hurt. He paid his fine, never even went to court. I can't see him having anything to do with this. He lives up in Scranton, I can have someone from up there track him down and talk to him."

"I think that's a good idea. Brad can you make that happen? Let's see where he was on Saturday and Sunday, just in case," Sam said. "What about the owner of the parked car?"

Newberry thought a moment and said, "Well, I never really talked to them. It was for sale. The gun shop owner, McFadden, was selling it. The owner was from New Jersey, McFadden had the title."

Sam handed the report to Adams, "Run the VIN and see who owns it now and check for a phone number of the old owner in New Jersey, okay?" Adams nodded and left. To Newberry he said, "Thanks, trooper, every little bit helps," Newberry headed back out on patrol.

The captain made her exit next, reminding Sam and Sgt. Dawes to let her know if they needed anything. Sam didn't have a chance to speak to her privately. When Adams came back, he gave Sam the printout of the current Pennsylvania owner of the car and a New Jersey phone number for the previous one. The car now belonged to someone who lived in the town just east of Porter.

Sam called the New Jersey number and spoke with a very confused woman. He had to explain twice that he was calling from Pennsylvania about her old car. She finally told Sam that her son wrecked the car and the insurance company paid them for it and took the title. They hadn't seen it since. She gave Sam the name of the insurance company and the name and phone number of her agent.

It was well after the end of Sam's shift, but he didn't worry about that. He spent over an hour with Calvin after Calvin got back from the magistrate's office with the now signed search warrant for the computer. They settled on an 8:00 AM start for the next day and Sam took the printout of the address of the new owner of the hit and run car and told Calvin he would stop there on the way home and talk to them about the car.

It was dark and the outside air had turned damp and raw. Sam could feel the weather changing, a new cold front was heading their way. Clouds were covering all but a very few stars and sliding toward the northeast. The Pathfinder started right up and Sam fiddled with the radio while it warmed. He settled on the country station in Hershey. That new pretty dark haired singer was belting out a sad song about her man not being kind to her soul. Company for the ride.

He made it to the address in less than forty minutes. It really wasn't a house, sort of a trailer with add ons. Zoning laws out here aren't what they should be sometimes. The street was mostly well kept brick or sided homes on small lots. This place was back from the street a ways and had a small pasture and barn off to the side. The Mustang was parked in the dirt drive. Sam pulled in and shut down the Pathfinder. He didn't jump right out. Sam knew it was smart not to be in too big of a hurry to climb out of your car out here in the country. Best to wait and see if the usual big nasty dog runs out from under the porch first. No dog, at least not showing itself yet, so Sam got out and walked up to the door. It opened before he could knock. Sam looked up into the hairy face that greeted him.

"We don't want none," the big man said in his deep voice. He was even bigger than Ozzie and wore filthy jeans and what used to be a white long underwear shirt. It was sort of brown colored now. "Get your ass back down offa my porch and be on your way."

Sam gave him the famous Deland all-purpose grin and said, "I'm Corporal Deland, state police. Mind if I have just a word with you?" the badge went up for Goliath to ponder.

His big shoulders slumped and he started to laugh. "Man, I thought you was a salesman or a bill collector. I'm sorry, buddy. Now, what is it I can do for you?"

Sam was glad this was friendly territory, this guy was as solid as he was big. He came out with Sam and explained how he saw the car at McFadden's and bought it for his daughter. She didn't really like it, especially on wet or snowy roads, so he drove it now. Got it for a real good price, over a thousand less than any other similar ones he'd looked at. Killed his back getting in and out of it. The minor damage from the accident had been repaired before the man bought it. He didn't even know it had been hit. Didn't know anything about McFadden either.

Sam used his flashlight to look at the VIN and compare it to the printout. He didn't mention it to the man, but Sam thought he saw just the slightest bend in the VIN plate and one of the rivets holding it in place seemed to tilt just a bit. Those little hairs on the back of his neck were standing up now. He knew he would have to come back again, but with another set of eyes that knew just what to look for.

~ * ~

Grandma was real glad to hear from Calvin. His mom wasn't home, but he said hello to one of his sisters who was there visiting. She brought her new baby over and Grandma was already starting to spoil him. Calvin promised her he would come down to visit as soon as he got some free time from this murder investigation, maybe Saturday night. Grandma got all excited and said she would make up a pot of beef stew and biscuits. When he hung up the phone he smiled to himself. He shut off the lights in the crime room and checked out with the desk man.

His personal car was an older Bonneville that still looked like new. Calvin kept it immaculate and fussed over it, having anything that even looked like it was worn or tired replaced or fixed. He headed east toward Allentown and hoped she would be there waiting for him. The little club was just off the lobby of the hotel and served overpriced drinks. But it also brought in jazz musicians from as far away as New York and was one of the places Calvin liked to hang out. He saw her sitting at a small corner table bouncing to the up tempo song the piano man was playing for the small crowd. "Hey, Jennifer, I'm glad you waited for me. I got tied up."

Jennifer was all dressed up. She went home after her shift at the barracks, took a long hot bath, and put on her designer black jeans with a tight, black knit top and teal jacket. Her hair was swept up on top and she had just the right amount of make up on. Calvin was in love, again.

"I've only been here a little while, will you get me another drink?" she turned sideways and crossed her legs. Calvin could see she had on black heels and a gold chain around her thin ankle. He signaled the waitress and ordered a bourbon and another vodka Collins for Jennifer. The piano switched to a mellow sound and Calvin looked into those big brown eyes of Jennifer's. This was going to be all right.

They talked and listened to the music for quite a while. After several drinks they even got up and danced to the slow songs. She pulled him in tight and ran her hand up the back of his neck and massaged the muscles. He could feel her breasts on his chest and her hips tucked in against him. They moved well together, not hurrying, but easing along with the melody. After a while they both knew, and without saying anything, she picked up her small purse and walked out with his hand in hers.

~ * ~

As he pulled into the lane, he remembered he hadn't picked up the mail yesterday. He stopped the Pathfinder and walked out to the box. He didn't usually get much mail and only had two letters in the box. In the dome light he could see one was the electric bill and the other was addressed to him and Ken with the return address of a well-known Bank and Trust in suburban Philadelphia.

The little beagle wiggled with excitement when Sam appeared on the driveway, pulled into the yard and down to the garage. "Hey, baby, you ready to come inside?" Sam said as he walked out to her run and unsnapped her. She jumped and circled under his feet until he bent down to get his mandatory slobbering.

Sam fixed her a small snack and got the stove going to heat up the house. He carried an armload of wood back up stairs and made a small fire in the big stone fireplace. He was dead tired. Not enough sleep last night and the pressure of the murder investigation were working together to knock the stuffing out of him. He turned the case over and over in his mind and kept thinking that the longer this took, the harder it would be to find the killers. It was coming up on three days since the McFaddens had been gunned down and Sam didn't have the slightest idea who did it. That really bothered him. He was hoping that if they kept filling in the details, they would strike upon an answer. But knowing who did it and proving it in court were quite different tasks indeed.

He made himself a peanut butter and jelly sandwich, poured three fingers of Jack Daniels, and sat down on the overstuffed couch in front of the fire. He was half way through the sandwich and finished with the drink when he picked up the envelope from the bank and read the contents. The mixture of emotions he felt when he got these letters always confused him. He was supposed to be this responsible government official, but he read the letter and felt sad and guilty and very helpless. Sam tried to have control of the events taking place around him, most cops were funny about that. The letter reminded him of a time over eighteen years ago when he had very little control over his life and when, three years after that, his world took an unexpected spin out of control.

~ * ~

She parked in the apartment lot and waited for Calvin to find a spot for his Bonneville and get out. She kissed him and squeezed him around the waist when they got to her door. "Don't go, come in with me, please," she cooed.

"I really should be going, I've got to…," her hand silenced him. It was difficult to talk with what she was doing to his anatomy at that moment. "Okay, Jen. How can I refuse?" She let them in and caught him again with an embrace and a very passionate kiss. She took off his coat and suit jacket and started to loosen his tie. By now he was fully aroused and figured which way the bedroom was and started toward it with Jennifer in tow.

She stopped him long enough to put on a CD and light a candle. He sat on the bed and she slowly removed her jeans and slipped out of her top. She hadn't been wearing a bra and her small breasts bounced a little as she pulled it over them. Calvin reached out and cupped them, letting his warm hands slide over her skin until his fingers found her nipples. She unbuttoned and pulled away his shirt and kissed his chest and neck. They rolled together onto the bed and he wrapped his arms around her and kissed her for a long time. His hands worked their way down her lean sides and found the elastic of her lace panties. He didn't stop there and went under them to touch and knead her backside. She had tight buns and responded to his touch by tightening them even more and pushing herself into him. She pulled at his belt and managed to take his slacks and underwear off all at once. She reached down with both hands and worked her way over his thighs until she had him fully in her grasp. He liked that and told her so. He found her moist opening and worked two fingers inside and rolled the folds gently until he found that special spot. She let go with a low moan and bit him on the shoulder. It got a little blurry for Calvin after that, but it was beautiful and they both went after it with real energy.

Wednesday

When he woke up, the fire was down to coals. Molly was stretched out in her usual spot on the rug in front of the fireplace, snoring softly. The rest of the peanut butter sandwich was gone and the paper towel it had been sitting on was on the floor next to Molly. It was after midnight and Sam labored up the stairs to bed and reset his alarm for 6:00. He'd give himself a little extra sleep tonight.

~ * ~

The witness would tell the Jefferson Township Police that the car that left the scene was small and red, maybe foreign, maybe not. It sped away toward Lancaster. That and a dead Hispanic male surrounded by shell casings in the parking lot of the Dutchland All You Can Eat Restaurant on the old Philadelphia Pike was all they had to work with.

~ * ~

Sam only got a little of the wood from the spreader stacked inside the stove room. He cut his run short this morning also. Molly got a treat of an extra half bowl of food before Sam was on his way down the drive. He wasn't sure what time he would be home tonight.

When he made it to the barracks, he found he was the last to arrive, again. Calvin was having coffee in the squad room and reading interview reports. He looked pretty sharp again today in a charcoal pinstriped suit and gleaming black tasseled loafers. His silk tie was a splash of colorful reds and purples.

"I'm going to break down one of these days and have your tailor do me one of those pinstripes, that's a nice suit," Sam had to admire Calvin's taste in clothes. Sam was in his usual blue sport coat and button down shirt. Of course the coat came off as soon as he got to his small office to check for messages.

Calvin followed him into the crime room and said, "Ozzie and Johnny took off about 7:00. Said they'd call later if they found out anything."

"Let me make a call down to Philly and then we can go over the financial stuff," Sam looked up Frank Dugan's number and Calvin started laying out some of the documents from the McFadden's house on Ozzie's desk.

"Frank Dugan, please," Sam told the woman who answered the phone at the Philadelphia Police Major Crimes Unit. Like many of the units in Philadelphia, Major Crimes borrows space in one of the police districts. The conditions are often not ideal and supplies, working equipment and morale are often in short supply. None of which ever seemed to bother Frank Dugan.

"Detective Dugan," Frank's voice did not match with the rest of him. He was soft spoken and seldom shouted or cursed.

"A voice from your past, you owe me ten bucks," said Sam. "The Lions beat Temple by more than twenty points," Although he never graduated, Frank had taken classes at Temple University and when Sam worked with him on the task force, always bet on Temple.

"Yeah, but you didn't bring your snooty statie butt down here to shake on it, bet's off. You forget about your old friends?" asked Frank.

"You know I'd never forget your ugly, old, scarred puss, how are you, anyway?" Sam once asked Frank about the small white scar over Frank's left eye. Frank was embarrassed to tell him he got it from a woman who hit him with a baby bottle, back when they were made out of real glass, in the lobby of the police station after he arrested her husband for beating her up. She was madder at Frank than her idiot husband.

"I'm just ducky, Sam. What have you been up to?"

"Busy Frank, real busy. We found a double murder Monday morning up here. Patrick McFadden and wife, Ginny. Late of West Philly. He used to run a gun shop on Oregon Avenue west of Broad. He moved up here a few years ago and had a shop in a little town out west of the barracks. Both were shot in their living room probably late Saturday night," Sam was looking out his window as rain started to spatter against it.

"Jeez, I remember that gun shop. There was something about it that rings a bell. I can't remember what it is, but I can find out. I didn't know this McFadden guy, you say he was from West Philly?" asked Frank.

Sam gave Frank the address of the shop and of the McFadden's former home, their birth dates, and Social Security numbers. Sam knew Frank had access to real estate, utilities, and police records through the computer system at Major Crimes. If it was working. "Two of my troopers are down in the city today checking for old neighbors at those addresses. Could you dig around and see what you can find? I would appreciate it."

"Yeah, no problem, I'll call you...no, you better call me back in about an hour, these phones are screwed up again. It's almost impossible to call out of the city sometimes. When are you coming down here again, the girls at the FOP still ask about you," Frank laughed as he said that.

"I don't know, Frank, I haven't had my shots lately. I get down to the main line once in a while with my son, but not into Philly at all. I'll have to find an excuse to stop in and take you to lunch. I'll call back after a while, Frank. See you," Sam hung up and looked at the stack of paperwork on his desk. He'd neglected his other duties, but couldn't put it off any longer. The memos, reports, and time sheets needed to be signed and sent along the chain of command or the paper monster would get angry.

~ * ~

Trooper Mitchell was scratching his beard as he sat in front of the computer terminal waiting for it to respond to his sign-on password. He was sitting in the traffic warrant section on the first floor of the barracks. Several troopers in plain clothes were busy with stacks of papers trying to run down the hundreds of suspended and revoked driver's licenses and auto tags generated by the population of the largest city in Pennsylvania. This computer was different from the state police computer system. It tied directly into the Department of Transportation in Harrisburg and contained much more detailed information about motor vehicle records.

Mitchell got the okay to enter information and put in the VIN of the van Trooper Damon gave him. The first screen showed Mitchell the same information Damon got out of the state police computer, the name and address of the registered owner and the tag number. Mitchell fed in additional commands and the next screen popped up. Mitchell let out an audible "Humpf" when he saw the information. The van came in from out of state and had been reconstructed from a salvage title. With the description Damon gave him, Mitchell now was very suspicious that the van was not right and may be stolen and disguised with a VIN plate from a wrecked van. Mitchell was just getting started.

Trooper Mitchell picked up the phone next to the computer and as the printer spit out a copy of the van's information, Don dialed a familiar number in New York. "Automobile Theft and Fraud Bureau," said the nice lady who answered.

"Hey, sweetcakes. It's Don Mitchell from down in Pennsylvania. How's your corn crop this year?"

The nice lady recognized his voice and said, "Lousy, honey, no rain to speak of. Is your daughter still in the school band?"

"Yep. She graduates this year. She says she wants to go to college. I guess I'll have to work a few more years," Don had been talking to the nice lady for several years whenever he called in for information.

"You want one of the records clerks?"

When she patched him through to the back, Mitchell asked the clerk to run the VIN through the company's computer and found out that the van had been owned by a resident of Point Pleasant, New Jersey and after a crash, was totaled and salvaged by one of the big insurance companies. Several hundred insurance companies fed claim information into this computer system and it was invaluable to cops working theft and fraud investigations. Mitchell got the claim number and the address of the salvage auction in Pennsylvania. Don recognized the name of the auction and knew it was about five miles west of the Quakertown exit of the turnpike. This was getting interesting.

~ * ~

"I gotta piss, want a coffee?" Ozzie asked Johnny as he pulled into the restaurant parking lot. They were just a few blocks from the McFadden's old house. Ozzie knew he better take advantage of a pit stop while he could.

"Naw, I'll come in and hold your hand, I've got to go, too," Johnny thought he could get in a quick smoke and buy a fresh pack. Ozzie wouldn't let him smoke in the car. The occupants of the small, run down café almost looked up in unison when the two white guys in coats, ties, topcoats, and shiny shoes came through the steamed up front door. It didn't bother Ozzie, who went straight to the men's room in the back. Johnny bought a pack of smokes from the young black woman at the register and scanned the room. The place was quiet except for the noise from the kitchen. Johnny opened the pack and faced the stares of the patrons. "Used to be thirty-five cents when I started," he said in the direction of the register girl. He made his way back to the rest rooms and met Ozzie at the door.

"I'm gonna get a bagel, you want anything?" asked Ozzie.

"No, I'll be right out."

~ * ~

Mitchell put in a call to Harrisburg and got a trooper assigned to the Bureau of Motor Vehicles to put in an order to pull all the paperwork on the van. The state kept photocopies of all the title and application for registration forms submitted for each vehicle in the state. Don figured he would get the forms Friday, or Monday, at the latest, and he could start to figure out this deal. He probably could have run down most of the information about who bought the van by calling the auction, but learned over the years that not everyone could keep their mouth shut, especially civilians. He would wait for the documents from Harrisburg. He called Trooper Damon and told him that it looked like this was a possible stolen van and if the lieutenant said anything more about it to have him call Mitchell. Don knew the lieutenant wouldn't bother.

~ * ~

They cruised around the block twice before they saw the number under the porch of the row house. It hadn't started raining yet, but it looked like it would soon. Ozzie parked the black Ford at the corner and they walked back to the middle of the block. They started with the houses next to the former McFadden house and worked out. They found that most of the residents either weren't home or chose not to answer their door. The few they did talk to came there after the McFaddens moved out and didn't know them.

An older lady just across the street did remember them and was shocked to hear that they'd been murdered. She didn't know of anyone who would want to hurt them. Everyone they did talk to, except the old lady across the street, was black. She looked like the only white resident on the block. They talked to a minister who was home for the day and he told them the neighborhood began to change from all white several years ago

98

and the McFaddens stayed after many of the white people left. Now, he said, young toughs caused so many problems with drugs and guns, nobody walked outside very much and many were afraid. He was trying to get a neighborhood watch group together so they could make it safe.

Johnny said they should go and see if they could get any information from the business address on Oregon Avenue and they walked back to the car. There were four of them. Two were sitting on the hood of the Ford and the other two were on the curb. They were all about eighteen or nineteen and dressed in oversized coats. Each had on a baseball hat from a different team. They watched the two suits walk up to them and kept looking down each of the cross streets. Ozzie almost stopped about ten feet from them, but Johnny kept moving right at the two on the hood and picked up the pace. The kids weren't expecting that. The tough guy looks disappeared as Johnny reached out and grabbed the biggest kid by the throat and pulled him right in, chest to chest. Johnny caught him with three quick blows to the stomach and the kid went limp. Number two on the hood started to get to his feet, but bumped into Ozzie and fell on his ass. The big folding knife in his hand fell to the sidewalk unopened. He popped back up, then joined the other two and they ran like greyhounds to the alley. The one Johnny had by the neck looked at Johnny and then at Ozzie. He realized now that he was all alone and these big fuckers were going to kill him. Johnny sat him down on the sidewalk and dusted off his shoulders like a mom sending her kid to school.

He told him, "Son, that's how the FBI takes care of little shitheads like you who mess with our cars. Now get before I really turn mad." The punk caught his wind and stumbled down the street to find his pals and tell them about how he really scared those two FBI agents back there.

Ozzie laughed until tears came to his eyes driving toward South Philly. "F, fucking, BI, You see the look on that kid's face? Oh, man. They thought they had some insurance guy or something and ran into the Golden Gloves Kid instead. They better find a new career, they're rotten at being muggers," Johnny just shook his head and wished he had a cigarette.

~ * ~

The wind began to gust just a bit and the first drops of rain started to fall. The smell from the sewage sludge piles was awful. Afif woke and was sick to his stomach from it. This was a terrible place. The people here did not like him and he had no privacy at all. He needed a hot shower, but hated to use the filthy bathroom in the apartment. He had all day today to rest and he did not intend to stay in this dump.

He slipped into the bathroom and washed as best he could. He dressed with what few clean clothes he had. There was no toothpaste so he brushed with a bit of the soap and tried to rinse the bitter taste out of his mouth. Back in the bedroom again, he gathered his dirty clothes and left without waking the several children asleep on a mattress on the floor. One of the women was in the kitchen trying to cook something and yelled at him as he went out the front door, "Hey, where you goin'?"

"To do my laundry," he called back to her and hurried down the block and past the bus stop. He carried his clothes in a backpack and quickly walked the few blocks to Passyunk Avenue. There he found a small laundromat and put his clothes in. It had a bathroom in the back and he used it to get himself really clean. Next door was a small bakery with a sidewalk booth that sold coffee and warm rolls. Afif ate three and then ordered a large hot chocolate with whipped cream. He went back to the laundry to put his clothes in to dry and sat on a plastic chair and savored the chocolate. It was the best he'd felt in days.

~ * ~

Calvin traced the pattern he put together of the business and personal records of the McFaddens. He showed Sam the list of income and expenses and the checkbooks the victims used. "See, Sam, it just doesn't add up. It wasn't costing them much for the mortgage on the place. The car was probably paid for, and he didn't buy a lot of extra inventory for the shop. But the sales still didn't cover it and the nursing home, too. I didn't find anything showing a safety deposit box and we didn't find any cash in the house except what they had on them. That's even more indication it wasn't robbery. Look in the checkbook. Here's a deposit of $3500 and then he writes a check to the nursing home. And again back here, and here, each month he drops between $3000 and $4000 into the account and then writes the check. Like it falls out of the sky."

"You said he didn't have a car payment? They have a late model Olds, right. A nice four door. Do we have the keys?" asked Sam.

"Yeah, I kept them until we can release it to the family. I thought I'd go over and take another look today and then get the husband to start cleaning up the place before his wife sees it. I want to talk to the other daughter later today anyway," said Calvin.

"Okay, don't release the car yet, there may be a problem with it," Sam explained to Calvin about the suspicious VIN plate on the Mustang he looked at last night. "If McFadden was making a buck on the side selling funny cars, his own may be bad, too. Doesn't Johnny know a trooper down in Philadelphia who messes with stolen cars?"

"Yeah, I can't remember his name. He might have retired by now. He and Johnny used to ride their Harleys together. Weird dude, he's worked cars for years, though," Calvin was stacking the papers in separate piles for the house records and the business stuff.

Sam placed his call to Frank Dugan again. Dugan said, "I found the property owner for the shop. Probably the same one from when your guy was there. But better than that, I found why I remembered the place. McFadden used to have a cop working for him in the shop. A black guy named Sylvester. We caught him buying guns off the street and selling them out the back door. Sold one to a stick-up guy who shot and wounded another cop in the Northeast. The stick-up guy got picked up and rolled on Sylvester. We let him out on bail and wired him up. Got Sylvester on tape selling him another gun. The snitch introduced one of our Major Crimes officers and an Internal Affairs detective and they bought two more from him, including a full automatic 9 millimeter."

Sam was getting real interested, "Where's this Sylvester now? Any chance he's our shooter up here?"

"Not unless he escaped. He's doing major time in Graterford State Prison. Besides, McFadden testified as a character witness for him. I talked to the ADA who handled the case. McFadden came real close to getting locked up himself. He moved out not long after that."

"What about hot cars? Anything on that?" Sam explained to Frank about McFadden selling cars on the side and his suspicions about them.

"No, not that I've found so far. I can check with the Auto Squad later and see if any of these names mean anything to them. Have your guys stop by here and I'll have copies of this information ready for them," Frank gave Sam the landlord's name for the former gun shop and they agreed to stay in touch.

Sam called Ozzie and relayed the information he received from Frank to him. "How's the big city, Ozzie?"

"It smells like shit, no I mean really smells like shit. They empty out the sewage plant and dump the stuff out in open fields to dry. You can't believe what it smells like," Ozzie was finishing the delicious roll he had just bought from the sidewalk stand on Passyunk Avenue just above where it meets with Oregon Avenue and the expressway. The smell didn't seem to bother his appetite. "We'll run down the landlord and see what we come up with."

"Ask Johnny what the name of the stolen car trooper from Philadelphia is for me," said Sam.

Johnny was leaning against the Ford smoking a cigarette and sipping his coffee he bought from the stand. He told Ozzie to tell Sam the guy's name was Don Mitchell and to hurry up, it was starting to rain again.

The computer geek from headquarters called Calvin. Sgt. Dawes made his only contribution to the effort and had a patrol trooper run the battered McFadden computer out to Harrisburg yesterday and they got right on it. The geek found a list of phone numbers, dates, VINs and amounts.

The fax machine spit out copies and Sam whistled a low tone as he looked at the pages.

"I'll bet we just found McFadden's little golden egg," said Sam. "A complete list of all the cars he sold in the past year, no, over a year. Everything except who he sold them to and who he got them from. We'll find out where they are with the state computer. Where they came from, or should I say, who they came from, will be a little more difficult."

The faxes continued to print out. They found the inventory records and an unusual list of three to five letter and number combinations with dates and amounts. Nothing else seemed to unravel what the list was. "I hope McFadden didn't take the key to this with him in his head," said Sam.

Sam thought it might be more to do with the cars or maybe dope, he knew they had to find out. Another lead to run down.

~ * ~

When he found the empty lot where a building used to be, Trooper Mitchell added one more piece of the puzzle. Trouble is, these puzzles have a lot of empty border pieces to them and very few that are easy to put into place. The empty lot was supposed to be the address of the woman who owned the van. It was obvious that no building had been here for years and the registration on the van was only months old. The woman's name was real enough. She had a suspended driver's license, was registered to vote, and had been arrested for dope. But this was her only listed address. Mitchell didn't give up easy, though, next stop was center city.

Sam left a message at the front desk for Don Mitchell to call back. Calvin still had a ton of reports to do and Sam settled in to go back over everything once again.

Ozzie and Johnny talked to the landlord in his barber shop about three blocks from where McFadden's gun shop used to be. "He was a good tenant. Always paid right on time. It was a shame about that policeman who worked there. He made it bad for Patrick."

"Did Mr. McFadden ever talk to you about that?" asked Ozzie.

"Oh no. He only told me they were selling their house and moving up to the Poconos to retire," said the landlord. "Lovely people."

The landlord didn't know anything about cars for sale either. Ozzie was way past hungry by now, so the interview was officially over. They drove east then turned on 9th Street to a little restaurant just below Christian Street. Ozzie knew about restaurants in every town east of the Susquehanna. This one was a four table and counter affair run by an Italian couple and their grown daughter. It had the best cabbage and sausage soup on earth. Ozzie squeezed the car into a tiny parking space and wasted no time getting through the door. They were lucky. Most days, people stood in line for at least a half an hour to get a table. Three construction workers were just getting up when Ozzie and Johnny came in. On any day you could find all sorts of people eating there. Five hundred dollar suits sitting next to blue jeans. Philly detectives and mob "associates." Old men and teenagers. Everyone fit in and enjoyed the food. Johnny groaned as Ozzie started in on a huge bowl of the cabbage. It would be a long trip back north today.

~ * ~

When his clothes were finished, Afif folded them and stuffed them into his backpack. The rain was turning into a mist and Afif didn't want to get soaked walking around. He decided to drop his clothes off at the apartment and go shopping for a present for his mother. He was expecting to get a day or two the next week to go back for a visit and wanted to buy her a silk scarf and some slippers. He jogged back up the street and turned into the project at the corner. He didn't knock at the door and just walked in. He was halfway across the living room when Jamal appeared in front of him in the hallway. The two women were at the kitchen table watching.

"So you don't believe me when I say things to you, is that what we have here?" Jamal glared at Afif with cold hard eyes. "You think you can just slip out and do as you please? I thought I was very clear when I told you not to go anywhere without my permission."

Afif looked at Jamal and then at the women. They turned their heads. "Jamal, I only went to the laundromat to wash my clothes, I...," Afif started to unsling the backpack when Jamal hit him over his left eye. Afif was shocked at first and then his knees weakened and he started to go down. Harold, the big driver, caught him from behind and locked Afif's arms in the straps of the backpack. Harold hit him hard with a punch between the shoulder blades that knocked every bit of air from his lungs. Jamal hit him again in the mouth and Afif could hear the laughing of the women as he lost his sight and fell hard to the bare floor.

~ * ~

The cop on duty at the rear entrance to The Roundhouse, Philadelphia Police Headquarters, recognized Don Mitchell when he came in. "Hey, trooper. How youse doin' ta' day?" the cop pressed a hidden button and the electric lock on the bullet proof door buzzed to admit Mitchell. Don bullshitted with the old cop for a bit and then clipped on his police ID card and went to the elevator.

Don had a special relationship with the Philly cops. Not too many years ago, the state police were on the other side of several corruption investigations of the Philadelphia police, and many of the local cops still had hard feelings about it. Mitchell worked car cases in and around Philadelphia for so long and always played it straight with them, that he earned their respect. He was one of the few staties that could walk into the Roundhouse without question.

He made his way to the records room and checked in with the clerk. He gave her the name of the woman who was the registered owner of the van and asked for her arrest report. Mitchell knew that the phony address on the van registration might fool some title clerk in Harrisburg, but wouldn't get past the Philly cops. He was right. The woman's real address was near the phony one in West Philly.

~ * ~

When they finally finished lunch, or rather, when Ozzie finished eating soup, veal, salad, and dessert, they made their way back across the river past the University of Pennsylvania and out Lancaster Avenue to the police station where Frank Dugan's office was. Dugan got Johnny a coffee and showed Ozzie the men's room. Johnny explained to Dugan where the investigation was and Dugan gave him the copies of the reports about the former officer, Sylvester.

"He had trouble from the time he came on. Always getting called to The Front for stupid stuff. He had a couple of suspensions, but managed to hang onto his job until he finally got locked up," said Frank. "He's not due out of Graterford for another three to five years, if he gets parole." Frank also told them a few good "Sam on the task force" stories before they left.

~ * ~

It was near the end of the block. A duplex set in among row houses and other duplexes. All were tight together with small yards and fences between them. The street was tree lined and wasn't as run down as most of the rest of West Philly. The old, confiscated Pontiac station wagon Mitchell drove was tired and beat except under the hood. It sure didn't look like a police car. That was one of the few advantages Don had.

He parked across the street and just past the house where he could see it in his rear view mirror. Even if they saw the bearded white guy sitting there, they probably wouldn't be concerned because he was looking the other way. The van wasn't there. Before he parked, he slipped through the alley behind the row to check for it there, too. He had a small tape recorder on his lap and read off the tag numbers of the cars he could see the back of.

He learned his lesson years ago while on a rolling stakeout. He was trying to write something on a pad on the seat next to him and rammed into a parked car. He decided to stay at least until it was almost dark before he would head back to the barracks.

~ * ~

Sam pulled Adams in off the road and asked him to start running the VINs from the list out of McFadden's computer. Calvin was phoning some of the suppliers that dealt with McFadden. It was very quiet around the barracks. Sgt. Dawes was in Bethlehem for a staff conference and Corporal Dickson was back in Porter checking with the victims on several burglaries that had never been cleared to see if they had anything to do with the murders. Sam hadn't heard a word from Yakavich and personally briefed the Major in BCI Headquarters earlier by phone. He called the prison and arranged for Sylvester to be available for an interview tomorrow, if he was willing.

It was the other list they found in McFadden's computer that was curious to Sam. It didn't make any sense, "21RNY 6/3 $4200, 17R6LRMA 7/19 $5500, 29R15LRIN 7/22 $11050, 12 RIL 9/10 $2400, 14R10LRMO 10/1 $6300." He finally had to put it aside, it was driving him nuts. Johnny and Ozzie were due back soon and he had plenty to do.

~ * ~

When Trooper Mitchell got back to the barracks, he found a note on his door to call Corporal Deland. Mitchell tried to place this Deland, but couldn't. He could wait until tomorrow. Don wanted to run the tags from the block in West Philly to see if any of them also came back to the van lady.

~ * ~

His dream was confusing. He could see the money on the floor, but couldn't make his arm move out to it. It was blowing around from the open door and he wanted to pick it up. Afif woke with a splitting headache. He was on the floor of the bedroom and alone. His head wasn't the only thing that hurt. He was sick to his stomach and found it hard to breathe from the pain in his shoulders. He couldn't tell if it was day or night and didn't care. It was the women laughing at him that hurt him the most. *Why would anyone laugh at what happened to him? They were just cruel.*

Jamal was impossible to please. No matter how hard Afif worked, it was never good enough for Jamal. Afif just wanted to go home. Jamal is mad, Yusef is mad, and these women do not respect him. Afif had had enough. No matter what these crazy fools might think is worthy and a service to God, it was not what Afif also wanted. It was too high a price to pay. He would stop it now. But first he had to get up.

~ * ~

Sam quickly looked through the Philadelphia police reports Ozzie brought back on the cop turned bad, Thomas Sylvester. The reports didn't say that McFadden was involved in Sylvester's scheme to peddle hot guns, but it looked like Sylvester couldn't have pulled it off without McFadden's help. Hot guns and hot cars, little nibbles at the other side of Patrick McFadden, the dark side.

Sam looked up as Trooper Adams came into the crime room with a computer printout in his hand. "Take a look at this, Corporal. It came in over the scope while I was running the VINs. Jefferson Township, Lancaster County, had a homicide last night. Victim shot multiple times with a 9mm. The victim had a record for Receiving Stolen Property, Burglary, and firearms offenses. No suspects, just a red car leaving eastbound from the scene."

Sam took the paper from Adams and turned to Ozzie. "Ozzie, give the township a call tomorrow and see if we have an interest in this, just in case. Thanks, Adams. We'll make a detective out of you yet."

"Let me get dry behind my ears first, Corp, I'm outta here, see you fellows tomorrow." All four of the crime room staff said good bye to the young trooper as he turned and left.

Sam eventually chased them all out of the place and told them to go home. Johnny had them all laughing hysterically with his recounting of their exploits in Philadelphia for the day. Ozzie had an attack of cabbage and sausage on the way back and almost lost his handcuffs in the woods off the turnpike. Sam told Calvin and Johnny to plan a trip to the prison tomorrow to talk to Sylvester and grounded Ozzie to work up the McFadden's phone bills. It was raining steadily and had been since earlier that afternoon. Sam just wanted to go home and do nothing, but couldn't tonight, someone was expecting him. He said goodnight to the desk man and headed for the Pathfinder in the back lot.

~ * ~

Johnny was pissed by the time he got home. The oil light kept coming on in his "wife's" station wagon. He only drove it when his pick-up truck was in the shop. He drove the Harley in clear weather. His pick-up needed a muffler for inspection and he hadn't had time to do it himself so it was either the station wagon or walk. Annette caught a ride with another woman to the truck assembly plant for work and would be home any minute now. He wondered how long she had let this go on.

For a woman who spent eight hours on a truck assembly line, she knew nothing about how to take care of a car. She didn't do much better with the house either. Johnny pulled the wagon into the small garage and popped the hood. He ran inside to change while the engine cooled. The breakfast dishes were still on the table and the bedroom looked like a tornado hit it.

Annette was from southern California. Her mother named her after the girl with the mouse ears on TV. She had singing, dancing, and acting lessons and ended up working in a truck plant in Pennsylvania, married to a trooper, divorced him and then three years later, married him again. Ain't life funny? Johnny added his mess to the room and was coming into the garage to look at the car when Annie got dropped off out front. She was blonde these days, but that could change, five feet tall and built for speed.

She stumbled into the garage lighting her cigarette and looked surprised to see Johnny and the car with the hood open. "What's wrong with the car?" she asked.

"Nothing a new payment book couldn't cure. How you doin', sweetie?" he stepped to her and hugged her tight. She planted a big kiss on his lips and turned her head to blow the smoke she had been holding in. "Old wagon's gettin' tired. Oil light's popping on."

"Oh, yeah. I've been noticing that. Does that mean it does or doesn't have oil?" she asked honestly.

Johnny groaned and said, "Oh, baby. It's a good thing I love you so. No, it's bad when the light comes on. It's called an idiot light because by the time it comes on, it's usually too late and the idiot who owns the car gets to buy a new one, ready or not."

"Well Mr. Idiot, Mrs. Idiot is going to order pizza delivered. It's too shitty to cook or go out. You want a beer?" she pinched his backside as she passed him to go into the house.

"Many," he told her and started in on the car. Johnny had learned to love her a lot. Even more than the first time around. He went through two other wives before he found her under a smashed up Charger and pulled her out. The first marriage ended shortly after it began, but they kept in touch after the lawyers were paid off and one thing led to another.

~ * ~

It was just a purely miserable night. Cold and wet. Thank God not cold enough to freeze and ice up the roads, yet. Sam drove through the traffic into Allentown and onto a quiet street of well-kept small brick homes. He pulled into the driveway of a house in the middle of the block and shut down the Pathfinder.

Peggy managed to keep the house after the divorce by working two jobs. Her shithead ex-husband wasn't content to make her miserable while they were married, he continued to cause her grief by not paying child support on time or in the right amount. He always seemed to have enough money for golf and booze, but not for his kid.

The "kid" answered the door. She was turning into quite a young lady now. Fourteen and full of fun. "Hey there, copper, get in out of the rain."

She had her hair up in rollers and was wearing an oversized sweatshirt. "Hi, Amy, how's school?" Amy just laughed and shut the door behind him before she disappeared up the stairs.

"I'm in here, Sam," Peggy called from the kitchen. Sam dropped his coat on the steps and went in. She was still in her dress clothes from the airport and cooking something that smelled real good on the stove. He moved beside her and bumped her hip with his.

"Hey, you sure are making me hungry," he gave her a hug and kissed her cheek. She returned the kiss, but nailed him square on the lips and held it. When she let him up for air he said, "Hard day at the office, honey?"

She crossed her eyes and stuck out her tongue at him and poked his ribs with the handle of the spatula she was holding. "The office is just fine as long as you hotshots stay out of my way. Sit down, I'll pour you a drink. We have a lot to do tonight. Amy would like you to look at her science project, too," Sam dropped into a chair at the small table in the kitchen and looked at the pile of books and papers already there.

Only part of it was Amy's. Peggy was well into her second year of part time college and Sam was her coach. When they first met it was a physical deal between them, but much had changed over the years and they tilted on a fine line. Mostly Sam helped her and Amy with their school work and ate her good cooking. He didn't think Peggy liked it that way and wanted something more. She was one of the few people that knew how hard it had been on Sam when he lost his wife. She told him she understood and didn't push him too hard for a more serious commitment.

He picked up the folder containing the science project and began to correct the punctuation and write a comment here and there in the margins. Amy had school by the tail and it looked like she was on her way to a good start for high school and college.

Sam got through the first few pages of Amy's treatment of fungal growth on corn crops in the Mid-Atlantic States before his thoughts turned to his own son, Ken. Raising a two year old with no mom was the most difficult job Sam had ever tried. He ended up having to admit to the limits of his abilities and got Grandma Landis and Grandma Deland to step in and help. Sam tried not to think about Ken's mom, but the memories only become easier to live with, they never go away…

~ * ~

Lt.(jg) Sam Deland was inbound from a navigation training exercise in the Mediterranean Sea. The run had been smooth and the right seater in the EA-6B was sightseeing out the window as they ate away the distance to the carrier when the radio call for Sam to "report to the CAG" came through.

Lt. Billy "Ramrod" Reager looked over at Sam and punched the intercom, "What the fuck did you do now, asshole?" Reager knew lowly jg's don't hob knob with Commander, Air Group three stripers unless serious good or bad shit is about to happen.

It took all of Sam's concentration to land the EA-6B, even though it was a beautiful clear day with calm seas. He kept trying to think of all the dumb things he'd done and what it could be that he finally got caught doing. The electronic warfare jet pitched and rocked as he rolled into the groove on final. He forced himself to breathe and set up for hitting that small area of wires at the rear of the deck. Somehow it all came together and his considerable pilot skills took over, he nailed the second wire as he plunged onto the deck. Sam pushed the throttles to full power at about the moment he felt the hook take hold on the wire. The yellow shirt forward and just starboard of him signaled to Sam that he was safely hooked and Sam cut the engines and taxied to the elevator area. Before he could get all the way turned onto the elevator, he spotted his executive officer moving quickly toward him with his plane captain.

Reager whispered into the intercom, as if anyone else could hear him, "XO's on deck and heading this way, Sam. We must be in deep shit."

"As long as no marines with guns are with him, I think we can weather whatever it is," laughed Sam. "Let me do the talking, you plan an escape route to Malta," Sam and Billy were setting switches and getting the EA-6B ready for the elevator as the XO, Lt. Commander John "Padlock" Simpson, climbed up to the cockpit.

"Sam, I'll take your plane. Meet the CAG at the island," Cmdr. Simpson pointed to the base of the carrier's superstructure and Sam saw the Air Group Commander standing at an open hatch.

"Do I need a lawyer, commander?" Sam said with a half grin.

"Padlock" hit him with that grim look that earned him that call sign. "Sam, just go meet the CAG, okay?"

"Aye, aye, sir," Sam said and shut up. This was not looking good at all. That empty feeling in his stomach began. Sam survived Naval R.O.T.C. at Villanova, flight training and carrier qualifications by hard work and keeping out of the kinds of trouble that many young, smart, energetic officers too often find to halt their careers. He unstrapped and squeezed past Cmdr. Simpson to the deck. The walk to the island filled Sam more with curiosity now than fear. He hadn't done anything that bad, *lately. He walked quickly across to Commander Anthony "Thunder" Malzone and said, "Kestrel reporting as ordered, sir."*

"Thunder" Malzone was in his forties, but his jet black hair did not have a single grey strand in it. His call sign "Thunder" had to have something to do with his voice. He sounded like a radio announcer and his deep voice seemed to start and stop with normal volume, but in the middle he boomed out the words loud enough for the neighbors across the street to hear.

Sam thought that it was odd today because Malzone could barely get out the words, "Sam, the captain needs to see you, follow me please," the voice was quiet and direct.

Sam tucked his helmet under his arm and squeezed through the passages to several stairways leading to the ship's command area. Sam was here only once before during his time on the Kennedy and that had been on the tour the Kennedy's operations chief gave to the "nuggets," new flight officers assigned to the ship. Sam had since learned how to navigate from his quarters to his squadron's ready room and to the hanger where his EA-6B was parked and maintained. Young pilots did not go to the island, they had no business there. Young pilots usually only see the captain on the ship's television. This visit was really out of left field.

Malzone turned a corner and Sam followed into a short hallway. They stopped in front of a polished wooden door with a brass plate that read simply "Captain." Malzone reached out to Sam. "I'll hold your helmet," he said and knocked on the door. Sam couldn't hear if anyone responded from inside, but apparently "Thunder" did and opened the door, motioning Sam to step in.

The captain's quarters were spacious by carrier standards and paneled with spotless polished wood. Captain Theodore "Dagger" Boone was a trim fifty something year old former fighter pilot who'd survived real combat. He now had one of the most coveted commands in all the military, reached not by those with political pull, but with guts and brains in bushels. He rose out of a rocking chair, fashioned after the one used by

President Kennedy in the White House, and faced Sam and Commander Malzone.

Sam came to attention and the captain said, "Please gentlemen, come in and sit down," he motioned toward a small couch and two chairs opposite the rocker. Sam looked to Malzone for guidance and received a slight nod toward the couch. "Thunder" moved to one of the chairs and the captain to the other. Sam took the hint and settled nervously on the edge of the couch. He didn't want to look too relaxed.

"Nice landing you just made, Lieutenant. I'm sure you'll get good marks for that one," the captain smiled slightly and glanced at Malzone.

Sam looked at Malzone and then said to the captain, "Thank you, sir. I'm still learning a lot each flight." Sam tried to look right at the captain without showing just how nervous he really was.

The captain shifted in his chair and cleared his throat. "Sam, your wife has been in a terrible auto accident. I'm sorry to have to tell you that she didn't make it. The doctors say she felt no pain and that she died immediately. I'm so sorry for your loss, Mister Deland. I..."

Sam felt the fear and the tears well from inside, "My son, Ken. Is Ken all right? Is he hurt? What happened? How...?"

"No, Lieutenant, your son is fine, he's with his grandmother. He wasn't in the car. Look, this is going to be very hard for you, but remember, your son will need his father. We will help you in any way we can. You are part of our family here and we take care of our own people. Commander Malzone will take charge of making all the arrangements."

By now Sam's head was spinning and tears were running down both cheeks. He tried to talk, but he couldn't. He felt like throwing up. The ache was growing and he didn't know what to do.

Malzone spoke, "Captain, if I may? Sam, it happened yesterday. Your father called and got through to someone at the Pentagon. She was on the turnpike and got hit by a truck. We need to get you off the carrier, probably to Naples, to fly back to the states. You'll be on the COD run this evening, Lieutenant. Reager and your XO will help you get packed."

There was a soft knock on the door and the captain turned and pronounced, "In."

The ship's protestant chaplain entered and greeted the captain. He turned to Sam and offered his hand and sadly said, "Mister Deland, I will pray for your wife and your family, and for you. Do you want to talk..."

Sam held up his hand in a stop motion to the chaplain and managed to stutter, "Chaplain, thanks, but I think I just need to deal with getting home right now. I'll need a minute of your time before I leave the ship this afternoon. Is that okay, sir?"

"Absolutely, Lieutenant. I'll look forward to speaking to you. You have my deepest sympathy. However I may help, just let me know. Captain, with your permission I'll be on my way," with that he spun and left through the still open door. The captain stood up and both Sam and Commander Malzone did the same.

"You have to think of your son now. I know I speak for the ship when I tell you that our prayers go with you," the captain shook his hand and put his other hand on Sam's shoulder.

Malzone took Sam by the arm and led him out of the cabin. Sam managed to mutter, "Thank you, sir," as they left, but he could not speak otherwise and barely heard anything Commander Malzone said about his travel schedule as the CAG half carried him through the ship toward Sam's small room.

~ * ~

The science paper appeared to materialize before his eyes and Sam realized he had only gotten to the third page. He cleared the old thoughts from his head and quickly corrected several more pages before he heard Peggy shout, "Ayyymmeee, it's ready!" Sam thought to himself that he seemed to always think about those old times while he was at Peggy's.

Dinner was a blast. Peggy and Amy got him to laughing so much he spit food back onto his plate. They talked and gossiped about the stupid boys in some of Amy's classes. Sam would imitate the goofy teenage talk to Amy's delight. Peggy and Sam cleared the table and Amy did the dishes while the grownups did Peggy's homework. Before they realized it, the kitchen clock showed 11:45.

Amy called from the stairs, "I'm outta here to bed, Mom. Night, Sam."

Peggy looked up at Sam and started to say something, but Sam beat her to it, "It's going to be a long day tomorrow, I'd better head on up the mountain. Thanks for the grub, missy," she grabbed his ear and kissed him.

Sam slowly stood and pulled her up into a long hug. "See you at the office Friday night. I'm picking up Ken in Lansdale before I come up," Sam was quickly out the door before he changed his mind. The cold air woke him a bit before he got the Pathfinder warmed up and headed west.

Thursday

The women put the children to bed and were sneaking a smoke at the back door to the kitchen. Afif could hear rap music coming from a car in the lot across the courtyard. He sat up and tried to think, to plan. What was he going to do? He hated living this way, always afraid. This had not been the first beating he'd taken from Jamal. *Where was Yusef? Why didn't he protect his own cousin?* Afif knew he had to leave, *but how?* Jamal needed his skills with the cars and would be dangerous if provoked. The abuse was not part of the bargain though. He came here to do an honorable thing. To help in the struggle. Now Jamal was acting without honor. Afif gritted his teeth and buried his head in his arms, trying to pull the strength from inside.

~ * ~

While he drove, the memories of that sad time began to come back.

The flight from the carrier and then to Philadelphia were only a blur. He made it to his mother-in-law's house in Sellersville in the middle of the night and considered sleeping on the porch so as not to wake anyone, but she must have had her mom radar on and met him at the door. Mrs. Landis didn't look like your typical German American grandma. She kept her figure over the years and much to her husband's delight, kept her grey hair tastefully hidden by Clairol. She was as sweet as her daughter had

118

been sour. Linda never cared for following her young naval aviator from air station to air station while he learned to fly navy jets. Since they met at a watering hole near the Villanova campus, it had been a stormy up and down ride. They married during one of the up times and for a while Sam thought his spirited wife was happy. He thought he was happy, too.

The navy has its own version of how ensigns in flight school should live and this did not suit the new Mrs. Linda Landis Deland. Not long after each move, Linda would declare the place a "shithole" and head back to Pennsylvania. Sam would talk on the phone to Grandma and try to get Linda to come back. Grandma would tell Sam he was right and even she didn't understand her daughter and that Sam should be patient and Linda would come around. Ken's birth only made it worse. Sam cried himself to sleep many nights, big tough jet jockey sobbing because he missed his wife and son. It didn't bother Linda. Grandma kept the baby while Linda went out with her friends. Sam would spend too much of his meager pay calling long distance trying to soak up as much of Kenny's childhood as he could.

Sam went in to the baby's room and even though he was sound asleep, picked him up and gently laid him across his shoulder. Ken smelled wonderful. Grandma kept him clean and powdered, like he was her own. They rocked while Grandma quietly told Sam what happened. Linda had all but moved out since Sam went aboard the Kennedy. She ran the roads to all hours and most nights didn't bother to call or show up. Grandma filled the void and without complaint, lovingly cared for Kenny. Linda called that day and said she was coming up from King of Prussia. On the Northeast Extension of the Turnpike, traffic was backed up solid in both lanes for a boat and trailer that had blown a tire and caught the inside lane guardrail.

The state police told them that Wayne Pollack was driving a Yellowbird Express tractor trailer about a half mile behind Linda. Wayne was a little tired. He'd been driving without sleep for the last day and a half. The vodka, speed and marijuana in his system backed up on him and when he crested a slight rise in the northbound lane, he never took the time to slow down. The tractor hit the back of Linda's Mustang and pushed the crumpled mass into several stopped cars in front of her. Wayne survived,

Linda and two others did not. Grandma said the troopers wanted to talk to Sam when he was ready. In spite of how Linda was, Sam still cried and his chest bounced the baby up and down for quite a while. Little Ken never stirred and slept peacefully on his dad's shoulder for the rest of the night.

~ * ~

Sam felt the Pathfinder begin to lose traction as he passed the dog food plant on 309. He slowed and cursed. He hated driving on icy roads. Only drunks and cops out on a night like this. The rain was freezing on the surface of the road and was invisible to the eye. He engaged the 4 wheel drive and dropped to 35. If he lost it now, at least he might live through the crash. It was after 1:30 when he pulled past the orchard. Molly was out and jumping into the air as far as she could as he lit her up with the headlights. No fire tonight, Sam just cranked up the pellet stove and fell into bed.

He had his Linda dream again. Linda was walking around the edge of an empty swimming pool while he watched from a house. Only the pool had no water and was bottomless. He yelled at her, but no sound came out. She just smiled at him as she stepped off into the pool. Sam started himself awake soaked in sweat. His eyes picked up movement at the side of the bed and there was Molly looking at him. She tilted her head to the left and stared. Sam just moaned and rolled back over. He could hear her nails on the stairs as she went back down to lay by the stove. She did her duty, made sure he was okay. Now she went back to the serious job of sleeping.

~ * ~

He could hear the snoring of the fat one coming from the other bedroom. The children in his room had been sleeping for some time. His backpack was in the corner by the door where Harold dropped it. *They think I'm so frightened of them I won't run away,* he thought. He was afraid, but now more afraid to stay. He knew what Jamal and Yusef could do with their guns. He overheard them talk of the killings once when they thought he was asleep. He knew they would not hesitate to kill him when they did not need him. Now was the time. He had to get to his family. They would decide what to do.

He eased slowly up from the floor and stepped into his shoes. His coat was the problem. He would not last long outside tonight without it and he had no idea where it was. Stepping carefully over each child, he quietly picked up the pack as he moved into the hallway. There it was. His coat lay on the floor of the living room.

He never looked back as he closed the front door behind him and quickly went along the wall and around the backside of the building. Not a soul was around. The rain was still falling and the air was cold. He wondered if it was snowing at home. He checked each street before stepping from shadow to cross. Jamal would not find any humor in this and Afif did not want to ever see Jamal again. It took almost half an hour to reach Broad Street. Afif found a northbound bus and began his journey.

~ * ~

"Oh, God. You big ox, what did you eat yesterday? It smells like something crawled up inside you and died," Marie quickly put the bedcovers back down to hold in the smell and rolled over the side and into her slippers. "Need a gas mask to sleep with you. You want coffee or hot chocolate, Ozzie? Ozzie?" she poked him in the ribs. "Oz, wake up, it's time," the huge mass in the bed moved slightly and made a rumbling sound. "Stop that, you'll blow up the house with all that gas!"

The former Marie Gianelli, mother of five, five feet one inch tall and still under one hundred and twenty five pounds, reached back under the covers into the fouled air where Ozzie's naked butt lay and grabbed a handful of Ozliewski manhood. His eyes popped open and looked at her.

"Now either you get your stinking ass outta the bed now, bucko, or I'll drag it…" She tightened her grip which widened his eyes. "…and you, if you're still connected to it, out my own self," her dark brown Bambi eyes flashed at him and she smiled just a little.

"I love you, hon. Come on back in here for just a little…," Ozzie lost his voice as Marie cranked down on the throttle handle. "Okay, okay, okay, okay, hon, hon, I'm up! I'm up!" she let go only after he started to unwind from the bed and leaned over to give him one on the cheek.

"That's my big boy. You get Junior moving and I'll start on the girls. Coffee okay?" Marie was up and out the door. Her days started early with the house, the kids, the rental properties, and Ozzie's side remodeling business to run. She didn't slow down. Ozzie watched her backside through the nightgown and thought how beautiful she still was and just how much he did love her, even though she was a pain in his considerable ass sometimes.

He pissed and started down the stairs to wake up his oldest son and caught a glimpse of Marie standing at the front picture window looking out at the front lawn. A coating of very light snow had fallen during the night and it looked like powdered sugar sprinkled on the trees and grass. He came up behind her and she said, "Isn't it somethin', Oz?" they both liked the first snows, though Ozzie knew it meant real winter was bearing down on them. Marie reached up and brought his arms around her. They stood there for a bit before Marie moved away to the kitchen to get ready to feed her Polish Italian army.

~ * ~

Afif waited at each stop for the next bus to move him north. Commuters moving into the city and others moving out to early jobs in the suburbs, passed by without taking any notice. He stayed out of the lights at each station, though he didn't think Jamal would know he was gone yet.

Jamal would have Yusef call Afif's father to track him down so Afif knew he couldn't go straight to his home in east Allentown. He had other cousins and planned to go to one of them first for a place to stay until he could figure out what to do.

Jamal's behavior was impossible to predict. The past weeks had been so filled with turmoil. Afif was only able to find out bits and pieces, but Jamal came to the house with Harold one night in a rage about someone turning traitor on him and swore to kill whoever it was. Jamal summoned Yusef and they talked for several hours alone in the living room. Awful talk of the punishments they would inflict upon "the old man" and the "greedy spics." Since that time, Jamal tried to speed up the cycle of changing the identity of the cars and moving them and the guns to the ships in Camden.

Afif knew Jamal was capable of quick and severe violence. One of the women who lived there, the middle one Afif knew her as, was keeping company with a new man at the time Afif arrived to stay in the project house. Jamal would come in and eat or meet with Harold and then retreat to one of the bedrooms to spend his time with the youngest of the three women who lived there. The oldest and biggest of the three was the boss in Jamal's absence. Afif was in bed one night and just before midnight, Jamal arrived at the house. The story Afif heard later when the boss told Harold was that Jamal found the middle woman's new boyfriend spread out on the couch watching a blaring television. Jamal walked by and turned it off. The boyfriend sprang to his feet and tried to get into Jamal's face to protest the interruption. Before more than a "Hey you...," got out of his mouth, Jamal hit him with a lamp and wrapped the cord around his neck. Only when the boyfriend passed out and dropped to the floor did Jamal release the wire and let him suck in enough breath to keep from dying.

Finally a bus with a sign for Montgomeryville/Allentown pulled to the curb. Pellets of sleet were mixing in with the rain and ticked off the bus windows as it pulled out heading north. Afif sat all the way in the back and offered a silent prayer to his God that Jamal would not find him.

~ * ~

Somehow he was awake even before his alarm would have gone off. He debated with himself about just turning back over for a few more minutes, but got up and dressed anyway. Molly looked up as he piled down the stairs and followed him down to the stove. It took Sam only a minute to kindle a flame and put in enough small and middle size wood to get the fire going. Then he was out the door into the fresh thin layer of snow and sleet with Molly at his heel. He snapped her to her run and stretched against one of the trees near her barrel. Just enough to keep from popping a muscle and he was off out over the little ridge and down into the creek bottom along the deer and woodchuck paths. He knew he didn't have enough sleep, but he would catch up tonight, if the murder case didn't break, that is.

He ran and felt his strength coming back. Pressing harder, he was able to drive his body and clear his mind. He thought about Ginny McFadden on the floor of her small kitchen. Something had to give them a break. Time was now working against them. Maybe the ex-cop in prison would shed some light on all this.

He came up out of the bottom as he neared the back of his property where the ground leveled for a bit. The wet and snow made his steps almost silent. Running cross wind now, Sam glanced ahead and picked up some movement about fifty yards in front near a pile of thorn brush he'd pushed together last spring. Sam almost tripped when the movement turned into a beautiful eight point buck rising from his bed. The buck wanted no part of Sam and accelerated from zero to hauling ass in no time. Sam yelled "buck, buck, buck!" and watched the magnificent animal bound across the open field and disappear into the woods. His white tail seemed to dance through the trees and was the last thing visible until that too was gone. There was just enough light that Sam could make out the outline of the house and he knew that it was time to head back and get ready for work.

~ * ~

Ozzie ambled into the big kitchen and joined Junior and the other four Ozliewski children at the table. It actually was an eight foot picnic table Ozzie made from cedar he somehow overbought for a deck he built for a customer several years ago. Marie had been complaining that since the youngest was out of a high chair the old table wasn't big enough anymore. Marie came home from grocery shopping one Saturday to find Ozzie and Junior assembling their new table in the kitchen. He joined the top boards tightly together to make a smooth, even surface and had the first of many coats of polyurethane already on. Marie at first thought he was nuts, a picnic table in the kitchen? But the kids loved it and they all fit, so what the heck.

"Oz, you want some pancakes with your eggs?" Marie asked. Ozzie was struggling with his tie as he sat down at the end of the bench nearest to the stove. The big .45 and handcuffs were attached to his belt and seemed to go unnoticed by the kids.

"Yeah, baby and some bacon. Maybe some a them biscuits, too," Ozzie forgot about the tie and got serious. He generously buttered a biscuit from the basket in front of him and popped it whole into his mouth. Marie piled the food onto a plate and slid it in front of Ozzie. When she turned to go back to the stove he grabbed her waist and pulled her down to him. He planted a big kiss on her neck and squeezed her.

The kids snickered and the youngest, Katie said, "Oh, Daddy, give me a kiss, too!"

Ozzie released Marie and with one hand slid under Katie's bottom, picked her up over his head and balanced her there. "Mow's mat, mittle mon?" Ozzie grinned and pieces of biscuit fell out of his mouth.

"Stanislaus, you put her down before you drop her and don't talk with your mouth full, you big ox!" Marie sputtered. He knew when she called him by his middle name she was not amused. He returned little Katie to her seat and winked at her.

"Your mom's right, it's not polite to talk with your mouth full, you should whistle!" Ozzie puckered and blew biscuit across the table toward Junior. Marie screeched and Junior ducked. Katie nearly fell off the bench laughing. Just a routine start to the day in the land of Oz.

~ * ~

When he woke, he realized the bus was stopped. He could see bits of snow here and there on the ground. Snow was something he hadn't gotten used to since he came to America. Sometimes, when the storms traveled up the Jersey coast, it would dump a foot or more of snow on Allentown. Most winters, though, were not too bad. A lot of clear sunny days and a few inches of snow a few times each year. It didn't matter, he wasn't going back to the West Bank, that much he knew.

His father and mother were determined to give Afif and his sister the chance to grow up in America. So much wealth and opportunity. Afif's father was a good mechanic and expanded his repair shop into a small used car lot as well. It was from his father Afif learned how to "rebuild" the damaged cars they purchased from the salvage yards. Sometimes with parts purchased with cash and no receipts from the back of vans and sometimes by sliding a whole car under the VIN plate from the wreck. Afif's father saw nothing wrong with any of this. He would have beaten his children if he caught either of them stealing from a neighbor, but had no remorse about taking money that came from rich insurance companies anyway.

He left the bus and walked east through the cold air. Only a few cars and trucks were moving through the early morning Allentown streets. Several blocks from the bus station he passed a small coffee shop wedged into the space between two office buildings. Other than the waitress and a grey haired security guard at the counter, the shop was empty. Neither even looked up as Afif entered and slid onto the last stool. He realized how

126

hungry he was now that he could smell the food. He needed some time to think about what he was going to do next. "Orange juice and a cheese omelette, please," he told the waitress.

"Sure thing, hon, want toast?" she asked. Afif nodded and then noticed the newspaper the security guard laid on the counter between them. "DA, PSP still puzzled by Porter double murder" was the headline.

"May I look at this please?" Afif asked the guard.

"Yeah, keep it. I'm too bushed to read it now anyway. Goin' home ta' bed," he said and yawned loudly.

Afif tried to eat as he read about the Porter murders. He tried, but a cold chill ran up his back and he couldn't finish his meal. He knew that name, McFadden. He'd heard it from the bits of talk between Jamal and Yusef. He looked around and saw the pay phone in the back of the shop. His hands trembled as he dropped the coins and dialed his father's number.

~ * ~

Before he was even out of his lane, his phone vibrated. Sam turned onto the hard road and tried to get the thing off his belt and not put the Pathfinder in the ditch. The Township salted and cindered the road, but there wasn't much ice to melt off and the snow hadn't been heavy enough to leave more than a thin layer of slush. The Pathfinder held traction and Sam got the phone out where he could see the number was that of the Bethlehem Barracks. He shook his head, not a good way to start your day.

The captain laid it straight out for Sam. The Commissioner was up early watching the morning news. It wasn't kind to the state police. Citizen interviews called for better police protection. That's when he called her at home at 6:45 that morning wanting to know just what the fuck was going on and why the fuck the goddamn newspapers are printing editorials and the television is blaring about how it isn't safe even in the rural areas covered by the state police. And didn't he promote her to captain and put her in Bethlehem to straighten out the mess Lt. Harman was causing in the crime unit there. Or did he have to find someone with real balls to step in and lock up murderers. "I reminded him Harman was on vacation and that we were really on top of this murder and expected a break at any time, right, Sam?"

"Yeah, Captain, you're right. Harman is on vacation. The rest is subject to debate. Did the colonel suggest that maybe Harman ought to be put in charge of the horses at the Academy. Be right at home with the rest of the horses' asses," Sam wished he hadn't said that, sort of.

"He's not really the issue here. This has got people scared. They think we're being invaded. You don't have to listen to the dozens of phone calls I have to. Every township supervisor and party committeeman within fifty miles is screaming for an arrest. The newspaper loves it. They sell bundles with this stuff." Sam didn't know what to say. "Look, I know your guys are good and something will break on this, but if it starts to get out of control we have to get the DA to work the politicians to give us some breathing room. I'm setting a meet with him for 1:00, meet me at the courthouse, we'll have lunch with him in the seventh floor snack shop. He won't like it, but we should all be seen together," she had a good instinct on this kind of thing.

"Okay, boss. See you there."

~ * ~

The little one bedroom apartment had a tiny bathroom and Calvin had to wade through towels and dirty clothes to get to the toilet. He knew he was running late, but the pretty little waitress delayed him when he tried to get up twenty minutes ago. Calvin had been sporting her for the last three months and when she called him the night before to come over, he hadn't figured to spend the night. She used a little wine and probing fingers to convince him to stay. Now he had to get moving. He hustled out of the bathroom grabbing jeans and boots. She was awake, barely, and she was naked and still on the bed where he'd just eased away from her moments before. "Can't you stay with me today, baby? It's gonna be cold out there. I'll keep you all warm..."

He dropped down next to her and leaned over. "You know I would if I could, but I can't today, call you later," he kissed her and scooped her up, pressing her breasts against his still bare chest. Slowly he released her and she ran a hand up his jeans. Calvin only hesitated a second and with a groan pulled himself up, threw his hooded sweatshirt over his head and walked quickly out the front door. In the glove box was a small battery operated razor. Calvin had been here before and could make the turnaround if he hurried. He shaved while he drove. The slick streets slowed him down, but he didn't have far to go to get to his place. He was in the door, showered, dressed and back on the road to the barracks in no time.

Johnny was standing just outside the back door smoking when Calvin got there. Sam's Pathfinder and Ozzie's pick up were already in the lot. As Calvin walked up to Johnny, he heard Johnny say, "Good mornin', alley cat. You ever stay at home? Why don't you rent out your house, man? You don't need it. I tried callin' you. Why have a cell phone if you don't answer it? Gave up at midnight."

"Fuck you, I don't talk to rednecks 'less I'm paid to. Why didn't you leave a message?" Calvin said, grinning a wide smile.

"Fuck you, too. I don't talk to voice mail. You missed the chance to have a beer with me and the old lady. Your loss," Johnny took a deep drag on the cigarette.

"Another great cultural experience missed. How will I ever improve my social standing? You ready to go to prison today?" Calvin punched in the combination on the door lock and held it open for Johnny.

"God, I hate going in those places, gives me a major case of the blackass. Doggone creepy." Johnny flicked the cigarette into the coffee can near the door that served as an ashtray and hopped up the two steps and into the hallway leading to the squad room.

"You southern boys sure do have such colorful speech patterns, 'doggone'?" Calvin shook his head and followed Johnny inside.

~ * ~

"The phone is fo' you," Jamal opened his eyes and saw the small woman was holding Jamal's cell phone over the bed. Jamal rubbed his eyes and sat up on the side of the bed. He took the phone from her and held it face down on the bed.

"Go find something to do for a bit, girl, okay?" she shrugged her shoulders and walked out of the room so Jamal would be alone. "What?" he said roughly.

The woman's voice on the phone said, "The little A-rab fella' be gone. His shit, too," Jamal slammed the phone onto the bed without saying another word. He quickly picked it back up and sent a short text message. Jamal stepped to the shower and tried to think what he would do next.

Not far away, the driver's phone displayed the text, Harold knew it was time to pick up Jamal at the West Philadelphia house of Jamal's current girlfriend. The one with the new red Lexus.

~ * ~

The paperwork never seemed to slow down. Sam tried to keep up with it so that his men would get their overtime pay and the bosses stayed off all their backs. Time sheets, car logs, reports, follow up reports, interviews, stacks and stacks of it. Sam also knew that he had precious little time for it with all that was left to do on the McFadden murder. He was in early today and moved much of the paper before Ozzie and then Johnny arrived. Each talked about the ideas that came to them overnight. Sam gave up on the office paper and started helping Ozzie with the phone records. It didn't take long to realize that, other than the daughters in Pottstown and California, the calls mostly went to Philadelphia. Sam told Ozzie to check the Internet for the most frequently called numbers and then call Detective Dugan in Philly to see if any popped in Philly's system. Sam told him to start court orders for the non-published numbers to be served on the phone providers after he heard from Dugan.

Calvin and Johnny were getting ready to leave for Graterford to interview Thomas Sylvester, the ex-cop who used to work at McFadden's Philly gun shop. Ozzie had a phone to his ear and said, "Johnny, phone's for you. Some guy wants to know if you got a girl's Harley for sale."

Johnny looked at Ozzie and thought for a minute before he picked up on the extension at his desk, "Is this the old fart who rides side saddle?"

"Shit, ride circles around you, girly boy," it was Trooper Don Mitchell from Philadelphia. "You don't remember your first Harley had training wheels?" Mitchell never let Johnny forget that Johnny bought a used Sportster, a smaller version of the Harley, before Johnny moved up to a full sized Hog.

"Well, old man, have you t-boned any Buicks lately?" Johnny was one of the few who could kid Mitchell about that. Twenty years ago Trooper Don Mitchell was nearly killed when a drunk pulled out in front of Don's bike and Don remodeled the drunk's driver's side door with his right shoulder. Mitchell still carried the scars from that one. Almost cost him his job. It took months of painful rehab before he could write and shoot well enough to go back to work. "How the hell are you anyway? Haven't talked to you for quite a while."

"Busy like always. Nobody else wants to mess with cars. Too much work. You got a Corporal Deland up there? He the same guy that worked the road down here and was on the task force a few years ago?" Mitchell asked.

"Yeah, Sam Deland. Wants to ask you about a double murder we're working up here. Something strange about cars the victim had. I got to run out to do an interview, I'll put him on. Let's go ridin' when the weather breaks. Sam, line two, Don Mitchell from Philly. See ya, old man," Johnny pointed the phone at Sam and hung up when Sam picked up the phone in his office.

"Don, thanks for calling back. We met a few years ago at Philly. I was in off the road working with the Marshals down there," Sam remembered the beard and the flannel shirt.

"Yeah, Corp, you were kickin' down doors and duckin' bullets. What can I do for you?" Mitchell was standing in his small, second floor office looking at the piles of paperwork on his desk that never seemed to get any smaller.

Sam explained the murders and how they found out that Patrick sold cars and the list from the computer. Sam described the Mustang VIN he suspected was bad and asked Mitchell if he could come up to look at it and any others Adams turned up from the list. "We don't have anyone we're looking at right now. We really need a break on this one," Sam sounded just a bit worried.

"Sure, glad to. Give me a chance to have lunch with Johnny, too. How soon you want me up there?" Don flipped open his notebook and checked his court dates. "I've got a few things working, but I can break loose. No court until after Thanksgiving."

"I was hoping you could at least look at the two cars we already have tomorrow," Sam pulled a copy of the McFadden car sales list and put it in front of him.

"Can you clear it with my captain? I can run the numbers through BMV today and be up there in the morning," Mitchell lit a cigar and opened his office window so the smoking police wouldn't swarm down on him.

"No problem, my captain has already been brought up to speed and will pull the strings. Let me give you these numbers," Sam read off the list of VINs and included the Mustang and McFadden's car. "Thanks, Don, see you tomorrow."

Mitchell sat down and started a folder for the Straus Valley cars. He probably wouldn't get a chance to do his regular work today, let alone look for the van in West Philly. Within twenty minutes, he had printouts of the VINs and started getting a good idea of what he had. All of the cars Corporal Deland had were reconstructed wrecks. Mitchell moved from the Bureau of Motor Vehicle machine and hotfooted it, in his own lumbering way, back up the stairs to his office. Once there, he dialed Harrisburg and connected with a trooper assigned to the BMV. He ordered title histories, the rush version, for the cars and asked that they be faxed backed to him as soon as they came from the microfiche operators. The Harrisburg trooper promised Mitchell he'd have the documents before end of shift that day.

~ * ~

The ride to the prison passed quickly for Calvin. He went over the case file, now several inches thick, and bounced his thoughts off Johnny. Calvin didn't like the way this was going. "We're losing the time thing, JB. It's Thursday and I don't think we've talked to the shooter yet."

Johnny flipped his cigarette out the window and rolled the glass half way back up. "Prison's comin' up around the next bend. Beautiful downtown Graterford," the town wasn't much. Just an old hotel and a few houses perched on the banks of the Perkiomen Creek. Downstream, the creek fed into the Schuylkill River, which led eventually down to Philadelphia. They turned left over the bridge and drove through the prison farm and up the hill to the series of drab brick and concrete buildings that made up what was considered the toughest of Pennsylvania's prisons.

Johnny put the Ford into a "Police Only" slot next to a marked PSP car from the local barracks. The front entrance to the prison was a wide concrete porch covered by a steel overhang. At the top of the steps was a red barrel filled with sand. Johnny and Calvin unloaded their pistols at the barrel and checked in at the desk. The sergeant took their pistols, magazines, handcuffs and phones and slid them through a slot in the wall of bullet proof glass behind him where another guard locked them up. The sergeant said, "You guys here with the other trooper?"

Calvin looked at Johnny and then back at the sergeant. "No, we're here to interview an inmate, Thomas Sylvester. Supposed to be set up yesterday by...," Calvin opened his notebook and read the name of the Graterford assistant warden who he talked to.

"Yeah, that's what I mean. The other trooper is in with him now," the sergeant looked puzzled.

"Him who, Sarge?" asked Calvin.

"Sylvester, in the infirmary. The uniform trooper's in taking the report now," said the sergeant.

"What the heck are you talking about, Sarge? We're here to interview Sylvester about a murder up in Lehigh County. Used to be in business with the victim," explained Calvin. Johnny just stared blankly at the sergeant, not really understanding what was going on.

"Look, Sylvester's up in the infirmary, if he's still alive. Got beat almost to death last night and wasn't found until about 6:00 this morning. The doctor may send him down to the hospital in Norristown or Phoenixville. We called the barracks and the other trooper came out to take a report. You want to talk to him, have the guard inside walk you up," the desk man waved through the bars and the guard inside tripped the electronic lock to admit Calvin and Johnny. Once through the first set of bars, they were enclosed in between them and another set. The lock on the inner set tripped and they moved inside the confines. Johnny shivered. Man, he didn't like jails.

~ * ~

Afif tried to explain to his father what happened. His father was not pleased. "What are you going to do now? Why do you want to make trouble for us?" his father asked. "These are not people you can disobey, you are in much trouble!"

"My father, I think they are pulling me into a deep well from which I will never escape. I used my skills for them and for our brothers, but I am not able to go on," Afif was cut off by his father.

"Stay away from here. Yusef may come for you. I don't want him to find you here," Afif's father lowered his voice. "Go to the old water plant at the river. Hide there and wait for me. I will bring you some clothes and money. Don't let anyone see you."

Afif felt empty. He wanted to see his mother and his younger sister. He wanted to lie in his bed and sleep. But he knew his father was right. Yusef was family, but he was also quite dangerous. Better to avoid him and especially Jamal.

~ * ~

Sam buried himself in the paperwork. Calvin had started the Homicide Book, a three ring binder sectioned off to hold the various types of reports generated during the investigation. Interviews, property receipts, press clippings and so forth. Sam filed several pages in the book and re-read much of it for the third or fourth time. Ozzie stepped into Sam's office and dropped the telephone records court orders on the desk. Sam didn't bother to read it. "Fax it over to the DA and give him a heads up. We'll get the judge to sign them and serve them on the phone companies on our way in to meet with the captain. Give the judge's office a call and let them know we're coming," Sam said.

"Already done. Judge will be there at eleven thirty," Ozzie grinned his shit eating grin at Sam. "Relax, Sam. This will come together. One step at a time."

"I hope we haven't missed something obvious. I keep thinking Philly is going to be a part of this," Sam said.

~ * ~

"Thomas, you look like you had a bad day," Johnny said as he walked into the infirmary. Sylvester was bandaged around the head and his face was bruised and swollen. Both arms were wrapped in what looked like splints and several IV bags hung above him dripping fluids. The uniformed trooper standing over the patient looked puzzled as they walked up to the side of the bed.

"Szul right? Met you at wiretap school a few years ago. How you doin'?" Calvin put out his hand. "I'm sorry I don't remember your first name. This is my partner, Johnny Bonner."

"Carl, it's Carl. What, may I ask, are you guys doing here? You're out of Straus Valley, right?" Szul asked.

"Well, we came to talk to Thomas here. Before the train ran him over. What did happen to him?" asked Calvin.

"Looks like somebody got into his cell before lights out and beat the piss outta him. He laid there all night. They found him when they opened up for breakfast. Doc thinks he'll live. Might need plastic surgery, but I don't think the state is going to pay for it. Give him some bed time and send him back. Doesn't want to tell me who did it. Says he must not have seen them. Tough guy," Szul turned back to Sylvester. "You ready to cooperate yet?"

Sylvester stirred just slightly in the bed and tried to speak. His lips were so swollen he looked like he had a pair of those wax Halloween gag lips. "Fug ou," he mumbled.

Johnny stepped over and thumped heavily onto the hospital bed beside Sylvester. The movement of the bed caused obvious pain and discomfort to the patient. He groaned loudly and a tear made its way out of his right eye. Johnny grabbed an arm and moved it out of his way and Sylvester bellowed in pain. "Thomas, my friend. You are a lucky man. Looks like you get a few weeks of comfy bed rest out of this," Johnny looked over at Trooper Szul. "Mr. Thomas Sylvester here is a very special guest of the state. In his former life, he was a Philly cop. A bad one. Got caught sellin' guns and got locked up. I'm amazed he's lived this long in this fine establishment. Looks like it's finally caught up with you, Thomas.

136

Someone here doesn't like you very much. Fuck me? No, I think it's fuck you, Thomas. Looks like it's fuck you real serious."

Calvin said, "See, Thomas used to be partners in the gun business with another guy down in Philly. Thomas got caught, but the other guy didn't and the other guy kept his mouth shut and walked away. Skated through while Thomas goes to prison. When's the last time you saw Patrick McFadden, Thomas?"

Sylvester's eyes moved from Calvin to Johnny and back to Calvin. Calvin saw the fear in them. "Well, Thomas. Last I saw him was three days ago and he was in a lot worse shape than you."

Johnny leaned over closer to Sylvester's ear and said, "Look, I think you know that the fucks that did you are gonna be pissed you're not dead. They ain't givin' up. They'll be back. How is it that your old pal Patrick gets dead and you almost get dead all in the same week? You better think about who you're afraid of the most right now. Me or them."

Calvin said, "We're going to find who killed Patrick. You know how this works. The sooner you jump on the bus, the better your deal. Witness or defendant, it's up to you," Calvin was freewheeling now. Making the connection that until a few minutes ago didn't seem to exist.

Johnny picked up on it, "Right in their living room. The wife got all chopped up. Real nasty. Lots of bullets. Lots of blood. You run with a real sweet crowd," Sylvester closed his eyes and shook his head slowly back and forth.

Trooper Szul took it all in and said, "This guy's pal got killed?"

Johnny replied, "Yeah, his old friend and the wife got murdered up in Porter over the weekend. Hell of a coincidence that Thomas here gets left for dead, too, right, Thomas?"

"Last chance, shithead. We walk out of here with nothing from you, you might not get another turn," Calvin moved slowly toward the door.

Sylvester made a gurgle sound and looked over at Szul. Johnny said, "Carl, why don't you check with the guard captain and see if we can get a visitor and phone sheet on this fella. We'll babysit him a bit."

~ * ~

Afif knew the building where he was to meet his father. They used it before to work on the cars that they didn't want anyone else to see. He made his way across downtown toward the river and warmed himself with the walk. He began to piece together more of the talk he'd heard between Yusef and Jamal. How Jamal bitterly complained to Yusef about loyalty, but had become quickly quiet when Afif walked into the house. Afif also now knew he had heard the name of the town Porter before. He heard Jamal and Yusef talk about that town, about going to Porter and deal with loyalty. The water plant appeared ahead down the hill along a section of the river front that was mostly empty buildings. Afif slipped around the back and pulled away a sheet of plywood over a window and went inside to wait and become even more afraid.

~ * ~

Sam just shook his head and smiled as Ozzie climbed back into the car. "Oz, we're going to be eating in a little bit. You're going to spoil your meager appetite."

"No pwawbum," Ozzie mumbled between gulps of the microwave burrito as they pulled out of the Turkey Hill parking lot and onto the highway for the trip into Allentown. Ozzie parked in a lot behind the federal courthouse and they walked up the hill and over a block to the county building to meet with the judge. Once the telephone court orders were signed, they crossed the street and walked the three blocks to one of the phone company offices where the order could be served. The head of security promised he would have the listings later that day and would fax them to the barracks. They would fax the other two orders to the security departments of the cellular companies that held the records.

Sam looked up at the increasing cloud cover drifting in from the west as he and Ozzie walked slowly back to the county building. He calculated the arrival of the cold front and didn't like the timing. Rain and wind were bad enough, but the temperature could turn downward and form ice on wings and runways. Sam still flew because he liked the mental and physical challenge of it. He always looked forward to the time he could spend with Ken at the gliderport and flying the towplane or running along under Ken with the Pathfinder and the trailer as ground crew. The flight he was clicking through his mind for Friday night would be very different, though.

Sam incurred some wrath from the state police before he ever made it out of the academy. His background of flying jets for the navy brought him to the attention of certain captains and majors at headquarters and they recruited him for the Aviation Bureau. Though most of state police aviation centered around helicopters, fixed wing pilots were used for high altitude surveillance and transportation of VIPs. Mostly though, they drilled circles in the sky over a stretch of interstate, timing and calling out speeders for the hidden marked units below. Not what Sam wanted to do.

Since Sam didn't volunteer to go to aviation after graduation, he drew the bottom of the assignment pile: road patrol on the expressways around Philadelphia. His choice to go upstate closer to his folks was laughed at and he was sent to Philly to learn his lesson. Sam, of course, made the best of it and with Grandma Landis pitching in to help with young Ken, proceeded to put the past behind him and work his way up out of patrol and onto the task force and eventually to promotion. He still had to fend off the weenies at headquarters each time a new boss found out about his pilot status. They didn't give up.

They stopped briefly at the entrance to the courthouse and exchanged a few minutes of bull with the sheriff's deputies at the metal detector before lining up at the elevator for the ride to the seventh floor snack shop. Early, neither the captain nor the DA were there. The lunch crowd was busy talking and eating and paid no attention to Sam and Ozzie walking into the crowded cafeteria. That is, except for one set of experienced eyes belonging to a white haired, rumple suited chap off in a corner. The newspaperman knew all the players in the Lehigh Valley and recognized Sam and Ozzie. He continued to eat and watched Ozzie line up at the sandwich counter. Sam said something to Ozzie and walked back out to the hallway.

"Hi, Mrs. Tuttle, it's Sam," Sam said into his cell phone.

"Yes, Sam. Johnny called. He and Calvin have a name. The prisoner gave them the name of someone connected to the victim. Hold on, I've got it right here. Here it is, Jerome Yancey, Y-a-n-c-e-y, from Philly."

"What are the boys doing now?" asked Sam. He fumbled out his small notepad and jotted down the name.

"On their way to Philly. They wanted you to call Detective Dugan and see if he has a last known address for this Yancey," Mrs. Tuttle said. "I ran Yancey through criminal records and came up with a couple of possibles. The closest one is about thirty and has a rap sheet for robbery and theft out of Philly and Chester County," She gave Sam the date of birth and Philadelphia police photo number of Yancey. The two others were both from Pittsburgh.

Sam caught sight of the DA and the captain emerging from the elevator together and told Mrs. Tuttle, "Tell Calvin I'm at the DA's office, call me here in half an hour," without waiting for a reply, he waved for Jess and the DA to stop, clicked "end" and dialed Dugan in Philly.

~ * ~

Yusef didn't like it at all. This little cousin of his was becoming annoying. Yusef didn't handle annoying things very well. That had been a problem for him since he was very young. The beatings his mother gave him for even the most trivial infractions had lasting effects on his personality and behavior. Long ago his temper developed into a lethal tool he wielded without any feeling of guilt or remorse. Yusef had become a very dangerous individual. His flight from Detroit to Philadelphia left behind several cold bodies, including more than a few women. Yusef didn't like much of anyone, but he really didn't like women. He never dated and only rarely gave in and found a hooker to relieve his sexual tensions. That often proved more of a problem for him and then the girl. Yusef couldn't always get things to work when he wanted them to. He thought he could, but sometimes when face to face with some junkie waif, nothing came up. More than a few took a bad beating from him. Some simply disappeared.

Yusef was in that kind of a mood now. Looking for Afif at the projects and the old warehouses, he found nothing and now he was mad. Jamal was calling him every couple of hours and Harold was getting tired of driving around in circles with Yusef ranting curses in Arabic.

"You better come up with something soon," Harold told Yusef. "Your cuz causin' too much shit. We got work to get done. No time fo' this."

The van made another circle past the shops on Passyunk and rolled back north toward the project. A yellow Mazda cut out from a side street and Harold slammed on the brakes just missing the rear of the car. Within a block they were stopped in traffic and Harold heard the side door of the van open and Yusef blasted out toward the offending car. The woman in the Mazda never saw Yusef until after he shattered her driver's side window and cracked her windshield with the stubby ball bat Jamal kept in the van. He screamed at her and she ducked and covered her head from the flying glass. Harold sounded the horn and waved at Yusef to get back in the van. Yusef stood next to the Mazda for a moment and after one last swat of the bat on the door jam, trudged back to the van. Harold backed up and went the wrong way in the next alley until they were a block over.

"Fuck, man. You tryin' to get us busted? You got that fuckin' machine gun in the back and you out makin' big noise like that? You fuckin' nuts!" Harold was one of only two people that could talk to Yusef like that and not face a fight. "Get the fuck out! You walk now, you stupid fuckin' greasy A-rab motherfucker! Get the fuck out!" Harold yanked the van to the curb. Yusef pulled the black gym bag from under the middle seat and slid back out of the side door. Harold squealed away and left Yusef standing in the middle of the block. He was on his own now. He would find Afif and teach Afif some respectful manners. Cousin or not.

~ * ~

Ozzie had two cheeseburgers, fries, a strawberry milkshake, corn chowder soup, and a jelly doughnut in front of him when he looked up and saw the captain signal him to "come on" from the doorway. Torn over what to do, he hesitated and the captain waved again. Ozzie stood up and retrieved the serving tray he had just put on the stack of trays near the trash can. He gathered up his little lunch and followed the captain over to the elevator where Sam had the DA pulled aside. The captain smiled and shook her head from side to side. Ozzie was Ozzie. He stood there waiting for the elevator holding this pile of food on his tray. Take out service.

Sam grabbed a handful of fries as the elevator doors closed. "Calvin's got a name from the guy in prison. Gonna call me here. Some guy hooked with McFadden and him. Good fries, how's the soup?"

~ * ~

Calvin opened the door and surprised the small woman coming out of the dining room. "Hi, Momma."

"Calvin, my God! And Johnny!" she tossed the dishtowel on the couch and was grabbed up by the big trooper. "It's soooo good to see you two. Oh my, oh my," she leaned over and smooched Johnny on the cheek and grabbed his ear. Lots of hugs and kisses between the three of them. Johnny felt good being here with his second mom again. It had been a while since he last saw her. Grandma hollered up from the basement and started up the stairs. She still amazed Calvin.

"Got only a few minutes to visit, Momma, okay? We're in between the prison and Philly. Thought this would be the place for a coffee break," Calvin grinned his magnificent smile and Momma turned to the kitchen to pour cups of coffee for them.

~ * ~

"We thought you were to stay in there longer. What will you do? Are these people looking for you?" Afif's father was trying to understand what was going on. The water plant had been closed since the late 60s. It was one of several old brick monsters looming over the river. More trouble to maintain than it was worth, the latest owner declared bankruptcy and disappeared behind a corporate disguise. Now it looked like the city would have to step in and demolish the structure before it fell in. It dripped and smelled. Afif and his father had been here a few years ago and late at night practiced their art on cars, at a nice profit.

"Yes, they will look for me. Yusef may help them. He is one of them now. At first it was just the cars they had me for, but now it has changed. Something is wrong. Not at me, but they are angry at some others that have not been true to them and I think they have killed some. I am afraid I will be killed also. They have become cruel and even though I work hard, it is still not good enough for them," Afif sighed and slumped his shoulders. His father poured tea from a thermos for Afif. "It is best if I stay hidden for a while. Maybe they will...," Afif stopped as a truck passed slowly outside.

"Clothes and some money," Afif's father held out a duffle bag. "That is my ride back. Go to Ali's place in Emmaus. Help him with the car lot. He will keep silent until we learn what is to be," Ali ran Al's Used Cars. Another cousin from his father's side who had no use for Yusef and could be trusted.

~ * ~

The Chief of County Detectives watched the parade come through the office. The DA, followed by the short blonde state police captain, Sam, and Ozzie with his lunch tray. Sam said to the DA, "I'll be in here with the Chief," Sam wanted to avoid Assistant District Attorney Bitch Asshole Janice if at all possible. Ozzie plopped down in one of the Chief's guest chairs and finally got to eat. Sam and the Chief gabbed about their mutual friends and went over the McFadden murder.

"Your call on one," the DA, now in shirt sleeves, stuck his head in the office and nodded to Sam. The captain slipped past him and took the guest chair next to Ozzie. She watched in awe as Ozzie put the last half of the second cheeseburger into his mouth in one bite.

"Calvin, Dugan will have what he can find on this Jerome at Major Crimes by the time you get there. What did Sylvester tell you?" Sam asked.

"Not much at first. Found him in the infirmary beat up last night and left for dead. Gonna transfer him to Phoenixville Hospital later today for surgery, new face. Johnny had a heart to heart with him in the way only Johnny can and we convinced him we were his pals. Jerome Yancey is a former cellmate. Got out last year. Sylvester set Jerome up with McFadden to buy guns, military theft stuff. Something about gang members and hangers-on in the National Guard. Steal guns and wholesale through places like McFadden's. Mostly Latin types, Midwest and upstate New York. Sylvester didn't know about McFadden being dead. Says there's been some rip offs. Bad blood. Thieves stealing from the thieves. McFadden was mad, Jerome was mad. I guess Jerome was madder," Calvin winked at his mom and Johnny at the kitchen table. Mom was trying to get Johnny to eat some shortbread cookies she made yesterday. Johnny just wanted a smoke and ducked out the back door with his coffee. "Funny thing, though, not a visitor or any outgoing calls made by this dickhead. Makes me wonder how he kept in touch."

"Good work. This might turn into something. Nose around the last known address and see if you find him, see if he'll talk to you. Ask Dugan to tap his sources. He's got good eyes and ears out on the street. And be careful," Sam gave the captain and Ozzie a thumbs up. "Who did Sylvester?"

"No go on that. He wants to settle it himself. Local guys are gonna do a crime report, hold it open for a while. Maybe after the pain medication wears off, our punching bag may change his mind," Calvin said. "Probably got into the middle of whatever killed McFadden. They just didn't finish the job."

Sam thought a minute. "Why don't you call Phoenixville security. Might be a good idea to have extra concern for this guy, while he's a guest there."

"Already done, the boss there is a retired trooper," Calvin told Sam. "We're at my mom's. We'll be heading into the city and hook up with Dugan. Call you later."

Sam briefed the captain and Ozzie and thanked the chief and the DA for their hospitality. Ozzie didn't quite know what to do with the tray of dirty dishes until the chief said he was going up for coffee and would take it. Sam and Ozzie didn't make it to the city limits before Ozzie jerked the Crown Vic into a Burger King and announced, "Gotta hit the head, want anything?"

~ * ~

By the time he got back to his rented room near the Italian Markets, Yusef was steamed. He dumped his stuff and got on his phone and tried to reach Jamal. No answer. Jamal was being very careful. He didn't like cell phones. Jamal warned Harold and Yusef several times to stop using their phones so much. Jamal tried to use pay phones as much as possible. That was becoming harder as pay phones disappeared from the streets. Harold just rolled his eyes when Jamal wasn't looking. After twenty minutes, Yusef was about to give up when his phone rang. It wasn't Jamal, it was the girlfriend and she told Yusef Jamal didn't want to talk to him until Afif was standing next to him.

~ * ~

Things didn't work out for Trooper Mitchell. A pile of reports showed up on his desk with correction memos on them. Then the phone rang and the Harrisburg BMV trooper told him the system was acting up and the title histories were coming in a lot slower than expected. Don looked at the reports he needed to correct and told the BMV guy to hold the histories until the end of the day and fax them to Corporal Deland at Straus Valley. He'd pick them up there tomorrow. He hung up and dug into the pile.

~ * ~

Sam called Peggy on his cell phone and found out the latest weather was not all bad. The front was coming through tomorrow, but didn't look as strong as it did earlier in the week. Sam told her he was in the middle of something and may have to cancel his Friday flight, but would let her know by tomorrow morning, probably, maybe.

"Sam, you make me nuts," she said as she hung up on him.

Sam didn't want to miss this flight. It was one of the few times Ken could go with him on these out of town hops. Flying the Lear was not especially fun. It was a slippery little jet with not enough room in the cockpit for his size. The military jets Sam flew were as fast, but handled better and were more forgiving, except on final over the wake of a carrier.

For several years now, Sam had flown for Peggy's charter service. He was the main guy a group of too rich Penn State alumni counted on to deliver them to away games and to short hop them from Allentown to State

College on home game weekends. Of course, Sam didn't mind since he got to combine trips to Penn State with his favorite type of flying at the little gliderport down the mountain from Beaver Stadium. Tomorrow he was flying the group to the away game at Champaign-Urbana in Illinois with Ken and flying back Saturday night. Somehow he was able to juggle the details of the McFadden murder and plan for the flight at the same time.

Ozzie came back to the car with a huge drink. "Supersize, baby!" Ozzie grinned as he hopped in. "Wonder if our Jerome is at the other end of any of the phone calls on McFadden's bill? Guess we'll know once Calvin finds him in Philly."

"I don't bet, but I'd bet you a supersize beer Jerome doesn't live wherever he used to anymore. We tracked ex-cons all over and you can forget what's on the books as an address. This Jerome isn't gonna come to the door when Calvin and Johnny knock. Hopefully Frank Dugan can sort it out with them," Sam said as he looked out the window at the thickening cloud cover.

~ * ~

Calvin looked at the mug shot Detective Frank Dugan showed him. "Not a peep out of him since he got out. His last address is in West Philly about a mile from here, but according to the sheet it was his dead brother's ex-wife's house. No phone," Dugan slipped the stack of papers into the copy machine and waited for it to spit out Calvin's copies. "I'll ride over with you and we'll see what or who's there now. Ready?"

~ * ~

Afif caught the bus at 4th and Hamilton and it swung around for its stop and go trip back through Allentown. He would have to transfer at Dorney Park, but would be in Emmaus just before dark. Unsure of what to do now, he allowed himself to relax and drifted into a cat nap as the bus rhythmically sped up and slowed down at almost every block west across town.

~ * ~

Sam got Mrs. Tuttle on the phone while Ozzie maneuvered them back to the barracks. "Can you get me a number for the Army Criminal Investigation Division, probably for the Midwest, Illinois, Indiana and also for New York if it's separate. Call me on my cell if you get it before we get in."

~ * ~

Calvin and Johnny's luck was used up for the day. The address turned out to be a burned out shell where a row house had once stood. Burned down a year ago according to the neighbors. No one had heard of Jerome, the dead brother, or the dead brother's ex-wife. Dugan said he would check the property records for the owner on the tax rolls, but didn't hold out much hope. Yancey's record had the name of an accomplice from the robbery that got him sent to prison, but Dugan found him awaiting trial on new charges in the city jail system. Dead end. Calvin reluctantly decided that was enough for one day and asked Dugan to press his sources for the latest on Jerome. Johnny drove them back to Major Crimes to drop the detective off and call Sam.

~ * ~

Mrs. Tuttle was about to punch in Sam's number when Sam and Ozzie trudged in through the back door of the barracks. She waved Sam over and Ozzie headed for the locker room to empty out from the supersize drink.

"What a run around, Sam. Army CID is lost in space. I got transferred four times and still ended up leaving a message at some 800 number God knows where. Hopefully they'll have someone call you back."

~ * ~

Don Mitchell was rubbing his eyes from the fatigue built up from pounding his computer for most of the day. If he was taking his road trip up to Straus Valley tomorrow, he knew he had to wade through this mess. One of the other crime troopers stuck his head into Mitchell's office and waved several sheets of paper. "Just came in for you from BMV," the young trooper said.

Don thought a moment and didn't understand why he would be getting stuff from BMV. He remembered telling them to fax the title histories directly up to Sam Deland. He hauled himself up and took the papers. As he stood there and looked them over, he realized this was the title history for the van he was helping Trooper Damon with.

"Afil Achmor? Shit I can't read this scratch," Mitchell was trying to decipher the signature on the reconstruction affidavit. The van was sold at auction by a Jersey insurance company and then rebuilt. "Lehigh Valley Rebuildables," Mitchell read out loud. Up in Allentown. Well, he was sort of headed that way tomorrow anyway. Mitchell threw the papers into the folder he set up for Straus Valley and went back to his typing.

~ * ~

He was going through the McFadden's stuff again when the phone rang. Sam answered, "Corporal Deland." Sam agreed with Calvin and told them to drive safely on the way back. Safely meant that Johnny would cover the distance in the inverse proportion to the square of the angle of Calvin's anatomical grip on the passenger seat. Barring deer crossing or Penn Dot repairing the roads. The listings for the phone numbers were coming in on the fax machine and Ozzie was sorting through them trying to match up times, numbers and names.

"Sam, looks like some of these calls went to pay phones in Philadelphia. 5200 Chestnut, South 56th St., 1800 South 22nd Street..."

"West Philly and South Philly," said Sam.

"Quite a few to a cell phone listed to a business on Market Street," said Ozzie. "The rest are private residences all over, a few in Philly. Ozzie sorted out the list and set up folders for the numbers that showed up the most. Ozzie got on the phone to the security unit at the cell phone provider they served with a court order earlier and ordered the call records for the past month.

Sam glanced through the phone numbers and names then tossed the folders to the other end of the desk and went through the door. "I'm outta here, Oz. Molly's gonna get supper on time tonight," without looking back, he hit the parking lot and had the Pathfinder headed up the mountain for home. Ozzie wasn't far behind. Marie was making kielbasa and sauerkraut and he had shutters to stain.

It always got dark quicker on a cloudy day in November and by the time Sam crested the ridge and started down, he needed headlights. He had an old Haggard CD playing and thought about how they could connect this Jerome to the McFaddens. If Sylvester would even testify, he would be a lousy witness. Discredited cop and convict. Somehow Jerome smelled right. That's real nice, but murder? Tough to prove.

Making the case and getting it to court. Sam didn't like courtrooms. He lost control there. Running the investigation, at least he had some capability of steering things. The lawyers and the judge took that away from him at trial. His mind suddenly flashed a clear picture of the courtroom in Norristown thirteen years ago.

The lawyers huddled in the empty jury box and the judge hid in his chambers. Months of meetings and depositions where he had to endure the personal, and often pointless, questions from the lawyers for the trucking company. Linda died instantly in that crash, but she left a little boy behind who never knew she was screwing with some slick at a motel. The company was trying to salvage something from the disaster. The driver who slammed into Linda's Mustang was drunk, high, sleep deprived, and operating on two phony driver's licenses and three log books. One of the licenses was suspended for a prior drunk driving arrest and Sam's lawyers were able to find a former company clerk who remembered the dispatcher warning that driver not to get caught and get back on the road.

It was a fight to the finish, but the company lawyers knew if it got to a jury they were screwed. Sam reluctantly became the only multi-millionaire trooper on The Job. The settlement agreement specified secrecy, but he still had to eventually convince the Colonel he intended to keep working. The money went into investments for Ken's future. Young Kenneth still didn't fully realize how much was there. It kept growing and by the time Ken turned twenty-one, he would be a very wealthy air force pilot.

Molly popped out of her barrel as Sam pulled up through the dormant orchard and down into the garage under the barn. She barked and howled and Sam could see her tail slap back and forth waiting for him to release her from the run. After Sam got the lights on and got the wood stove going, they both got something to eat.

~ * ~

Calvin saw the note Ozzie left on the desk explaining the phone records and that Sam called Army CID. Johnny begged off and put his leathers on for the ride home on his Harley. The lights stayed on late in the crime room. Calvin had a lot to sort out.

~ * ~

Sam threw some socks and a set of sweats into the washer and loped up the stairs to pack. He had to pick up Ken in Lansdale at 5:00 the next day and wouldn't have time to come back home from the barracks before they flew out at 8:30. He called Flight Services for the weather and pulled his flight bag out of the closet to go over the maps and approach charts for Champaign, Illinois. Sam was thorough and reviewed several alternative airports along his intended flight path, just in case. It would be a long day tomorrow, he hit the bed before 11:00 and didn't last long after that.

Friday

Afif's father was startled awake by the ringing phone. The red glow of the digital clock read 12:45 as he picked up the receiver next to the bed. Before he could say anything he heard, "Put Afif on the phone."

"He's not here, who is this?" Afif's father asked.

"Uncle, put him on the phone. Tell him everything is okay now. It's Yusef, uncle, put him on the phone," Yusef tried not to sound as angry as he was. He waited quite impatiently to call this late so that he would be sure to catch Afif at his father's house.

"Yusef, I told you he is not here. Isn't he there in the city with you?" the father asked. He hoped his lie sounded like the truth.

"I need him for some more work. I thought he was coming to visit you there. Has he not arrived yet? I hope nothing has happened to him. He told me he would come right back if I needed him. Where is he, uncle?" oh so sweet, slippery sweet.

Afif's father now knew Yusef was hunting Afif for sure. "Well, my wife's nephew, I have not had a visit from Afif. Surely he is either still on his way or has returned and you have missed him. I will tell him to call you right away should he come here tomorrow," Afif's father yawned loudly. "Now, it is very late and I do not wish to wake my wife. Goodnight, Yusef," Afif's father slept very fitfully the rest of the night.

~ * ~

Jamal wouldn't go with Yusef. Grumpy at being up so early, Jamal slid over and let Yusef drive the red Lexus. "Drop me at Harold's," growled Jamal and tilted the seat back almost all the way. Yusef's mission today was to round up Afif and try to beat some sense into him. Jamal wanted a load from the auction that afternoon and needed Afif to make the buys. "Pain in the ass, causin' me to lose money. Fuckin' problem if we got to switch to another mechanic. He's either in or..." Jamal fired a deadly look at Yusef.

That time of the morning, the light traffic in the city allowed Yusef to make his way across the river into West Philly quickly and drop Jamal in the alley behind Harold's. Yusef stopped for gas on Girard Avenue and merged onto the Schuylkill Expressway west toward the Blue Route.

~ * ~

The dryer had stopped and the coffee was down by the time Sam got back from his short run down the drive and out on the hard road. He didn't work too hard this morning. Had to save something for later. Molly was in the barrel back asleep. A dog's life. Sam had to decide early if he was going to make Peggy livid and cancel his flight. He hated to crap out on Ken and knew it would put Peggy on the spot to replace him with a qualified jet driver at the last minute. He grabbed the clothes from the dryer and got coffee on his way to the shower.

~ * ~

Don Mitchell pulled into the lot at the Coopersburg Diner and put the big Pontiac wagon into a space near the front door. This was a regular stop for Mitchell, but usually on the weekends when he was heading north to hunt or fish upstate. He grabbed the Allentown paper from the box and went in to breakfast. He had his squirrel rifle and hunting vest in the car just in case he got done early at Straus Valley.

~ * ~

She banged around in the kitchen loud enough he could hear her from the bathroom upstairs. Johnny lit a cigarette and foamed up his face to shave. Deftly guiding the straight razor around the Marlboro and flicking the ash with the thick part of the blade. He had the television on in the bedroom and he could hear the Weather Channel forecast of light rain later that night. Johnny decided, screw it, he would ride the bike anyway.

Flight Service gave Sam the latest update. It didn't sound too bad. No ice, that was the main thing, and winds well within limits. The weather in Illinois would be clear and cold through their departure back to Allentown on Saturday night. Sam hefted his flight bag and his overnight suitcase and was out the door. Before he left, he walked over to Molly's house and reached in to give her a scratch behind her ears. "See you tomorrow pup. Get a couple fat bunnies for Junior, okay?" she snorted and curled herself up into a tighter ball. So much for fond farewells.

~ * ~

Calvin was the last out and the first in. He wasn't all that excited about this Jerome character just yet. He looked right, but if McFadden and Jerome were dealing with gangs, Jerome could be dead now, too. Besides, not too many graduates from the University of Graterford were very cooperative with law enforcement types without some sort of big hammer hanging over their heads. Without something physical linking the shooter to the shoot, Calvin would have to rely on loose lips. Right now he didn't have many hot prospects to tell him what happened last Saturday night in Porter.

He sat down with the phone records and got out a city map of Philadelphia. Using markers, he noted each pay phone location and each

155

residence. He did the same for the few phone calls not to Philly on a Lehigh/Berks County map. He would have to wait for the cell phone subscriber records to be faxed or e-mailed from the providers' security shops. It didn't take too long before he found the pay phones were within a half mile of each other in West Philly and another group in South Philadelphia. He got some coffee and called to say good morning to dispatcher Santiago.

~ * ~

Sam stopped on the way in and bought a sheet carrot cake from the bakery at Pleasant Corners. He figured it was going to be a busy day, why not start it with sour cream frosting. He beat Ozzie in, but he could see Johnny and Calvin were already on station. As he walked into the squad room he could hear the fax machine whirring through the open door to the front desk. Mrs. Tuttle spotted the cake and met Sam at the big table.

"All for me, or do I have to share?" she asked.

"Get some before Ozzie gets here. Breakfast was over a half hour ago, he'll be starving again," Sam laughed. Calvin waved off the cake and refilled his coffee cup at the other end of the room.

"Bunch of faxes from Harrisburg coming in for you, Sam," Mrs. Tuttle said as she got plates and forks out of the cupboard next to the coffee machine table.

Sam walked over to the fax machine and began to sort out the papers. Title histories on the McFadden cars, Sam figured. He was reading through them when the front door opened and Don Mitchell walked in. Dressed in a heavy black leather jacket and jeans, he looked more like a customer than a Member, but Sam recognized him and reached over to hit the inside door buzzer to let him in. "Good to see you again, Don. Thanks for coming up. Looks like this is the paper on the cars we talked about," Sam held up the stack.

"No problem, Corp. Glad to get out of the city for a bit. I told the BMV guys just to fax that stuff up here, their system was coughing blood yesterday," said Mitchell.

"Hey, we have coffee and cake, help yourself. You know Calvin and Johnny's around here somewhere. Mrs. Tuttle, this is Trooper Don Mitchell from Philadelphia. He's up here to help out on Calvin's shooting case," Sam handed the faxes to Don and they moved over to the cake table.

"Oh, Jesus," Sgt. Dawes looked at Sam, the cake, and Don Mitchell as Dawes walked in from his office. "Oh, Jesus, Sam. That looks good. I know you, you're Don Mitchell, right?" the sergeant shook Don's hand.

"Yeah, I taught the Auto Theft part of the in-service at the Academy. We met there a few years ago. Good to see you again. I thought you retired," said Mitchell.

"Oh, Jesus, no. Not yet. Soon though. Got to get the wife convinced of it. Don't want me hanging around the house," Dawes replied.

The back door slammed open and Ozzie flew past in a real big rush for the locker room. He spotted the cake and seemed to hesitate, trying to decide if carrot cake was worth shitting his pants for. Shitting into a toilet won and he threw his overcoat on a chair and headed down the hall yanking at his belt. "Hi, everybody, be right out."

"I know the feeling," quipped Don. Mitchell had the papers separated into individual piles fanned out in front of him on the table. "Look at this, Corp. All of these cars are reconstruct titles. Means they are rebuilt salvage wrecks or burn jobs. Let's see, this one's outta' Jersey, this one, this one, yeah, this too, yep, yep.... Oh, boy."

Sam looked puzzled, "What's up?"

"Same inspection mechanic did all the reconstructs. As a matter of fact, that same guy showed up on a van a turnpike car spotted. Got that title history with me," said Mitchell.

"With you, why?" asked Sam.

"Guy's out of here, in Allentown," Don opened up his folder. "Lehigh Rebuildables, can't read the name, but we can run his mechanic's number, it'll give us his driver's license. How 'bout runnin' this number for me, hon?" Don handed a slip of paper to Mrs. Tuttle who went in to the computer. "Yeah, turnpike guy, Damon, spotted this van and a rollback at the Quakertown exit. Thought they were actin' funny and wrote a narc slip on 'em. Asshole lieutenant kicked it 'cause the VIN was screwed and Damon asked me to unravel it. Came back reconstructed with a minivan VIN on a big full size job. Address in West...," he stopped mid-sentence. "I'll be damned. You got a Lexus in your stack registered at the same address as Damon's van. Broad's name's the same. It's a phony address, but I found out where her real house is. And look here. All the salvage was bought at the Pennsburg Auction. Less than five miles from the turnpike."

Calvin saw Mitchell and Sam huddled over the table and made his way over to them. "What's up, Sam?" he asked.

"Don's got us a bit of a puzzle starting to shape up. Where's the real address in Philly? Calvin you have a Philly map?" Sam asked.

"Yeah, I put the pay phone locations on it this morning," Calvin put his pen on the real address for the van and Lexus and they all just looked at each other. The pay phones fanned out in a neat semi-circle around the address. Although not perfect, close enough for government work.

"Johnny, go in and pry Ozzie out of the john and everyone, my office," Sam ordered.

Calvin was about half way through his rundown of the case so far, when Mrs. Tuttle stuck her head in and handed Don a computer printout. "Your mechanic," Don said and handed the paper to Sam, "lives in Allentown."

Sam looked at all of them and said, "Okay, we have cars sold by McFadden reconstructed by this Allentown guy, showing up sold to folks around here and in Philly. The van's acting creepy meeting a rollback near the auction where the junk cars are bought before they get reconstructed. Two come back registered to the same woman in Philly and McFadden is calling pay phones close to that address. What's any of this got to do with this Yancey cellmate of McFadden's stolen gun contact in prison? Nothing, that's what. Not yet. We don't know yet that any of these cars are stolen. But I think Don would tell us that's what we're gonna find. Stolen cars worth killing someone over?" Sam took a deep breath and scratched the side of his head.

"That's what we have. Let's run with it for now and see what shakes. At least until something better comes up," offered Calvin. "Yancey had a place in West Philly at one time, worth a shot."

"At least you close the loop on that part of McFadden's scam," Don said.

"Johnny and I can go down to Philly again today, check out the address of the woman. See if she will talk to us. Might know Yancey," Calvin suggested.

"Okay. Don, Ozzie and I will look at the cars here and try to find ...," Sam looked at the printout, "Afif Ahmed, inspection mechanic at large."

~ * ~

No sign of Afif. Yusef had been watching the shop and needed to piss. He drove to the nearest McDonald's and relieved himself. Yusef used the pay phone outside so his cell number didn't show on caller ID and dialed Afif's house. When Afif's mother answered, Yusef hung up.

~ * ~

McFadden's car was hot. Stolen out of Bensalem a year and a half ago. Sam would have to tell the daughter in Pottstown she couldn't have it back.

They got the Mustang from the big man next. He was out of work and was home when they pulled up. Sam watched Don check the confidential VIN and when Don came over to them, he told the big man it was probably bad. Don called in to get the final word. Stolen from Camden. Don told the man he might be able to make a deal with the insurance company that owned it now. Sometimes they were willing to let people buy them back. For now, though, they had to take it. Don drove it back to the barracks and they decided it was time to go talk to Ahmed.

~ * ~

Yusef didn't knock. He went to the back and used his buck knife to jimmy the kitchen door. Afif's mother was upstairs putting laundry away. Yusef stood quietly in the kitchen and listened for conversation. If Afif was here, he would find him or he would find out where he was. Either way, he wasn't leaving until he had one or the other.

She thought she heard the stairs creak. Like at night when one of the children tried to sneak down to the kitchen for a snack or a drink. She thought, *why would he be home from work now* and turned expecting to find her husband on the stairs. She gasped when she saw Yusef standing on the landing holding the big knife. "Hello, Aunt," he moved on her and she, without realizing it, backed into the bedroom away from him.

"Yusef, Yusef, what...what are you...?" it came out as a whisper. She cleared her throat and squared her shoulders. "What do you want? Put away that knife!" she was up against the dresser and couldn't go back any farther.

Now he circled left and stepped between her and the bed. "Where is Afif, dear Aunt?" Yusef growled. The knife was in his right hand and stayed at his side. He rotated it slightly back and forth and smiled when her eyes snapped down to it and then back up to his.

She hadn't seen him for several years, but knew him for what he was and what he was said to have done. She heard the men talking lowly about him and his father and mother. Her dead sister was an evil witch and her son had been tortured by her beyond what any child should have to withstand. Now she was face to face with him, and that knife. It frightened her more than she thought she could ever be frightened. "He... Afif is not here. My husband told you last night he is not here. Why do you want him?"

"Shut up! Stupid old woman!" Yusef quivered and screamed at her. *She sounds like her, my mother. She sounds just like her. God in heaven.* "He's here, somewhere, and you are going to tell me."

160

"Please don't...," She felt sick and flashes of light, sparkles, jumped in her vision. The room swirled and Yusef moved to her.

~ * ~

This was not good. The three big men, two in coats and ties coming into his shop, he did not like this. Afif's father put on a big smile and greeted Sam. "Yes, what can I do for you?"

"Looking for Afif Ahmed," Sam showed his badge and ID.

"I am sorry, sir. I am Afif's father. Afif has done something?" asked the father.

"I need to talk to him. Does he work here?" asked Sam. Don and Ozzie fanned out a bit and Don's expert eyes went to work while Sam talked.

Afif's father glanced past Sam at the other two and then back to Sam, "He is away visiting with relatives, in Detroit. His cousin has had two babies since he last saw her and he is there. He does not like the weather there, though, much colder than here, you see."

"Okay, you'll do. I'd like to see your records on the salvage you buy for parts and to rebuild. No problem with that, is there?" Sam caught the flicker of worry in his eyes. "You do have all that, right?"

"Well, you see, of course we keep excellent records. As you know, we are a state inspection station. I myself am licensed and my inspection book is always okay when your troopers come to check it," Afif's father started the dance. "It is in the office over here. Please come and look."

Sam didn't move. "No, sir, you didn't listen to me. The purchase records, parts and salvage. Pennsburg Auction ring a bell?" Sam picked out the spot between the older man's eyes and locked in. It was too much for Afif's father. He had to look away.

"Well now, you see. Yes, we do buy parts and we do sometimes buy and rebuild cars, but we have been so busy with repairs for our regular customers it has been some time...," Sam cut him off by walking past him

161

and into the small office area where Don and Ozzie had already gone. "Wait, wait, please sir, please wait," Don started looking in the desk and Ozzie was into the filing cabinet.

Sam turned to him, "I'm going to ask your permission to look through this. You don't have to give me permission, but, as you know, we can look over all your inspection records anyway. It's up to you. You're not helping yourself by lying to me about Afif. I know he's not in Detroit. I just want to talk to him. What do you say? Can we look?"

"Well, well, I guess it's okay. I have nothing to hide. Nothing. But you must believe me about Afif. He is not able to talk to you right now. He is not here. I will tell him you wish to talk and I'm sure he will be happy to," Afif's father sat down in a chair and watched the troopers sort through his files.

"It's a question of how long I can wait for him to decide to see me. The longer this goes, the more difficult it's going to be. He has some questions he needs to clear up, right away," Sam walked back over to Afif's father. "Understand me?"

He nodded. "Perhaps he will call, maybe later today and I will ask him. I am so sorry that I do not have the telephone number of his cousin. They...they moved just recently, you see."

The sight of the shiny unmarked police car in the lot at Afif's father's garage startled Yusef. He pulled into the curb quickly rather than drive past slowly as he intended to do. The mother knew Afif was here in Allentown, but didn't know where he was. Yusef was sure she told him the truth. She would not have lied to him after what he'd done to her. She begged him not to hurt her anymore and he believed her. That's why he let her live. Yusef decided he would have to go back to trying to spot Afif at the garage or at one of the other relatives. He wasn't worried about her calling her husband. She wouldn't dare.

He watched for a little while and decided the car was definitely a police car. He had to get out of there. He needed to figure this out.

~ * ~

Johnny and Calvin came in for a landing off the expressway and decided to drive over to see the woman the two suspected stolen cars were registered to. They had the tag numbers and at least knew the van was blue. They had no idea what model or color the Lexus could be.

The address was a huge, old, three story duplex. Run down now, at one time this block must have been something. They cruised around the block twice and didn't see any vehicles with the two tags. "What do you think, Johnny?" Calvin asked.

"Why not?" said Johnny. He pulled the Ford to the curb in front of a hydrant and they got out and went to the door. They knocked, rang the bell and even pounded on the porch window. No answer and no sounds from inside. "Gonna have to wait it out. Let's talk to Sam."

~ * ~

When they all got back into the car Don said, "Not a scrap. Nothing. Gonna have to go to the auction and pull their records to find the rest of the cars. I can run 'em multi state and try to get current registrations for the ones that 'er not showin' up."

Sam looked at his vibrating phone and turned back to Don, "Let's hold off on that right now. Just pick up the ones we know about and interview the buyers. See if any know anything about why McFadden should die for some hot cars." He opened the phone to talk to Calvin.

"Kinda ironic, Sam," Calvin said. "Standing by one of the pay phones on the phone bill. About six blocks from the woman's address. No cars there and no one answers the door. Johnny and I are gonna cruise the area in South Philly where the other pay phones are and interview some of the people McFadden called the week before. Keep checkin' back here and see if Jerome shows up."

"Don't hold your breath, Calvin," Sam said. "Look, I have to make a decision if I'm going to fly out to Illinois tonight. I'll be back tomorrow night, but I hate to leave in the middle of this. What do you think?"

"Ahh, go man. We'll keep punching the numbers on this. Something's got to loosen up. We're getting there. It's just taking longer on this one than I'd like," Calvin watched Johnny fiddling with the car radio, trying to find the country music station.

"Ok. I'm drafting Don Mitchell onto the team. He's got the car thing under his wing, they're all gonna be stolen. He can help Ozzie pick up the rest and do interviews. I'll get the captain to pull the strings and go for the overtime. You can buy a couple 'a new suits," Sam replied. "I'm having them drop me at the barracks and then I'm leaving at 4:00. I'll be at the Marriott in Champaign if my cell phone is off. Good hunting."

~ * ~

He couldn't believe how late he slept. It was hard getting to sleep last night, another strange bed. Once he finally got settled, though, he didn't even stir until mid-morning. The luxury of a quiet room and a long hot shower to wash away the weeks of accumulated grime the cold water from the project sink left behind. Cousin Ali didn't want to be called Ali anymore. He thought of himself as Al and his wife Americanized her name to Sara. Afif was surprised at just how western his cousin's family was. Sara and her daughter did not wear the traditional clothing and the house was furnished like those Afif had seen on television and in magazines. His mother still kept much of the old ways in her house and the filth he saw in Philadelphia had not prepared him for the luxury he found here.

Sara made him hot oatmeal and biscuits with her homemade raspberry jam. He enjoyed each mouthful. She had the television on and the talking twosome was gleefully gushing over some movie star plugging his latest film. Sara told him, "Al wants you to go over to the lot when you're ready. No hurry. Your father said you were having some problems right now and Al is glad to help out."

Afif was a little surprised to hear Sara talk so openly of his father and her husband's business. Afif was used to the women staying away while the men talked. "Thank you, Sara," he had to catch himself and pronounce her name in the new way.

~ * ~

"Where we going to eat?" asked Ozzie.

"Jeez, Oz. It's not like you're gonna fade away or anything. Drop me off first, then you guys can eat and screw the colonel for some overtime," laughed Sam. "Don, you're welcome to stay over if you want. The 'Hotel Deland' will be empty for the night. Goofy plumber coming in the morning, though. Probably wake you up with sewer gas."

"You wanted that toilet upstairs out in the middle of the hall, right?" Ozzie grinned.

Don replied, "Naw, I got the state car, I'll run back and forth. Suzie would be too lonely without me. Reckon we won't fire up until noon tomorrow anyway. Break these people's hearts when we take their cars away from them, though. What you want to do with them? Looks like we got about eight more on the list and probably more n' that once we get to the auction."

"Park them behind the barracks for now. That's one of the calls I have to make," Sam started a list as Ozzie roared west in trooper/warp drive toward the Valley.

~ * ~

They shook Afif's father's hand as they left. Yusef watched the three plainclothes cops pull out. He didn't move for almost a half hour. Just in case they came back. Still no sign of Afif and Yusef was getting itchy. He decided against jacking up the father, let the mother work on him. Afif would get the message and scramble to Yusef to keep Yusef away from his mother. In the meantime, Yusef would check with the other relatives in town. He eased away from the curb and drove east.

~ * ~

The interviews went uneventfully. Former friends and church members that the McFaddens kept in touch with. They all were shocked when they heard about their old friends. Couldn't understand why. Calvin and Johnny went from address to address and, in between, located the pay phones and tried to make sense of what was in the area that could link any of them. Enough work for a couple more days. Several weren't home and they left business cards asking them to call for an interview. At lunch time, they drove to Major Crimes and hijacked Frank Dugan. He moaned, but let them buy him lunch. The least they could do for all the favors they kept asking of him.

~ * ~

Sloppy work. As careful as he was with his father to avoid any problems, Jamal wouldn't let him take the time to make the cars right. Now the police were asking his father about him and the auction. Afif sadly realized this wasn't about any cause. It was about money. Money for Jamal. Greed. Afif's father assured Afif they found nothing at the shop, but they pressured him to produce Afif. He read the name of the state police corporal from the business card they left him. "What will we do now?" his father asked him.

"If they know about the auction, they will find what they need. My name is on the papers. This wasn't supposed to happen," Afif sadly told his father. "I have to think about this. Think about what to do now."

"Yusef will find you if you stay there. It will take him a while, but he will find you. What will he do then?" his father sounded worried.

"I don't want to find out. I'm leaving here, I'll find someplace and get word to you," Afif hung up and shrugged his shoulders when Al asked if everything was all right.

~ * ~

Sam wasn't hungry, but grabbed one of Ozzie's Pepsi's from the refrigerator. Ozzie was taking Don to the Chinese buffet. If the owner was smart, he'd close before those two buffaloes got there. Mrs. Tuttle handed Sam several phone messages as he passed on his way back to his office. Sam stripped off his coat and made the first call. "Hey, Peg."

"Don't talk to me unless it's good news, you," she snarled.

"I'm going into surgery. The doctor says I'll be okay, but I'll have to be diapered for six weeks. Want a part time job?" Sam asked her.

"I know an ex-pro wrestler. He'd, well it's she now, she'd be perfect for that job. Hold you up by the ankles and powder your ass good," Peggy gave as good as she got.

"How's the weather, Peg. You have my full attention," Sam said soberly.

"'Bout time you realized who's the real boss here. Clouds down to 3200, possibly 2800, up to 9000. Scattered showers, winds 265 at 10 to 15. Piece of cake for a hot shot jet pilot like you, sweetie. Destination is clear with winds at 310 15 to 20. Right down the runway. We on for tonight?" Peggy asked.

"Love to, but I gotta fly for this mean old woman with no sense of humor," Sam said.

"Good decision. Keep your priorities straight. See you about 7:00?" she asked.

"Yup, I pick up Ken and I want to stop at his grandma's for a minute on the way up," Ken missed Grandma Landis. She did a lot of the hard work when he was little. After Linda was killed, Sam took Ken to his folks upstate for a while until the navy decided if they could let him out to be the kid's only surviving parent. Sam brought him back down to Sellersville several times to get spoiled. Grandma Deland and Grandma Landis built up a friendly rivalry for the little guy, but kept Ken's best interest on top. Sam eventually decided he didn't want to drive his dad's fuel oil truck up and down people's driveways for a living and made the move to the state police. Kenny and Sam finally moved into a rental house in Perkasie, the town next to Grandma Landis, who babysat while Sam worked as a road trooper.

That was the next call. "Hi, Grandma, it's Sam," she was real glad to hear from him. It had been a while. She worked around to ask him about his love life. She seemed real interested in getting Sam married off again, but had not been very successful. Sam bounced around lady friends. He knew that after Linda, he couldn't seem to get real close to any girl. It hurt too much. They would reel him in, but he would break the line before it went too far. Safer that way, at least he thought so. He thought about Eileen at that very moment. *That was odd.* He'd just met her. "Ken and I can stop by about 5:30 for just a minute. We're flying out to a Penn State game tonight. I know he'd like to see you, me, too."

"Your ears must have been burning. I was just telling my friend about you. She has a niece..." Grandma could picture Sam and Ken in tuxedos.

"Wow, that's great, but my social calendar is pretty booked up right now, plus it's the busy season with the games and work. Looks like State is going to the Orange Bowl this year. Ken and I might get to spend New Year's in Miami," Sam tried to steer her off the track. "We'll see you this afternoon, love ya," Sam hung up before she could plan the engagement party.

"Eileen, it's Sam Deland. How are you?" Sam even liked the sound of her voice. He could hear Dutch woofing in the background.

"Great, better now. Dutch, shut up, you mutt! Semi just went by and thumped in the pothole. You the guy I call to get that thing filled in?" she asked.

Sam thought of a smutty come back but restrained himself. He didn't know her quite that well yet. "How much did you give to the supervisor's campaign last year. Your name up high on the list?" Sam heard her snort on the other end.

"Doesn't matter, it's a state road. Penn Dot only gets through here when they need a new place for their crews to sleep. You still wining and dining me on Sunday?" she asked.

"If you insist, my lady. I'm at your service. About 4:00 okay?" Mrs. Tuttle stuck her head in Sam's office and held her hand up to her ear to tell Sam he had a call waiting for him. "Look, I hate to rush off, but we're dealing both decks here right now, see you Sunday?"

"Sure, I'm game. See ya," Dutch was in full roar now. That truck woke him up and had to pay the price.

"Army CID calling, I'll put them through," Mrs. Tuttle scurried back to the front desk and Sam's phone rang.

"Corporal, this here's Master Sergeant Walls from CID out in St. Louis calling. Understand you fellas called our 800 number about stolen mil'try hardware. You anywhere near Lancaster?" he had a deep southern accent, but sounded smart enough.

"About an hour and a half north and east of Lancaster. Why's that?" Sam replied.

"We got one a our chief warrants up thar a doin' some nosin' 'round on a folla up case outta Chicago. Armory thefts some boys from the wrong sida the tracks cooked up to boost the generous salary the gov'ment pays 'em. Truly ungrateful lads. His name's Johnston with a t. Ya can call him at, hold on lemme see he'ah, looks like Jeff'a son Township po-lice," the master sergeant gave Sam the number even though Sam already had it. Sam confirmed they were the same from the folder in front of him he was digging out of the pile that needed more follow up work. Sam thanked him and dialed out again.

~ * ~

Yusef was having no luck at all. He put on his smile and tried to be friendly and polite to the cousins. He despised his mother's side of the family. Somehow his own transgressions didn't enter his mind. They got all of his blame. He thought himself a man of action. This digging for the little shit Afif was beneath him. He would let the mother be the reason Afif would come to him. Yusef left Allentown and drove cautiously back south toward Philadelphia.

~ * ~

Chief Warrant Officer Thornton Thomas Johnston III was known as T to everyone. He respected his momma for wanting his father's family name and tradition to be honored and carried on, but at six foot three inches and two hundred and sixty five pounds, Thornton didn't work. As a small kid, he took his licks for the name, but that all ended at thirteen after a growth spurt of a few inches. It was T from then on and it stuck. T stood out in the group of police officers and detectives, not just for his size, but there aren't too many black people in this part of Lancaster County, especially in full camouflage BDUs. The portable radio the detective carried burped a request for the detective to ask CWO Johnston to call the state police corporal at Straus Valley. The crime scene tape had been cleaned up, but you could still see the dark stain from the blood left by the young Hispanic victim of the shooting earlier in the week. CWO Johnston popped a cell phone from his belt and called Sam.

T's case was not a good one. He had a bunch of rifles and LAW rockets missing from several armories from Chicago to Akron, Ohio. Another CID group was working on similar thefts out of Lynn, Massachusetts and Plattsburg, New York. Gang members serving in Guard units were suspected. T was in Lancaster because the shooting victim there was the younger brother of one of his Gary, Indiana suspects. "Word is the group was breaking up. Too much heat from us and they couldn't get the price they wanted. Asshole snitch I got even said 'the profit for risk factor' was unacceptable. You believe that? Fuckin' gang bangers talkin' like Harvard pukes," T told Sam. "Cops here figure our victim wasn't alone. Too far from anything to walk out here. Whoever drove him to this parking lot must a got away, or set him up. Might actually have a witness. Spooky country out here, ever see that movie about the Amish kid sees a murder in Philadelphia?"

Sam agreed to share his information with T and told him he would send Ozzie and Don out on Saturday to sit down with him.

"What'd your ballistics guys say about the weapons used?" asked T.

"Ours is a .45 and a 9mm," replied Sam.

"Yeah, this is, too. The detective here says he sent the slugs in to the state lab. I was wondering if they matched up?" T waited for the answer.

"You got me there, Chief. I should have been notified if they did. I'll check for you. I'm sending what we have with Trooper Ozliewski tomorrow. If I find out anything new, Ozzie will let you know. 2:00 tomorrow at the township PD, okay?" T told Sam that was fine, give him time to hit the outlet shops for his wife.

Sam almost got into a screaming match with the sergeant at the ballistics lab. Why, sure the slugs from Lancaster and Porter were from the same two guns. The letter he was preparing to send out so stated. Why, no he didn't think it was at all necessary to go running around calling people on the telephone with the results. A formal report was the proper format for these technical issues. "What an IDIOT!" Sam said in total frustration when he hung up the phone.

He called the captain to brief her and get her to pull Don Mitchell out of Philadelphia for a few days, at least. Oh, by the way, he needed a fenced lot for twenty or thirty recovered stolen cars, thank you very much. He also mentioned he would probably be home on Monday night.

He talked to Calvin and then Ozzie. He called Flight Service again and called Scotty to brief the flight. He returned the call of the lawyer for the McFadden's daughter about the car they wouldn't be getting back. By the time he finished, he looked at his watch and it was a quarter to four. Sam wrote a quick note to Sgt. Dawes and dropped it on his desk on the way out the back door. "Oh, Jesus" would shit about the overtime, but so be it.

~ * ~

Even though Ken was in civilian clothes, the young eighth grader manning the checkout desk snapped to attention. "Good afternoon, sir!"

Ken gave him a close look and approved of the uniform's neatness. "Gonna have to start shaving soon Cadet Simmons. Take your seat," Ken signed the log and noted his return for 2000 hours on Sunday. "Carry on, Cadet"

He snagged a ride from one of the ROTC sergeants assigned to the Academy. The reserve army enlisted man liked the duty there. They provided him with a small house and since he was divorced, he had plenty of rich, beautiful girls to chase at nearby Cabrini College. On the short ride to the train station, they talked about Ken's appointment to the Air Force Academy. The sergeant wished him luck and dropped him off at the front of the station.

~ * ~

Calvin kept looking at his watch. Johnny let it go for a while, but couldn't resist. "She's gonna keep. You're worth waiting for, sweet cheeks," Calvin shot him the finger. They were back at the West Philadelphia address. Again no movement.

Calvin said, "Let's wait for dark, see if any lights are on inside. I'll call her and change the time."

~ * ~

Of the four cars they tried to locate, they only found one. A nice Toyota. The lady didn't really understand what it was all about, but when Don told her they would have to take the car, she cried and wanted to know if she could get the baby seat out of the back. Ozzie felt terrible, but there was nothing they could do. The car looked good, but drove like crap, needed struts. By the time they got to the barracks, Sam was gone. They stayed in and did the three vehicle reports and property receipts.

~ * ~

After he gassed up at the Turkey Hill, Sam jumped on the turnpike and headed south for Lansdale. He was on time, but got to thinking about the case and let his speed creep up over eighty. Traffic was heavy northbound, but he was able to hog the left lane on the southbound side and eat up the miles. He came back to reality going down the hill of the Perkasie ridge. He remembered the turnpike troopers liked to sit just over the crest of the hill and zap speeders on the downslope. He eased back to just under seventy and sure enough passed a marked unit running radar right where Sam thought he might be. Trooper Damon never noticed the Pathfinder amongst all the other cars flying past. He still hated traffic enforcement.

~ * ~

Ken got lucky. The train ran smooth and he was able to get some reading done while it made its way through Center City and north to Lansdale. When he arrived, Sam was standing next to the Pathfinder waiting for him. "Come on, you drive. Let's stop at Grandma's on the way," Sam tossed Ken the keys and threw his bags into the back on top of Sam's next to Molly's box. Ken drove like he flew, flawlessly. Hand eye coordination by the bucketful. He changed the radio station to the All News channel to get the weather and talked to Sam about the flight. Sam went over the set up and talked about how things were so automatic now. The Lear was run by computers. Punch in flight levels and airport designators and it flew itself.

They drifted into talk about the glider and Ken said he was hoping the weather would cooperate at Thanksgiving so they could run the ridge. Sam told him that he had the Cessna 182 reserved for that long weekend and they could fly to Wellsboro to have Thanksgiving dinner with his folks. Before Sam realized it, Ken was exiting off the 309 Expressway and they dropped down into Sellersville.

~ * ~

He put the Lexus into a parking space out on Washington. Jamal would want it right away. The woman had to have the car back. *Possessive bitch. Like it was really hers to begin with.* Yusef dialed Jamal's cell number. Jamal told Yusef to meet him and Harold at the corner to give back the keys. Yusef bought a container of corn chowder soup at the deli and sat down to eat and wait for Jamal. He was careful not to drip any of the soup on the black gym bag between his feet.

~ * ~

It was past dark now and Johnny was out of cigarettes. "Let's go, man. Start fresh tomorrow," Johnny said.

"Okay, north, my man. Maybe she won't hate me for being two hours late," Calvin said and slipped on his seatbelt for the ride home.

~ * ~

Marie was all slicked up. Earrings and all. "We're going out," she announced as Ozzie threw his keys up onto the kitchen counter. "Friday night or not, I don't care if it's crowded. Don't even change. Turn around and march." The babysitter was rolling on the floor with Katie and the television was blasting MTV. "We'll stop at Sam's and feed Molly and go to the fish fry up at the Elks. You can ask me to dance later."

Ozzie couldn't even get a "but" out. She pulled him by the topcoat and they left. Ozzie managed to grab the keys to the minivan before Marie slammed his hand in the door. You didn't argue with her.

~ * ~

The noodles and tuna smelled real good to Sam. He forgot he hadn't eaten all day until he smelled Grandma's cooking as he and Ken walked in. She fussed over Ken and marveled at how good he looked. "Straight as an arrow and you have my father's square jaw. I wish I knew where the black hair came from."

"My dad's side, I think. Seems like I remember a picture of his father in his marine uniform with real dark hair," offered Sam. He quit after a small plateful. Didn't want to load up and get sleepy. Ken ate like he hadn't all day. Sam did butter a piece of her brown sweetbread. That was good. Almost taste the molasses dripping off from it. It was a record. They were back out the door within a half hour, Sam insisting they had to get to the airport.

Ken picked through the Friday night traffic and they crested over the top of South Mountain to a view of the broad valley holding Allentown, Bethlehem and several smaller towns, all in lights. The airport was fifteen minutes farther and Ken turned onto the road for the charter and private aviation buildings at the west end of the airport complex. As they pulled into the parking lot, Sam reached across behind the driver's seat and slipped his big automatic and his cuffs into the lock box with the snubby derringer. He didn't like having to explain the hardware around airports. They each hefted their bags and walked over to the entrance to Peggy's office.

"Kenny, and his grumpy father, too," Peggy came around the counter and grabbed Ken. "You married yet?" she asked.

"I'm saving myself for you, or maybe your daughter. Whichever is richer," Ken laughed.

"Well, I guess she's out of the will then," Peggy said and looked at Sam. "Scotty's getting the latest weather, looks okay. Want to sign the paperwork and preflight?"

"Sure, our guests all still coming?" Sam asked.

"Yup. All but the one. Got trouble at the bank and has to work this weekend." She stepped back to the counter and spun a clipboard around for Sam. He read the top sheet and signed off for the airplane. The maintenance reports all looked good. He spent a few minutes more checking each line item. Ken took the bags and went through the office and out the side door to the ramp. The Lear stood gleaming white in the sodium vapor lights. The chief mechanic was snapping open the luggage compartment and waved at Ken as he approached.

"Gonna teach your dad to fly one of these things tonight, Ken?" the mechanic asked.

"I'm gonna let him drive. He let me drive him up here," Ken said and loaded the two suitcases into the compartment. He took his dad's flight bag and his own soft briefcase and walked to the steps just behind the cockpit. As he went into the plane, he smiled at the familiar smell. Each plane had its own and he'd been on this one several times before. He turned left to the flight cabin and looked at the amber glowing control panel. The jet was hooked up to an auxiliary power cart and the instruments and computers were on and standing by for engine start.

Ken put Sam's flight case in the slot just behind the left pilot's seat and turned to drop his bag on the first passenger seat to the rear of the flight deck. Sam poked his head into the plane and asked Ken to get out the flashlights for them to preflight. Ken walked all around the plane with his dad as they carefully checked it for the flight. They met the co-pilot, Scotty Jamison, as he walked out to the plane carrying the weather printouts and the official passenger list. Scotty and Ken shook hands and Sam did the preflight again with Scotty.

Ken went back inside and spent a few minutes with Peggy. The first of the passengers arrived and greeted Ken. The group was made up of wealthy Penn State graduates who had enough money to avoid the traffic jams surrounding State College on game days and were rabid enough fans to charter Peggy's jet to haul them all across the country for away games. A couple of bankers, a tool company executive, construction company owner, an orthodontist, a stockbroker and one even Sam wasn't too sure what he did. They all knew Ken and considered him, Sam, and Scotty part of the group. Though they drank some, they behaved themselves and saved their enthusiasm for the games.

Sam was in the left seat running checklists with Scotty. Ken helped the group with the bags and suffered the gags and teasing well. Ken was as smart as any of them and wasn't intimidated at all by them. The construction company owner insisted Ken come to work for him this summer, but Ken had other plans and would be off to Colorado anyway.

By 8:30, everyone was in their seat and comfortable. Sam supervised Scotty begin the startup and the hatch was dogged and secured. Ken knew he wasn't needed anymore and dug out his calculus book and got to work.

"Two good engines," Sam reported to Scotty. "It's yours tonight. I'll handle the radios for you. Ready if you are," Sam set the frequencies and scanned the instruments for anything not secured or set for flight.

"Let's roll," said Scotty.

Sam contacted ground control and received taxi instructions for runway 24. Scotty increased the power and the small jet shuddered slightly and began to move forward. They were starting from the wrong side of the airport and it took some time to taxi the distance out to the apron for the active runway. Sam used the time to recheck everything and preset the computer to control their flight path. A long way from when pilots used road maps to navigate. Now satellites and advanced electronic navigation beacons made cross country flight navigation a matter of pushing buttons.

Both Sam and Ken appreciated the little glider they owned. The only thing electronic on it was the two way radio. Every movement of the sailplane was as a direct result of what the pilot did. Stick and rudder. In the Lear, other than takeoff and landing, little human touch on the controls was really necessary. It was an easy decision for Sam when he got released by the navy. Commercial aviation would have taken him on, but he didn't want the routine. After flying off carriers, commercial passenger service would have been too tame for him. He flew these charters to keep his ticket and because he liked the company. Didn't want to be one dimensional.

"Corporate Charter Lear November 15 Quebec, clear for takeoff, fly runway heading, contact departure at the outer marker," the tower radioed Sam.

In his pilot voice, Sam replied, "15 Quebec, good night, sir." Scotty pushed the throttles to takeoff power and they rolled down runway 24, gaining speed rapidly. "Rotate...gear up... Flaps coming up," Sam called the progress for Scotty. They were into the clouds now and the lights of the valley below were gone. Blank space out of the cockpit window. Scotty didn't need to see out the windscreen, he monitored the ascent on the sophisticated instruments and knew exactly what the plane was doing. They were cleared by departure control to 16,000 feet and made their course correction to almost due west. By the time they were between Hazleton and Harrisburg, they were directed up to their selected cruising altitude and Scotty engaged the computer and autopilot. That was it. Unless something weird happened, the jet would fly by itself all the way to Illinois.

Sam unbuckled and slid out of the small seat. He found Ken in a serious conversation with one of the bankers about price theory and international trade. Ken's laptop was open and he was pulling up a file to show why his opinion was more correct. The screen materialized a set of four graphs that Ken then actually set in motion with a series of commands. He pointed to the lower left graph and the banker let out a low whistle. "Got me, Ken. You can have my first born daughter."

"Hey, genius, you want to go up and babysit the computer with Scotty?" Sam asked Ken.

"Sure, want to end up in Alberta or Cabo San Lucas?" he grinned and rubbed his hands together. Everybody that heard laughed and Ken slipped past Sam and disappeared into the cockpit.

~ * ~

The effect was narcotic. She had great hands and pair of legs to match. The dinner she carefully prepared for him sat under warming covers in the kitchen. That could wait. This was their third "date" and she met Calvin at the door just a little peeved because he was so late. When he produced the box with a dozen roses, she only hesitated a bit before she forgave him and helped him with his appetite. She was kneading the stress knots from his lower back and letting her nipples lightly rub across his shoulders and neck. Yep, narcotic, he had to have some more. She was ready, too.

~ * ~

Old habits. The Harley cranked and set into a throaty rumble. Johnny zipped his leathers all the way up and snugged his helmet strap. The cigarette between his teeth glowed brighter as he left the bar's parking lot onto the street. A couple of beers after a long day felt good. He kept it down to two glasses of draft. Top that off once he got the bike home. Treat the old lady to clams at the tavern.

~ * ~

She must be in one of those moods again. Didn't even speak to him when he came home from the shop. He didn't intend to tell her about the police and Afif. She had no need to know. Just didn't concern her. Still, he would have liked to have his supper ready. Very unusual. His daughter was trying to make a stew from what she found in the refrigerator and doing just fine with it. He went up and found her lying on the bed. "You all right?" he asked her.

"I'm just tired and my stomach is upset. Please may I just rest here? Is she getting you something to eat?" Afif's mother struggled to keep her voice from wavering. Trying to sound just ill, not in pain and scared to death.

"I will have her bring you some tea and honey. Have her bring it right up," he said.

"I'm missing my son, you know," she needed to talk to Afif, right away. "He has been gone and I miss him. Can he at least call me, or come to visit, do you know?" the pains in her gut came stronger and she stifled a cry.

~ * ~

A five hundred dollar leather briefcase serving as a poker table for the quarter game. Big shot rich guys whooping at taking a buck fifty from each other. Sam shot the bull with his friends and caught up on sons and daughters. Rich people have just as many problems as anybody else. No immunity. The guy who was self-employed and kept his business very private, was asking Sam's advice about his twelve year old son. Real hard head. Didn't listen. Time, Sam told him. Put in the time with him. Gotta cut back on the outside stuff and put in the time.

Ken came back out and shook his head at the raucous poker game and sat back down with his textbook. He had more work to do. Sam excused himself and made his way back to the left seat and strapped himself back in. Everything was still in the green and Scotty had little to do but scan the panel. The young co-pilot was a "college boy." No military time, but came out of school with a commercial rating. Until he started getting some charter time, he was flat broke and washing planes for flight time. Sam felt very comfortable with Scotty on the flight deck. It wouldn't be much longer before one of the major airlines scooped him up.

The flight took just about two and a half hours. It wouldn't be much longer before the controllers started bringing them down over Indiana. Sam noticed the cloud cover over Ohio and Pennsylvania had slid beneath them and even from this altitude, he could see the patches of light from the cities. It was going to be a clear landing.

~ * ~

It was small but clean. The motel had several cabins at the back that usually only rented out in the summer. The owner was glad to take the cash from the scruffy looking kid. Thought he must be some kinda towel head foreigner, but business is business.

~ * ~

Junior was asleep in Dad's recliner. Marie was driving the babysitter home and Ozzie shook his son's shoulder. "We're up and out early tomorrow, gonna' run Molly and finish the upstairs bathroom at Sam's."

"Ok, Dad. Goodnight," Junior wrinkled up his nose. "You guys went up to the fish fry, didn't you?"

"Big night out on the town. See you early," Ozzie went down the hall stripping off clothes as he went. He wanted to smell good when Marie got back.

~ * ~

Yusef walked the ten blocks down to the theater complex at the river. He had the gym bag over his shoulder like a backpack. It was busy on Friday night with groups of people going in and out of the theaters and the shops nearby. Across the wide street toward the river was a union hall that was dark and empty. Yusef bought a flavored cup in the coffee shop and surveyed the crowd through the window. She was in the parking lot with two other girls smoking and acting bored. Couldn't be more than fourteen. Tight jeans with holes in the knees and one over her left ass. Her brown wispy hair was swept up in a blue bandana and she had on a dirty brown coat that looked like it was her older brother's. Something about her mouth made him nuts. Snarl to her lips. *So sure of herself. Ha! Fourteen and acting like she was all that.* Yusef watched her. He couldn't take his eyes off her. She really was making him mad. Real mad.

~ * ~

Jamal parked the Lexus in the alley behind her house. Backed it in so the tag wouldn't show. In a couple of weeks he'd buy a new tag for it. Sell it on paper to a phony name and get her mom's name off the title. She'd be pissed, but he'd get her another car eventually. She'd just have to live with it. *What's she going to do, cut him off now?* He didn't think so.

He let himself in the back door and slipped it closed quietly. He stood still and listened for a few minutes. He didn't hear or sense anything unusual. He could hear her television on upstairs. Her mother wasn't home.

She'd have been parked on the living room couch if she was. *Good.* He eased into the house and went up the stairs to her room.

~ * ~

When he came out of the shower, Ken was gone. The note on the desk said he was ordering food and would meet him at the pool. "Hormones," Sam muttered. He slipped on his trunks and put his clean sweats on over that. A few twenties and his room key card went into his ID case and he headed down to rescue Ken.

He found him swimming laps backstroke while a slender young woman was pounding out a decent freestyle trying to catch up to him. They reached the other end of the pool almost together and both did quick flip turns for the lap back. She drilled him by a forearm. He went under and came up blowing water toward the deep end.

"I can't believe it! You have to give me another chance," Ken said, gasping breath. He turned to see Sam approach the gathering group of stews in and out of the water and in various states of undress. Two poolside tables were pulled together and a waiter was placing pitchers of soft drinks and plastic glasses down. Another waiter was coming out from the bar with a big basket of nacho chips and bowls of salsa.

"She's the fastest thing I've ever seen," Ken laughed to the group.

One of the girls started trying to push another into the pool, but slipped and lost her hold. At that, the other girl grabbed the first by the back of her top and swung her around and into the pool. The tossee was quickly followed by the tosser and several others. Ken was surrounded by splashing, giggling women. You couldn't have blasted the smile off his face with dynamite.

Sam caught the waiter and gave him an additional series of requests and turned back to the noisy pool. He noticed Ken and the slender girl off to the side in the shallow end floating just out of range of the rest. Ken was looking at her and she was looking right back at him. *Oh, oh,* thought Sam. He'd seen that look before. Her hair was the same dark black as Ken's.

Although his was cut so short the white of his scalp showed through. Even though wet, hers was full and touched the top of her shoulders. She had a strong, but quite proper nose and her skin looked clear and a shade more olive than Ken's. They weren't saying anything now, just looking.

Sam stripped the sweats off and did a cannonball between them. He came up to find her paddling away and Ken looking him square in the eye.

"Chicken fights!" tossee shouted and climbed up on to Sam's shoulders before he could protest. One of the other ladies grabbed Ken and forced him down so she could mount his broad shoulders herself. Someone threw a towel into the pool and the women each grabbed an end and the fight was on. The object started out to be, pull your opponent's team over by yanking on the towel. That changed, in short order, to pull your opponent's top off. Titties all over the place. Only Ken's swimming challenger didn't get mixed up in it. She managed to slip out of the pool and was cheering the topless troops on from the impromptu buffet. Eventually the girls got themselves covered back up and began to slide out for refreshments.

"Sammy! You came through!" shouted the banker. He was followed into the pool area by two of Sam's other passengers. "You promise a party, it means a party."

Things moved right along then. More food and bottles of tequila, vodka, and peach schnapps appeared. The bar music got switched on to the pool speakers and the dancing began. Sam relaxed and let himself enjoy the evening. Their group was joined by stragglers from the bar and by midnight everyone was old friends. The construction guy slipped out with the tosser and Sam found Ken in quiet conversation with the little dark haired girl at the other end of the huge pool room.

"Dad, Sam Deland, I'd like you to meet Grace Echaverria. Grace, this is my dad," Ken said straight out. She stood up and shook his hand.

"I'm very pleased to meet you. Thank you both for this nice party," she looked back at Ken with those big, soft, brown eyes. Sam knew this was going to be trouble. Not bad trouble, but trouble, you know.

"I'm glad you're enjoying it. Ken, can I get you kids anything?" Sam didn't know what else to say. She looked younger than Ken except for her shape. Tiny waist, strong legs, real biceps.

"Grace just got her wings, she's the rookie. Swam for Florida State. She's from Florida, Sarasota. That's why she gave me such a good race," Ken bubbled.

"Well, Ken's second sport is swimming, he's really a baseball player. Hope he makes the team at the Academy next year," Sam dropped the hint, just in case Ken hadn't been forthcoming about his age.

"I think that's spectacular he's going to the Air Force Academy. I only managed two years before I had to go to work. I want to go back and finish my degree someday. Ken you stick with it. Don't let anything stop you," she advised him.

Amen, thought Sam. "Ok, you kids," *Didn't I just say that?* "I'm going back to the bar." Sam wasn't sure what just happened, but knew he'd be seeing that girl again if Ken had anything to say about it

Saturday

The party lasted until about 1:30. The Penn State alumni delegation crapped out on the remaining flight attendants and they took a last swim with Ken before gathering their things. Sam badged the security guard so Ken and Grace could side stroke and talk a little longer. The pool was supposed to close at 1:00. The guard was retired from Chicago PD and was living down here in a mobile home park. He and Sam watched the two youngsters paddle slowly around the pool.

"Your boy's got a real pretty girl there, trooper. Make nice grand babies for you," the guard innocently said.

Not right away, I hope, thought Sam.

~ * ~

The arcade had a machine that changed bills to quarters. Yusef got five dollars' worth and moved back to where he could see the group of three girls. He was trying to be patient, he didn't know how he was going to get her away from the other two. One of the other girls said something and his little snarly girl shook her head. The other two got up and walked toward the coffee shop. *Pee break*, thought Yusef. *Silly girls got to go together and babble while they piss. Stupid.* He watched until they were inside the shop and he stepped out onto the parking lot.

He didn't go directly at her. He slipped out toward the street and came back at an angle. He walked about three feet in front of her and let the quarters drop to the pavement. She couldn't stop herself. She leaned right out and reached for the coins. Yusef dropped down beside her as if to pick up his lost money and put his left arm around her shoulder. He hit her hard and fast with the heel of his right hand just below her right rib cage. The blow landed solid and she expelled a rush of air and slumped into him. He hit her again just a little higher and heard the crack of her lowest right rib as it broke.

"Let me help you, I know it hurts, doesn't it. I'll help you," Yusef spoke softly into her ear. He lifted her up and turned her around to cross the street. He timed the traffic and moved her across the lanes quickly. Her mind couldn't put together what had just happened. It hurt so much. No air. She actually helped him by walking a bit on her own. She worked hard to catch her breath and took it in gasps. To anyone watching, it looked like she was sick and her friend was helping her find a place to throw up.

When the two others came back out of the bathroom they didn't see her in the lot. But hey look, someone dropped some money. They hoped it was enough to buy a pack of cigarettes. Maybe she went to get a soda or something.

~ * ~

They slipped out of the pool and Ken put the towel around her shoulders. She walked over to Sam and said, "Goodnight, Sam, thank you again, I really had a nice time." When she bent over and gave him a peck on his cheek, it took him by surprise. Sam hadn't expected that.

"Your welcome, Grace. Have a good flight tomorrow," Sam thought he could see a glow around her head and shoulders. Must be the chlorine.

"I'm going to walk Grace up to her door, Dad. Catch up to you later," Ken said as they turned to go back into the hotel.

"Yeah, really peachy grand babies, trooper," the security guard chuckled as he left Sam all to himself.

~ * ~

"Coffee's ready, Dad," Junior said softly through his parent's bedroom door. Ozzie opened his eyes and for a moment had to think where he was. Marie was cuddled up bare naked under his right leg. And the pillows were all on the floor. Wow, she was full of it last night.

He thought a quick shower was in order and groaned when he saw that it was only 5:30. Well, it was going to be a busy day, might as well get started. Up and out.

~ * ~

It looked like a piece of plastic sheet in the dim light. Radio Patrol Car 310 stopped and the driver sat for a minute before getting out. He'd pulled behind the union hall to take a leak before daylight and caught the shimmer of the thing in his headlights. He took his heavy flashlight with him and made his way over to the edge of the lot at the river. He stopped a few feet away and muttered, "Aw shit."

His portable radio microphone was clipped to his jacket lapel. He reached up with his right hand and keyed the button. "Three ten, I need rescue rear 'a the union hall Washington and Columbus. Have three Andy meet me here also. Looks like a female down." Man, it was almost time to go home.

~ * ~

They finally moved to the bed to make love again at midnight. Sleep came sometime after that. When Calvin's watch alarm went off, he was already awake and softly rubbing her upper thigh. He liked to just touch her. He'd never felt such smooth skin. She must really take good care of herself. "I have to go, baby. Is that okay?" he whispered to her.

"Nooo, please stay, please?" she purred.

"For a little while, then. For a little while," he guided her hand over to his fully awake male self and she let out a deep, soft laugh.

~ * ~

The truck windows were frosted over and Ozzie cranked it up and turned on the defroster. He tilted the bench seat forward and slid the two shotgun cases behind it. Junior picked up the paper from the driveway and tucked it into space between the storm door and the porch door. Mom wouldn't have to sneak out in her robe to get it so she could check their stock prices.

It took a little scraping so Ozzie could see well enough to miss Marie's van and they were down the drive and headed for Sam's. Well, after a stop at the diner. Ozzie always treated Junior to breakfast out on these Saturday hunts. Part of the dad-son deal.

~ * ~

He heard it before he saw it. That unique scraping sound of squirrel claws on bark. Don put the cigar down on the log next to him and eased himself a little to the left in the direction of the sound. There was just enough daylight he could make out the shape as the squirrel worked its way from the tree trunk out onto the limb. He watched it move from that tree to the next and then to another. Squirrel highways in the sky. Don eased back on the hammer of the long thin rifle. The .36 flintlock was an antique. One of the few from the 1800s that wasn't converted to percussion. Don found it in a hardware store in Pike County just hanging over a door frame. The owner said it didn't work and he just kept it to look at. Don knew what he was looking at and paid the man cash on the spot. He nursed it back to life and had hunted with it for years.

One more tree, thought Don. Then if the critter would just slow up. He brought the rifle up, laid the front sight on the spot where the head met the shoulder and tracked the moving target. The squirrel leaped the distance to the next nearer tree and Don let out a bark, "Woof!" The squirrel stopped instantly and looked for the danger. Don was squeezing the trigger and the ignition of the pan powder was followed quickly by the main charge in the barrel.

The squirrel dropped straight down and landed with a thud. The smoke from the shot hung for a moment in the air and Don pulled the gun slowly back to him. He didn't make a move for a few moments to let the noise die down then quietly set about reloading. He blew through the touch hole to expel any remaining embers and uncapped the powder horn he had over his shoulder, adding what he knew by experience to be just enough. He pulled a strip of pillow ticking from his possibles bag and cut off a swatch with a stubby little knife dangling from the strap of the bag. Next, he fished out a small lead ball and wrapped the ticking around it. With the butt of the little knife, he worked the ball into the end of the barrel and slid the ram rod out from its holder on the underside of the bore. He started the ball and then pushed it firmly to the base of the barrel with the rod. Replacing the rod, he pulled out a much smaller powder horn and added a few grains of finer black powder to the pan beneath the lock.

The whole operation took less than a minute and Don watched the trees the whole time. He knew squirrels were real curious little guys and it wasn't unusual to be looking for one you just knocked down and have another come scampering across the trees to see what was going on.

~ * ~

Yusef was at the corner waiting for them when they pulled up in the blue van. He went in through the sliding door and moved all the way to the back seat. Jamal was stretched out on the middle seat and Harold, as usual, was driving. Not a word was said. They stopped on Broad Street for Harold to get them coffee and then they cut back south for Oregon Avenue to pick up the Expressway. Yusef ignored his coffee and fell asleep. It was the first he'd slept all night.

~ * ~

Sam heard him counting under his breath. He got up to one hundred and switched to crunches. After sixty five he went back to pushups and did another twenty five. Thirty more crunches and he was up stretching his hamstrings. "Morning, Dad. Gonna run with the wild dogs this fine day?" Ken asked.

"Run your young butt into the ground," Sam sat up and swung out to slip into his sweats that were in a lump on the floor. "God, what time is it?"

"Our time or their time?" Ken grinned.

"Aw, that's right. We're an hour behind here." Sam slipped his socks and running shoes on and began to stretch the sleep out of his legs.

Sam couldn't believe Ken could talk. Sam was breathing hard trying to keep Ken's pace and the kid was jabbering on about Grace this and Grace that. Jeez. After two miles, Sam had to slow down and Ken finally shut up. They settled in to a more sane speed and finished back at the hotel with just a little over four miles for the morning. Ken found the pool unlocked and stripped down to his shorts and dove in. He did lap after lap, changing stokes from crawl to butterfly, breast to back, and finished with a two lap freestyle sprint. Sam found them coffee and a paper and plopped down in a pool chair to let his legs stop burning.

"Let's put in a pool, Dad. Molly will love it. We can play hockey on it in the winter," Ken said half seriously.

"Only if we have lifeguards like on that old TV show, the girl ones," Sam said over the top of the paper.

Ken's head snapped to the left and a big smile appeared on his face. "Hi, Grace. You're up early, too?"

She padded into the pool room wrapped in a big striped towel. "Good morning to both of you. I ate too much of your food last night, have to burn it off if I'm going to fit into my uniform tonight." The towel dropped and Ken stopped breathing. She had on a different suit. Half again as small as the one last night. She was built for speed, Sam thought. Fine lookin' woman.

Ken sat with his feet in the shallow end while Grace swam her workout. She started slowly and completed several laps before she first increased her leg kicks and after a few more laps, put her arms into high gear also. She surprised both of them with her stamina. Finally she slowed her pace back down and did the last two laps at a leisurely breast stroke.

Ken slipped into the pool and floated with her. They touched accidently several times and then Ken put his hands at the back of her head and let her float totally relaxed for a while. Sam figured you can't live on love alone and left briefly to order breakfast for them. He anticipated Grace might not want too much greasy food and asked the waiter to bring fruit and some cereals also. They sat and ate together. Sam felt himself being drawn into this thing, whatever it was. He really didn't seem to mind. Grace just turned twenty two and Ken would be eighteen next month. Ah, well, what will be will be.

Her college life had been cut short by the death of her father in a boating accident. He'd been water skiing with a real estate client and was struck by a jet ski. Grace found out a week into her junior year and couldn't go back. Her mother finally forced her to apply to the airline and she found she rather liked it. Her mother ran the real estate office now and was dating one of the city councilmen. She said she missed Sarasota, the beaches were beautiful and she loved the water. She wouldn't go skiing anymore, but had a small sailboat at her mom's house and tried to get out on it whenever she could.

Sam watched Ken all but drool while she talked. She finally said she was sorry. She hadn't talked this much at once since her dad died. She thought she must be boring them terribly.

When Ken told her about his mom, she reached across the table and put her hand over his. They held each other's eyes for almost a full minute.

192

Sam noticed just the slightest glint of a tear in Ken's eye. Grace squeezed his hand then took Sam's hand also.

~ * ~

They weren't out of sight of the house before Molly hit the first time. She bellowed and with a furious set of twists and circles struck on the bunny, shot down next to the streambed and was gone up the gully. Ozzie signaled Junior to go up on the bank to the left and watch the high side for the rabbit to circle around. Ozzie followed Molly's backside for several yards past where she struck and stopped to let her work. It was up to her now. She yelped steadily and by the sound, kept the bunny moving straight up the creek. Wouldn't be long now before it turned either left or right. Ozzie was betting left. They usually didn't cross the creek unless it was almost dry. There it is. Molly broke left and her yelp was coming from up on the bank. Ozzie glanced over where he knew Junior was standing.

Crack whoom! "Got 'em, Dad!" Junior shouted. Ozzie heard Junior pump the shotgun and eject the spent shell. Ozzie cleared the bank and was next to Junior and Molly in a few steps. Molly was all excited. Junior let her muzzle the rabbit a bit and praised her lavishly. Ozzie snuck a peek at Junior's shotgun and was pleased to see he'd put the safe back on after the shot. Good. One in the bag and we is jest a startin'.

~ * ~

"No, I insist. You don't get a chance like this very often. They're going to be the national champs. You and Ken will enjoy it a lot more than I would," Sam had just decided to give his ticket to Grace and let Ken take her to the game. She didn't have to be back to the airport until 7:00 tonight and was going to have to check out of the hotel and hang out in the general aviation employee lounge. The game would be a lot more fun, for Ken, too. That earned Sam another kiss from her.

"My Cuban father kissed everybody. My mom was a cracker Baptist. She would shudder when he would walk right up to one of her uncles and plant a smack on his cheek. Daddy thought it was the thing to do. I thought it was sweet. Mom kinda loosened up and started the kissing thing herself. Helps her sell a lot of houses," Grace explained.

"When's it my turn?" Ken asked.

"You, I think you have to wait for me to figure out what I'm going to do with you," Grace cocked her head and gave him a sly look. "Take me shopping, I have to get something to wear to the game, okay?"

Without skipping a beat Ken said, "Okay."

"Go ahead, kids, I'll do the dishes," Sam waved them away.

~ * ~

Now ain't that somethin', Don said to himself. He'd been hearing the rustling behind him for several minutes. He thought it might be a squirrel, but then it didn't move. The sound kept coming from the same place. Maybe a deer deciding if that was the right spot to bed down for the day. Don began the slow process of turning his bulk around without spooking whatever it was. It had taken him a few minutes but he finally spotted the movement behind some thin berry bushes.

"Nice fat ringneck," Don muttered. Must have snuck up along the edge of the cornfield. Now he was in a fix. He had his squirrel rifle, not his scatter gun. Well, a head shot is a head shot. Slowly, ever so slowly, he eased the rifle up onto his right knee and steadied his left arm by bracing back against his leg. The bird wasn't cooperating. It stayed behind the bush and strutted back and forth without giving Don a clear shot at its head. Don's arm was losing circulation. He either had to take the shot or chance a reposition. Birds have a lot better eyesight than squirrels and any movement can be a giveaway. The ringneck made the decision for him. It paraded right out into the clear and looked straight at the .36 ball coming out of the cloud of smoke.

~ * ~

They ran out of hot water. That signaled when it was time for them to get out of the shower. Calvin dried her with the big fluffy towel and rubbed baby powder on her back. "You are my beautiful girl, aren't you? Look at you. Pretty, pretty," she soaked it up. He pulled her to him and kissed her gently on the mouth. He kept kissing her down her neck and shoulders. She got goose bumps. What she did next convinced him they could find something to occupy their time while the hot water built back up.

~ * ~

The Fire Department rescue unit got her stabilized and a regular ambulance transported her to Jefferson Hospital. The detectives tried to get a statement from her, but she couldn't even look at them. She needed to be in the hospital and soon. There was no ID on her and she couldn't tell them her name. Either she would come around or someone would call in that she was missing. She looked about seventeen or eighteen to the older detective. His partner bet him lunch she wasn't a day over fifteen. "Whoever did this to her was a brutal motherfucker," the older detective said. "Looks like he stuck a fireplug up inside her. Beat her tits purple."

"How 'bout pancakes, you feel like pancakes while we wait for Cinderella here to get her voice back?" the young one asked.

"Yeah, the joint on Pine Street. Got good pancakes there. On the way to Jeff."

~ * ~

"Hey, hon, mornin'. Gotta work today?" Johnny lit her cigarette for her and sat back down at the table to finish his coffee.

"Nope. Me and Donald Trump are gonna have lunch. Wanna join us?" she smiled at her own joke.

"Got a hot date with Calvin, overtime! Pay the 'lectric bill this month," Johnny stubbed his smoke out and stared at the refrigerator for lack of anything else to do at the moment.

~ * ~

One of the nice things about the blue van was cruise control. Harold set it on 65, the posted speed limit on that part of the turnpike, and let his right leg take a break. Jamal was stripping the shells out of his magazines and reloading each of them. Yusef was still asleep using the black gym bag as a pillow.

~ * ~

"No, sir. That's been all taken care of. The breakfast, too." His tie was crooked and his sport coat was a size too big, but he was polite. Sam was trying to pay the bill for the pool party, but the Penn State crew had beaten him to it.

"Let me have an envelope, Son," Sam asked. He was pretty sure there had been three of them working the crowd. Policy usually was to add 15 percent right on to the bill, but he wanted to be sure the waiters were taken care of. The young desk clerk handed Sam a hotel envelope and Sam asked, "Where's the bar manager's office?" He was directed around the corner and told to turn left at the next hall. He slipped three twenties into the envelope and wrote on it 'For the pool waiters.' The manager assured him she would see that her night crew got the envelope.

Now, what the heck was he going to do until late in the afternoon? He walked back to the elevators and thought he might as well enjoy a few hours with no one to answer to.

~ * ~

They stopped at three. The creek banks sort of flattened out up into the University property and they worked back along the field edges. Ozzie got the last rabbit after it fooled him and cut away from Junior back into him. Junior clipped the short lead on Molly and they walked back to the house through the big field. A lone hawk circled out over the hard road and screeched a high pitched warning. The clouds were breaking up and blue sky was showing to the west. The wind had increased since daylight and was pushing at the tops of the bare maples along the edge of the field. Ozzie figured the venison chili would be about ready in the crockpot he started before Molly took them out for their exercise. Just a little snack while he put the PVC together.

~ * ~

They don't have real telephone booths anymore. The one on the outside wall of the gas station worked fine, but there was no shelter from the wind and the cars passing by made it hard to hear. That, and his mother was almost whispering on the other end. She wanted to see him.

"I'll try to come tomorrow, Mother. Today I have much to do." It was a lie. He didn't know what he was going to do. "Tomorrow, but I can't be sure," Afif felt better to say it that way. "I need to speak to Father now."

~ * ~

"See if there are any crackers up in the cupboard. You want another bowl?" Junior shook his head and went to the sink to rinse out his dish. He handed his dad the box of crackers and Ozzie crumbled a half a stack into the big soup mug. "Why don't you feed Molly and bring my green toolbox in from the truck. I'm going to get to work upstairs." He carried his chili with him and took the stairs two at a time.

Ozzie was real proud of this house. Sam even let Ozzie use photos of parts of the house to show to people that wanted Ozzie to do work for them. The success he had with this project gave Ozzie a lot of confidence and he'd increased his remodeling business to the point that it was going to make college possible for any of his kids that wanted to go. That and the account Sam set up for each of the kids. But Ozzie and Marie didn't know about that, yet.

He stood in the room gulping down chili and figuring what he was going to do first. All the fixtures were stacked in the tub and he had earlier brought up several bags from the home supply center. *Well,* he thought, *if this chili goes to work, I'll need the crapper first.* He unwrapped the wax ring and set about installing the toilet.

~ * ~

Calvin thought about it for a minute. Not wearing a suit was out of character for him. But, it was Saturday. Well, they would be looking for the Yancey cat down in Philly, but still had a bunch of straight interviews to do. Sounds like sport coat and slacks, blue button down shirt and striped tie. Good enough. He was rushing now. Trying to get in to the barracks. He wanted to have some time to work alone in the quiet before the rest got there. Try to link all these loose bits together.

~ * ~

He couldn't remember the last time he took this long to shower, shave and get dressed. Usually, he was planning the use of every minute of the day and trying not to end up pissing anyone off by cutting them short. He still had a couple of hours until checkout time, but was carefully packing for both himself and Ken. The lad wouldn't be thinking about such mundane details right now. He looked at the phone and figured it would be about time.

"Hi, Junior, it's Sam."

Junior heard the phone and picked it up. "Yeah, she did real good. She's sleeping off breakfast. We left a few behind for another day. I cleaned 'em and stuck one in a freezer bag for you. Mom's going to crab a little, but she'll cook them for Dad. I'll get him for you."

"Hey, Ozzie, shit in the new toilet yet?" laughed Sam.

"How'd you know? You got cameras in here? She works like a champ. Just have to finish the trap on the sink and screw in the shower head. Junior tell you that beagle is about as good a bunny dog as I ever seen?" Ozzie was holding Sam's portable phone from the bedroom against his shoulder and fitting the trap to the bottom of the sink. "Hope that CID guy has something we can use. Military ain't known for cooperatin' with us mere civilians, you know."

"Doesn't hurt to do a sit down and see where it goes. His suspect's brother gets smoked with the same two pieces that our job has, maybe his suspect will want to know where these guys are as much as we do. I got a feeling more bad guys are gonna get an early visit from the grim reaper," Sam said. "I'll be back on the ground just after 9:00. Anything shakes, leave word with Peggy. My cell will be off for the flight home," he let Ozzie get back to work.

~ * ~

When the cab dropped them at the mall, it was just opening for the senior citizens to walk. Most of the stores were still closed, except for the news stand and a few shops selling coffee and juice. They were both full from breakfast so they joined the walkers and window shopped. They drew a lot of looks from the old men and the women all smiled and remembered those days when they were young and in love. Ken kept slipping a half step behind to just look at her. She would reach back and hook his arm and pull him back up next to her. Someone had Tommy Dorsey on the mall sound system and a couple in their seventies up in front of them were holding hands and dancing along.

They found what she wanted in the shop that sold Irish wool sweaters. The cream colored cable stitching looked great against her rich black hair. She matched that with a long red wool blend skirt that didn't hide her feminine shape at all. "I have just the boots to go with this. It's perfect. And you thought you'd be here all day, I'll bet," she said.

Grace turned to the register and slid her credit card out of her purse. Ken said from behind, "I don't have much patience for shopping, but I like being with you." The girl at the checkout counter didn't notice Grace smiling, she was trying not to be too obvious about looking at the hunk standing next to her customer.

~ * ~

It smelled like a restaurant in the barracks. Don made a stop between the woods and Straus Valley and had the meat sizzling in a skillet with onions and garlic. Once it browned, he would debone the squirrel and drop it into the pot with the vegetables and other spices. The thick stock was almost to a bubble and he was peeling potatoes and carrots to put in the roasting pan with the pheasant. He had to keep it simple and brought an apple pie and vanilla ice cream for dessert. Lunch was on him today. Trooper Miles was on the desk and kept coming into the kitchen to supervise. Man, did that smell good.

Calvin was separating out the last of the interviews and other work they needed to do today. He and Johnny would take the ones down in Philly and Ozzie and Don would finish up locating the cars left in and around Porter when they got back from Jefferson Township. Don wanted to put some more pressure on the inspection mechanic's father to produce the kid, if he wasn't on a plane back to Jordan by now.

Calvin planned on meeting with Detective Dugan again and checking the woman's address for the cars. He was getting frustrated. Was he missing something? He needed a link, a solid knot between the shooters and McFadden. Usually he figured out fairly early who the killer was in a murder investigation. The trick was getting a confession or enough other evidence to prove it. Everyone seemed to think it could be this Yancey dude, but he needed something, any piece of solid evidence to make him sure of it. Then he could concentrate better. Eliminate all this bullshit distraction, routine, fill in the blank, run around in circles, type of nonsense. *And damnit, why the fuck does it have to smell like a...*

"Hey, Calvin, gonna be a heck of a meal in a bit," Johnny said cheerfully as he walked into the crime office and peeled off his leather jacket.

"Fuckin' Davey, fuckin', Crockett out there smellin' up my clothes with his rat soup, fuckin'..." Calvin mumbled the last of it as he stormed down the hall to the locker room.

"Yeah, had a great night, how about you? Jesus Christ, he didn't get nothin' last night!" Johnny tossed his leathers onto his desk and dropped into his chair.

~ * ~

"We see if they want to make money or die for their foolishness. Can't do both. We gonna be set up long before they get there and we watch them come in. They slip in early and try to set up on us and we decide if we do the deed there or disappear out and fight a different day," Yusef listened to Jamal set the play. Harold didn't say anything, as usual. "We got the money, they got the guns. They don't get anything close for their stuff anywhere else like they get from us. Motherfuckers try to rip us off again, more of 'em die again. They got to learn this is business, not some fuckin' movie," Harold was easing them through another construction zone and picking up speed again on the other side. Jamal looked at his watch and said, "No problem, plenty of time."

~ * ~

Now he was worried. She hardly moved in the bed all night and when she did get up to go to the bathroom, she moved very slowly. He heard her make several gasps and moans and she kept turned away from him the whole night. No breakfast either, until the girl quickly made hot oatmeal and tea for him. He only heard her speak when Afif called and once to the girl about cleaning up the kitchen for her. He left for the shop thinking he would have to be paying a doctor bill if this didn't clear up soon. He didn't need this now with the police coming around asking about Afif. *What had Yusef gotten Afif involved in?* He had always been so careful with his special cars. None had ever been discovered. He was very proud of that. Maybe if he could have Afif visit her, she would feel better. Tomorrow he would arrange that. And have a serious talk with him about Yusef and what has gone wrong in the city.

~ * ~

The Weather Channel drifted across the screen and Sam made mental notes of where he expected the position of the clouds and rain would be at takeoff time tonight. They were lucky again. The weak front that moved across home last night wasn't followed by another until late Sunday or Monday morning. Clear flying meant a lot less hassle.

He heard the door latch click and Ken burst into the room. He glanced at the weather maps on the screen and did a quick mental calculation before speaking to Sam, "Gotta change into something warmer, it's chilly out there in the wind." He hesitated just a bit when he found his bags on the bed and packed for the trip back. "Maid service, I see. Hope you took care of her, Dad."

"You're lookin' at the head maid right here. I'm trying to decide if I want to see the latest movie massacre of a Clancy book, or Redford aging," Sam hadn't been to a real movie for quite a while. "I'm gonna eat greasy popcorn and five dollar candy. See if I can stand the surround sound. Might have to stuff tissue in my ears to get through it."

Ken didn't seem to hear him. He rummaged through his bag and came up with a heavy Varnum pullover and slipped it on. "What do you think of her, Dad, seriously?"

"I seriously think you're seriously silly about her and in serious need of a serious cold shower. Other than that, she's just about the nicest girl I've ever met. She was ten years older, I'd fight you for her," Sam deadpanned.

Ken straightened up and turned to face Sam with a bit of surprise on his face, "Well, if we survive the game sitting next to my 'foster uncles,' I'll meet you at the airport. Her pals are going to take her bags over for her. See ya," and out the door he went. Sam thought he might have just lost a little bit of something right here.

~ * ~

"Thought the prissy little lieutenant was going to break out in hives," Johnny was laughing trying to get the story out. Ozzie was standing in the back door and Don and Johnny were just outside smoking. "Don's out in Greensburg at the Southwestern Training Center to teach a week of Auto Theft to the rookie class they had running out there. Second week of buck season and Don's pissed that the dipshits planned his block during hunting season. So Don, he don't let the bosses get him down and he's out every morning with his suit on under his blaze orange coveralls and gets a couple hours in the woods before rushing down the mountain and teaching the boys and girls. Well, he's got that monster old Pontiac wagon and one morning he pulls into the training center and damn if there ain't a six point buck flopped halfway out the back window of the state car. Blood and hair all over. Old Don here, he drags the fuckin' buck outta the wagon and strings it up in a maple outside the gym. Standin' there spreadin' the carcass open when the CO drives past him and damn near plows into the cadets running in formation down the drive,"

Tears were running down Johnny's cheeks and Ozzie's belly was heaving he was laughing so hard. "Stripped off his coveralls and has a big blood stain down the front of his suit pants. But the balls on old Don here are legendary. He goes in to one of the sergeants and says, 'Can you get a camera out of the equipment room and take a picture of me and my deer?' The pussy lieutenant tried to ding him, but the captain in Philly told him to get a life and leave it alone," Don was turning a little red. "Couple weeks later, the UPS truck delivers a cooler to the lieutenant with deer steak packed in dry ice. Little note attached thanking him for his hospitality."

"Hey, life's short, gotta live it every day. Boys 'er coming in, let's eat," Don said as two marked units pulled into the lot. The citizens of the county would have to remain calm while their protectors ate some squirrel stew and roasted pheasant.

~ * ~

They really let her have it. "Seminoles, Ha! If they don't all get arrested before the season's over, they might get to the Fiesta Bowl, maybe. No way are they going to stay undefeated," the tooth doctor told Grace when he found out she'd gone to Florida State.

"What's the coach going to use for linebackers, their parole officers?" the banker commented on the recent troubles members of the Seminoles defense had encountered with Leon County Sheriff's deputies outside Tallahassee.

She withstood it all and still made them laugh with her. The Marriott van dropped them a block from the stadium and Grace tucked in tight to Ken for the walk to the gates. Each of the men shared Ken stories with her while they waited in line to enter, much to Ken's embarrassment. Grace just loved it. Before they even got to their seats, she felt familiar and comfortable with them, especially Ken.

~ * ~

It was way too loud to suit him. He passed on the popcorn, but made lunch out of a huge box of Raisinets. He was a little surprised how full the theater was for the afternoon show. He sat all the way in the back and tried to follow the story. His mistake was that he'd read the book. Bad move. Hollywood chopped it to pieces. He kept thinking that what he was seeing wasn't in the book. Characters blended together and whole parts were missing. Somewhere late in the first hour one of the bad guys, who everyone thought was a good guy, was screaming at his accomplice about the computer not spitting out the secret information the way he wanted it to.

Sam stopped in mid chew and the movie went away in his mind. He sat there for a few more moments and then got up quickly and stumbled over two teenage boys between him and the aisle. He dumped the candy into a big plastic trash can at the door and squinted into the light of the lobby. He pulled out his cellphone as he went out through the front doors and dialed the barracks.

"Naw, Corp. They all left after we had lunch. You missed a good one," said Trooper Miles.

"Get Ozzie on the radio and have him call me on my cell phone," requested Sam. He sat down on the bench outside the movie complex and tried to remember.

~ * ~

They were a few minutes early and stopped at the roadside stand. The little Amish girl had honey, several kinds of apples and bunches of Indian corn for sale. Ozzie was loading a half bushel of green apples, the kind Marie used to make pie and cobbler, into the trunk of the Crown Vic when he heard Miles calling him on the radio.

~ * ~

Her mom wanted a new television. Her mom's boyfriend complained that the one mom had, was grainy and he was coming over to watch the Eagles on Sunday. She wasn't too sure it would fit into the Lexus, but she would figure that out when she had to. She made her way down Cobb's Creek Parkway and eventually got onto I-95 from Island Avenue. It wasn't too long of a trip down to Delaware. It was worth it to save on the sales tax. Delaware had several malls just over the border and a lot of electronics and appliance stores. She knew she would not only get a good deal for her mom, but would save six percent on top of that. Maybe they could make an afternoon of it and find a nice Red Lobster for dinner. She had been gone for forty-five minutes when Johnny cruised by the rear of the house looking for the Lexus or the Ford van.

~ * ~

Yusef had to piss. He and Jamal were watching the parking lot of the Dutch Restaurant from the rear window of the van. Harold was pretending to read a girlie magazine on a bench outside the trucker's lounge across the big lot near the fuel pumps. Traffic flowed in and out of the busy interchange and people were milling all around the shops and other restaurants at the Breezewood exit of the turnpike. Interstate 70 up out of Maryland hooked into the turnpike here and made this one of the busiest places in this unpopulated area of the state. "I'm going in to the bathroom. You want me to bring you anything?" Yusef asked.

"Leave the Uzi here. I don't want you walking around with it," Jamal ordered. Yusef hesitated, but decided he would be okay without it for a few minutes. "Don't just walk right back. Watch Harold for the signal before you leave the restaurant." Yusef went upfront and got out on the driver's side. As he walked toward the building, he put his right hand to his head to signal Harold everything was still clear.

~ * ~

By the second half, Penn State had the second and third string mixing in with the starters. They still couldn't be stopped. Penn State was twenty four points ahead and Illinois only managed a field goal and a few first downs. The action on the field wasn't holding the attention of the boys from Allentown. They kept switching seats to get to sit next to the dark haired beauty. Ken picked up several more pieces of information about Grace as she talked easily and freely with these businessmen. Her dad and grandparents came over after Castro began to clamp down on the island's educated people. Her grandparents escaped with almost nothing. Her grandfather owned a Ford dealership in Santiago and started over again in Miami. Her father was able to go to college and got into real estate with a fraternity brother in Sarasota. Only her Cuban grandmother was still living and her mom's parents used to have a hardware store in Arcadia.

She really liked working for the airline, but was getting bounced all over. It would be a while before she could bid for a regular route. She shared an apartment with six other flight attendants outside of Atlanta, but only ended up there about four or five days a month. The rest of the time was spent in airports and hotels. They were lucky the Marriott was the contract for here. In some places the accommodations weren't nearly as nice.

~ * ~

"No it was worth it just to see the look on Ken's face. He's stuck on this girl he just met and would have been miserable company anyway. He'll be like a wet puppy tonight on the flight back," Sam told Ozzie. Ozzie was trying to steer the troop car, eat an apple and talk on the cell phone at the same time. "In the homicide book is a section on the computer search. The stuff the headquarters geeks got out of McFadden's smashed up computer. There should be a printout of a series of numbers and letters with what looks like dates. Chief Johnston mentioned his armory thefts were spread out from Chicago to Massachusetts. Have him look at that printout and see if it means anything to him," Sam told Ozzie. "Heard you fellas had quite a spread at lunch."

"It was great. We didn't save you any. Even had Brad doing dishes. Look, we're going to try to pick up a few more cars later and talk to a couple of the phone call people. You want us to work tomorrow, too?" Ozzie asked.

Sam thought he could tell what answer Ozzie wanted to hear. "If the CID guy gives you anything that has to be done right away you guys can, otherwise we'll regroup on Monday. Take a day to let all this settle."

~ * ~

The utilities and the taxes were in the woman's name. Detective Dugan looked at the printouts and told Calvin and Johnny that she had an arrest record and looked like she'd lived there for quite some time. "Maybe she's down south visiting relatives or something," Dugan said. He had come in on his day off to meet with Sam's men. "I'm pushing my snitches hard on this. Anything that even smells like Yancey and McFadden were hooked up. You're going to need more than Tom Sylvester for court. His record, even before he got sent to Graterford, was lousy. Any good defense lawyer will find a way to bring out the departmental dirt, too."

"We're going to keep on the house as much as we can. We probably won't be back tomorrow unless we shake the cars or Yancey," Calvin said. "I'm going to find what I need. Can't let this one go cold. I'm beginning to take this personal."

Johnny could tell something was bugging Calvin. They stopped on the way to Major Crimes and interviewed one of the people on the McFadden long distance list. Nice lady who said she talked to Ginny about tickets to the Christmas bazaar at Ginny's old church. Calvin snapped at her and made it sound like the woman was hiding one of the murder weapons or something. Got real ugly for a minute.

~ * ~

Harold saw Yusef come out of the restaurant and gave him the clear signal. Yusef went around the lot and made his way back to the van. "Nothing yet, they're late," Jamal muttered. "We'll give 'em a while longer."

~ * ~

Afif ate and slept and thought. He had nothing else to do.

~ * ~

T ran through his case. He didn't have much. The thefts had been getting more frequent and when not only M-16 rifles were coming up missing, but LAW anti-tank rockets also, it got a much higher priority. The military was having a lot of problems with gang members and associates in recent years. They couldn't keep them out and it was impossible to exclude them from details where security was an issue. Besides, money talks. What the gangs couldn't get themselves, they bought. Finally a source of information developed and a suspect from the Gary, Indiana area was identified. When Chief Johnston began to question servicemen who had access to the weapons, the suspect went AWOL and disappeared. His little brother got dead and here was T. Johnston looked at the printout Ozzie pulled from the book and studied it for a minute. He opened one of his folders and compared them. "Look at this, trooper," he showed them to Ozzie and Don. "On Memorial Day weekend, twenty-one M-16s go missing from Plattsburg, NY. On July 4th weekend, seventeen M-16s and six LAWs from Lynn, Massachusetts, and twenty-nine M-16s and fifteen LAWs from Gary. Labor Day, twelve M-16s from Chicago and our boy goes AWOL at the end of September just before fourteen rifles and ten LAWs from Springfield, Missouri. Looks like your victim kept track of his customers. His list fits. If my math is right, I'd say, let me add this, I'd say two hundred for the rifles and three fifty for the rockets. Damn cheap for what you're getting, but the upfront costs were pretty low."

~ * ~

No one could ever accuse State of running up the score. In the fourth quarter, Illinois finally sustained a drive against the sophomore and freshman version of the Penn State defense and scored a touchdown. Ken lost all interest in the game long before that. The only thing that he was thinking about was what would happen in about two hours when she had to go back to her world and he flew back to his. "Would you mind if we slipped out and made our own way back to the airport, Grace?" Ken asked.

She looked into his eyes and smiled. "I really don't want to go to the bar after the game, sounds like a good idea, we can talk and grab a cab."

Ken made their excuses and told them he and Grace were going to skip the after game stop and he would meet them back at the airport. They protested loudly, but relented and each received the Grace peck on the cheek. They pressed business cards in her hand and made her promise that if she ever needed them for anything, to call. The tooth doctor pulled Ken back at the very last second and told Ken what Ken already knew. She was special, take care of her.

~ * ~

The bags were safely stored at the desk where Sam left them when he checked out earlier. He helped the cab driver load them into the trunk and left for the short ride to the airport. Sam hoped Scotty had survived and would be in shape to help him deliver his cargo back to Allentown. The weather was breezy, but clear and Flight Service wasn't predicting anything unusual for Pennsylvania. He didn't mind getting to the airport early, give him plenty of time to nose around the plane, and think.

~ * ~

Ozzie called Calvin and brought him up to speed on the military connection. Calvin thought for a bit and said, "So, the only people in this mess that are still alive are the AWOL and Yancey. I wonder for how long."

~ * ~

The door on the passenger side was unlocked and Jamal slowly looked all around and checked the floor of the back seat before he started to open the door to get in next to the dark skinned Hispanic driver. The driver came into the lot alone and parked between the pumps and the restaurant, just like they agreed. Harold watched him and anyone else coming onto the lot for fifteen minutes before signaling Jamal that it looked clear. Yusef had his ugly gun out and four spare magazines tucked into the back of his belt. He could have the rear door open and thirty-two rounds on target in seconds if he needed to. Jamal calmly sat until Harold's signal and then took his time before he slipped out on the side the new arrival couldn't see, and made his way around the lot to the car. Jamal put his right hand behind his back and gripped the Colt as he moved to sit down next to the driver and pulled the automatic free before his hand got trapped between his back and the seat. The driver never saw the gun come out and Jamal kept it low to his right side between his leg and the door.

Both of them looked at each other and back out to the lot again. The driver spoke first, "Why'd you have to kill him, man?"

"Who says I killed anybody, my friend. They're others in this thing. I'm just one part of it," Jamal was looking right into his eyes now. Jamal knew to watch the eyes. They told you if something was coming.

"He was supposed to just talk. He didn't have anything with him. Now he's dead. Someone has to answer to me for him, he was my brother. He was part of me," the driver growled. "If I wanted you dead, you would already be dead."

Jamal increased the pressure on the safety. He carried the .45 cocked. "See, my people don't always tell me everything that they do. I get what I need. You know the problem. You can't change the deal. You can't hold back for more. Your brother found that out. The question is, do you know that?"

Before he answered, he looked away. Jamal shifted in the seat and the rustle of his coat covered the small sound of the safety being fully released.

"For now, I choose to grieve for my brother. There is plenty of time," he slowly took a pack of cigarettes from the dash and held open his coat to show Jamal he was getting his lighter from his shirt pocket. He lit the cigarette and said, "I have some increased expenses. It's only fair that I pass some of that along," he turned back to look at Jamal. "I understand I may have a more direct route to deliver the articles."

"That's right, your people go through me from now on. It was a mistake to use the old man to bargain for you. The deal stays the same. Handle your own problems, don't bother me with anything but deliveries," Jamal watched him look away again. He was thinking that over.

"Take this message back with you. For now we do business. I will decide when the business is through so I can collect the debt of my brother's life. You won't know when that is," he flashed a thin, steely grin at Jamal.

He knew he had to decide right now. He stared back at the driver. His finger was over the trigger, but he hadn't put any pressure on it yet. It had come down to this moment. "Go have a sandwich, don't try to look around after you walk over. I'll be ready when you have the next delivery. Now go get your supper." The driver sat there for a moment and then opened the door and got out of the car. Jamal checked quickly behind the car and didn't see anyone close to them. He waited until the driver was going through the glass door of the restaurant before he put the safety on and slipped the pistol back under his coat. He quickly got out of the car and got the clear signal from Harold. Jamal walked away from the van and toward Harold. They both walked around opposite sides of the truckers' lounge where Yusef picked them up in the van. Harold took over and they went cross country, making several turns and stops to make sure they weren't followed, before stopping to eat.

~ * ~

They ended up sitting at the counter in a small coffee shop just a few blocks from the stadium. Ken ordered coffee and Grace had tea and honey. They were both quiet. She complimented him on his friends.

"You're very lucky to have them," she told him. "You'll find it hard to keep in touch with them when you go out to Colorado to school. My high school and college friends are all scattered. When I get home, it's usually just me and Mom. Everybody gets so busy."

"I don't want you to get scattered from me, but...," she put her hand into his and he stopped.

"Ken, we have to be realistic about this," a tear started down her cheek, "I'm just starting out and you're, well, you're going to be so involved with the Academy. I know how hard you're going to have to work."

"I'm not thinking about anything but when will be the next time we can see each other. I don't care. We have to see each other again," he said with conviction.

"I, I," both cheeks were covered now, "I know, Ken. I know," she reached out for him and right there in front of everyone, he scooped her up and got his kiss. Not on the cheek. The waitress nearly dropped the coffee pot.

~ * ~

They found one at the first place they stopped. The man remembered Patrick and said the Buick was a good car and he got it for a real good price. No, he didn't know anything about where Patrick got the car and other than the woman he assumed was the wife, no one else was involved in the sale. Bought shotgun shells from him earlier this year, too. Don confirmed the VIN in the dash was different from the hidden number and called Trooper Miles on the radio to run it for stolen. It was, over a year ago from Philadelphia. They let him get his fishing poles and tackle box out of the trunk before Don drove it back to Straus Valley.

~ * ~

Johnny handled the interviews. Calvin was in an evil mood. "Come on, baby. We're makin' a ton of money. Try to relax," Johnny told him. Calvin just told him to shut his cracker face.

~ * ~

He found Scotty on the phone in the General Aviation building checking the weather. Sam left his flight bag and Ken's leather case with Scotty and humped the suitcases out to the jet. He made a second trip and got the plane unlocked and started his preflight. In a few minutes, Scotty came out and they walked the preflight together. They would have time to sit for a while and swap stories before everyone started to arrive.

Grace insisted on saying goodbye to Sam. Ken got them a cab and they found Sam and Scotty stretched out in the cabin of the Lear. "We had a great time at the game. Thanks for being so generous. We have a lot to think about now. I wanted to let you know how important I think Ken's Academy appointment is. He knows I want him to be the best cadet there. I want him to be proud of himself and that will make all of us even more proud of him. What I'm trying to say is, we're all going to see each other again and I'm happy because of that," she tried to make her voice sound clear. Ken had lipstick just on the edge of his mouth and Sam watched him beside her.

"Grace it's been a pleasure for me, too. I'm glad you two had such a good time. I'll bet young Ken here will figure some way to get you two moveable objects within the same orbit. He's a whiz at physics," Sam smiled at them. He gave her a strong hug and saw Ken grinning at them.

"I'm gonna' make sure she gets over to the terminal and I'll be back," Ken said. Grace gave Sam a double peck and the two youngsters were out the cabin door and gone.

The driver of the hotel van was thinking about where he was going to spend the hundred dollars. He waited outside the bar and his special passengers were in very high spirits as they came out and got in. They didn't want to have to deal with taking cabs so had arranged for the van to have their luggage on board and take them directly to the airport. The driver was more than happy to provide the service.

~ * ~

The second car was there, too. Working people aren't usually home during the day and you have to catch them in the evenings or on weekends. Another of Patrick's customers. A deal too good to pass up. Fifteen hundred dollars less than others the man had shopped. Paid Mr. McFadden cash he did. No one else there. McFadden even did the notary work for him. He wasn't at all happy about these troopers telling him this was a stolen car and they had to take it in. He called his lawyer to complain. Cost him to find out the lawyer couldn't stop the troopers. They had to take it if it was stolen.

By the time they got the car back to the barracks, Ozzie announced it was time to eat. "I know this good rib place, all you can eat for $11.95, that sound okay?" he got no argument from Don Mitchell. Both of those big boys could eat.

~ * ~

Now he was getting angry. The door slammed behind him as he stormed out and the girl watched a picture on the front wall rock back and forth and then fall to the floor. When she opened her eyes, she was glad to see that the glass didn't break. She replaced the picture and cleared his dishes from the table. At first she was going to wrap the food to save it, but thought it would be better if she threw it away. His mood darkened when he came home from the shop and found her preparing the meal. Her mother was still in bed and getting worse. The girl was up and down the stairs trying to follow her mother's directions on how to cook the meat and vegetables, but it didn't work. It would have been better if she'd just heated up soup for him.

Now he was off to play cards without his dinner. She rinsed the dishes and slipped on her coat. The money her mother gave her was in her pocket. The bleeding wouldn't stop and she had to walk to the store for something to soak it up. Her mother told her to get the pads, two packs. "I'll be right back from the store," she called up the stairs on her way out. She wished she knew where Afif was, he should know his mother was very sick.

~ * ~

Calvin only picked at his cheese steak. Johnny was enjoying the food and the atmosphere. They took a break from interviews and checking the pay phones. They sat at an outside table on the famous corner of 9th and Passyunk in South Philadelphia. The two steak shops on opposite sides of the angled intersection each had their following and anyone who was anybody eventually passed through here for a sandwich.

"You gotta lighten up, Calvin. Something's going to shake loose. We just got to keep at it," said Johnny between bites of the steaming sloppy lump of meat, onion and cheese filled roll. "You gonna finish that or take it back for Ozzie?"

Calvin looked blankly at his food, rolled the wrapper back around it and stuffed it back into the sack. "Yeah, Ozzie will appreciate it a lot more than me," he pulled out his small notebook and sat quietly studying it.

"You're missing the show here, pal. South Philly on a Saturday night, look at those two over there," Johnny nodded toward two well-developed teenage girls, fluffed and painted, standing in line at the steak shop across the way. "Does my old heart good." Calvin wasn't biting.

~ * ~

"I have to go, the fellas will be getting back and Dad will want to get them on the way home," Ken sighed to Grace. They'd been caught once already in the middle of a long kiss by a surprised captain and his first officer coming down the hall to the crew lounge. Grace still had to locate her bags and get changed, but she was finding it hard to pull herself away from him. Ken straightened his shoulders. "I'll e-mail you every chance I get. This has got to work out somehow, we have to give it a chance." He pulled her in and kissed her for the last time. She responded by melting into him and holding on tight. They held it for a moment more and then she pulled away.

"I can't say goodbye, just, just...," tears streamed down her cheeks and she quickly turned and went through the door. And was gone.

He stood there wishing the door would open back up until he heard voices approaching from the outer part of the hallway. He stuck his hands in his pockets to keep them from strangling himself and walked out.

It was actually pretty quiet in the van as it pulled up in front of the general aviation building. The men worked their way out between the seats and lined up to get their bags from the back compartment. The driver picked up another quick fifty dollars in tips by helping with the bags and holding the door for them. He hoped they would come back this way soon. Good group.

Scotty was there to greet them and walked out to the plane with those that didn't pay a last minute visit to the bathroom. Sam was in the cockpit setting up for the flight. He could feel the plane vibrate and move as the bags were loaded into the baggage compartment and the men come up the steps into the cabin. Sam looked out the windshield and saw Ken shuffle out of the glass doors and head down, walk to the jet. Now Sam could hear the men's voices retelling the plays they remembered and ribbing each other about last night. It didn't take long, they were experienced fliers, too and Scotty buttoned up the cargo doors before his last walk around.

"Hey, Dad," Ken stuck his head in the cockpit. "Everything okay? You need me to do anything?"

"Yeah, cheer up to start with. She's a great girl. The right things will happen, trust me. It's only logistics. Time and space. Keep it simple, understand?" Sam said.

"You know, I think I know what you mean. When does this canyon in my stomach go away?" Ken asked.

Sam touched a lever over his head and scratched a note on his clipboard. "It doesn't. The one I had for your mom is still there. You learn to work around it. See if everybody is tucked in, we're ready to go."

Ken slipped by as Scotty secured the door and did a quick walk around to everyone and thanked them for being so nice to Grace. He slowly made his way back to his seat and strapped in. He had a lot to think about.

~ * ~

"Now, Yusef, we're back to the car problem. Your little skinny cousin's got to get over his crisis here real soon and get back to work. Do what you have to do. And Harold is going with you this time, understand?" Jamal wouldn't talk business in the diner. Now they were making their way back to the turnpike, one exit east of Breezewood. "Go tomorrow and bring him back, in a sack if you have to. We're goin' to the auction on Monday."

~ * ~

The television just did fit in the back. She had to move the passenger seat all the way up for the salesman to cram it into the Lexus. It seemed like a nice area, but they parked where they could see the car out of the window of the restaurant. Shrimp and scallops were on special. That and a couple of tall draft beers. They settled in for a good meal.

~ * ~

Three for three. This one turned in to a screaming match. Ozzie tried to stay calm, but the old woman and her middle aged son both sounded like cats with their tails in a fan belt. Don was trying to call into the barracks on the radio and the noise could be heard by every trooper on the air. Miles asked Don if he needed another car there and at first Don said

219

no, but the decibel level was increasing and he asked for the nearest Straus Valley car to start their way. Ozzie was a pale shade of purple and deepening. "Just give me the keys and I'll let you get your personal things out of the car. It's going with us, we have to take it." Don stood there on the porch and tried to stay out of it. She was spraying spit as she screamed at Ozzie and her son was in the door repeating everything she said, "You can't just come in here and take my car!"

He would then scream, "Come in here and take my car!" like some falsetto parrot.

"I paid good money for that car!"

"Good money for that car!"

No letup appeared in sight. Don took it for a few more minutes and walked past her to the door and said to the son, "I hate to ask, but could I please use your bathroom? I have this medical condition, you know how it is?"

He missed the last stanza and appeared caught off guard by this big bearded man in leather and blue jeans. Don smiled sweetly at him, "Please?" the fellow stepped aside to let Don in and picked back up on the chorus, "Better things to do!"

Don went in through the kitchen and looked on the top of the microwave and then spotted them hanging on a Garfield magnet on the side of the refrigerator. He deftly slipped the car door and ignition key off the ring and replaced the set. Then he went in and took a leisurely crap in the garish pink bathroom. He passed on the muscleman magazines and read about radish spot in the garden magazine. Never knew that before. Every day is a learning experience.

Ozzie was passing purple to deep burgundy by the time Don came back out to the porch. Don walked past Ozzie and winked as she said, "Goddamn bully trying to rob an old woman!"

"To rob an old woman!"

She was in mid-sentence when she suddenly stopped her tirade. Ozzie heard the engine start on the woman's car and as it began to back out of the drive, the lights blinked on and off twice. Goodbye, lady! Ozzie was speechless for a brief moment and then turned to her and exclaimed, "Don't worry, ma'am, I'll get him for you!"

Ozzie whirled and flew down the steps to his Crown Vic. He spun the tires in the dirt and turned quickly around. The last thing the woman and her only son saw was Ozzie's big hand put the flashing red light on the roof and disappear out the drive, siren wailing.

The landing gear gave a solid thump and the indicator told Sam it was up and locked. Scotty brought the flaps up and got clearance for their departure heading and altitude. Sam visually checked for traffic and made the left turn to start around to the east. The stars spread out above them in the crystal clear air and Sam climbed rapidly and leveled out on course for home. Ken had his laptop out and shut out the conversations behind him so he could think of just the right things to put in his e-mail to Grace. They decided it would be the easiest way to keep in touch. Ken wasn't allowed to have a cell phone at school and Grace was in the air with hers shut off most of the time. The new electronic age.

"Take me home, I'm tired," Calvin said as Johnny rolled past the West Philadelphia house again. "I got a week's worth of paper to catch up on and I need a day to forget this for a while."

"Just need one little piece to sew this up. You and I both know this Yancey is probably good for this. What'r you gonna do if you find him and he tells you to talk to his lawyer?" asked Johnny. Calvin didn't have an answer for that right now. He needed to go back over every scrap from the beginning.

~ * ~

The Straus Valley car roared down into the little stream bottom and his headlights caught Don and Ozzie pulled over in a small area just beyond the bridge. They were standing outside the cars laughing. "You guys all right?" the uniform trooper asked.

"Yeah, thanks for coming by. Don let off a gas grenade in the house and they gave up the keys voluntarily, sort of," Ozzie said. "We're on our way back in."

~ * ~

She felt warm to the touch and the girl asked her mother if she wanted a doctor. Her mother sobbed and tried to put a clean pad between her legs to soak up the blood. "Go back downstairs and wait for your father. When he gets home, tell him I need him," her mother said between her labored breaths.

~ * ~

Ken took a break on the third page. Two of the passengers were asleep and he spent a while talking with the others. They avoided the subject of Grace until one of them reminded Ken that they were probably going to Miami for the Orange Bowl. That is, if the Penn State defense could stop Michigan and Perdue in the last two games. Ken remembered that Grace had a grandmother in Miami and just how far is Sarasota from Miami anyway? He slipped back to his seat and brought up the maps on his laptop.

Sam told Scotty to stretch if he wanted to. They switched for the flight back and Sam was monitoring the autopilot. "I'm punching in the tailwind numbers for a revised ETA," said Sam. "See if Ken wants to come up for a bit."

"So maybe we can rent a car or maybe Peggy will let you fly the Lear up there and...," Ken was sputtering.

"Whoa there, lad. There's a couple of good teams they have to knock off yet. Michigan is undefeated and Perdue, well you never know with them if they show up to play," replied Sam. "You have to be back at school on the third. That's cutting it close."

"Yeah, but Miami's only about three hours flight time, if that, and if she can be at her mom's or her grandmother's in Miami...," Ken kept trying.

"Sounds like a plan, Ken. Pencil it in for now and we'll see," smiled Sam. Better not fight it.

~ * ~

Ozzie was pounding away at a computer and Don was on the phone when Johnny and Calvin dragged themselves in through the back door of the barracks. Calvin dropped a white paper sack on Ozzie's desk and went back out to the refrigerator and got a bottle of cold water. He pried off the top and drank half of it in one gulp. Ozzie walked out to the squad room a happy man. The cheese steak was just what he needed to top off the day. He found some salt and shook a generous portion on the sandwich. He palmed one of his Pepsis out of the fridge and sat down at one of the report writing tables to eat. "Thanks, Calvin. You're a sweetheart. You guys have any luck in Philly?"

Calvin stood motionless and stared at the wall. Johnny sat down across from Don and said, "Still no cars or people at the address in West Philly. I think they might be out of town. Dugan says the utilities and taxes are in the woman's name. He's got his sources trying to locate Yancey. We're at a point something's got to break to move this along. You guys gonna try to shake that mechanic out again on Monday?"

Don answered, "Yeah, his name is all over the paperwork. He's probably got a lot more cars we won't know about until we get over to the auction. Probably do that on Monday, too. One of the buyers may have seen

McFadden and this Yancey together. Maybe get lucky and find Yancey's name on one of them."

"You guys better get out of here. I'm just gonna reshuffle some of this paper and get us set up for Monday. Go on, go home, I got this under control," Calvin shooed them all away with a wave of his hand and went back to the crime room alone.

~ * ~

Not much traffic on the Expressway tonight. Harold eased them off at Passyunk Avenue and made his way up to Washington to drop off Yusef. "Call me tomorrow, I'll tell you what time to be ready," Harold told Yusef. Yusef got out of the side door and quickly blended into the dark.

"I'm not ready to see her yet, let's go to one 'a the clubs up on the river, look at the ladies," Jamal said to Harold. The van drove east on Washington and mixed in with the city traffic.

~ * ~

It had been a late night and a long day. Sam could feel the fatigue start to set in. "I've got to stretch. Give me a few minutes, okay?" Sam asked Scotty. He unbuckled and went to the rear. Ken was tapping away and Sam touched him on the shoulder as he walked by. He found a cold cola in the small refrigerator and took a few generous drinks. The passengers were quiet and all but three now were sleeping. The tooth doctor was reading a medical journal and the banker was pushing at his tablet computer with the stylus. Sam stopped in the aisle next to Ken and leaned over to read over his shoulder. "Looks like English composition," Sam said.

"No, actually it's Economics. Critical analysis of some stock market guru who published a magazine article on how to get rich by not doing market research. I'm writing his literary obituary. It's for extra credit," Ken yawned and began to flip back through the paragraphs editing for mistakes.

"I'm really too tired right now to do this. Making too many mistakes. I didn't get much school work done today, kinda busy."

"Was it worth it?" Sam asked.

"No 'bout a doubt it," laughed Ken.

Sam made his way back to the flight deck and went back to work. It was time to start getting ready for the descent into Allentown.

~ * ~

Junior had the television on in the living room and Katie was asleep next to his feet at the end of the couch. "Where's your mom?" Ozzie asked as he tossed his keys on the kitchen counter.

"Went up about twenty minutes ago. I'm gonna put Katie in bed and stay up a while. How was your afternoon?" Junior asked.

"Got your mom some pie apples. Get the twins to peel some tomorrow, maybe she'll bake us a couple. I'm gonna have a beer and hit the sack. See you for mass in the morning," Ozzie easily screwed the top off from a beer bottle and started for the stairs. Halfway there he stopped, turned around and went back for a second beer. With ammunition in hand, he took the stairs in his usual two at a time fashion.

Marie was curled up in the bed with a towel around her head. She was reading a paperback and had a candle burning on each bedside table. The room smelled like bubble bath. Ozzie stopped just inside the door and the picture he was seeing registered in his head. *She's fired up again tonight*, he thought. "Hey, beautiful. Ya miss me?" he offered her the beer, but she shook her head no.

She put the book down and snapped off the small light on her side of the bed. "Come here, Ozzie," she said softly.

"What's wrong? Everything all right?" Ozzie asked and threw his sport coat over the soft chair in the corner. "You sure you're okay?" He sat down next to her and gave her a big kiss.

"I'm fine, honey. You ready for some news?" she patted her tummy and said. "I hope it's a little brother for Junior, you're a daddy again. I was pretty sure yesterday and the test came back today. Now, get rid of that beer and let's put a seal on this envelope."

~ * ~

Calvin called her and canceled. "I'm sorry, but I have to work. Tomorrow for sure," he told her. It was real quiet in the barracks. There were two cars and Brad Dickson out on the road and a trooper on the desk. Calvin was the only other person in the place. He went at the case file and read everything from start to finish again. He had to make something happen.

~ * ~

"Lear 15 Quebec, good night, sir," Scotty thanked the ground controller who gave them their parking instructions. Peggy was watching from the door as they put the plane in its spot near the office. Sam had everything shut down in short order while Scotty did the paperwork. Ken got the door open and pitched in with the guys and their bags. He took care of Sam's, too. Peggy walked out to greet her customers and got hugs from most of them. They gave her a quick gossip on Ken and Grace and her eyebrows went up several times during the story. She caught Ken as he was going back up the stairs into the plane.

"So you finally threw me over for an older woman, did you?" she said to him. "You had a good time?"

"Peggy, it was a great time. She's something else. I'm not sure what's going to happen from now on, but I'm going to see her again. I just don't know how or when," he told her.

226

"Well, I'm the last person to give advice. I haven't got a very good scorecard on that issue," she said. "I hear the plane was okay, everything ran smooth?"

"Yeah, we wrung it out with a few snap rolls and a couple of loops. Just had to replace the right wing. Minor inconvenience," he laughed and she punched him in the arm. Sam appeared and Scotty was right behind. The mechanic took the clipboard and the plane was his again.

"You want to go get something to eat?" Sam asked Peg and Scotty. Scotty had a date, as usual, and Peg said she wanted to get home to Amy before it got any later.

"Food or home, Ken?" Sam asked as they walked out to the Pathfinder.

"Let's go rescue Molly. I'll eat after she does," said Ken. He had the keys and unlocked the Pathfinder so they could throw their gear into the back. "I'll drive, Dad, you can zone out," he got absolutely no argument from Sam.

~ * ~

He'd been drinking, she could smell it in the cold rush of air that followed him through the door. That was very unusual for him. He came in much quieter than he had left earlier. Fumbling with his keys and nearly tripping over the rug just inside the door. The girl was dozing on the couch and sat up when she heard him. "Oh, it's you," he grumbled.

"Mother says she needs you. She's very sick," she said, unable to look him in the eye. She expected him to be angry again. Instead, he stood there looking at her as if he didn't hear her. He then took off his coat and hung it in the small closet by the door.

"She's still sick? What's wrong with her?" he asked her.

The girl shrugged, not sure what she could say that would not upset him. He waited for just a moment and when she didn't answer, he went upstairs to her mother.

227

~ * ~

Sam didn't say a word until they were almost to the mountain, "We're gonna have some company for the ride back to Varnum tomorrow," he let that sink in for a moment. "Nice girl I met the other day. She has the grocery down in Porter. Beautiful black shepherd," he realized how odd it was to describe her to Ken by talking about her dog. "Taking her to Mama's for a veal sandwich after we dump you."

Ken looked over at him, "Filling up your social calendar, I see. She got a daughter? Or maybe a sister?"

"If she did, they'd be too young for you, she must be all of thirty. Now that you're into older women," Sam quipped.

"Ha! Can't take the competition!" Ken teased.

"Just drive the truck, genius," Sam closed his eyes again and felt them begin the climb up Blue Mountain.

Ken felt like he was really coming home. Bounced around when he was so young between both grandmas and the rented house with his dad. Grandma Deland in Wellsboro took care of him while Sam went through the hiring process for the state police and the six months his dad was at the academy in Hershey. Grandma Landis took over his day care when they moved into the house in Perkasie and he'd grown real close to her ever since. He didn't get to see his dad's folks that often now, but was looking forward to Thanksgiving there. The old house in Wellsboro was on a small creek and he knew every riffle and rock in it for several hundred yards in either direction.

Grandpa Deland had slowed down a bit lately, but still drove his fuel oil truck in fall and winter and farmed corn and hay on leased land the rest of the year. Ken's summers were filled with the outdoor adventure in limitless amounts that part of this beautiful state provided. He learned as a young kid how to navigate in the woods and had been doing overnights with a bedroll and a book on the constellations since he was eight. Grandma even went with him once and never complained about the bed of pine he made for her. She woke up the next morning to his hot chocolate and bacon over an open fire and pronounced it a fine way to start the day. Grandpa taught him how to drive the old John Deere and he only burned out one clutch.

When his dad first brought him out to the old barn and burned out house, he was excited about having a place to camp and run in the stream catching crabs and minnies. He was in military school by then and reveled in the freedom the property gave him. He realized that having his time so committed to other things made this place even more special. Just for a moment he pictured Grace laughing and happy swinging under the big oak on the rise above the milk house. "Hope Molly likes her," he said out loud before he could stop himself.

"She will, Eileen's a dog person. Gonna have to introduce Molly to Dutch, too," Sam said without opening his eyes. Ken had to smile at that.

Ken hit the turn just a little fast, but compensated and made the township road without squawking the tires. They didn't pass another car all the way in to the lane. Ken eased into the drive and stopped after about twenty feet. "Give me a couple of minutes, I'm gonna see what Molly does," Ken said quietly to his dad. He slowly opened the driver's door and closed it behind him with just a muffled snap. In an instant he was gone through the orchard on foot. Sam got out and quietly walked around. He wished he could be watching Molly's barrel right now.

Ken moved in near silence through the underbrush. He caught his coat on a low hanging apple branch once, but went with the pressure and reversed the fabric off the stick without any sound. He began to make out the shape of the house and the yard from the outside light on the end of the house. He stopped while still in the darkness. He could see movement and picked out Molly pulling on her tether in the direction of the drive. She obviously heard the Pathfinder even from that distance. He smiled to himself and slowly walked out of the orchard and past the old house site. Molly picked him up before he got too far and exploded into a howl. She barked and jumped straight up in the air. Up and down straining on the rope about to strangle herself with the force. Ken gave in and broke into a trot down to her and let her jump right up into his arms. She poured a pint of dog spit onto his face and jiggled and moaned in joy. "Oh, my Molly, I missed you, too, little doggie. How's my baby?"

The Pathfinder eased into the yard and the garage door started up. Molly saw the truck and yowled again. Both her men were home. A beagle couldn't get any happier unless a rabbit was involved.

~ * ~

Jamal got quiet when he was drunk. Harold knew that was a good thing. Harold nursed his third light beer and watched Jamal stir the whiskey and soda before slugging it back like he'd been doing since they got here. Jamal sure wasn't looking at any of the ladies like he said he wanted to. Other than ordering drinks, Jamal hadn't said ten words to Harold since they got there. Finally he said, "Think I shoulda' ended it there? Could have been over quick."

That surprised Harold. Jamal rarely asked Harold what Harold thought. Hardly ever happened before. "Give 'em another chance. Might be tough finding another source for the stuff," Harold offered.

Jamal waved for another whiskey and smacked his lips. "Our A-rab brothers gonna have to come off some a that A-rab money. Ramos says he got expenses, shit probably live like a cockroach. I got you and too many others count on me fo' the nut. Makin' almost as much on the cars. Gonna have ta come offa some a that oil money."

Harold wasn't positive how the deal worked, but was pretty sure he had most of it. He knew Ricky took the cars to Petty Island and they got shipped to San Juan. Couldn't figure out where the guns got separated out to go on to Africa, but didn't want to ask. That was a bad thing, asking Jamal questions. Better to watch and be ready if Jamal slipped. Move right on up. He sipped the foam from his beer. Jamal drained another glass. He was really drunk.

~ * ~

"How about Vincent?" she asked Ozzie looking up from her paperback full of kids' names.

He took a long drink of the second beer and thought about it. "I don't want to pick one. I did that the last four times and wasn't close. Let's wait until the ultrasound and then pick."

She elbowed him in the ribs, "You're no fun at all, well maybe sometimes," she gave him a gentle touch where he most appreciated it. "I like Vincent. Vincent Gianelli Ozliewski. He can pick Saint Stanislaus as his confirmation name."

"Jeez, Marie. You got the color of his tux for the wedding picked out, too? Vinny, huh? Yo, Vinny! Get your mudder a be-ah he-ah! Yeah, I like that." She hit him with the book of names.

~ * ~

Molly gulped her food down and drank the bowl almost dry. She padded around the kitchen and belched, loudly. Ken laughed, "Ladies must mind their manners, missy," he finished spreading mayo on the bread and folded the turkey and cheese over. He grabbed his dad a beer and took a Sprite for himself. Sam had the wood stove and the fireplace going and the chill was starting to come off the big house.

"Wow, Hazel. That looks good. I'll run my bags up and be right back. See if the late sports is on. I didn't get to see the game, remember?" Sam started up the stairs.

"That's okay. Neither did I. Too busy gawking at this beautiful girl sitting next to me. They replay the whole game at 11:00 on cable," Ken said over a mouthful of sandwich. He kicked off his shoes and fell into the chair. Molly was up with her front paws on his knees waiting for the sandwich to fall out of his hands.

"Ladies and gentlemen, we have a go for launch, 5, 4, 3, ignition, 1, liftoff!" Sam yelled from upstairs. With that Ken heard a toilet flush. "God bless Ozzie! It's a baby toilet. Listen to that wonderful sound!" Ken was startled to see his dad dancing all around the loft and singing, "Oh, when the saints, go flushing in. Oh, when the saints go flushing in...," Molly looked up at him and tilted her head.

"Hey, Dad, who's Hazel?"

~ * ~

"No. Take me down to the women in the project. Can't go to the other one tonight," Jamal slowly told Harold. "Call me tomorrow about Afif," Jamal lay down on the middle seat and fell asleep.

~ * ~

The doctor was grim faced and had trouble finding the right words. "She says she fell on the stairs while you were at work. Frankly, Mr. Ahmed, I don't think it could have happened that way. Before I have to involve the authorities, I thought I should talk to you. See if you have any other information that might be...useful."

They were in a small office just down the hallway from the reception area in the emergency room. Several old police report forms were on the small desk and a calendar that hadn't been changed from October. He made the girl stay at home. She would be all right alone. Afif's father thought the doctor sounded like he was talking down to him. He was good at picking that up from people. He often used that to his advantage. "Since yesterday she has been in bed. Yes, I was at work and my daughter was at school. Will she be all right, doctor? I have been so worried."

The doctor wrinkled his nose. These foreign people, they all drink so much. All the time. He'd seen their livers in the x-rays. "She's in critical condition, Mr. Ahmed. She has lost a great deal of blood. Her injuries are quite severe. Don't you think you should tell me everything? We need to know so we may treat your wife more effectively."

"Please, sir. May I see her now? I want to be with her, please," Afif's father lowered his eyes and folded his hands in front of him.

"All right, but the nurse must stay in the room...You know, to a...to a, monitor the equipment," the doctor stuttered. "Come with me," the doctor led him to one of the rooms that had the beds separated by curtains and left him with the patient and the nurse. The doctor went to the desk where he told the clerk to telephone the police.

~ * ~

Calvin slipped into his bed and shivered at the cold sheets. He needed sleep tonight. Needed it more than anything else.

~ * ~

Steam was rolling out from under the door to the bathroom. Sam had to rig up a big towel as a makeshift shower curtain. Water still splashed out onto the plywood floor. He didn't care. He was going to cover it with cement board and ceramic tile first chance he got. He just wanted to break in his new shower. Man, did it feel good. Ken put his dad's sandwich back on the kitchen counter before Molly got to it. The game was on and Ken wondered if it was the same game he'd actually been to earlier today. He didn't remember the touchdowns. Must have been distracted.

"Dad, you're missing it," Ken hollered up to the loft.

"I'm coming, get me a beer," Sam replied from the bedroom as he slipped on his flannel robe and hunting socks. Real fashion plate.

"Oh, wow! Look, it's Grace!" Ken shouted. "The camera is on Grace, and me, too!" a crowd shot by the director required a pretty girl. The camera just found the one Ken thought was the prettiest in the stadium. "I can't believe it," Ken turned to see his dad leaning over the rail trying to focus on the TV image. "Shoot, that reminds me. Gotta send her my e-mail. Be right back."

Ken raced into his room and extracted his laptop from his bag. He fired it up and logged onto the Internet. A few commands to the machine and his first note to Grace went into cyber space.

~ * ~

Ozzie fell asleep with Marie cuddled up tight with her butt into his belly. One from two now would be eight. The Ozliewski legend continues.

~ * ~

Sam couldn't make it past the first half. Ken was still wide awake. Molly gave up after the food was out of sight and was in her spot in front of the fireplace. "I'm done. See you in the morning," Sam announced as he got up from the couch and went for the stairs. "Throw a couple of pieces on the stove before you turn in," Sam stopped half way up the stairs and looked back at Ken. "Use my cell to call her if you want. I love you, Son."

Sunday

It lasted until well after midnight. An Allentown uniformed officer responded to the emergency room and spoke with the duty nurse. She explained what the doctor found in his examination of Afif's mother. Of course, the doctor was gone for the night. The officer looked at the exam notes and could actually read most of it. He interviewed Afif's father in the same room the doctor used and asked the same questions. He then said he was going to talk to Mrs. Ahmed, with only the nurse present. He told Afif's father to wait and he would be back. The officer spent about a half hour with her and came back into the room to talk to Afif's father.

"Look, Mr. Ahmed. Your wife is injured very seriously. She's been assaulted and probably raped. That means we're talking felonies here. You've obviously been drinking and you don't seem to want to cooperate. Why not make this easier on yourself and tell me the truth about what happened."

"Excuse me, officer. What are you saying, she was raped? The doctor did not say she was raped," Afif's father stood up and the officer put his notebook down on the desk, not sure what was going to happen next.

"Sit down, Mr. Ahmed. Sit down now," the officer ordered in his command voice. "Let me see your hands."

Afif's father could not believe this. This policeman was examining his hands to see if he had beaten his own wife. Afif's father pulled his hands back and said, "You are very wrong, officer. I have done nothing. What did she tell you, who did this to her?"

The officer sighed and said, "This will go a lot better for you if you just tell me the truth. The detectives are on their way down here and they aren't going to fool around. They're gonna get the whole story, you can count on it, so why not help yourself and tell me what happened."

This couldn't be happening. Had she lied to the police? Who had done this? Why am I being accused of this?

The officer didn't give up. He kept talking, trying to get Afif's father to talk to him. Using the threat of the detectives to get a confession.

Two Allentown detectives eventually arrived and spent the next two hours questioning Afif's mother and father. She was groggy, but able to tell them over and over that she fell down the stairs. Afif's father tried to tell them he had not hurt his wife and when they kept asking him to tell them what he had done, he just stopped talking.

They talked in the hallway before they came back in and told him they should arrest him now, but they were going to continue their investigation. He was free to go, but they would talk to him again.

~ * ~

His internal alarm clock woke him at 5:00. Sam started to get up and remembered it was Sunday. He rolled over and told himself he would just lie there a few more minutes. It felt like only a moment and he woke hearing sounds. He couldn't be sure what it was and his body gave him a shot of adrenalin. His heart rate increased and he thought, *what was that?* He got another shot of adrenalin when he suddenly remembered that his handguns were still in the truck. More sounds. *Definitely not Molly.* Sam remembered the shotgun. He kept an old Savage single shot 12 gauge loaded with double ought buck in the closet. It had a nylon holder with five more rounds strapped to the stock. Just cock the hammer and go. *What was that sound?* Sam felt awful when he heard the tractor start up. It flashed into his mind that it must be Ken. *That's right, Ken was home.*

236

He groaned and stretched in the bed. There was no light coming in through the window. *Should be by this time. Must be real cloudy out today. Oh, that's right. A real bathroom up here now.* He treated himself to his first morning piss in his new toilet.

Ken was up and made coffee before he went down to get the stove fired back up. There was still a good bed of coals and he stirred them and added some split pieces of oak. He took Molly out and got to work unloading the wood out of the old manure spreader under the deck. He made short work of it tossing the logs with his strong arms and then quickly stacking the pieces up against the wall. Once the spreader was empty, he opened the last garage door and checked the tractor for oil before starting it up. He backed it slowly out and hooked up the spreader for the short pull up around the house to the woodpile just up the hill.

Ken let the tractor run while he pulled the maul from the rack under the spreader and began to split another load. He worked up a good sweat and was surprised to see Sam come around the end of the house and walk up to him. Ken stopped and went over to turn off the tractor. "Why aren't you sleeping in?" he asked his dad.

"I need the exercise. Getting too lazy in my old age." Sam pulled the heavy ax from under the spreader and moved to the other end of the pile to work on the smaller pieces. They chopped for over an hour and filled the spreader. Both were soaked and ready for a break. Sam took both tools and replaced them in the rack while Ken started the tractor and moved the wood back down to the deck. Sam followed on foot and supervised Ken backing in. Sam unhitched the wagon and yelled over the engine, telling Ken to pull the tractor over to the garage so they could hook up the plow.

They worked a few minutes making the connections and Sam said, "Could get snow that sticks anytime now. I don't want to get caught without the plow on."

By the end of that chore, they were ready to go in for coffee and some breakfast. It wasn't even 7:30 yet.

~ * ~

"Get up, Son. It's 7:30. You want the shower before the girls get up, now's the time," Junior looked at Ozzie and crossed his eyes. Ozzie chuckled and took his coffee cup out to the kitchen. Marie was slicing sticky buns and spreading butter on them. They always waited until after nine o'clock mass to eat breakfast. Made a brunch out of it. The kids and Ozzie would have the sweet cinnamon rolls to hold them until then. It was tough on Ozzie. He could have eaten the whole plate, but, like a good dad, he just took one and left the rest for the kids. Marie had an orange and a cup of tea.

"Come on, girls. Get ready for church," she yelled down the hallway. She could hear little feet hitting the floor and her mommy super hearing detected four sets. All up and accounted for.

"Ozzie, we're going up to Hazleton to my mother's this afternoon. We'll have dinner there. Don't plan any work for after 2:00, okay, hon?" she winked at Ozzie. "She probably already knows. Can't get anything by her so we better tell her before she gets her feelings hurt. We'll tell the kids after church."

Ozzie thought she was beautiful when she was pregnant. Ah, heck. She was beautiful anyway. "Ya wanna take anything special up to her?" Ozzie asked. He opened the kitchen door and stepped out on the porch. He came back in with the half bushel of apples and set them on the floor. "How 'bout one a them cobblers you make up? Get the girls to peel and I'll make my special crust for ya," Ozzie was a good baker. Something he learned from his mom, may she rest in peace.

"Ozzie those are beautiful apples. I'll make enough for a few pies, too. We can freeze the filling," she said.

He put the basket back on the porch and refilled his coffee. He had just enough time to glance at the sports page before getting dressed for mass.

~ * ~

He spent a few minutes with his wife, who had been admitted and was in a room on the fourth floor. He hated hospitals and was glad to get out of there and go home. He thought the girl was still asleep when he got there. He fixed himself some warm milk in the microwave and dialed the telephone.

The girl could hear him talking. She was very worried about her mother and snuck out of her room to listen to what he was saying.

"I know, I know. They kept questioning me. She won't tell them who did it to her. No, I don't know. I fear she has been unfaithful to me and her sins have caught up to her. No, they don't know how long, maybe a week. This is going to cost a fortune. No, the police said they would want to talk to me some more. I am afraid they will arrest me no matter what. Yes, yes, but I don't know where he is staying. No, there is nothing Afif can do, except weep with his mother. I worry about him. I am tired and must get some sleep. No, I don't want anyone visiting her. I don't know what to do. I have to sleep and think about all of this. Yes, yes, goodbye."

The girl quickly moved back to her bedroom and hid under the covers. Afif must call today. He will know what is wrong. She began to cry and couldn't stop.

~ * ~

Sam grabbed an empty plastic grocery bag as he came through the kitchen and told Ken, "Let me get my stuff out of the, I mean, your bathroom, and take it upstairs."

Ken ignored the coffee and poured himself a big glass of juice from the refrigerator. "How's French toast sound, Dad?" he checked the shelf and found eggs and a half gallon of skim milk. "Don't you have any high octane? Just this diet stuff?"

Sam stuck his head out of the bathroom and said, "There's bacon in the freezer if you want to thaw it out. But I've got real maple syrup, not that sugary, store bought stuff, for the French toast."

"Sold," said Ken.

~ * ~

Marie only had one unbreakable rule about church. No jeans. Black, brown, green, it didn't matter. Oh, and no shorts in the summer. And no shirts with writing on them. It didn't bother the girls too much, but presented a weekly dilemma for Junior. It was more a matter of taste than economics. He stood in front of his small closet and considered the options.

Ozzie was dressed and had his bar-b-q apron on while he threw flour and sugar all over Marie's clean kitchen. He mashed and beat the mixture with his big hands. He figured the quicker he got his part done, the quicker he could sample the magic result. Besides, he had two days' worth of remodeling jobs to get done between brunch and the two o'clock departure to Hazleton. Junior just got drafted into the fetch and tote squad. "Junior, I need you today after we eat," Ozzie hollered.

He figured the khaki cargo pants would pass inspection, but didn't think he could get the Nike shirt by her. He settled for the tan button down. The collar bothered his neck, even though it wasn't buttoned at the top. Thank God she didn't make him wear a tie. He smiled and remembered his nutty dad and the big boo boo. One summer Sunday before Katie was born and Mom was still carrying Connie up and down the stairs at the time, Mom had been loudly instructing the children on the proper attitude and respect for the dignity of the Holy Mass and how what you wore was a reflection of how you felt about the baby Jesus. Later that week, Dad made a trip to the cheap clothes store in Walnutport and bought white t-shirts in appropriate sizes for the Ozliewski tribe. On that next memorable and fateful Sunday morning, he snuck out to the garage and used a can of red spray paint to inscribe a careful 666 on the front of the t-shirts in time for them to be dry and ready for the kids to slip on.

Mom pounded down the stairs demanding an immediate gathering of her three little ones for church. Impatiently standing next to the open kitchen door, she was urging them to get moving toward the car. Dad was trying to keep the twins from giving it away with their giggling and asking if they were going to get a big treat for playing this special surprise on Mommy. Mom ordered them out, now, and the three of them marched out of Junior's room in step and down the hall right up to her horrified look. Dad couldn't keep it in and belly laughed from behind, which started the kids and all four of them broke down.

Mom didn't find it the least bit funny. Even after Ozzie tried to assure her the kids didn't have a clue as to the meaning of the numbers. She refused to go to church with them even after they stripped off the offending shirts to reveal their legal church clothes. She ran upstairs and wasn't seen until after they got back. Dad did dishes and brought flowers home for three days before she finally cracked a smile and forgave him for his bad taste. Junior didn't push the issue after that.

~ * ~

Sam came down from the shower and found Ken at the kitchen table with his calculus book and a stack of syrup covered toast. "Yours is in the pan," Ken said.

Sam put two of the four slices onto a plate and dropped just a small amount of the golden syrup over them. He topped off his coffee and sat down with Ken at the table. "This is good service. You available for parties, too?" Sam joked.

Ken shot him an annoyed look. "I have a couple of hours of work to do and I should be out of the weeds. You want to hit me some grounders at the middle school field a little later?"

Sam said, "Sounds like fun. We have to pick up Eileen about 4:00. I'm going to get a few things done then while you study." Sam dug in to his breakfast. Nothing like the real thing.

He rinsed their dishes off and loaded them into the dishwasher. Between last night and the bits and pieces of eating Sam had been able to squeeze in during the week, the dishwasher was full enough to run. Ken added his laptop to the table with his other books and papers and was taking a break to start another e-mail to Grace. They talked while they both worked.

Sam pulled out a covered roaster and a short legged rack that fit into the bottom. He cleaned the big pan Ken used for the French toast, saving the left over two pieces for Molly. Into the pan he poured a bit of pure olive oil and a big hunk of butter and let it begin to heat. He chopped a sweet onion, celery and a red sweet pepper into tiny pieces and dropped them into the hot oil. The effect was immediate. The kitchen filled with that delicious ethnic smell Sam loved. He added salt and pepper, a little sage and saffron. The Cuban part of Grace would appreciate that. Sam learned about the spice in the navy and used it for light meat. The mixture sizzled and began to reduce. Sam opened a jar of good quality chicken broth and poured it into the pan and stirred until steam just began to rise. He turned the heat down to simmer and covered the pan.

The rabbit Junior left for them came out of the fridge and Sam rinsed it thoroughly under the faucet. He placed the meat into the roaster and sprinkled it with coarse black pepper. To the roasting pan, Sam added washed red potatoes, carrots, small whole onions and two sweet potatoes. The oven clicked that it was preheated and he took the skillet from the stove and poured the contents over the rabbit and the vegetables. He covered that and put it in the oven to slow cook. The rack would keep the liquid under the rest and steam everything. He set the timer for two and a half hours and cleaned up the kitchen again. Ken paid little attention, other than to say that it smelled good, and was back into the math book.

~ * ~

The readings reflected thoughts of the upcoming celebration of The Glorious Birth and in his homily, the priest reminded the congregation of the wonder of The Miracle and how special it was for the children of the parish. He appealed for generosity in their hearts for the collection of unwrapped presents for the poor. The homily ended with his admonition to love their own children and not to put their needs aside for other things. The children, he said, were a gift from a loving God, one of the greatest gifts He had to give. Marie squeezed Ozzie's hand and sighed as the priest walked back to his place behind the altar.

~ * ~

Afif went to the mini market and got hot coffee and a Tastykake. The phone smelled like beer. He dialed and heard it ring once before his sister answered in a hushed voice.

"Let me talk to Father," Afif told her.

"He is sleeping," she said.

"Oh, well, and how are you?" he asked.

She was silent for a long moment. "Mother is in the hospital."

"What, why, what's wrong?" he was caught by surprise.

The girl told him what she knew.

"I must speak to Father, go wake him up," Afif ordered.

"There is something else. I think Father is going to be arrested for hurting Mother," she knew she had to tell him, even though her father would be angry with her. She tried to remember all of her father's phone call and relayed that to Afif.

"Do you think he knows I'm on the phone now?" Afif asked her.

She told him to wait and she slipped upstairs and listened at his door. He was still snoring. She went back down and told Afif.

"Tell him I made you tell me that she is in the hospital, but let's keep the police business between us," Afif told her and hung up. He needed to see his mother.

~ * ~

Laundry was next and he ran the sweeper through the living room. He took it upstairs, but left it in his room for later. Back down and pulled the Pathfinder out for a good wash and dry. He used an old whisk broom to brush out the accumulated pebbles and pulled Molly's box out and stored it up at the milk house.

"Dad, come in here a minute," Ken called from the deck.

Ken was all smiles. "She's in Denver," he handed his dad a printed e-mail.

Dear Ken (show this to Sam, too),

It was a long and dreary night. How much longer before I can pick my flights? I finally found a terminal here at the lounge in Denver and the time to sit down and write you back. Thank you for the lovely note. You're so sweet. I think I've been in and over ten states since last night. At least on the late flights everybody is quiet and sleepy. Only one grumpy lady who we finally got settled down with a glass of wine, on the house. All the girls are quite taken with you and Sam. I lied and told them I didn't get your number. Am I naughty?

We all really thank you both for a real special night (and next day, too, Ken). We usually sit at the hotel bar and whine about the company. That party gave us all a chance to let loose.

Ken, you don't know how lucky I feel that we met. I think we share so much. The same feelings about so many things. Sam, I look at you and I know that Ken is a very lucky guy. He has such a great opportunity for his future and with you to support him, he can't lose.

I have to run now. I'll try to think of more to write about next time. Ken, please write to me often. Anything at all. I can see you sitting there when I read your note.

Love, Grace

"Slick, genius. Nice girl, you don't deserve her," Sam said and Ken punched him in the shoulder. Sam spun and grabbed him by the back of his pants and Ken lost his balance for just a second. That was all Sam needed and he turned into the movement and had Ken under him in a flash. "Just to show you that if I did want to fight you for her, I'd win," Ken smiled and Sam was helpless as Ken bench pressed Sam's whole body straight up and did three reps before he put him down.

"Thanks for the workout, old man," Ken said and they both laughed and rolled out flat on the floor.

~ * ~

"Hey, Momma. How are you?" Calvin talked to her for a long time and got all the news on Grandma and his sister and the kids. Grandma got on the phone and quizzed him about what he was eating, and if he was taking those big vitamins he was supposed to take every day. He always called on Sunday. Even if he'd been down to visit. It was the only chance she had to really talk to him. He told her he was real down about this case. Didn't like not having it in his hand. She told him he was smart enough to figure it out and not to get discouraged. Grandma told him to drink apple vinegar, clean him out good.

~ * ~

Ozzie spent a few minutes in the shop organizing his truck and tools. After he ate, he was taking Junior with him to finish cabinets at a house in Northampton. Probably take until it was time to get back and load everyone in the van for Grandma's. When he went back in the house, Marie and the girls were in full battle mode in the kitchen. Junior was helping, too. Food was out on the table and everyone was ready to make a plate and spread out in the family room. The cobbler was baking in the oven and Marie asked Ozzie to say the grace.

245

It took a while for everybody to fix their plates. Connie helped Katie with hers and the twins tried to make sure they didn't get the same things. They were in to being different now. Something about having their own thing.

Marie lagged a little behind and after the chattering family was all settled, Marie came in and sat next to Ozzie. She had her own plate and something else. Everyone was eating and talking. Connie was the first to spot what Marie was doing. On the small end table between her parents, she saw her mother place a plastic baby plate with teddy bears and balloons painted on it and a small matching cup. Both were empty. Connie nudged Junior and when he saw the items he let out a, "Shhh". The twins took a bit before they saw something was happening. Their mother was eating her brunch and looking at their father. Katie was the first to ask.

"What's the baby plate and cup for Mommy?"

Marie didn't answer, she just looked at Ozzie again.

Slowly she put her own plate down on the little table and picked up the one with the teddy bears.

"This? Are you wondering why we have this little empty plate here with us?" she asked Katie. Katie nodded. The twins sat with their mouths open at precisely the same width. "Well, kids. This is so that the newest member of our family doesn't feel left out. Right now your new brother or sister is being fed inside Mommy's tummy, but when the new baby is born, we'll have to set another place when we eat."

Junior said it all, "Wow, that's great! When? Are you all right, Mom?"

"I want to name him Justin," announced Connie.

"Taylor," the twins said in unison.

Katie wrinkled her forehead and after thinking about it, shuffled over and sat on her mom's lap. "Do I still get your hugs, Mommy? You always save the best hugs for me," she sounded very sad.

Marie squeezed her warmly and said, "Oh, Katie. Of course you still get the best hugs and it will be your job to pass those best hugs on to the new baby. Mommy will just have to give you extra ones now."

Katie chirped, "Yippee!" and mashed her face into her mom's belly. "You, little baby in there, I'm Katie, your big sister and I can hug Mommy and you at the same time."

Every one of them came over and kissed their mom and then their dad. Junior leaned back to his mom and said, "Congratulations. Can I hope it's a boy?"

Marie winked at him and said, "Don't worry, Mom's know. His name is Vincent."

~ * ~

Afif was walking fast, almost running. It was up hill to the hospital, but he wasn't thinking about that. He just wanted to get there and find out what happened to his mother. He thought it impossible that his father would ever raise his hand to her. He was sometimes rough with words for her, but that was the old ways he couldn't quite overcome. Everything was to be his way, no questions from her. Afif didn't try to ever go against him. His father was a good man and a hard worker. He did everything he could, even things that would put him in trouble if the authorities knew. But his father did it all for his family. There was no way he hurt her. Afif had a very bad feeling about this.

~ * ~

Harold said they were going to stop at the Turnpike rest area to eat. They had good fried chicken and he didn't mind paying the high prices they charged. Yusef mumbled something and then just kept quiet. The ride up from Philly was slow, an accident at Lansdale. Now they were stopping to eat. Yusef just wanted to get there and end this business with Afif.

~ * ~

The girl heard him up washing and cleaning his teeth. She quickly prepared his coffee and his boiled egg and toast. She dreaded having to tell him about Afif, but would. When he came out, he was putting on his shirt and tucking it in. He didn't even say good morning to her, he just sat down at the table and waited to be served. Now that her mother was gone, it was up to her to do the work. She didn't complain, she just hoped she did it right so he wouldn't get angry with her.

"Father, Afif called while you were asleep. He said...," he put up his hand to silence her.

"Why didn't you tell me so that I could speak to him, girl?" he said with a touch of disgust.

"He told me not to wake you. He wanted to speak to Mother. He made me tell him she was in the hospital," there she said it. She waited for him to react.

But he didn't say anything for a few moments. "I'll see him there, then. When she's better, I'll take you to visit with her. She would like that," he ate his egg and drank his coffee.

The girl hadn't expected that. Not at all.

~ * ~

Molly got all new straw in her barrel and Sam fit a better flap over the opening to keep out the cold wind. Molly almost always slept inside the house, but on those nights Sam was late or gone, she needed all the protection from the cold Sam could give her. He went back into the kitchen and checked the roast. It was almost done and he took off the cover and basted the meat. When he slid it back in, he left it uncovered to brown. He then cut a cabbage in half and grated it into fine pieces. With that he mixed in a bit of purple cabbage and a carrot. His special sauce consisted of bleu cheese dressing and wine vinegar with a dash of sugar.

"Ken, this will be ready in about fifteen minutes. I thought we would eat just a little early so we can have time to burn it off over at the field before we get cleaned up for the trip back," Sam said.

"Fine with me, I'm finished with the book work and just have a small load of skivvies and socks to put in the machine. Yell for me when it's ready, I'm going to send a short e-mail to Grace," Ken said, as he passed through on his way to the laundry.

~ * ~

The Bonneville started right up and Calvin let it idle until warm. He had a file folder of interviews he was reading for the third time trying to find anything that had been missed. He put the folder away and drove out of his apartment complex lot and on to 7th Street. He wasn't sure where he was going to eat, he'd know that when he got there. Earlier, he canceled another date for today. He just wanted to be alone and think.

~ * ~

Yusef just picked at his chicken breast. The crust was greasy and tasted mostly like salt. He drank his Coke and tried not to look at Harold eat. Harold didn't have what even Yusef knew to be table manners. He took big bites of chicken and chewed with his mouth open. Harold didn't seem to be in any hurry. "We gonna stop at that mall on the way. I gotta get something," Harold said. Yusef rolled his eyes.

~ * ~

He was tired and a little warm. The clouds broke up and the sun was slipping through. The reception desk was a curved wooden thing topped in a pinkish purple hard plastic. The older woman sat on a high stool with a computer in front of her and asked Afif if she could help him. She gave him directions down the hall to the elevators and his mother's room number on the fourth floor. Afif hurried to catch the car as the doors were closing and rode up with the cleaning lady.

She looked terrible. She was thinner and so pale. The IV bag dripped into the clear tube that ran down under white medical tape on the back of her hand. She looked like she was sleeping. He pulled one of the padded chairs from the corner over beside the bed and sat with her for a while. Slowly she opened her eyes and saw Afif. She turned her head away from him and closed her eyes again.

"Mother, it's me. Tell me what's wrong. What has happened?" Afif asked her.

She kept her eyes closed. "I, I can't tell you," she turned and finally looked at him. "Don't be concerned, Son. I'm getting better. The doctor won't tell me when I can go home, but I know it will be in just a few days. Don't worry."

She closed her eyes again and seemed to go back to sleep. Afif sat with her and tried to think how he was going to ask her if his father had done this to her. He wasn't sure he really wanted to know.

~ * ~

The temperature was rising. Sam was glad they were getting a nice day. The forecast was for rain later that night. Warm air rising up from the south was preceding a stronger front and the possibility of snow or freezing rain existed for Monday. But today it was going to be partly sunny and go up to almost sixty. Sam took mats and silverware out to the table on the porch on the north side of the house out of the wind. They would have their lunch overlooking the big field and the wooded mountain on the University property beyond.

He took the rabbit out of the oven and cut off a big piece for each of them. He pulled some of the meat off the smaller pieces and put it in a dish. Molly's reward for a job well done. He dished vegetables and coleslaw for both of them and took the plates out to the porch. "Ken, grab a pitcher of ice water and two glasses and come out here and eat."

A moment later Ken appeared and poured them each a drink. "Looks really good, Dad. We haven't eaten out here since September," Ken remembered because they were having a snack just before dark then and he spotted a woodchuck lumbering out of the edge of the field into the standing corn.

Sam kept an eye on where it was going and Ken went in the house for a minute and came back out with his .222. He used a chair cushion to support the rifle on the porch rail and began tracking the feeding rodent through the big scope mounted on the sleek little rifle. Sam and Ken didn't like woodchucks at all. They dug holes in places where tractor wheels and ankles seemed to find them and break. It was their mission to rid the farm of them. It seemed like a never ending job. They would stalk and nail two and another would appear the following week.

Sam stuffed pieces of a napkin in his ear and did the same for Ken. Ken kept the big scope on the brown shape. He didn't have a good shot lined up and waited patiently. Sooner or later the whistle pig would stop and poke its head up looking for trouble. Ken made sure the critter found it, less than a minute later. The chuck stopped and raised its head and then came all the way up on its back legs. Ken squeezed the trigger just enough and the little rifle cracked and bucked just a bit up off the cushion. They took a long handled shovel and walked down the field and found the varmint rolled and very dead. Sam took the carcass and shoveled it back into the hole at the edge of the field. He dug the loose dirt from around the hole and filled it, smoothing the top. That would keep other chucks from taking over the den, discouraged by what was left of the previous tenant.

They talked about school and what Ken did and didn't like about it. He'd been at Varnum since the seventh grade and adjusted to it well enough. He didn't like some of the other kids, though. Schools like Varnum attract several different types. Some are there because they are military brats and carry on a family tradition. Others, like Ken, begged and badgered their parents to send them there because they wanted to go, had to go. Glory, honor, and a cool uniform.

Ken realized in his second year he'd made the right decision, but for the wrong reasons. The group Ken avoided were the ones sent there because they were too young for prison and their parents had money. Trouble followed them day and night. Ken, on too many occasions, had to stand up to the senseless bullying those kids seemed determined to practice.

Either when he was the intended target, or when he found one of the snots preying on a younger, smaller cadet. By the ninth grade, Ken had the reputation that he was to be avoided unless the challenger wished to call Mommy for new teeth.

As they sat on the porch they watched several types of birds working the field. Fattening for winter. The corn at the far end was still standing. It wouldn't get knocked down until heavy snow or ice fell. The wind would swirl past the house in little gusts. They both noticed. "Thermals cooking off," said Sam. The sun was heating the ground just enough that the ground then warmed the air above it and the warm air would lift upward, causing breaks and disturbances in the wind direction and flow. Fuel for gliders.

"Look, see that hawk? Looks like a Red Tail," Ken pointed to the far end of the field. The big bird was circling, rocking in a thermal and being lifted higher with each turn. They both had many times used the keen senses of soaring birds like hawks and buzzards to find thermals for them while flying in sailplanes. The bird gained altitude rapidly and then banked out of the circle and flew straight ahead out over the creek and east, eventually going out of sight.

"You remember your first cross country?" asked Sam.

"Oh, yeah. Short but...a learning experience," Ken replied. "I wasn't afraid, I guess. There was too much going on for that. I can still hear you saying to me 'Now, Ken. Don't leave the thermal until you're high enough to glide to the next landable field.' I kept flying in a triangle over the airport until you radioed that if I was going to fly to Morgantown I had to go now."

"You did learn a lot that day as I remember," Sam said. "There were some pretty good thermals cooking, but the down air was strong, too. You hit four, no five good thermals before you got out ahead of yourself." While Ken ate rabbit, Sam tried to remember.

Ken was in the 1-26 and Sam was ground crew and following under him with the trailer. It was only about twenty-five air miles from Kutztown south to the glider strip at Morgantown. Sam planned this as Ken's first

252

time to fly out of range of the airfield and navigate to another gliderport. They spent a lot of time planning and talking about the trip and waited for two weeks that summer before the weather gave them the right day.

Sam told Ken, "Climb until you get within three or four hundred feet of cloud base or the lift starts to drop off to less than two hundred feet a minute, then fix on the next landable field on your course line and put the nose down and run. You have to watch the variometer. It's going to show you how fast you're going down. You'll feel the next thermal and the needle will bounce to the plus side. Between thermals, watch your sink rate. You may think everything is fine, but you can get into an area of heavy down air and that needle will pull the glider right down with it. If you don't get out of heavy sink, you're going to be on the ground, hopefully in a nice smooth pasture. A lot of good glider pilots bust out of a booming thermal and don't pay attention to what's happening around them, positive that the next great thermal is just ahead. Before they know it, they're at decision altitude and have to set up for a landing."

That day, Ken banked out of the thermal over Kutztown and headed south. He found a series of fields that looked like they would be big enough and flat enough to land in and flew toward them at sixty-five MPH. The 1-26 loses about one foot of altitude for every twenty feet forward it flies, in smooth air. Air on a warm sunny day isn't smooth. It rises and falls in irregular masses. And it falls the fastest just outside of the columns of rising thermals the sailplane needs to stay up. Sort of like water rushing down the sides of a full bucket with a garden hose filling it.

Ken was feeling great. He had the 1-26 moving fast and before long, felt the plane bump and watched the variometer jump to the plus side. He pulled up on the nose and rolled the glider into a steep left bank and was rewarded with eight hundred feet a minute of upward rising air. He keyed the microphone and shouted, "Got a good one. Gonna ride this up!" Three or four more times he punched out and flew on course, trading altitude for distance forward. Each time he found the next thermal and regained his height. Sam was following and talking to Ken on a hand held aircraft radio from the car. They were within ten miles of the grass strip at Morgantown and Ken said the thermal was giving out and he was heading out on course. He would need only two or three more to assure he would arrive with plenty of altitude to enter the pattern and land. Sam moved with him, stopping every few miles to try to get a visual on the 1-26.

"Dad, I'm not finding anything. See any birds?" Ken asked.

"Stand by, I'll pull over on the next hill and look around. What's the vario showing?" Sam asked.

"Four... no, five hundred feet a minute down," Ken said with hesitation.

"Try heading for the next cloud. That down stuff is too strong, you've got to get out of that bad air," Sam told him.

Sam found a spot to pull the trailer off the road and jumped out to try to spot Ken. He looked where Ken should be and didn't see him. Sam checked the air chart and found a lake that should be between Ken and him. "Do you see the lake east of the high power lines?" he asked.

"No, I'm heading west trying to get out of this heavy down stuff. Six hundred feet a minute, no let up. I'm down to 2800 feet," Ken sounded defeated.

Sam figured out what was happening. Ken was turning with the sink and following it instead of breaking out. Unless he hit a good thermal, he would be at pattern altitude in less than four minutes. "Have you got a good field in sight?" Sam asked.

"Ahh, stand by, I did just a minute ago...," Ken answered.

"Ken, watch your sink rate! You've got about three minutes to pattern altitude. Forget finding a thermal, find a field and get started setting up. Give me landmarks so I can find you, you're off course," Sam was all business. He got out his binoculars and tried to find the sailplane.

Ken started checking off ground features he could make out. He finally saw the lake and the power lines and let Sam know about where he was, "Looks like two fields separated by a tree line. I can put it in either one. Vario's settled at three hundred down and I'm at 1700 feet. Go south then west at the white barn you'll see woods, then an opening. That's the two fields."

Sam radioed back, "Wind is from the southwest at ten to fifteen, have a good landing. Keep calling once you're down, I'll find you."

"Just when you think everything couldn't be going better, the bottom falls out. Taught me something, all right," Ken said and saw that his dad was staring out over the field. "What is it? You see something?"

Sam realized he was thinking about how Patrick and Ginny McFadden must have been sure they were doing just fine and had everything under control last week.

~ * ~

Afif's father ran a few errands before going to the hospital. Some things at the store and letters he wanted to mail. He needed the time to think about what he was going to do.

~ * ~

He knew he would end up here. Calvin parked the Bonneville and took his roast beef sandwich into the barracks. The trooper on the desk told him he was nuts for coming in on a Sunday if he didn't have to.

~ * ~

When everything was put away, Ken gathered two gloves, his good aluminum bat, and a bucket of baseballs from his room. Sam took the leftover rabbit out to Molly and they got into the Pathfinder and headed for the school. The sun was up as high as it would get for the day and it was hard to believe it was two weeks before Thanksgiving. Even the leafless winter countryside doesn't look too bad if the sun is shining.

The school baseball field wasn't in great condition, but it had a clean infield and a good wire backstop. They played catch for a while to warm up and then Sam took the bucket and bat to hit grounders to Ken. Ken mostly played second base, but his coach at Varnum was beginning to use him more at third at the end of last season. Ken's throwing ability made him able to reach the first baseman from deep behind third better than anyone else on the team. Sam had to stand well out of the batter's box to avoid the mud filled depression. Ken took grounders and threw the ball to the backstop hard and straight. He moved from second base to third and then to shortstop. Sam refilled the bucket between each switch.

"Okay, let's see if you can hit," Sam said and Ken jogged in and warmed up with the bat. Sam took the bucket out to the mound to pitch. Now, Sam never played baseball on any organized team. He learned his game on summer days with his pals. If they had six, they played three on a team with ghost runners. If they couldn't get more than two or three together, they played 500. Sometimes they got lucky and one of the kids would get a new baseball for a birthday gift and they got to play with one that had all the cover on it.

Sam couldn't put much curve on the ball, but after about ten fat sweethearts that Ken blasted deep into the outfield, Sam felt warmed up and started giving Ken a pretty decent fastball. On about the eighteenth pitch, Sam smiled to himself and put Ken on his back.

"Hey! You tried to bean me!" Ken shouted, almost angry.

"Wanna quit?" Sam teased. He had three balls left in the bucket.

Ken answered by getting back up and standing in for another pitch. The look on his face was like a four letter word. Sam threw as hard as he could without tearing his arm loose from his shoulder. Ken met the ball and sent it beyond the outfield and under the bleachers in the soccer field the other side of the fence. He dropped the bat and bowed to Sam. "Now that was a homer," the pitcher said. Sam knew his arm was done and they both walked to the outfield and tried to find as many of the baseballs as they could.

~ * ~

Marie had the girls ready and let Ozzie and Junior alone so they could get cleaned up for the trip to Hazleton. She did put a small cobbler in a dish for Ozzie and he gobbled it down while he got dressed in clean clothes. "This is great, Marie. Did you freeze the filling?" Ozzie asked.

"Yes, dear. Enough to make a bunch of pies for Thanksgiving and Christmas," she assured him. It didn't take much to make Ozzie happy.

~ * ~

It was locked. Yusef tried the same trick with his knife and once again the door opened. The girl stepped into the kitchen and was shocked to find cousin Yusef and a very big, very black man there looking at her.

"Yusef, what...why are you here? Who is this man?" she fired questions at him. He stepped over to her and she tried to back away, but was blocked by the refrigerator. He slapped her hard across the face.

"Shut up!" he shouted at her. "Where is your brother? Is he here?" He didn't wait for her to answer and walked by her and started going through the house. The girl looked at the big man, but he didn't frighten her. She thought that was odd.

The man motioned with his head for her to move out of the way and he looked in the refrigerator. He came out with a carton of milk and a bowl of green Jell-O. He found the glasses in the cupboard and poured himself some of the milk. She went to a drawer and got him a tablespoon.

"Thanks, I ate some chicken didn't 'gree with ma' stomach," he sat at the table and ate the Jell-O and drank his milk. They could hear Yusef slamming doors and yelling for Afif to come out. "Where is yo' brover, girl?" he asked between gulps of Jell-O.

"I don't know, that's the truth," she said. "He was in Philadelphia the last time I knew where he was."

"Well, he ain't there now and he got work to do. We got to get him back there today," Harold drank a whole glass and poured more. He belched loudly and shrugged at the girl.

Yusef came back into the kitchen and grabbed the girl by the hair and slammed her to the floor. He kicked at her, but she blocked the kick with her arms. Harold said loudly, "No! Don't touch her," and stood up. Yusef looked at Harold and then at the girl.

"Then I'm taking her and they can have her back when I get Afif," snarled Yusef. He snatched her arm and pulled her toward the door.

Harold reached up and pulled Yusef away from her. "You a fuckin' idiot," Harold said to Yusef. The girl scooted to the other side of the table and put Harold between her and Yusef. "She gonna do what she can do. Better she be here to do it."

"Find Afif, and tell him to be back in Philadelphia by tonight. Or I'll come back by myself and finish you and your mother. Just ask her if she wants another visit from her favorite nephew. Just ask her. Tell him, by tonight," Yusef spit on her and turned for the door.

Harold told her on his way out, "Member, by tonight. I ain't gonna stop him afta that."

~ * ~

The Eagles were playing the late game on television. Frank Dugan never missed a game. He scrounged tickets to most of the home games or caught them on satellite. He planned his Sundays around the TV coverage of the away games. He'd been to church, the market, raked some leaves and had a pan of sausage and peppers on the stove simmering. His team had only won two so far this year. The starting quarterback was out and the best running back they had seemed to always be a half step slower to the hole than the opposing linebacker. The rookie was starting at quarterback today. Frank didn't expect too much, but would watch anyway. For some reason the games were bumped up a half hour today and the 12:30 game was on in the living room. The Eagles were next up at 3:30.

~ * ~

While Ken was using the shower downstairs, Sam ran the sweeper in the loft and put his bathroom articles in the cabinet over the sink. He would have to stop tomorrow and get a shower curtain and rod. The temporary beach towel curtain would do until then. He remembered the Pathfinder was below a half tank and hollered down to Ken they were going to leave a couple minutes early to gas up on the way.

Ken's bags were by the kitchen door and he was packing his laptop into the smaller one. "Last minute e-mail to Grace. I think I have everything. Maybe we'll get a run on the ridge at Thanksgiving," he said to his dad. They were both cleaned up and ready to go. Sam had his leather navy jacket over his arm just in case it cooled off later.

~ * ~

Marie's mother was not a typical Italian grandmother. She wore eye shadow and had hair that made other ladies in their fifties jealous. She never put any color in it and was just starting to show a bit of grey. Her clothes were always tailored to fit and even though she didn't have a lot of money, looked like a million bucks. Marie's father had been dead for seven years and Marie suspected her mom was keeping company with several local wolves. The twinkle in her eye gave her away. The kids loved her and got to spend a lot of time with her. It wasn't unusual for her to drive down and capture one or all of the girls for a day and the twins spent most of last summer with her traveling through upstate New York and over to Maine. They did all the forts, historic places and clothing outlets.

It didn't take thirty minutes before her mother figured it out. She kept looking at Marie while she quizzed the girls. Marie finally sat her down and confirmed what her mother already knew.

~ * ~

Sam drove and when they stopped, Ken got out and pumped the gas while Sam checked the oil. A car full of teenage girls was across at the other set of pumps and had their music vibrating loudly. Sam stuck his head around the hood and gave Ken a pained look. Sam hoped someday Ken wouldn't feel like he missed out on all the public school foolishness. Well, Ken didn't complain at all. Sam guessed Ken liked his busy schedule and just didn't let any of that social garbage bother him. His heavy academic load, platoon leader, flight lessons, and now add to that this thing with Grace, Ken would be very busy this winter. No time for "poor me."

~ * ~

Yusef was glad Harold didn't want to stop anywhere on the way back. When they got onto the expressway at Conshohocken Harold said, "So, how you gonna make it right wif Jamal, Afif don't come back tonight?"

Yusef stayed quiet for a minute before he replied, "He'll be on the bus tonight, I know him, he's a coward and a pussy. Besides, the money's better than he can get bullshitting around with his father. He wants his own shop away from the old fool so he needs this money. He'll be walking through that project door with his little backpack, I guarantee it."

~ * ~

The trooper on the desk was back in the squad room with Calvin watching the end of the Oakland game on the television. Calvin had his folders out on the work table and was listening while he read. He would watch if the play was worth it, like an interception or a good run.

"How's the murder job going?" the trooper asked.

"It's not. Dead end. We've got a good suspect from Philly, but can't put him with the victims that night. Got another body out in Lancaster was killed with the same two guns. Probably gonna get Ozzie and Johnny pulled off tomorrow. Captain's been getting scorched by the newspapers and Harrisburg. They won't be able to justify the overtime any longer. All the other work's been backing up. Going to be up to me to wait it out, see what breaks. I think the brass is going to use the publicity from recovering the stolen cars to deflect some of the heat." Calvin watched the last minute of the Raiders and it went directly into the Eagles game that had already started.

~ * ~

They parked in front of her small, neat, white house. It had black shutters and several big evergreen shrubs around a front porch. The yard had a few flower beds, now covered with leaves. As they walked up to the door, they could hear him barking. "Sounds like he means it," Ken said.

Sam knocked and the dog was banging on the door trying to get at the intruders. "Best burglar alarm on the market," Sam joked. When she opened the door, she smiled and looked back and forth at both of them. Dutch had his black nose pushing at the storm door and Ken didn't look too sure that the big dog wasn't going to eat the glass and then him.

She ordered Dutch to quiet down and unlocked the outer glass door for them to come in. "Hi, I'm sorry about him, he was sleeping all day at the store and now he has too much energy. I'm Eileen, you must be Ken," she stuck out her hand for Ken to shake.

"Are we early?" Sam asked.

"No, right on time. I'm ready, but I want to let him out a bit before we go. Come on through, we'll put him out in the yard," Sam reached down and grabbed Dutch by the ears and gave them a good rub. Ken was a bit surprised, but figured the two met already. Dutch moved his side into Sam's leg and his tail slammed back and forth. The dog kept looking over at Ken and had to pull away from Sam to stick his nose to Ken's leg. Ken squatted down to level out with the dog and they stared at each other for a bit.

"You going to be friends with me, too?" Ken asked. Dutch looked at Ken then Eileen and back to Sam.

"It's okay, he doesn't bite," Sam said to Dutch.

Ken offered Dutch the back of his hand and Dutch put his nose to it. He must not have smelled any fear and didn't mind when Ken stroked the underside of his chin and his neck.

"You are a big dog. I'm used to little Molly. You must cost a bundle to feed," Ken had Dutch lifting up his paw to shake and the tail started up again.

"It's not too bad when Mom owns the feed store. He gets to eat whatever breaks open that week," Eileen laughed. "Are you excited about having two old folks hanging around on your day off from school?" she asked Ken.

Sam said, "Oh, no. Ken really enjoys the company of older people, don't you Ken?"

"Private joke, I'm afraid. Dad is just jealous of my youth, superior intelligence and good looks," Ken said.

Eileen led them through her small house. Everything was neat and very clean. They went through her dining room and in to a good sized kitchen. She had a commercial gas stove and a real butcher's block in the middle of the room. Sam spotted a fresh pumpkin pie on the counter and the room smelled like cinnamon.

Dutch passed them all when he figured what was going on. He waited at the kitchen door and as soon as Eileen cracked it, bam, he was out. Sam just turned to talk to Eileen when Dutch came back up onto the small porch and pushed his muzzle against the screen door. Sam looked down and Dutch had a tennis ball in his mouth. Eileen said, "Looks like he remembers your game with him the other day."

Ken went to the door and turned to Eileen, "Is it okay if I throw the ball for him?"

She said, "Oh, sure. Go ahead. He'll love it," Ken went through the door and roughly snatched the ball out of Dutch's mouth. They went into her fenced yard and Ken had the dog running in every direction chasing the ball and bringing it back.

"Kids. Aren't they great. Everybody ought to have some," Sam said looking out at Ken and Dutch romping in the yard. "If only all of them were as well behaved as ours are."

"Do you want coffee or anything before we go?" she asked.

"Oh, no thanks," Sam replied. She looked good today, just like he remembered. She had on a denim shirt embroidered with colorful butterflies on the front under each collar with the waist loose over tight ski pants and those soft cowgirl boots. Her hair looked like it might have been cut a bit, but was still over her shoulders and shiny. She was wearing some fragrance that made Sam's insides stir each time he got close enough to get a smell of it. He thought it was safe, "I like your hair like that."

"Oh, I thought I'd try a little something different. I keep getting told that I should get it cut short, but I'm not convinced yet," she said.

Sam reached over and cupped the end of it in his hand and felt the texture. "No, I like the feel of it. It would be a shame to shorten it too much." She looked up at him and smiled.

"Thanks, Sam. You've convinced me," she said softly.

Ken flew into the kitchen from the yard and Dutch was right on his heels. The dog went for his water dish and lapped loudly. "He's fast and strong. My arm is really gonna be sore tomorrow. Eileen, can I wash up?"

"Sure, right here at the sink, soap is there and here's a towel," she handed him a clean towel from the drawer by the big stove. "You fellows ready to go?"

~ * ~

Three possessions, two punts and an interception. The Packers scored a touchdown and were driving for another. Frank Dugan threw the magazine section of the newspaper at the television and stormed out of the house in complete disgust. He wasn't sure where he was going to go, but he didn't think he could watch any more of that fiasco. He got into his Taurus and made his way out to Henry Avenue. Frank figured a ride along Kelly Drive might calm him down. He turned onto Hunting Park and past the cemetery down the hill to Kelly Drive. It was nice even this late in the afternoon. Might be some good looking girls jogging or biking along the river. He spotted a few, nothing to bring his bachelorhood to a halt, though. He passed Boat House Row and rounded the turn at the art museum. *Oh, what the heck,* he thought, *might as well take a ride by the house out in West Philly. Maybe the woman's back from wherever she was. The troopers haven't been having much luck on this job.* He reached down and adjusted the position of the Glock 9mm pistol on his belt under his light jacket. Reflex.

~ * ~

Ken was in the back, chatting about Grace and the party in Champaign. "Sounds like she's a nice girl, Ken. When will you get to see her again?" Eileen asked. She was scrunched around in the seatbelt so she could see Ken.

"Not soon enough to suit me. I'm hoping things will work out at New Year's. If she wants to see me, that is," Ken said.

"Whoa!" Sam interrupted. He reached down for his phone and held it up to see the number. "Sorry, guys. It's the barracks. Yeah this is Sam, okay, okay. Hey Calvin, what's up?" Calvin told Sam that Frank Dugan spotted a red Lexus, with the tag number they were looking for, at the house in West Philadelphia. Might mean that Yancey or the woman were at the house. Dugan was going to Major Crimes to get a city car and a radio and would meet them there if they wanted to try to question Yancey.

"Sounds like we better take the chance while we can. Get Johnny and see if Don Mitchell is available to check the car while you're there. I think it's worth the overtime. I'd meet you, but I have people with me. Just call me later and let me know what's happening. Ozzie and I can come down if we need to," Sam told Calvin.

"Sorry Eileen, I have to make another call," Sam went right over Yakavich's head and called the captain at home. He knew the number without looking it up.

~ * ~

His father was shocked that Afif would think such a thing. Angrily, his father stormed off to get a drink. Afif told his mother that he didn't believe her about falling and hurting herself. She got quiet and wouldn't talk to him. He decided to let her cool down a bit and went to the phone in the lounge and called his sister. He wanted to ask her a few more questions.

She was crying and didn't make sense. "I'm trying to tell you he was here with a big black man. Yusef was here looking for you. He was angry and said you had to go back to the city or he would..."

"What did he say, little sister, you must tell me," Afif knew she would do what he told her to do.

"Mother. Yusef is the one who hurt Mother. I think he was trying to get her to tell him where you were and he hurt her. I'm so afraid. Mother, what if she dies? The police are going to arrest Father, they think he did this to Mother. Then what do we do, we will be all alone...," she sobbed loudly into the phone.

Afif felt anger. He seldom ever felt that, but now it was growing fast inside him. "That devil, Yusef..."

"He hit me and kicked me. He tried to take me away, but the black man stopped him. I'm frightened of him. He's coming back and he will kill us all, you know how he is. He can kill anyone," she kept on crying.

Afif had to do something. This was out of control. It was his fault. He went with Yusef with some foolish idea he was helping the cause of the fighters for true religious freedom. The struggle much like his people's own in Jordan and the West Bank. Help do a good thing. But he was greedy and now he had to pay for his weakness. Yusef was insane. Someone had to realize that and stop making excuses for him.

"Leave the house. Take warm clothes and any money you can find and get out. Go to the house of the woman who Mother sews with. She is a kind woman and her husband is a good man. Tell them I sent you and tell them Yusef has gone crazy again. They will understand. Her husband knows the truth about Yusef. Hide there until I send for you. I'm going to get Mother out of here tonight. Now, go. Be out within ten minutes, go," Afif hung up the phone and stood there to think.

~ * ~

Johnny was outside when Calvin pulled up. Calvin got out and moved to the passenger seat. Johnny's driving skill would be put to the test tonight. "You got me just as I was making a big whiskey and soda. Fifteen minutes later and I'd a been snockered and you wouldn't get the driving lesson of your life," Johnny said as he punched the big Ford and pushed Calvin back in his seat. "I called Don, he's got the state car at home and will meet us there. Said he'd be on Tac 2."

~ * ~

The captain wasn't real sure about this at first. She told Sam she's been keeping the press off his back, but they were looking to make something out of this. Her troop had an unsolved murder of a teenage girl in Nazareth from last year and the paper was going to start a series on whether the state police were properly trained in investigating homicide cases. "If we don't get something on this soon, Harrisburg might be finding us new places to work. Ever been to Corry in the winter?" she asked.

"Calvin's the best we have at wringing the fixes out of these tight cases. I have to give him the chance to go for it. I know it's not guaranteed, but Jess, it's what we have to work with right now," Sam finally convinced her. She was ready to shorten his rope, though, and he knew it.

"Well, aren't you glad you came to work with me tonight?" Sam tried to pay attention to the conversation in the Pathfinder, but it was hard from then on.

~ * ~

Being in the car repair business meant that Afif got to meet all kinds of different people. He found a telephone book at the nurse's station and started making calls. He hoped his father stayed out for a while longer. Afif knew he had to get his family where Yusef couldn't find any of them. His father would just have to understand.

~ * ~

The blue van turned onto Washington Avenue from Broad Street and pulled over at 10th. "You better be right about that little creep," Harold said as Yusef was getting out. "I gotta go get Jamal, he ain't gonna be happy greaseboy ain't here."

Yusef turned and said, "Jamal needs to watch his part of all this. I can take care of mine. Afif will come running back. He's afraid of me and Jamal. But he's more afraid of me. Jamal should remember why that is."

~ * ~

Trooper Damon couldn't believe it. He wasn't getting any speeders in the light Sunday night traffic on the turnpike and all of a sudden his radar gun read 118. The lights of the approaching car crested the hill at Perkasie and was about to flash past him. He locked the speed gun and reached to put the Crown Vic cruiser into drive as the offender roared past. Damon hesitated. The dark Crown Vic was going fast, but Damon thought he recognized the burgundy flash as an unmarked state police car. He switched to the car to car band and said, "Southbound unmarked, you require any assistance?"

He heard, "Naw sir, we're runnin' in to Philly tryin' ta catch us a murder suspect. Thanks anyway, brother."

Damon thought that guy sounded more like he was an Alabama trooper than one of ours.

~ * ~

It was a really beautiful area. Eileen wished she could come back and see it in the daylight sometime. Tree lined streets and very expensive, well-groomed houses were all around. Sam pulled into the parking lot at Varnum and parked near Ken's barracks. Ken said, "Come on Eileen, I want to show you something."

They got out and walked in the now much cooler night air. Sam could feel the dampness and knew that meant the front and its cold rain was approaching southeastern Pennsylvania. They crossed the Quad and passed between two large, three story red brick buildings. The ground sloped down slightly and they came to the walk that led through a beautiful arched gate. Lights were directed to the ironwork and cast shadows, making the structure seem even more ornate and impressive.

Ken told them, "This is the Eisenhower Arch. It's wide enough to march a company sized unit through and is used for all the important ceremonies here. We have quite a few marriages performed here. It's covered in wisteria and climbing roses in the summer and fall."

Ken led them through the gate and out to an area that overlooked the parade ground. Spotlights were on the white reviewing stand and guest seating. A cannon was at each end of the big field and a huge American flag moved in the southwesterly wind. "I've marched out on to that parade ground a hundred times and each time, with the music playing, I still get a neat feeling inside. Come May, I'll be graduating from here and I'll march out there for the last time. We've had three Congressional Medal of Honor winners come through those gates and onto this field. Too many generals and admirals to count. A lot of good husbands and fathers, too," he turned to Sam. Eileen was standing close to him. "I just want to thank you, Dad. You gave me the chance to come here and so far it's worked out pretty darn well."

She thought she was going to cry. Sam did, just a little.

~ * ~

Jamal felt like crap. He swore he wasn't going to drink like that again. It had been a lousy day. His head hurt and he argued with the women in the project house on and off all day. He finally showed his temper and slapped one of them and knocked her down. They all shut up after that and left him alone. He spent the rest of the day on the cell phone and running out to the pay phones lining up his next set of deals. He had a list for the Monday and the Thursday car auctions and the gun guy had some items that could be picked up on Friday. He also found out the job in the prison didn't get done the way he wanted it to and now he had to go and straighten that out.

~ * ~

"Straus Valley 17 to Philadelphia 35 on Tac 2," Calvin reached out for Don Mitchell.

"Philly 35, go ahead," Don replied from his undercover Pontiac wagon.

"Where are you, 35?" Calvin asked.

"At the east end of the rear alley of the house. I have the red car in view. There's a Philly detective you know at the other end watching the front," replied Don. The state police radios can talk to a number of other departments, but not with Philadelphia PD.

"Okay, I'm gonna meet with him and I'll get back to you," Calvin told Don. Johnny drove past the house and turned on the next street. Frank was in a beat up detective sedan just at the corner. Johnny pulled past and double parked. Calvin got out and walked over to Frank Dugan.

"You work on Sundays now, Frank?" Calvin kidded him.

"Fuckin' Eagles stink. Couldn't sit and watch them any longer and took a ride. Somehow ended up here and, bingo. Found you a Lexus. Lights are on inside, but nobody's been in or out. The car's cold, been there all day probably," said Frank.

"We'll pull around and stop mid-block where we can see the front and you. Let's watch for a bit and if nothing moves, we'll see who's home and take the car. We'll flash the lights if we have to go in." Calvin patted Frank on the arm and went back to the car and told Johnny to pull around the block. Calvin radioed Don the plan.

~ * ~

"You are going to have the best veal sandwich in three states," Sam said to Eileen. After Ken said goodbye, they turned toward Lancaster Avenue to go to City Line Avenue. "The place was just a pizza and hoagie shop, but then they built on a dining room. It's always busy and the food is great. Just up from the Philadelphia barracks on Belmont Avenue. It's only about twenty minutes or so from here."

They were on a two lane street where the houses were a couple of hundred feet apart. The road curved and rose and dropped through the nice neighborhood. The trees looked like they had been there for a hundred years and many of the drives had fancy gates guarding them. They were about two miles from the school and Sam was enjoying the quiet conversation with Eileen. She was sharp and didn't let much get by her. She liked Ken, too. Thought he was 'a young gentleman.'

Sam started around a curve and caught the flash of lights ahead. As he crested a slight rise, he could see headlights facing him on the side of the road and the flashing red and blue lights of a police car behind it.

"Looks like someone's getting a ticket," Sam commented to Eileen. They were in Radnor Township. It was a good department and Sam new the chief and several of the officers from the task force days. It was hard to see because the cruiser's headlights were also flashing, but as he got closer, Sam could make out the shape of a person standing between the cars.

He slowed a bit and started to pass by the two cars. When he got even with them he blurted, "Shit!" and punched the gas. Eileen's eyes opened wide and before she could say anything Sam threw the Pathfinder into a hard tight turn to the left and hit the brakes.

"Cop's fighting with the guy!" Sam said loudly. What he thought was one person was actually the police officer and a big man grappling with each other. The turn threw them to the right and Sam hit the gas again. As they closed the gap between them and the cars, Sam reached across with his left hand and released his seat belt. He roared up to the rear of the police car and hauled the Pathfinder to a sudden stop.

He reached for the door handle and as he started out, he said loudly, "Cell phone, 911, stay here!" then he was on the ground and trying to move fast without tripping over himself. He got three steps and instinctively reached to guard his gun. It wasn't there. It flashed in his mind that his .45 automatic and his .22 magnum derringer were locked in the gun safe behind his seat in the Pathfinder.

He was covering ground quickly as he passed the police car. He saw that the fight had dropped to the ground and the cop was on the bottom. The man was holding the officer down and was over him hitting the cop hard in the face with his right fist. Sam could hear the blows thud against skin. The cop was trying to push the man off, but was only opening up his head and leaving it unprotected to receive more unblocked blows. Sam didn't have time to decide how to enter the battle and used his full force and weight to throw a body tackle on the upper part of the attacker. Sam kept his feet under him and drove his right shoulder into the neck of the bad guy. Sam hooked his arms in front of his own chest and as his shoulder contacted the man's neck his arms and chest met the left side of the attacker. The effect disengaged the man from over the cop and drove him sideways and into the shallow ditch beside the road. Sam didn't know if it was him or the other guy who let out a loud, "Uhh!"

The problem was, Sam's momentum and force wasn't completely used up on the target. It had the desired effect of removing him from the cop, but Sam and the man continued on over without stopping until Sam found himself now under this big guy. They landed hard and Sam felt his right elbow take a lot of the impact. He thought he heard the crunch of bone, too. For just a part of a second, everything stopped and Sam could hear the loud hiss of the policeman's portable radio with the squelch open and roaring.

The man looked right in to Sam's eyes from above and as if he only paused to change targets, drew his big right hand back to punch Sam's head. Sam's hands grasped the man's jacket and were now in front of Sam. He could see the blow coming and was able to roll his left forearm just enough to take most of the punch and deflect it to his left shoulder. It hurt. This guy knew how to fight. He immediately drew back again and got off another shorter punch and swung up and over Sam's forearm. This one landed square into Sam's forehead. It hurt worse. Sam again blocked the next shot and was shifting his legs trying to get leverage to move this maniac off him. He couldn't get around under the knees of his foe and took two more punches, one to his left ear and one to the left cheek. He had to do something and fast. He was losing this fight before he could get in it. *Where the hell is the cop?*

The man's left hand was gripping Sam's collar and was in range. He rolled his head slightly to the right and bit the big thumb to the bone. Sam absorbed another shot to his left ear before the pain registered with his opponent and the right hand stopped hitting Sam and felt for the source. That shifted the big man's weight just enough that Sam pivoted under and away and rolled him onto his side. As the man's head hit the dirt in the ditch, Sam released his thumb and slammed his forehead onto the bridge of the man's nose. He felt the grip on his collar loosen and Sam thrust his knee hard up into the man's groin. He knew that one landed solid. He glanced over the top of the big fellow to see where the cop was and saw an arm rise up and slam back down. It wasn't the cop's arm. Sam pulled himself up and out from under the big man's leg and saw a second guy was now pounding the cop and trying to get at the cop's holster. Fists were one thing but if he got the gun they were both dead.

Sam got his knee under him and launched over the moaning form toward the second man. He caught the man's arm as it was coming down and again he was pulled harder than he thought he would be. He saved the cop from another blow, but it pulled Sam down on his injured right elbow again. The second man was still yanking on the holster, but couldn't get the pistol out. The cop could only hold on to the man's arm. He didn't have the strength to push it away from his body.

Sam started to get up to stop him and was stopped himself. He felt the grip from behind and was pulled backward and down on top of the first man. The second man turned to Sam with a smirk on his face. He slapped Sam hard with a backhand and Sam felt an arm come around his neck from behind. The big man squeezed against Sam's neck and Sam felt the air stop. By now he was breathing real hard and he knew that without air he would be down or dead in moments. He reached up and under the arm and tucked his chin into the elbow. It didn't work. He still couldn't breathe. The white flashes started dancing in front of his eyes and he was passing out. His right arm didn't seem to have any strength. He was working it up under the big man's arm trying to force a gap. He just couldn't do it. This couldn't be happening. All these years, he'd never lost a fight.

The bad guys were yelling at each other. The second man pulled again on the cop's holster and out came the big automatic. He just kind of looked at it for a second and turned it on Sam. *Jeez, no. I have to see Ken. I can't get killed here, like this.* He thought about little Molly. He could see her tail wagging back and forth in front of that big black hole at the end of the barrel. The second man grinned at Sam again.

It came from Sam's left. Like a silver flash sort of, and the second man crumpled down on to the cop. The gun spun out of his hand and fell onto the cop's chest. Sam felt something like wind on his bloody left ear and a sudden jolt behind him. The arm around his neck loosened and he gulped for air. He couldn't hold himself up. There was no power in his upper body and he went backward onto something soft. He looked up at the streetlight above him and saw Eileen. She was standing right next to him and he looked over to his right and could see she had one of her soft leather cowgirl boots on the neck of the big man and Ken's aluminum bat in her hand. *That's funny,* Sam said to himself, *I thought I put that back in the house.*

~ * ~

Don lit a cigar and shifted around in his seat. He was trying to calculate how much overtime he was making out of this. The weekend had been pretty good so far. The camper needed new rubber and his son was ready for that muzzleloader for buck season. Don shifted in his seat. Suzie's Sunday ham dinner was sitting heavily and his stomach was pinching in against the short barreled .45 tucked into the front of his pants.

Before the state police switched to the semi autos, they carried big Ruger .357 revolvers. Don worked almost exclusively in jeans and t-shirts and found it impossible to conceal any revolver but a snub nosed .38. He wanted something that would actually stop a drug crazed biker and bought his own 3 ½ inch compact .45 semi auto and qualified with it each year.

The first sprinkles of rain, more like a mist, began to fall on his windshield and it was getting colder. He debated about turning on the engine, but decided he didn't want to attract any more notice. *The first rule of a good surveillance is not to attract any undue attention to yourself,* he remembered from the academy. He chuckled when he remembered a few years ago he was on loan to the narcotics team watching drug houses and photographing the foot traffic in and out. They had spotting posts set up in warehouses and vacant apartments. The teams would park a block or two away and walk separately in to the hidden vantage points and relieve the previous shift. The neighborhoods were filled with customers who would rat the narcs out in a minute so they tried to keep a very low profile.

Don was teamed with a hard luck case. The narcotics trooper was driving a borrowed undercover car because he'd just totaled his own in a particularly embarrassing wreck the week before. He was still writing memos and listening to lieutenants tell him what a serious matter this was. He'd turned left in front of a $50,000 BMW. The state lost a seven year old Toyota.

Well, "trooper down on his luck" was stuck with a beat up Monte Carlo, the old style with doors about five feet long. They drove slowly into the neighborhood and found a spot about two blocks from their stake out. They sat in the car a minute and Don told the other trooper he would give him about five minutes and then follow him in. The narc said okay and opened his door to get out. The door was pulled out of his hand in a tremendous crash and went down the street on the front of a black pickup truck. The narc was left holding air and thinking, *oh shit, more memos*. Don was laughing hysterically, once he was sure his partner hadn't been hurt. They were quite a show for the neighborhood while the local police wrote up the accident report. The team in the post didn't get relieved for a long time.

Johnny got the Crown Vic tucked in to a tiny space down the block from the house. They couldn't really see Frank Dugan, but he would see the lights flash if anything happened. Johnny was humming along to the sweet little girl singing on the radio and it was driving Calvin nuts.

"Shut the fuck up, hillbilly. Can't we turn that corn shit off? I'm trying to figure out what we're going to do," Calvin strained his neck to see the front of the house in the darkness. The street lights on this block were almost nonexistent. A few porch lights added dimly to the wet, misty glow of the street.

"Your people get cranky in the damp weather? Something I need to read up on so's I can more effectively comprehend the crucial diversity issues facing members of today's state police?" Johnny could be verbosely sarcastic.

"Fuckin' redneck," Calvin loved him just the same.

The headlights came in from the Market Street side and made the right onto the street. As the van passed Johnny and Calvin, they saw it was Ford and blue. Both looked for the tag but the tag light was out and it was dirty. Impossible to read, but Johnny said, "I think the first letter matches. Can't see the rest of it." He reached up and started the Crown Vic.

Calvin said, "He's slowing down." Just as he said that, the brake lights came on and the passenger door came open.

"Wait, Johnny. A man's getting out. Man, that guy fits Yancey's description!" Calvin had to make the call. He grabbed the mic and said quickly, "Valley 17 to Philly 35, blue van out front pulling away, grab Dugan and try to get it stopped, we're going in." Calvin popped the door handle and was out on the sidewalk. Johnny shut off the car and grabbed the keys. He was about six steps behind Calvin as they sprinted toward the figure walking from the van up to the front door.

Don thought he heard something on the radio. It was muffled from where he was standing in the dark alley just behind the big station wagon trying to piss as fast as he could. He drank a lot of Mountain Dew with the salty ham and it was catching up to him.

Frank Dugan saw the van pull up and the black guy get out. The light was better on his side of the house and he recognized Jerome Yancey from the mug shot. The van was driven by another, bigger, black male and it pulled quickly away as soon as Yancey was out. Dugan decided, *fuck the van*, he knew the troopers wanted to talk to Yancey. Now appeared to be the time. He popped his door open and figured he would meet up with the troopers and see what Jerome had to say.

"Hey, Jerome, got a minute?" Calvin called from two houses away. Jamal was on the step and turned to see two men, one black and one white, running toward him. He knew what that meant, cops.

"Valley 17, did you call me?" Don spoke quietly into the radio microphone. "Calvin, did you say something?"

Jamal accelerated into the front door and hit it hard with his left shoulder and turned the handle at the same time. It was locked, but only with the knob latch. That gave under his weight and the door burst inward with a crash. Dugan saw the suspect slam into the house and started running as fast as his out of shape legs could move him.

"Johnny, do you copy?" Don asked over the air.

Calvin got out, "Police, stop!" but only Jamal's back was visible going through the door. Calvin caught the movement of Detective Dugan to his left and shouted to Johnny, "He's gonna come out the back!"

The two women and the older man visibly jumped when Jamal exploded into the room from the front door. The mother got out a "Hey!" as Jamal leaped the coffee table and knocked over the bottle of beer in front of the man, flashing between them and the new television.

Calvin started his turn to the right and motioned with his left hand pointing to Dugan advancing on the front steps. Johnny was just registering Calvin's warning about the back and now tried to interpret what he meant by the hand signals. They hadn't gone over this part. Calvin was even farther ahead of Johnny by now and was up to sprinter's speed angling for the right side of the house. It flashed in Johnny's mind that Calvin wanted him and Dugan to go through the house to keep Jerome from going back in and they would grab him in the alley. *Yeah, that was it.*

Dugan huffed across the small lawn, almost tripping over the short step up onto the front walk and could see the front door was open and lights were on inside.

Jamal was through the dining room and into the kitchen in four long strides and went straight for the back door. His right hand was behind him reaching for the Colt and he extended his left to the lock set above the knob. He knew it would be locked. He reached the door and his forward motion pushed him into it hard. The .45 wasn't firmly in his grip and almost tumbled from his hand. He caught it by the barrel and held on.

Calvin crossed the yard and went down the side of the house. Several lawn chairs and a small table were on a concrete slab between Calvin and the back. He had to slow and clipped one of the chairs as he passed through them. His feet stumbled in the dirt and he had to slow even more to regain his balance.

Johnny watched Calvin pulling away and move into the dimmer light of the side yard between the houses. To his left he could see Dugan trudging to the steps and followed him up and onto the porch.

Jamal got it on the second try and yanked the door open. He took a quick step out, bringing his pistol up and out in front of him. Hesitating just a moment, he looked for any cops at the back before starting onto the landing and down the steps to the alley.

It was close enough to see the back door just past the red Lexus open and a figure step out. The figure sort of jumped onto the little porch and stopped. *Jeez, that guy's got something in his hand,* Don thought. The man on the porch then jumped down the steps and was in the alley looking to his right.

Dugan stopped at the door and Johnny almost ran him over. He sidestepped around him and brushed past to enter the house. Even with the television on, Johnny could hear the back door bang against the frame.

Calvin did a stutter step and got back on course for the right rear of the house. He took three more big steps and saw something move behind a big bush at the corner of the house. He knew it didn't belong there and as his body moved closer, the movement turned into the shape of a gun barrel. Calvin thought *gun* and started to reach for his Glock at his right hip. The next step he took was a bit longer than the last and his foot didn't hit the ground at the same level as the last one did. Calvin's left knee extended and his upper body began to drop.

Jamal heard the noise as he moved in the alley to the right rear of the house. The .45 swung at chest level toward the corner and he closed the distance in two quick steps. His thumb pushed the safety off and he started his trigger squeeze.

He couldn't move fast enough. Don saw the man take the steps down in a leap and swing the gun out toward the corner of the house. Don's left hand was on the door handle and his right was gripping his automatic, while his whole body moved left to get out of the car.

Johnny slowed to look at the occupants of the room. The younger woman was starting to get up out of the chair and the woman on the couch with the man had her hands up to the sides of her head and began a scream.

Calvin was falling and he knew it. The hole was only four inches deep, but the effect it had when he stepped into it with all his weight was to jolt him hard and force him down and to the left. He couldn't get his hand on the gun and now could clearly see it was Jerome standing just beyond the bush pointing the gun at his chest.

Jamal made the decision. The black man running at him was reaching like he had a gun. The trigger didn't need much more pressure and he gave it. The flash from the muzzle surprised him it was so bright. He didn't seem to hear the sound.

Johnny did.

Don saw the flash and cleared his car. His .45 was coming out and he brought it over the top of the door, staying behind it for cover.

Calvin thought he was diving head first into the blast. It seemed only inches from his face and he was sure he was going to die and he was angry. For falling, and angry because he couldn't get his own gun out. He wanted to fight back, he couldn't.

Jamal followed his target as the black man came toward him and went face first into the dirt at his feet. The shell casing was still tumbling through the air when Jamal squeezed again and the second bullet went into the man's back.

Johnny yanked his gun out and scrambled through the kitchen and to the back door as the sound waves from the second shot jolted him.

Calvin felt the hammer blow in his right shoulder. It didn't hurt so much as it seemed to knock the wind out of him. He couldn't get his hands out in front of him as he went down and hit the ground face first, sliding forward almost to the feet of the man trying to kill him.

Don started yelling before the echo of the second shot even reached him, "Drop the gun!" Don's .45 was double action. He didn't need to release any safety, when he pulled the trigger the gun would fire just like a revolver. He knew when he saw the second shot he would have to shoot this man. The range was a little over twenty yards. Don was a good shot, but any shot over about fifteen yards is difficult. Add fear, shock, darkness and a moving target and it's damn near impossible.

Johnny didn't even slow down at the door and went through gun first.

Calvin felt the heat from the second shot. The blow hurt this time and drove into his back and down his legs. It felt like his feet were going to explode. He was looking right at the legs of his attacker less than a foot in front of him. His right side wasn't following orders from his brain and he didn't know if he had his gun in his hand or not. He thought, *how odd it is that his guy actually has a crease in his jeans.*

Don put the illuminated front sight on the upper body of the shooter and pulled his trigger.

Jamal began moving and jumped up and over the dirt and dust kicked up by the man's slide to him. He was trying to put the pistol back under him to the head of the man on the ground when he heard the bullet hiss by and the crack of Don's gun. Instead, he whirled and began running into the yard.

Johnny looked to his right and saw Yancey's coat flapping behind him as he hopped over Calvin and went into the darkened yard. He swung his pistol in that direction to line up his shot when he heard what he knew to be the ripping of the air by a bullet passing before the sound of the muzzle blast reached him. The thud of the bullet into the back of the house and the sound of the shot reached him at the same time. He was confused where it was coming from. Too much to process all at once. Yancey getting away, Calvin on the ground, and shots ripping by him.

As the flash cleared, Don, for an instant, thought his target had stepped back to the landing. He swung to put the sight back on again and recognized it was Johnny. Don kept swinging to his right, clearing Johnny from the sight picture. He was glad he hesitated. His target wasn't in sight and he could see something moving on the ground and Johnny stepping toward that movement. Don was sure he'd dropped the shooter. He decocked the hammer of his .45 and started up the alley.

Jamal never slowed down. Hugging the front yards to stay out of the light, he crossed the street down the block at its darkest spot.

Johnny could see Calvin was moving. He went down to him and looked past him into the yard for Yancey. Quickly, he glanced down at Calvin and put his left hand on Calvin's back. He started to get up to chase after Yancey and pull Calvin up with him when he heard Calvin wheeze and cough.

"You okay?" Johnny asked still looking into the yard for the threat.

"Fuckin' peachy, Johnny. I'm shot, I think," Calvin hoarsely said.

"I hit him!" Don called to Johnny. Don ran up to where he thought Johnny was on top of the bad guy. He could see Frank Dugan with a gun in his hand coming down from the landing behind Johnny.

Johnny turned to see Mitchell coming up behind him and yelled, "He's over that way, running!" Johnny pointed with his pistol out into the yard. "Cavlin's hit! Get the motherfucker."

Dugan stopped for just long enough to let his mind absorb what had happened and he ran into the yard and after Yancey. Don looked down at Calvin and realized his target was gone. He yelled back to Johnny as he followed Dugan into the yard. "Put him in the wagon and take him to Lankenau. Up 63rd, west on Lancaster. Don't wait, go now!" Don didn't know how badly Calvin was shot, but knew Johnny could get him to one of the best hospitals in the country in less than ten minutes. It would take a rescue unit a lot longer than that to respond.

Mitchell was catching Dugan, who had a portable radio in his hand and was trying to yell into it and run at the same time. "D-Dan 615, assist officer, officer shot, 56th and Spruce, foot pursuit, black male, black coat, jeans, armed with handgun, southeast," he stopped and breathed and the radio squawked back. "Beep, Beep, Beep, all units assist officer, police by radio, officer shot, 18th District, 5600 Spruce, black male, black coat, jeans, last seen on foot southeast, all units use caution, male armed, plain clothes officers in foot pursuit! D-Dan 615 what is your location?"

Dugan hoped the fucker would keep going in that direction. He'd run right into the 18th District and West Detectives headquarters at 55th and Pine. He knew his transmission would have everything moving quickly and bad guys often ran right into the cops. He slowed just a bit to catch his breath and listen for garbage cans tumbling or dogs barking trying to track Yancey. They ran east to the end of the block and didn't catch sight of anyone moving. Frank gave the radio his location and called in the number of the woman's house as the crime scene. Dugan turned south and went another block. He stopped on the corner and Mitchell was beside him.

"Where...do you...think he...went?" Don struggled to get the words out while sucking in huge gulps of air.

Jamal knew where the police station was and when he came out from between the houses to the next street, he turned back to the west and crossed between the houses on the south side. He zig zagged west and south until he heard the first sirens start and dropped in under a big rhododendron hedge to listen.

Johnny tried to find out from Calvin where he was hit. He could see the blood on Calvin's ass and gently rolled him over. There was blood on the front of his pants, too. Calvin's face was covered in dirt and pieces of paper and little stones. Johnny brushed most of it off as Calvin struggled to breathe and talk.

"Right side, I think. Feels like my shoulder's broke," Calvin said. Johnny could see wetness on Calvin's shirt and his stomach went even hollower. It looked like Calvin took one in the chest. Johnny knew that meant heart and major blood vessels. He didn't want his friend to die.

He pulled back Calvin's jacket and popped the buttons on his shirt. He could hear Dugan yelling as Don and Frank ran out of the yard. He hoped he would hear them shooting. *Kill that bastard!* The hole was small. Just down from Calvin's right shoulder and on the right side of center.

Johnny had a little hope. Calvin was struggling to breathe and Johnny saw a bubble appear at the bullet hole.

Somewhere in the back of his brain the military and police first aid training film threaded into the reel and started to flash up on the screen. Instinctively, he placed his hand over the hole, but he knew that wouldn't be enough. He holstered his gun and pulled out his cigarette pack from his shirt pocket. He slid the cellophane wrapper from the pack and stuffed it into the hole, wedging it down in with two fingers. Calvin winced and groaned sharply. Johnny pulled Calvin's shirt tail out and ripped a piece from the bottom. Stripping that piece into a smaller one, he then jammed that on top of the cellophane. Blood from Calvin's butt wound was on the ground under where he had fallen. Johnny took out his ink pen and jammed it into the ground to mark the spot.

Now he could move his partner. He hauled Calvin up and onto his shoulder in a fireman's carry. "Come on, baby. We're takin' a little ride," Johnny covered the twenty yards to Mitchell's Pontiac in a shuffling duck waddle under the weight and opened the backdoor. Carefully he rolled Calvin onto the back seat and slammed the door. He found the keys in the ignition and got the big machine moving down the alley and out onto the street.

Left there and then a right. He knew Cobbs Creek Parkway turned into 63rd Street at Market. The wagon turned right onto the Parkway without even slowing for the light. Pushing the heavy wagon as fast as it would go, he roared down the center of the street past startled drivers in both directions. He managed to find the microphone as he blasted across Market Street and almost broadsided a van while he was switching to the Philadelphia frequency, "Straus Valley 17 to Philadelphia, I got an emergency. I'm en route to Lankenau with a trooper that's been shot. Be there in a couple of minutes. Call 'em and have 'em get ready. He's hit bad."

There was no answer. Then, just as Johnny was getting ready to broadcast again, he heard, "What unit is calling Philadelphia?"

But Johnny was in a four wheel skid trying to miss a bus and didn't need this aggravation. Man, this car would move. The big V-8 didn't give any back talk and when Johnny poured the gas to it, it jumped.

Once he got back up to warp speed he tried again, "Pay attention! I got a wounded trooper going to Lankenau. Call 'em and have them meet me at emergency." That was enough, time to drive. The radio mic went to the floor and the Mitchell improved engine did its job pushing the wagon even faster.

"Frank, this ain't gonna work. We don't even have a flashlight," Don grabbed Dugan by the arm and started pulling him back toward the house. Sirens were coming to them from all directions. "Come on, you should be at the house to control the scene. Get those people that were inside and find out what they know. I'm gonna go after this guy." They crossed back to the side the house was on as several marked units slid onto the block from both directions.

Don stopped at Johnny's car. It was unlocked, but there were no keys. He spotted a five cell Mag Light on the seat and grabbed it. Uniform cops were jumping out of cars up and down the block and running toward the house with guns drawn. Don pulled his badge case out and stuck it in the breast pocket of his coat so he wouldn't get shot by mistake. Dugan was waving his arms and shouting orders to the blue suits and Don went back to the spot where he last knew Yancey had been. He needed to see something.

"Shit!" Johnny's heart skipped a beat. He was looking in the rear view mirror looking at Calvin looking at him. "What the fuck, you doin'? Lay back down, you scared me to death!"

"I got it right here," Calvin said, just loud enough to be heard over the engine and road noise, and touched his chest. "I got what I need. I was beginning to wonder."

"You're nuts! What do you mean, you got it? Yeah you got shot, now lay back down!" Johnny was almost screaming.

"The slug, you idiot. Get the slug," Calvin said. Johnny went into the intersection at Lancaster Avenue with a green light and made the left turn hard and fast. Calvin fell to the right and stayed down.

"Fuckin' zombie motherfucker!" Johnny shouted at the back seat. He put the wagon airborne at City Line Avenue and regained control enough to turn into the hospital lot.

Don had to tell two cops to get away from the back of the house. They looked at him with curiosity, a heavy, grey bearded guy with a little gold badge on his coat, but they stepped back. He told them where the shots had been fired and noticed the ink pen stuck in the dirt over a spot of blood.

"Through shot, gonna be a bullet under there," Don said to a uniform sergeant that walked out of the back door. Don was holding the flashlight low to the ground and studying some marks in the dirt. He moved a few feet farther, stepping to the side and then he was gone. *Who was that bearded man?*

Johnny slid to a stop amid burning brakes, tires and steam from the engine. A security guard and a young man in a green smock were standing just outside the glass doors of the emergency room.

"Hey, you can't stop here!" the guard yelled at Johnny. "Move outta' here!" he stepped over to the car as Johnny was coming out of the driver's door. The guard stopped short and gasped. Johnny had blood all down the front of his coat and shirt. "Are you the ones' been shot?" the guard asked.

"In here," Johnny said and opened the back door. Calvin was actually pale. The young man pushed past Johnny and reached in to Calvin and felt for a pulse at his neck. He stayed there longer than Johnny expected he would. "Is he okay?" Johnny asked.

~ * ~

Don worked his way through the yard. He ignored the still arriving police cars and all the shouting and concentrated on the ground. He found the prints, or parts of them, angling east. He took his time and worked it out. This guy knew what to shoot, how to shoot, had been to the toughest prison in the state and ran some kind of a criminal organization. He wasn't dumb and Don figured he wouldn't just run until he dropped or stumbled in front of a cop. Probably he would hole up or find a car to steal. If he was still on the ground, Don would find him.

Don stopped and looked down the street. Here and there he could see people stepping out onto their porches to see what all the fuss was about and a few porch lights coming on. Then he saw it. The dark spot. About the width of three houses. A big pine tree and no street light on either side. *That's where he would cross.*

~ * ~

"He's dead, I'm sorry," the young man in the green smock said. "Help me get him onto the gurney, we'll take him inside."

"Ahh, no," groaned Johnny and leaned against the side of the wagon. "No, he talked to me on the way here, no," his chest started to heave and he began to cry. "Ahh, Calvin, baby."

The guard wheeled the bed to the other side of the car and the young man pulled Calvin up by the arms and out so the guard could lift his feet onto the stretcher. They tried to be gentle, but managed to bounce him a little before they could get him settled and strapped on. Johnny couldn't look.

"Oh, my. He's got a gun," the young man said with some alarm.

"Yeah, he's a cop. Let me take it, I'm a cop, too," Johnny said sadly and came around the car. Calvin looked peaceful. His face was still dirty, but he looked just like he was sleeping. Johnny loosened Calvin's belt and slid the gun and holster off and tucked it into his own belt behind his back.

"Come on, let's go inside, we'll take care of him now," the young man said.

The guard asked if Johnny wanted him to park the car and said he had a special place for the police and it would be all right there. Johnny said sure. He was numb and sick to his stomach.

286

~ * ~

It took some looking, but Don found it at the edge of a flower bed in the back yard. The direction was changing. *He went west.*

Dugan refined the description and added the name. The city police radio was broadcasting it on all frequencies and then began to relay the information to the surrounding counties. The captain in the 18th District called the barracks on Belmont Avenue and notified the lieutenant on duty. Lower Merion Township police were already on their way to the hospital to assist there. Every cop within twenty miles was looking for Jerome Yancey. Only one was within two blocks of him.

~ * ~

The glass doors swooshed open and the young man wheeled Calvin past the desk and into a hallway lined with curtained cubicles, each big enough for one of the beds. Johnny followed behind, his shoulders slumped and tears rolling down his cheeks. He didn't know what to do first. He knew he had to do something, but just couldn't get focused. The young man put Calvin in an end space and pulled the curtain all the way around on its overhead track to block the view to the hall.

"There will be someone in to speak to you and get the paperwork started. Can I get you anything, are you all right?" he asked kindly. Johnny just shook his head, no. Sitting himself in the only chair, Johnny sobbed and stared at the floor.

~ * ~

The shift lieutenant gave Sam and Eileen a ride to the station. One of the uniformed cops would drive the Pathfinder. The lieutenant wasn't happy. Sam had a cut on his forehead that bled a bit and another two cuts on his left ear. His cheek was swollen and turning dark red. The EMTs tried to get him to go to the hospital, but he refused. They put butterfly bandages on his cuts and gave him an ice pack for his face. He didn't tell them about his elbow. It felt like it had been hit by a sledge hammer. The EMTs didn't have anything to patch his pride. The lieutenant didn't want this statie passing out at the station, then it would be his ass.

"Some first date, huh?" Sam tried for humor with her when they got settled in chairs in the chief's conference room.

"I thought I left all this excitement behind when I split from my drunken, brawling marine ex-husband. I seem to attract it," she said dryly.

"Thanks again. You saved two lives tonight. The cop and I would have had to kill those two if you hadn't distracted them," he grinned at her.

She threw a yellow tablet from the table at him.

The uniformed policeman who drove the Pathfinder stuck his head into the conference room and tossed Sam the keys. "The detectives would like you to sit down with them for a minute, corporal. Ma'am can I get you something?" he asked.

"Scotch and soda, double," she answered without skipping a beat.

He looked out into the hall and then stuck his head back in, "You got it, be right back," he winked and motioned Sam to follow him.

He dropped Sam with the detectives and went to the locker room. *This lady can have the whole damn bottle if she wants it. Anything for her, she saved my friend's life tonight.*

Sam recognized one of them from the scene. That one introduced the other as his sergeant. They both looked tired and were dressed in what most cops would be wearing at home on a cool, rainy Sunday evening, jeans and sweaters. A portable radio on the desk in the back of the room was following the traffic of the cars on the street and at the scene. The detective showed Sam a short question and answer interview he printed from his computer, based on his conversation with Sam at the scene. He asked Sam to read it over and sign it. Sam read,

Q: Were you operating your personal vehicle in the company of Eileen Matthews in Radnor Township on the date cited above and observed Officer Paul Dietz engaged in a physical confrontation with a subject later identified as Georgi Pavluch?
A: Yes.

Sam crossed out *physical confrontation* and wrote in above it, *fight.* It went on like that, the questions taking in big gulps of the story to ease the length of the statement and allow for simple answers. Sam made several more corrections and added three more questions and his answers that seemed to flesh out the sequence of events. He signed the statement and said, "Let me see Eileen's before you have her read it."

The detectives looked at each other and the sergeant started to say something. Sam stopped him, "Professional courtesy. I trust you, but I feel responsible for all this. I want to be sure some hairball ADA doesn't twist this around a year from now. The one guy's got a fractured skull. I think he's gonna be okay, but you never know what he'll do civilly from jail." Reluctantly they agreed. Sam changed a lot of her questions and answers.

The detective was finishing the changes to Eileen's statement on his computer while Sam talked about mutual friends with the sergeant. They all got quiet when the portable radio on the desk sounded the three beep alert tone, "All east county units, flash information from Philly PD. Be on the lookout for Jerome Yancey, black male, 29 years of age, six foot tall, two hundred ten pounds, last seen wearing a black leather coat and jeans, armed with a .45 semi-automatic, last seen on foot 5600 Spruce Street, Philadelphia, wanted for the murder of a state police trooper this date, 18th District in West Philadelphia, any contact notify Philadelphia Homicide."

Sam stared at the radio with his mouth open. The detective and the sergeant sat silently. Sam stood up and exclaimed, "What!" Yancey was his suspect. "A trooper?" *No, it couldn't be.* Calvin, Johnny and Don were out looking for Yancey, *why hadn't someone called me?*

"I gotta go, now. That's my people," he turned for the door, but stopped before he got there. "Look, it's one of my men. I've got to get...," he was confused. The detective helped out.

"Use the phone and call Belmont Barracks, they'll know. We'll get one of our officers to take Ms. Matthews home. Don't worry, we'll take care of her. Use this phone," he slid the desk phone to Sam. "I'll go talk to Eileen," he got up and left Sam and the sergeant.

Sam quickly dialed the state police barracks on Belmont Avenue. The desk officer put him right through to the lieutenant and Sam got the bad news. Lower Merion Police just called from the hospital and Johnny brought Calvin in DOA. Sam found out no one else was hurt and the hunt for Yancey was on. The people from the house were going to be taken to West Detectives, but would probably end up at the Roundhouse in Homicide.

~ * ~

Don lost the track at the street. He was in a block of tight homes with little room between them. Slowly and meticulously, he worked up the street, checking each opening for the track. It took a long time and he kept doubling back on himself. Most of the attached houses had big concrete porches with wide steps and sturdy rails. It would be easy to run up the steps, cross the porch and swing over a fence into the side yard without leaving a footprint. Don was a good tracker, but not on cement. There was a lot of cement in the city.

~ * ~

"They're going to have an officer take you home. It's a lousy night for a ride in the country. I'm sorry about all this, but thanks. You did save my life and probably the officer's, too. You'll never get a speeding ticket in this town," Sam sat next to her and held her hand. Eileen drained the glass of scotch and crunched on one of the ice cubes. "I've got to get to the hospital and take care of Calvin and Johnny, my two troopers. I just can't believe that Calvin's dead. He was such a good man, a good friend, too. Johnny's his partner, he'll be...well, I need to get there to make the notifications. This isn't how it's supposed to happen." Sam ran out of words.

Eileen wrapped her arms around him and held him for just a moment. "I'll be fine, you take care of what needs to be done. When you feel like you can talk about it, I'll listen. You be careful, Sam. I still have a dinner coming," she leaned forward and gave him a kiss. Without hesitating, he returned it and tasted the scotch.

~ * ~

The Lower Merion cop said he was real sorry about Calvin and would be around to help Johnny. Finally the curtain parted a bit and a pretty young nurse in pink scrubs eased into the space. She had a metal clipboard and came over to Johnny and put her hand on his shoulder. He caught the smell of her perfume. So soft, but it seemed to overtake the air around him. It was real nice and made him feel better just to smell such a fresh scent.

"I need to check him and write up the chart, you can stay if you want. The Philadelphia detectives will be here in a while and will need to look at him, you know what I mean?" she said oh, so sweetly.

"Mmmm, that's nice," Calvin stirred and opened his eyes. He smiled at the two shocked faces he was looking at. "Did you get the bullet? I want the lab to get it right away. What is that you're wearing, darling? It's real nice."

"Calvin, You're, you're....," Johnny couldn't think of what to say.

"Don't tell Grandma, let Momma do it. Just tell Momma," Calvin started giving orders.

The nurse punched the call button and whipped off her stethoscope and put it to the good side of Calvin's chest. "Well, you still have a heartbeat. Going to be a very surprised young intern in a minute," she said.

"That kid was a doctor?" Johnny asked.

"Yep, afraid so," she answered.

The crowd formed rapidly. Two more nurses rushed in and before a minute was gone, an older doctor showed up and ordered IVs, x-rays and blood work. Calvin slipped in and out and kept trying to find out the pink nurse's name. He just wanted to do some of his talk with her, you understand. They fussed and poked and got an IV into him before they started for the operating room. Johnny was right with him. He wouldn't leave Calvin and wanted to get that bullet. The doctor stopped Johnny and asked if he was the one who did the plug for the chest wound. He told Johnny that Calvin would have stayed dead without it.

~ * ~

Don snuck up onto each porch. He checked for the track over the edge of each one and finally found what looked like a patch of dirt that had been broken loose behind a fence between two houses. He managed to get himself out onto the fence from the porch and went over, landing with a thud.

He was in a fenced side yard that was no more than ten feet across. Don dropped down and used the light to cast shadows over the grass and dirt. Working his way along the house to the back, he found one bit of a heel mark that by now he recognized just by the shape and depth. He cut the light and drew his .45. There was still seven rounds left in it, but his spare magazines were in his briefcase on the front seat of the station wagon. That would have to do.

He moved next to the house wall and stayed in the shadows. The yard was small and another section of the fence crossed the back. A big bush was in the corner of the yard. Looked like no one ever trimmed the thing. Hung all the way to the ground.

~ * ~

When the news about Calvin being DOA reached Frank Dugan, he knew he would be relieved by a Homicide team. He continued working the scene, assigning arriving detectives jobs and getting plenty of help from the uniform officers who remained after the excitement wore off. Most of the others resumed patrol and went looking for Yancey. The two women in the house refused to talk without a lawyer and were shuttled off to West Detectives. The man posed a special problem. He had a gun. Oh, it was registered and legal. After all, he was a prison guard at Graterford.

"You happen to know an inmate out there by the name of Thomas Sylvester?" Frank asked. Frank could see the guard's Adam's apple work up and down.

~ * ~

Sam leaned into the Pathfinder and got the gun safe open. He clipped the Glock onto his belt and slipped the .22 Mag into his back pocket. He took his cuffs and a spare magazine out, too. He wanted to go to the hospital first to see Johnny and figure out what to do about Calvin's mother and grandma. The Pathfinder was a quiet place for his short ride to Lankenau.

~ * ~

It sounded just like the noise he made when he jumped earlier. Jamal tensed and flipped the safety off on the .45. An all night stay in the darkness of the bush was what he planned to do. He knew he'd been sitting under it for quite a while and heard the heavy rumbling police car engines prowling up and down the streets on either side. Someone was in the yard. He watched the corner of the house where the noise came from, ready to do anything he had to do. He wasn't going back to that pit of a prison.

Don was an experienced hunter. He hunted wild critters when he was off and stolen cars at work. This deal was quite a bit different. Getting real serious. He slid to the end of the house and slowly peeked at the yard. That big bush was there. He asked himself, *where would I hide if I was in this yard?* He didn't want to just walk up and shine his light into the bush and see if Yancey was in there.

He had to do something. In the dim light, he looked to see what was near him. A coiled up piece of garden hose was on the ground about five feet back in the direction from which he came. Slowly he moved back and picked up the coil. He'd learned a squirrel hunter's trick years ago. Sometimes you walk up on one while you're moving through the woods and catch a glimpse of it as it scoots around to the other side of the tree. You move one way or the other and the squirrel moves around the tree some more, always keeping it between you and him. The trick was to toss a stick or your hat over to a spot behind the squirrel and make him put the tree between him and the new sound. Squirrel for dinner.

Not exactly the same here, but close enough. Don wrapped the coil tighter by pulling the end of the hose around the coil and lodging it between the circles of hose. He moved back to the end of the house and judged the distance to the bush and the fence. About forty feet, he thought. Don focused on the bush and rolled the hose coil out onto the yard toward the bush.

The hose was spinning along like a wobbly wheel and the bush exploded in flame and noise. Dirt kicked up around the hose and Don counted the shots. One, two, three...and the noise paused. Don pivoted left, braced against the corner of the house and fired into the bush four times. Two shots came back and one hit the wood of the wall at Don's waist showering his coat with shards of splinters and paint. Don returned two more shots.

Now he only had one left in his gun. Five hundred dollars of expertly crafted machinery in his hands that now functioned like one of his flintlocks. He pulled back behind the wall and waited for Yancey's eighth shot. Don figured Yancey didn't have a spare magazine either. Two into Calvin and five here, leaves one. If it wasn't one of the high capacity .45s they were making now. Then he might have five more rounds. Tough time for math.

~ * ~

His father tried to object but Afif wouldn't have it. "She's been hurt in her mind, too, Father. Stop worrying about how this matters to you and think of what has happened to her. I won't allow you to make this worse. She's going, tonight. I know you have the money, now is the time we need to use it. We have to get all of you where Yusef won't find you. He'll be coming back."

The nurse at the desk was trying to get the doctor on the phone. She said Afif couldn't take his mother without the doctor's medical release. Afif ignored her. He stood up to his father and told him to get the money and pay the bill, she was leaving. The private ambulance would be here any minute.

~ * ~

Don threw a rake and a basketball. No response from the bush. He found a shovel and took off his coat. He slipped the handle up one sleeve and hooked the end in the loop at the back of the coat collar. Trying to make it look like he was stepping out to fire, he thrust the coat out around the house and waited for the shot. Nothing.

Big balls time now. He didn't hear any sirens and nobody came out of the house. It was up to him. He put his coat back on and picked his spot. There was no cover except a skinny clothes line pole and he wouldn't fit behind that. Three deep breaths and he held the last half of the fourth and leaped into the yard. He'd seen it in the movies, but it was a lot different in real life. He took three quick steps and dove to the ground, intending to roll over on his right shoulder and come up dodging bullets and returning fire.

He hit the ground and crashed, sliding on his back and knocking the wind out of himself. A target for the monster in the bush. Still no shots came. Don struggled to his feet and flipped the light up under his gun hand with his other and illuminated the target. He was close enough to see in under the green mass and saw nothing but bare ground. He shuffle stepped over, ready to use his last round, but found Yancey gone.

The dirt under the bush was all pushed around and several shell casings were scattered among the debris. He saw something black and found an empty Colt magazine lying next to a couple of drops of blood. *Bad guess about the spare magazine, Don*, he told himself. The fence was rotted out under the big bush and the trail led through it. But now the runner was leaving more than footprints on the ground.

~ * ~

After the short ride in from Radnor, Sam found a spot outside of the emergency room entrance and locked up the Pathfinder. He rushed in through the door with his badge out and asked for Trooper Bonner. The lady in the glass booth told him to go to the waiting area for surgery and gave him directions. *Surgery?*

Sam tried to think. *Was someone in surgery? Johnny must be hurt, too*. They hadn't told him that. He made one wrong turn, but backtracked and came out of the elevator to see Johnny spread out in a small chair. He looked beat, but didn't look like he needed surgery. Johnny glanced up at the sound of the elevator doors and saw Sam.

"Who used you for a punching bag?" Johnny asked, looking puzzled.

"Never mind me, who's in surgery?" Sam demanded.

"That voodoo crazy zombie Calvin is. Dude's still alive. Some snot nosed intern couldn't find a pulse and declared him dead. Hope they used pencil on the death certificate, gonna have to change the date," Johnny needed a cigarette. "What'd you run into?"

"Rough date, hits right handed line drives. What happened?" asked Sam. Johnny started in the middle and had to double back a couple of times but got Sam filled in. Sam gave him a quick explanation of the gallant hero getting his ass kicked story or Johnny would never have shut up about it. "They tell you what they expect?"

"Tight lipped about it. Just to wait and see. A lot of lung damage on his right side. His ass has a new hole, actually two of them. I sure hope he gets well real quick, I got a lot of great material to try out on him," Johnny said. He held up a plastic bag that was on the floor at his feet, "I have all his stuff."

"Ok, how's this? You take Don's car and get up to Norristown and notify Calvin's mom, bring her down if she wants to come. Let one of his sisters take charge of Grandma, we don't want her dropping on us. Stop a few blocks away and call 'em to let them know you're stopping in so you don't shock them too much. I'll stay here with Calvin and get the bullet he worked so hard to collect. I'll have my cell phone on. And stop somewhere and get a clean shirt, you got his blood all over you, scare Grandma for sure with that."

Johnny said okay, Calvin should be out of surgery by then. He gave Sam the keys to the Crown Vic parked back in West Philly and was gone in the elevator.

Sam went to use the pay phone next to the elevator to conserve his cell phone battery, it was going to be a long night.

"Sorry we're not here, probably out drinking beer, love to get a message from you, right after the beep that you hear," Sam could hear Katie giggling in the background when Ozzie recorded that. Beep.

"Ozzie, saddle up, I need you down in Philly. Calvin's been shot and is in surgery. Yancey's the shooter and is on the ground in West Philly. Call me on my cell phone or at....," Sam gave the number of the pay phone.

He dialed Ozzie's cell next, left the same message when Ozzie didn't answer. He tried to alternate between the cell and the pay phone so one would be open. Every time he thought he had called each person that needed to be notified, he'd think of someone else. No, Calvin's still alive. Just a mistake. He's still in surgery. Yes, we know who did it. No, we don't have him yet. He could have made a tape and played it for each of them.

He started getting calls back. The first was from Frank Dugan at the scene. The Homicide guys were pissed that Calvin was alive. Not that they didn't like Calvin, but that they were called out of whatever bar they had been hiding in on a quiet, damp Sunday night and chewed a half a pack of gum for no reason. Frank told Sam that Don was still out chasing Yancey, alone. The uniform cars were looking for both of them and were supposed to "persuade" Don to check back in or take a couple of them and their police radios with him on his expedition into the wilds of the Cobbs Creek section of tightly packed houses. Dugan winced when Sam suggested the state police helicopter be called in to help with the search.

"Shit, Sam. Remember 1985?" Dugan asked. The Philly bomb squad borrowed the state police helicopter to lift one of their lieutenants up over a house with barricaded shooters and he dropped a pack of explosives on a log fort on the roof. Only burned down a few blocks. The police department has the reputation of staging the only successful aerial bombing of an American city. They still sell t-shirts with the likeness of the mayor piloting a dive bomber over a burning neighborhood. The fecal material hit the fan over that one. "It'll never make it past my captain, Sam. Christ, it's the same area that Yancey headed for."

"I don't care, Frank. I'm pushing for it. I want this guy. He's gonna go for three murders, at least, and the attempted on Calvin. I'm not holding anything back. I'll keep you out of it. For the record, I didn't ask you. Now, find Don or Yancey or both and call me back." Sam hated to be short, but didn't wait for a reply and hung up.

~ * ~

Don went over the fence and picked up the clear trail in the alley. There was plenty of loose crap lying around for Yancey to step in. Every few yards Don picked up a few drops of the runner's blood. Carefully moving from one bit of cover to the next, he expected to find him lying in a heap at every turn.

Yancey wasn't being careful now, he was trying to put distance between him and whoever was after him. *Man, my foot hurts.* His shoe was full and the blood was squishing out over the top every time his foot hit the ground. The crazy cop would find him quicker now. He'd run from the police since he was a kid, none ever caught him or even stayed with him after a block or two. This guy was something, *some kind of fuckin' bloodhound human mix.*

He had to get off the street and out of this area. He hobbled west and stopped in the shadows just before crossing Cobbs Creek Parkway. The traffic broke and he went across the street and into the thin strip of park along the creek. Turning south, he tried to stay off the dirt and in the grass, pausing every few yards to hide behind a bush or tree and look behind him. *Damn! That's him.* Two blocks back and crossing into the park. Jamal sucked it up, ran as fast as his wounded foot would let him and put another two blocks between them.

~ * ~

This phone call was hard to make. Sam knew what he was starting. He should have gone through his captain, but didn't want to put her in the middle of it, she was doing enough for him already. Frank Dugan was right. No one wanted the memories of the trauma the last helicopter flight over this neighborhood caused, to come out again. The deputy commissioner's prior job was as the major in charge of, among other things, the State Police Aviation Unit. His relationship with Sam had been a rocky one. Sam's flying skills should have, in the then major's opinion, been applied to official use with the unit and not simply for Sam's off duty personal benefit.

The major was unsuccessful in either yanking Sam into his command or screwing up the job with Peggy. It wasn't for lack of trying and Sam didn't like him. Now, he needed him. Headquarters in Harrisburg phone patched Sam through to the lieutenant colonel's home. The discussion that followed sounded more like the verbal banter just before two men went outside the bar and pounded each other into the dirt. It was ugly.

"I don't care, the press would cram this up the governor's ass and love it," the colonel finally said. "It can't be done. Unless..."

"Look, Colonel. You want something and I want something. There has to be a deal here somewhere," Sam started to back off a bit, leading him in.

"Deal? Yeah, deal me right into early retirement. If I'm going to risk my ass, I have to have some collateral to make it worthwhile," fired back the colonel.

"I'll officially volunteer, but no traffic. Crime work or VIPs, but no traffic. That's my end. You win," Sam offered.

"When I need you, no pissy attitude, no F.O.P. lawyers?" the colonel asked.

"No trouble, I'll fly for you on an as needed basis. Let the rookies clock the speeders," Sam had the deal. It left a bitter taste in his mouth.

When the pay phone rang it startled him a bit. Sam was in between calls and thinking of how relieved he was to find Calvin alive. Ozzie was calling from the road outside Hazleton, "Hey, I'm on my way home from Marie's mom's, what's going on?" Sounds of kids and Marie could heard in the background.

"Calvin's been hurt. He's in surgery. He took two shots from Yancey in Philly. I don't know if he's going to be all right yet, it's too soon to tell. One was in his right lung and the other in his, well, his ass," Sam said.

"Wow, God I hope he's gonna be okay. You want me to do anything?" Ozzie asked.

"Don Mitchell and half the Philly PD is chasing Yancey on foot now, but we're gonna have to put this thing together. I hate to say it, but if Calvin pulls through, this is all gonna end up on us. Our homicides are of no interest to Philly. We have a couple of women, who Yancey was sort of living with, in custody, but I don't know how long they can be held. One of them was dating a Graterford guard. He's talking to Frank Dugan. Come on down as quick as you can. I'm at Lankenau Hospital now and I'll stay as long as I can do something here. If I move before you get here, I'll call you again."

300

"Ok, I'm taking a van full of kids home and I'll swing by the barracks for a car. You want me to come by your place on my way home and feed Molly?" Ozzie was a real sweetheart.

"Thanks, Ozzie. She can stay out, it's not going to be that cold tonight. See you when you get here," Sam hung up.

"What did Sam want?' Marie asked.

"To pay for the first months diapers, I gotta go to Philadelphia tonight," Ozzie quietly told her about Calvin and they said a little prayer together for him as they passed through Tamaqua heading south toward Sam's, then home.

~ * ~

At this rate, he was going to jail or the morgue tonight. He had to find a way to get away from his human shadow. Jamal stopped and caught his breath at the edge of the playground parking area. There was one car in the lot and Jamal noticed the white Cadillac was running. The windows were steaming over and he moved in on it. All the windows were up and hard to see through, but Jamal could see the back of a man's head against the driver's window. He tried the door handle and found it locked. He tapped on the glass with the barrel of his gun and the man moved a bit, but didn't look out.

"Open the door!" Jamal shouted and as the man turned his face to the window Jamal pointed the .45 right between his eyes. "Open the fucking door, asshole!" the man looked at the hole in the end of the gun, but still didn't move.

Jamal smashed the gun against the glass and shattered it with the first swipe. The man was naked and in his lap the head of a girl of about fifteen was still rocking up and down on his penis as fast as she could. Jamal reached through and hit the electric door lock and pulled the door open quickly. He pulled the man out of the car by his hair and reached in for the keys. The girl smacked as she broke suction on him and looked up to see Jamal waving the Colt at her.

"Out, girly. In the trunk with him, you can finish earning your pay," he prodded them back to the trunk and forced them in. There was a first aid kit lying on the trunk floor and Jamal snatched it out before slamming the two inside. Neither of them even made a sound. He quickly got the car started again and pulled out onto the street headed south.

~ * ~

A lieutenant and a sergeant arrived from the Belmont Barracks and found Sam coming out of the men's room. The lieutenant introduced himself and Sam recognized the name as the one from whom he received the news about Calvin.

"He's alive and in surgery, Lieutenant. Some ER doc thought he was dead, but thank God he was wrong." While Sam was telling them about what brought everyone here, three more uniformed troopers and the crime sergeant showed up. The hallway and small waiting area were getting crowded. The crime sergeant was a road trooper when Sam was assigned here earlier and didn't like Sam. They seemed to disagree on how to conduct the daily affairs of the state police on most issues. He started making suggestions to Sam in front of the lieutenant about things Sam should have been doing and needed to get going on. Sam tolerated the interruptions until the pressure of the long day started coming out of his ears.

"Let me talk to you a minute over here, Bobby," Sam said to the crime sergeant and led him past the crowd of uniforms to the hall on the other side of the elevators. "Thanks for coming down, we can probably use some help from your guys on this in a bit. If you think of any more brilliant suggestions for me, why don't you get out your little notebook you use to keep track of all the stuff to rat out the folks that work with you and write me a short note. I'll consider it."

The sergeant started to say something, but Sam held up his finger to shush him. "I am getting to the point that I'm ready to forget that you outrank me and drag you out back and beat the shit out of you. If you think I'm going to let you fuck up this case with your stupid ideas, you've figured wrong." Sam kept his finger up in Bobby's face. "My trooper is in there with holes in him and I'm going to get the crazy bastard that did it, you won't stop me and if you try, I'll run you over. Now, before I have to have a talk with our captains, after which you'll be figuring patrol schedules in Erie, why don't you get on back to Belmont."

It was a risk Sam thought was worth it. He really wasn't very afraid of the sergeant, he'd backed him down before. When they were both troopers and Bobby got a little snockered, enough to think he could push Sam around one night after work, Sam set the record straight. Bobby's dentist made some money from that incident.

"Now why don't you tell the lieutenant that you will go back to your office and wait for the fellows from BPR to show up for the shooting investigation." The state police version of internal affairs, the Bureau of Professional Responsibility, would investigate Don's shooting along with the Philly PD. Once they found Don, that is. Bobby didn't think about it very long, he just mumbled something to the lieutenant on his way out.

Sam's cell phone rang. "We found him, just Don, not Jerome," said Frank Dugan. "Don tracked him all the way over to Cobbs Creek. Looks like he stole a car there and took off. Don wounded him, the guy left a blood trail. I've got the radio room calling all the hospitals if he shows up. We recovered the bullet that was under Calvin and Don shot up a backyard with Jerome a few blocks over. Gonna send another crime scene unit over there. How's Calvin?"

"Don't know yet, Johnny's gone to get his mom. I'm staying here until I know about Calvin. I'll send a couple of troopers over to you to help out," Sam said.

Next to arrive was a team of Philly detectives. They went straight up to the lieutenant and asked where the bullet was. Sam had his back to them, but turned sharply and said, "Well, thanks for asking, the wounded officer is alive and in surgery. He'll be so pleased that you were so concerned about his health."

The younger Philly detective smirked and said, "Fuck you, jitbag. We've got the shooting job, we're takin' the slug to our guys at the Roundhouse." Two of the bigger troopers had to pull Sam off of him.

When the dust settled, the lieutenant told the Philly detectives, "You've already got a bullet, from the same gun, recovered at the scene and I understand there's another shooting scene with more slugs. This one's going for a helicopter ride to Harrisburg so we can get murder warrants for this guy. No debate. Understand?"

~ * ~

Cobbs Creek Parkway turns into Baltimore Avenue, which took Jamal toward the University of Pennsylvania. He cut off at University Avenue and entered the expressway. No one seemed to notice the white Cadillac with no driver's window on this chilly, damp night. Jamal's foot hurt and he was freezing. He rounded the curve and passed by the project, exiting on Passyunk. Instead of turning back to the north to enter the safety of the project, he crossed down onto Oregon Avenue, went east then slipped a block north and parked next to a small park. He shut off the car, but left the keys in it, hoping it would be stolen again before the police found it. Still not a sound from the trunk.

The park was ghostly dark and deserted. Jamal hobbled in, found what was left of a bench and sat down. He carefully peeled off his shoe and blood poured out on the ground. He left his sock on and squirted half of the tube of antibiotic over the bullet hole an inch behind his second toe. It amazed him he'd only been hit once. The bullets passed him ripping branches and crashing into the fence. How foolish he was jumping for the movement of the hose and giving away his position.

He pulled the little first aid kit apart and placed gauze pads around the wound. With the shoelace from his other shoe, he wrapped the gauze tightly around his foot to put pressure on the bleeding. He put on the wounded shoe and laced it up as tight as he could, grimacing in pain.

Gathering up the remains of the kit, he tossed it into a trash bin and stumbled north out of the park toward the project, ten blocks away. He hoped the cops didn't know about this place, too.

~ * ~

Don finally got to look at the red Lexus. It had been forgotten in the excitement and they wouldn't let him do anything else. He knew once BPR showed up, he would be captured for a while. Took him all of fifteen minutes, it was an easy one. "Frank, not that it matters, the Lexus is stolen out of the 5th District. What else can I do?" Don asked.

Dugan was on the couch, next to the Graterford guard, writing. He slid the paper over to the guard and asked, "Like this?"

"Yeah, a grocery list or a set of names and phone numbers, regular stuff normally carried in anyone's pocket and a series of numbers on the bottom that look like lottery numbers," the guard explained.

Frank excused himself, walked Don into the kitchen and said, "They called Yancey, Jamal. The guard took messages into the prison for Yancey and gave them to Sylvester. Carried back the reply. They used a simple code in case the guard ever got searched. Common list or piece of innocent paper with numbers on the bottom. The numbers tell the reader which letters and numbers in the list go in what order. Took one of the lists from Yancey to another prisoner the day before Sylvester got almost killed. I don't think this guy even knew what he was doing. Sort of against the rules, didn't think it hurt anything. He's afraid he'll lose his job. He's more afraid of Jerome. He says he just got a girlfriend out of the deal," said Frank. "The younger one is tight with Yancey. She's not givin' up anything to the guys over at West Detectives. Shouting about a lawyer. I got an idea and you're the guy to do it. Listen to this..."

~ * ~

"Here it is," the OR nurse handed the lieutenant a small specimen jar sealed with surgical tape with the doctor's name, the date and time. Her name was next to that. Calvin's name was on a piece around the middle of the jar.

"How's it going?" asked Sam.

The nurse looked back over her shoulder and then back at Sam. "I'm not supposed to say, you didn't hear this from me. He's going to be down for a long time, but he's going to make it. He's strong and healthy. His hip is badly shattered. He'll probably have more surgery for that later. If we can keep pneumonia from setting in, he should recover from the lung damage okay. Two or three inches higher and to the right would have been the heart. You know what that means."

Sam thanked her as she spun and marched back to the operating room. The bullet looked good. Not too much flattening. Calvin did a good job collecting the evidence.

The lieutenant said, "Sam, I can designate a trooper as the custodian and hand carry that to the ballistics lab in Harrisburg. The helicopter will be landing at Belmont as soon as it gets down from Reading," Sam liked the idea and the trooper went to his car to get a property receipt and a lab request. He was going for a chopper ride.

Sam's next call was to the DA up in Allentown. He sounded a little drunk, but was polite and listened to Sam's report. "Yeah, sounds like enough for an arrest warrant, but I wouldn't want to go to trial with it," the DA said. "The bullets will put his gun as the murder weapon, but there was another gun used, too. Until we establish who that is, we still have a big hole of reasonable doubt. I'll approve the warrant. But Sam, you have to get me the other person, and a full signed confession would be nice, too. Good luck."

~ * ~

He passed within a block of the police station at 24th and Wolf and went in to the project. The wound should be cleaned and properly bandaged and he needed something for the pain. The women had plenty of good stuff for pain and could go to the drug store for sterile bandages; he didn't want to be seen. There were also more guns and ammunition in the crawl space over the bedroom. His phone vibrated and shrilled and startled him a bit. It was a number he didn't recognize. He ignored it for now.

~ * ~

"I'm Trooper Mitchell, Frank Dugan sent me over. You got a couple of women from the shooting in here?" the detective behind the glass looked at the big bearded man in black leather and dirty jeans standing on the other side. He didn't look like any trooper he'd ever seen.

"You got any ID, pal?" the desk man asked. Don produced his ID case and the desk man nodded toward the bench for him to wait. It took about ten minutes before the detective sergeant came out.

"Yeah, trooper, come in, we got the girls in the back waiting for lawyers. Real sweethearts. How's the other trooper doin'?" the sergeant was trying to be nice. His two detectives called from the hospital and were on the way back without the bullet. He could have told them not to fuck with the staties. It didn't get you anyplace. He knew from experience. Now they did, too.

"Still too soon to tell. Are these two separated?" Don asked.

"Yeah, the mom's in with the coffee and the spitfire's in the interrogation room. What a bitch. Wants E. Peter Lacertosa to come down and represent her. She ain't got the juice," the sergeant laughed. Lacertosa was the top dog of criminal defense lawyers at the moment. Big bucks and worth it. Send your limo with a briefcase full of hundred dollar bills if you want to see him. "One of the assistant flunkies said he'd be down after midnight, even the flunkies' 'indisposed', she'll have to wait until then."

Don was led back through the open squad room, cluttered with desks and papers and not too many people. The interrogation room was really just a big closet. Room for three chairs and a crooked little table. Jamal's girlfriend was handcuffed to a big metal ring in the wall and sat slumped in one of the hard wooden chairs. She smelled. That funky woman smell like she needed a long hot bath. Don stepped in and let her look at his badge.

"Well, hon. You're goin' home. Papers'll be ready pretty soon. Sorry for the inconvenience, but we had a lot to sort out with the trooper dying and all," well, the doctor said he was dead, for a while. Don let that sink in and sat down next to her. He got out his handcuff key and unsnapped her from the wall. She rubbed her wrists and the red ring where the shackles had been.

"You motherfuckers had no right takin' me and my momma down here, we ain't done nothin'. My lawyer, he gonna sue yo' asses off!" she spit out at him.

"Whoa there, missy. We know you haven't done anything, that's why you're going home. It wasn't real clear at first, but now we've had some time to figure a few things out and you're right. You have to understand," Don smiled his bearded smile at her.

"Who takin' momma and me home? I ain't walkin' no where's," she demanded.

"Oh, I'll take you. You can make the arrangements for your mother once you get home," Don kept smiling.

She looked a little puzzled for a second and quickly put her indignant face back on. "What? What 'chew mean, 'rangements? What 'rangements fo' Momma, she all right?" the girl snapped.

"Oh, my yes. She's fine. The legal arrangements, you know, bail and the lawyers. She's going to need all that stuff done for her while she's locked up," Don laid it out there.

"WHAT? Locked up? She goin' home wif' me!" the girl shouted.

"Oh, no. I'm afraid that can't happen. She has way too many charges against her. Probably will be a real high bail," Don strung the line out onto the water.

"Charges, what charges? She done nufin'!" she stood up and put her hands on her hips.

"Oh, my. She's in very serious trouble. The trooper being shot, her boyfriend being involved, the stolen car. All that adds up. Real serious. Probably even prison, with her prior arrest record," Don motioned for her to sit back down and she did, with a thud.

"My momma? You can't. She don' know nufin'," her hands folded over her heaving stomach.

"Well, it's her house, her boyfriend and her car. The DA won't need much else. She'll be all right, though. They'll put her in the women's prison, teach her how to sew or something. You can still drive out to see her. It's only about three hours from here, nice day trip," Don jiggled the fly on the end of the line.

She looked at it a bit before she rose to the surface. Her eyes went from Don to the floor and then to the ceiling. "Momma not in this. I ain't either. We jus' let him be in the house. He good to us. Treat me like I'm somefin. But Momma ain't in this. I didn't know this was goin' to happen. What can I do? You gotta get my momma off'n these charges," the first tear started to show in her right eye.

"Well, I can't promise you anything at all. You asked for a lawyer earlier, so I can't even ask you any questions about tonight. If you know something that will show me your mother didn't do anything and can tell me about Jamal, I'll let the DA know. That's all I can do," he spread his arms open and welcomed her to his side. "You're not being charged, you're free to go, so if you want to make a statement to me without a lawyer, I'll try to see that the right thing is done."

She thought that over and nodded her head.

~ * ~

Man, did that hurt. She eased off his shoe and let his foot rest on the towels at the end of the bed. The kids were all shuttled out and left Jamal alone with her. The training she had from the air force helped her decide how to handle this. "You need to go to the hospital. The hole might have cut through bone and tendons. Went right on through. Your foot ain't never goin' to be right. Might get all infected and you get blood poisoning."

"No hospital, fix it up. Do it right. Yow!" he yelped. She was probing the wound and swabbing it with peroxide. The liquid fizzed and turned white from the infection already setting in. He tried to figure out what to do next. Yow!

~ * ~

By the time he was heading south on the turnpike at a hundred miles an hour, he was awake and ready to work. Ozzie only had two beers that afternoon. He didn't drink and drive anymore. He used to. He needed to set a good example for Junior and now the twins. They were all getting older and noticed everything Mom and Dad did. He switched to iced tea before dinner and after, sat through the new baby talk playing Sorry with Katie and Connie.

Marie saved him and sent him and Junior out to the meat market for homemade kielbasa loaf before they closed. Ozzie stretched it and took Junior to the big sporting goods outlet to look at backpacking gear. Now, he was on overtime making the run down to help Sam catch Calvin's shooter. He had three big folders in the trunk with as much of the case file as he could round up in a flurry through the barracks to grab keys to the black Crown Vic. He hoped they had the prick locked up by the time he got there and would let him alone with him for five minutes.

~ * ~

When the phone rang, Grandma sat straight up on the couch from her sound sleep. Calvin's mother answered on the third ring and spoke quietly when she heard it was Johnny calling. This late on Sunday night, phone calls usually meant trouble. "Okay, Johnny. We'll see you in a few minutes," she said and pressed the button down. She dialed her daughter and told her to come over. "Yes, right now."

"Is he dead?" Grandma asked. "Our Calvin. What happened to him? I been dreamin' crazy dreams 'bout him when the phone ring. Mean's somethin' happened to him, what it means," she pulled herself up and trudged off to the bathroom.

"I don't know, Momma, Johnny's coming to talk to us. I'm scared," she said.

Grandma stopped at the door to the bathroom and looked back, "I don' think he daid, didn't dream that. Dreamed he fall down the stairs and get up and do it again. Keep fallin' down the stairs. Don't listen to me 'bout not goin' back up," she went in to pee and slammed the door. Calvin's mom went to the kitchen and started making a pot of coffee. Grandma was usually right about her dreams. She hoped it wasn't too bad. Anytime something happens to your kids, even if they're grown, it's bad, though.

~ * ~

"My name is Trooper Don Mitchell, I'm in the interrogation room at West Detectives, Philadelphia, PA. With me is Nancy Highsmith. Miss Highsmith, do you understand that this is being recorded?"

"Yes, I do."

"Do I have your permission to record this interview?"

"Yes."

"Earlier tonight, you requested a lawyer be present before any questioning, is that correct?"

"Yeah, but I don't want one now, jes axt me the questions."

"You are voluntarily agreeing to answer questions without a lawyer present?"

"Yes, axt 'em."

"You understand you are not under arrest and are free to leave?"

"Yeah."

"You are waiving the right to a lawyer of your own free will?"

"Yeah."

"I am showing you a piece of paper on which are written your Miranda rights. I will read each one and ask you if you understand each one. If you do understand each one, I want you to answer out loud and also to initial beside each. Do you understand?

"Yeah, answer and initial."

Don carefully went over the rights sheet and after, again made sure she understood she didn't have to answer anything and was not under arrest and was free to leave at any time. The courts didn't require all of it, but he was being very careful.

She told him about her mom and the guard and how Jamal introduced them, hooked them up, she said. She didn't know anything about their business, just that Jamal would take him into the kitchen to talk to him. She was pretty sure Jamal was giving him money. The guard always had money in his pocket and they didn't get paid that much, did they.

Jamal was her main boyfriend. He didn't want her hangin' with other dudes. He wanted her there when he showed up. Never called, just showed up. Would come in and wait in her room until she got back and yell at her for not being there. Always had the big driver drop him off. He gave her the Lexus for a present. Just this week. She didn't realize it was in her mother's name. Didn't even think about it. Pretty car. Fun to drive. Jamal took it for a couple of nights already, then brought it back. Told her to back it in so the tag didn't show. Thought that was odd, but did what he said, except for last night. Guess she fucked up. Oh, can she say that on the recorder, sorry.

Jamal used the phone sometimes, but his cell would go off and he would read this code on it and just leave. Or he would text someone, probably the big dude that drove the van. Yeah, she knew Jamal's cell number, it was...

~ * ~

No more calls to make for the time being, so Sam settled into a chair and fell asleep. He would stir when one of the radios would sound off, but then slip back into a cat nap. It didn't help much. The lieutenant signed the bullet over to the trooper who left to race to the Belmont barracks to meet the helicopter. The cloud base was holding just above minimum for the chopper to get in from the Reading airport where they are based for this section of the state. Harrisburg was more iffy, but the pilot was willing to risk it for this run.

~ * ~

There was a space just a few doors down and Johnny wedged the big wagon in. Momma was waiting at the door and looked tense. Johnny walked up to her and gave her a warm hug. She was almost his mom, too. "Calvin's hurt bad, but we think he's going to come out okay. I ain't prayed much lately, but I made up for it tonight. Me and God got this understanding now," she was crying and held his hands tight in hers.

"Come in, honey. Grandma wants to hear. Sissy's here, too," she pulled him into the house and he got more hugs from the other two. They sat here, lower lips visibly quivering, as he told them parts of what happened. He left out the stupid doctor at the ER. "He's still in surgery and I think you should be there when he wakes up," Johnny said to Momma. "I'll take you."

~ * ~

"Jamal, he talk to the big guy, Harold, yeah now I remember, Harold, that's his name. He talk to him on the phone sometimes, too. He don't think I hear, like I'm all asleep after he, you know, do the thing so good with me. He think he wore me all out an' he all the man. So he tell the dude, 'The skinny A-rab this or the crazy A-rab that.' They is two of them A-rabs, Skinny and Crazy. I don' know they names."

"Last Saturday, a week ago. Not last night, a week ago. Do you remember anything about that night?" Don asked.

"That before he give me the car. He suppose to take me to the big ship down on the Penn's Landing for some special dinner. I remember. Gonna dress all up an' go fancy. Big old sailing ship parked on the river downtown. Real 'spensive. Jamal he don' even call, just don' come for me. Sittin' there with a real nice dress he bought me. Real heels, you know, them 'fuck me' pumps. Says I got nice ankles, loves my skinny ankles. Well, finally he come in like one in the morning. All worked up. Pulls out his gun, that old Army gun he got, and he starts to clean the thing. See, but I'm real pissed by now 'cause he lef' me sittin' in the house when he 'posed to take me to the boat for dinner and he get all fussed at me 'cause I axt him why he do me that way. Start pointin' the army gun at me and shoutin' how he do me right there I don' shut up. Crazy motherfucker cocked the gun and shove me down on the bed and put the thing right in my mouth and yell at me how he done a old man and a old woman tonight and how it ain't no thing to him he do me, I don' shut the fuck up right now. He don' like no bitchin'. Real touchy 'bout that. Gotta be real careful what 'cha say to him, he real touchy, he is. Now, my momma, she don't know nothin' 'bout none a this here stuff, you see?"

~ * ~

When the cash was put on the desk there wasn't any problem. Afif said to the lady at the hospital in Phillipsburg that he wanted the name to be Mary Jones. "No one was to know her real name. Mary Jones, got it?" His father rode with her in the ambulance and Afif picked up his sister and met them at the hospital.

Afif told his father, "There's a hotel three blocks over. Get us a room there. I'm staying here with her for tonight. I'll need the car in the morning."

~ * ~

Ozzie got there just before Johnny and Calvin's mom came in and the whole group waited. The pay phone rang and one of the uniform troopers got it. "Hi, Don. Yeah, he's out of surgery. We're waiting for the doctor to come out. Here's the corporal," he handed the phone to Sam. Don repeated the important parts of the statement Jamal's girlfriend gave.

"Stay with her. We want to put her on ice until we grab this guy. We're going to need her for the trial. I'll have one of the uniforms bring Ozzie in to get Johnny's car and he'll pick you and the women up. Let them get some clothes and stuff and take them out to one of the hotels on City Line near the barracks. We'll treat them to a short vacation. Good work. You know, BPR is going to be in to see you, you okay with the shootings?" Sam asked. "I can make you disappear for a while if I need to."

"No, they're both good, I can't hit what I'm shooting at is the only problem. Gonna start carrying a sawed off shotgun," Don joked. "Listen, I smoothed things over with the sergeant down here, they're going to get a warrant punched for the Ag Assault on Calvin and when they get Yancey locked up we can put a hold on him for the murders. Less complicated that way."

Sam turned to Ozzie, "Once you get them settled in, go to the barracks and set up in Don's office. We're gonna run this out of there. Get an arrest warrant started on Jerome and call Jefferson Township, see if they want to get one started, too. The ballistics lab is going to rush this one, not like last time. We should have an answer by tomorrow sometime." Ozzie took Johnny's keys and left.

"Johnny, give the Philly detectives the pay phone locations we think Yancey might be using. I'll get the lieutenant to assign a couple of teams from the crime room at Belmont to work with them. Maybe we can find something useful for the dickhead crime sergeant to do," Sam said.

Calvin's mom was with him in the recovery room and watched his eyes open and focus on her. "Are you dead, too, Momma?" he asked. "I saw it, the light and the clouds. It felt real good. Then I remember a pink angel. I told her to get the bullet out. Now you're here."

"No, baby. We're all alive, thank God, honey. We're all alive."

The Last Day

Sam fell asleep on the carpet. Johnny went outside and smoked with the guard. The night slowly moved along, cold and wet. Sam dreamed about flying. When he was all wound up about something, he dreamt about flying. It didn't help. He was in control when he really flew. These dreams were like the ones kids have about not knowing the combination on their school locker, or showing up at a party with no clothes on. Out of control dreams.

Sam was in the 1-26 toying with cloud base in a boomer of a thermal. Up and up, strong solid lift pushing him up into the misty fog. He punched out and flew ahead. The ground was a mass of rocks and mountains. Even from altitude, Sam could see that landing out was impossible. But the thermals were so good. He felt he could go forever. One tiny field, miles ahead. Too far? He checked his altitude and watched the airspeed. If he held it just right, figured it out, even if he got no other lift, he could make the field. If he didn't, he would crash into the mountains. He flew on, knowing he would feel the glider bump and pull him into a thermal and take him back up. Nothing. He kept going lower. The field seemed to be just as far away. He couldn't make the sailplane fly closer to it and he kept going down. Got to be a good thermal here, look at that cloud, got to be here. Where's the field? Rocks getting closer. Can't make this mistake, can't do dumb things like this. Misjudge the sink rate and miss the safe field. The rocks coming up to the glider. How could this happen...

"Sam, wake up. I got some coffee for you. Sam...," Johnny shook him slightly. "Calvin wants to see you, he's awake."

The lieutenant was gone and only two uniformed troopers were in the waiting area. Sam didn't recognize them and then realized that the shift changed at midnight. "Give me a minute," he said to Johnny and went into the men's room to wash up and rinse the carpet dust out of his mouth.

He looked awful. The mirror didn't tell him any lies. The bruise on his cheek was darkening and the cuts were crusted over and swollen. Hot water to wash everything out and then cold to wake himself up. It was getting light outside. He thought about Molly. She would be fine as long as the temperature stayed up. Ozzie fed her last night and Sam expected to be home today, at least to get fresh clothes and come back. He rinsed his mouth with the hottest water he could stand and rubbed his teeth with his finger. Time to start on the second guy. *Who the heck is it?* Yancey might never tell them. *Got to get Yancey or the driver, Harold. Squeeze the second shooter, the 9mm, out of them.*

"Sam, you okay in there?" Johnny stuck his head in and saw Sam staring into the mirror. "Ozzie called, he's got Don and Frank Dugan over at Belmont hashing out the affidavit on Yancey. Be ready to fax up to the DA in less than an hour. Just waiting for the ballistics. Ozzie says it's still pretty circumstantial. He's leaving some of the more, shall we say, speculative parts out. Fill them in by trial he hopes. BPR's gonna want a statement from me, too. Gotta go over this morning sometime. I just love those guys."

"Stick to the incident, don't go into the investigation. They don't need to know the whole thing. They give you any trouble, ask for a break and get me," Sam knew some of the BPR investigators. Most were okay, some were real pricks. He didn't want them slopping up his case.

Calvin was smiling at Momma's joke. He couldn't laugh, it hurt too much, but he could sure smile. Sam waved at Calvin through the door and held up a finger to let Calvin know he would be just a minute. He found the nurse in charge and made sure she understood to take the uniformed troopers to the room with Calvin when he came out of recovery. The television crews would be letting everyone know about last night with the morning news and Sam figured Yancey might be upset that an eyewitness to his mayhem was still alive.

"You sure have unusual methods of evidence collection, Calvin," Sam said and leaned over the bed. "Supposed to use a water filled barrel to retrieve the bullets, not you. Had us very worried last night. Doc says you won't be dancing in the clubs for a while, but you're going to be fine."

"Johnny did the job last night. Saved me from the other side. I tried to go, but it wasn't my time. I had to come back to catch them. Couldn't leave without finishing the case," Calvin had to slow down and breathe. Only one lung was working right. "Any word on Yancey?"

"No, not yet. He'll turn up. Don got a piece of him last night. We got some leads on Yancey's running partners, a big guy named Harold and two Arabs, no names on them yet. We figure one of them is probably the inspection mechanic. Maybe he's the second gun, too."

"Yeah, need a break on the second gun. We got Yancey's now. Guarantee it," Calvin smiled and closed his eyes.

"They gave him something for the pain," Momma said. "He'll sleep now. I'm going to call home and let them know."

Sam sat with the sleeping Calvin for a while in the quiet room. He was out of things to do and didn't know where to look next. Philadelphia was a big city and Yancey could be anyplace, even dead. He needed something to keep him awake and focused.

"Sam, call Mrs. Tuttle at the Valley. Ozzie called and said she was looking for you," Johnny said. "Ozzie says the lab confirmed the slug from Calvin is a match with the Porter and Jefferson Township shootings. Pieces of the puzzle fitting together, Sam."

Sam held Calvin's hand for a few seconds longer and then walked out to the phone. "Hi, Mrs. Tuttle, it's Sam."

"I tried your cell, but got no answer so I called down to Belmont and got Ozzie. How's Calvin?" she asked.

"Out of serious danger. He's got a long way to go. We're optimistic, cautiously optimistic. Why did you need me?" Sam asked.

"You have someone here asking to see you, says you were looking for him. His name is...I can't pronounce it…A...Afif, I think," she just gave him what he needed to focus on.

"Ahh, thanks Mrs. Tuttle. Who's in the station now?" Sam snapped his fingers down the hall for Johnny and waved him over.

"Well, the sergeant's here and Corporal Dickson just drove out and signed on. Pretty quiet," she answered.

"Ok, call Brad back in and put him on the phone, I'll hold on," Sam requested. He turned to Johnny. "Call Ozzie. Tell him to get ready to go with me to the Valley with the warrant to get it signed. If it's back from HQ, get the chopper warmed up, we're going first class," Johnny nodded okay and went to the nurse's station to make the local call.

"Sam, he's here. Didn't make it down the hill, hold on," Mrs. Tuttle handed the phone to Corporal Brad Dickson.

"Hi, Sam. How's Calvin?" Brad asked.

"Out of immediate danger and awake. His mom's here with him. Look, see the guy out in the lobby?" said Sam.

Brad leaned around to see the chairs by the drink machine. A dark young man in cheap clothes was sitting with his hands in his lap. "Yeah, there's a guy looks Iranian or something sitting out there, what's up?"

"Don't let him outta your sight. That's the guy did all the paper on the stolen cars from the Porter murders. I can't say he's the second shooter, but the possibility exists. He came in asking for me, so that's a good sign as long as he doesn't have a bomb or a 9 millimeter on him. Mind escorting him to the squad room and entertaining him until I get there? I'm grabbing a ride in H-1 as soon as I can get to Belmont from the hospital."

"Shit, Sam. You owe me big for this. Only me and 'Oh, Jesus' on station. He's gonna have a heart attack," Brad protested.

"Don't tell him. Get the kid some coffee and a newspaper and correct some reports, I'm on my way," Sam hung up and grabbed Johnny. "Watch the fort here. Make sure the uniforms know the drill on protecting Calvin. I'm going to the Valley." Sam was in the elevator and gone.

~ * ~

Four Percocet, and a big glass of vodka got him through the night. Now his foot was throbbing again. She cleaned it and woke him up. Jamal knew if he took the pills he wouldn't be able to move anywhere real quick. Oh, hell. His foot hurt too much. He took two more and another glass of the fiery drink. He would deal with his next move later.

~ * ~

"You are Mr. Deland?" Afif asked Brad.

"No, but he's on his way here. Come on in and sit down. You can wait for him in the squad room. Would you like some coffee?" Brad closely looked him over. No bulges or clothing out of place. This kid was too thin to hide much of anything on him without it showing.

"Oh, yes. Thank you. I would really like one, with sugar, please?" Afif replied in his soft voice.

Brad put him all the way to the back where he could see him from the patrol office. "He should be here in just about a half hour. Make yourself comfortable. There's some magazines there, help yourself," Brad slid the coffee in front of him and retreated to his office.

Afif was so nervous he thought he would jump out of his skin. The officer was very polite and that eased his tension a bit. He sipped on the hot, sweet coffee and tried to get interested in the boating magazine. The pictures of the beautiful sailboats made him think of the time he saw the Mediterranean Sea and the fleet of small sailboats racing just offshore. They bobbed and pivoted around red buoys, frantic to pass each other and charge ahead. That was a very good day in a short life that hadn't seen many. He prayed this Deland would listen to him and try to help before they took him to prison.

~ * ~

Sam saw Ozzie huddled against the cold just outside the circumference of the whirling helicopter blades. He put Don's wagon in the visitor's lot and waved to Ozzie to get in the chopper and he'd be right there. Sam tramped up the steps and dropped Don's keys off with the desk trooper. He wanted to talk to Don for a minute, but wanted to get to the Valley more. He ran back down the steps and across the grass to the pad. Ozzie held the door open for him and Sam jumped up into the right seat. He knew the pilot. One of the best the state had. Sam put on the headset and greeted him over the intercom. "Thanks for the run to Headquarters last night. I hear the minimums were pretty close."

Sam heard the tinny reply, "We squeaked through. Busted out the hood a couple of times. Made a turtle out of the trooper who took the ride with me. Looks good for the flight north. Still cloudy, but the base is rising. Should clear by later today." The Jet Ranger spooled up, shuddered to full power and they were airborne. In forty minutes they were descending to the grass next to Straus Valley station.

Ozzie was out and into the back door headed for the locker room. Afif nearly jumped out of his seat when the big man burst in. Sam followed a moment later and the pilot was right behind.

"Hi, I'm Sam Deland," Sam shook Afif's hand and looked him straight in the eyes. "Let's go back to my office and sit down, this way," Afif followed the poor man who looked like he had been in a bad accident.

"My father told me you were at the shop asking about me. I know why you were there. It is hard for me to say these things to you, but I will tell you everything you want to know. But you must help my family. You must not let the things I have done stop you from helping my mother and sister. I can only do so much for them and I have come to that place and time," Afif took a deep breath and began before Sam could even ask any questions.

"My cousin Yusef is a crazy man. He hurts people and I believe he killed those two old people in Porter..."

Ozzie didn't see the thin little man in Sam's office when he came out of the head. The pilot was talking to Brad and the sergeant had his door closed. "I need one of the marked units, Brad. All the others are down in Philly. Going over to the Magistrate in Porter to get the warrant on the McFadden murder."

"Take four, it's just back from the garage," Brad tossed Ozzie the keys and Ozzie left through the back door just a little slower than he came in.

"Yes, I can show you the places I have seen them. I only know of the project and the empty warehouses. Jamal never came into the auction with me. Yusef lives not too far from the project, but I never knew any phone numbers for any of them. They dropped me off and picked me up. They wouldn't let me go anywhere," Afif explained.

Sam listened for a while, then Afif agreed to tape record a statement. Sam went back over it with Afif and believed the kid only did the wrench work and wasn't involved in the murders. Afif's identification of Yusef as the second shooter, at least circumstantially, set the next step in motion. It was just pieces of Yusef's and Jamal's conversations about the McFaddens, but it was enough to start with. Sam wanted Jamal and Yusef in a tighter noose.

Sam spoke toward the tape recorder, "You've told me that the guns were hidden under false floors in the stolen cars that you disguised with the wrecked cars identities. Do you know where the cars and guns went?"

"Jamal, Yusef and Harold would bring the guns to whichever warehouse we were using and leave them for me to hide in the cars. Ricky, he drives the tow truck, he said once to me that they go to boats at Camden and to Puerto Rico. I don't know what happens to them there," Afif said.

"We'll give the Allentown Police a copy of your statement about your mother and what Yusef did to her. She has assured you she will cooperate and testify against him in court?" Sam asked.

"Yes, she will. She knows he has to be stopped. He would hurt my sister, too, if he had the chance. He has a bad feeling about all women," Afif was both angry at Yusef and sad for him.

"Do you think Yusef and Jamal would talk to you if you went to see them, asked to get back to work with them?" Sam asked.

"Yusef would do what Jamal tells him and Jamal wants me to come back. He wants the cars. He needs them. He needs me. My work on the cars and my signature are worth a lot to him. He will be angry and punish me, but he will use me again. If I can find him." Afif was determined.

~ * ~

The shrill tone of his phone woke him. The foot was hot and pounding. He struggled to move and not disturb his leg. It was Harold. Where had he been? He wouldn't talk to Harold and simply let the call end. "Come in here!" he shouted at the door.

"Yeah, what?" the big woman stuck her head in the door.

"Go out to the phone and call Harold. Tell him to pick me up in an hour. Get me some more of that pain stuff, too," Jamal's day wasn't starting off well at all.

~ * ~

"Mrs. Tuttle, can you transcribe this for me in between calls?" Sam handed her the cassette he just copied. "When it's done, fax a copy over to the captain at Allentown Detectives. He'll be expecting it." The warrant for Yusef on the assault of Afif's mother would be based on her statement to the detectives now on their way over to Phillipsburg to talk to her. Afif's story might add something to that.

323

~ * ~

"Don't know if they Philly cops, but they cops. Big shiny car with two white men in it. They watchin' the phone boof," she told Jamal. "I went to the other one and they a car there, too. These was Philly cops in a detective car."

"What did you tell Harold?" Jamal asked.

"Don't come yet, let me talk to Jamal," she said.

"You need to borrow the lady's car from the next building. Give me one of them sleepin bags. You gonna take me outta here right now," Jamal ordered.

~ * ~

Sam got Afif another cup of coffee and got on the phone to Frank Dugan, "He's the kid that did all the cars for them. His cousin, Yusef Naji, carries an Uzi around in a black gym bag and likes to shoot people and beat up women. Jamal's partner. Looks like Skinny and Crazy to me. My nutty idea gonna fly with the Philly DA?"

"I don't know, Sam. Wiring up a bad guy is risky. You got a good feeling about this kid?" Frank asked.

"Yeah, he's not going anywhere. My biggest worry is we'll get his ass kicking on tape instead of Jamal admitting he jaywalked. Kid thinks they'll act real pissed, but won't rough him up. It's worth a try. Any admission we get tops off the physical evidence. At least he'll bring Jamal out of hiding. We can snatch Yusef on Allentown's warrant to hold him and if he's carrying the gun...well, we should be so lucky," Sam told Frank.

"Ok, we'll get an ADA out here to do the consent and find a judge to sign the order. You want to ride him by the address first?" Frank asked.

"Yeah, stuff him in a surveillance van and take a run down to South Philly before we do the court order. Another busy day. We're leaving as

324

soon as Ozzie gets back with Yancey's warrant. Our girl will put it in NCIC while we're on our way down," Sam was writing his to do list so he wouldn't forget anything. That reminded him. "Did you get cars on the pay phones?"

"They're all covered. Got a team on each one in South Philly and a team roaming by the shooting scene. Don't figure he'll be back to West Philly, Don scared him off. No, he's holed up down there somewhere in that project, I'll bet," Frank said.

"Ok, Frank. See you shortly," Sam hung up and checked on Afif.

~ * ~

The troopers covering the pay phone closest to the project didn't pay any attention to the beat up Dodge with the fat woman driving alone as it passed by, heading toward Passyunk Avenue.

~ * ~

She couldn't believe it. The flowers kept coming. A few little baskets from the troopers and their wives and then came the big sprays. The nurse saw that the cards were signed by women. And the phone calls. They wanted to speak to Calvin and didn't understand why he couldn't come to the phone. Eight so far.

~ * ~

By the time Sam was done with Afif's story, copying the tape and the phone calls, Ozzie was back. "Mrs. Tuttle, I hate to keep dumping on you, but could you enter this into NCIC. This is the warrant for the guy who killed the people in Porter and shot Calvin," Sam told her.

"My pleasure. I hope you catch him quick," she took the desk copy of the warrant and brought up the screen.

Sam went back to the squad room where Ozzie was talking with Afif, filling in the parts Ozzie didn't even know about yet. Sam said to them, "We'll add all this in later. We have to get down to Philadelphia now. Afif, my new friend, ever been on a helicopter?

"Might as well warm it up, we're ready to go," Sam told the pilot. "I have to make one more call."

Ozzie took Afif out to his father's car to get Afif's backpack. It would be useful later on. Sam retreated to his office and called Eileen.

"Good morning, have you saved any other helpless men today?" Sam asked.

"More like hopeless, don't you mean to say?" she replied. "Dutch didn't like the young cop that brought me home. I think he was expecting you or Ken for another round of dog spit ball. How's the trooper that got wounded? The Radnor cops told me that the hospital made a mistake about him dying."

"Calvin's gonna be okay. He'll be down for a long time, but he's out of danger. We could have used Dutch last night," Sam said.

"Speak for yourself, I did okay," she laughed. "How's your head today?"

"Filled with thoughts of the dinner we missed. Make it up to you tomorrow night?" Sam hoped for a yes.

"Okay, we can cruise the bars for fights, get your other ear to match. Pick me up at 7:00," she said. Sam heard the helicopter start to run up and told Eileen he had to go.

~ * ~

Jamal slipped out of the car and crossed the weed covered, cracked concrete lot to the loading dock. The building was once a milk plant and had several bays for trucks to back up to and unload. The plant had been closed for years and allowed to age terribly. He limped up the crumbling steps and found the loose plywood where he could get inside. The equipment and fixtures were sold and stripped out, leaving a large, open space supported by thick, brick covered steel columns. The east end of the building was partitioned off into eight offices, four on each side divided by a hallway. Jamal found one of the rooms fairly dry and no wind was coming through. He wrapped himself in the heavy sleeping bag he took from the house and settled to the floor to wait for dark. Then he could move again.

~ * ~

Sam had the request for the consensual interception written in longhand by the time they landed at the Belmont barracks in Philadelphia. All he needed was the address of the project house he would send Afif into with the transmitter. Ozzie stayed with Afif while Sam went up to Don's office to check in.

The room was buzzing. The small office was really a converted dorm room. A few years ago, troopers were given rooms to sleep in during the week. Each room had space for two wire framed twin beds, two sinks and closets. Now it served as office space for two troopers working crime or from special units like Don. Frank, Don, a detective from Major Crimes and one of the crime room troopers were all working the phones and computers. Frank's Philly radio was snapping out reports from the radio room and the units on the street. Don had a state police portable going, too.

"Got another job for you, Don. Can you get the typing started on the consent and the request for the court order? I roughed it out and I'll radio back the address as soon as we get it. Frank, do we want to wire him up here or at South Detectives?"

"That's a better idea. The ADA can get there by the time you're done running Skinny around and we can round up the troops from there. Here's the keys for the van. It's the dark blue one out back." Frank handed Sam the keys.

Frank got back on the phone and Don pulled up the forms on his computer. Sam escaped the office and went to find Ozzie and the newly dubbed Skinny. Now if they can just get Crazy to come out to play.

"I got the van, let's go," Sam told Ozzie and Afif. Sam remembered the combination to the punch lock to open the door from the front lobby to the stairs that lead to the back parking lot. The van was tucked in behind the big garage so that it couldn't be seen from either Belmont Avenue or Monument Road. The barracks sat in the V of the two intersecting streets and was, some thought appropriately, across the street from a psychiatric hospital and on the other side, a golf course.

Sam and Afif got in the back behind a curtain and Ozzie drove. The mid-afternoon traffic was light and it took less than half an hour to make their way to the Passyunk Avenue exit of the expressway. Ozzie slowed as they turned into the project and Afif gave directions over his shoulder. The shabby building had a hand painted number on the front and the little makeshift bench was still there. No one was stirring on the streets at all. The sun was peeking through skidding clouds, but it was windy and cold. "That's it. I'm sure," said Afif.

"See if there's a view of the back, Ozzie," Sam said. Ozzie found a spot that gave an angled picture of the back door and the dirt strip between the buildings. Sam didn't like the set up. "We're gonna stand out like a shiny penny. We can monitor the transmitter from just outside the project, but can't get an eyeball on the house."

Ozzie pulled through and turned around for another pass. "What about putting a car up on the expressway. Put the hood up like it's broken down. Keep the other cars out on 25th Street and use the expressway as an observation post."

"That'll do it, Ozzie. Good idea. Let's go look at the other spots. Lead on, Afif," Sam called Don on the radio and gave him the street and number for the paperwork. Don told Sam they would all meet him at South Detectives. The ADA would be there any time now. Sam settled back into one of the captain's chairs in the back while Afif gave Ozzie directions to turn right on Passyunk and go over the bridge.

Ozzie made the turn and spotted the bakery he and Johnny stopped in last week. So did Afif. In unison they said, "They have good rolls in there." Sam smiled and shook his head.

They passed the auto junk yards and parts stores. Cars were parked everywhere. Lot after lot filled with cars of all kinds and with the highest density of thieves per square mile in the tri-state area. Afif pointed out a small road leading back in behind the lots. The road was paved once, but was now mostly dirt. "I think two of the places are back here. It was usually dark when we came," Afif said hesitantly.

Ozzie managed to hit every pot hole large enough to rock the van and bounce them all around. They passed pieces of junk cars, some obviously stripped and left to rust. High weeds on both sides of the road didn't conceal the thousands of pieces of trash and car parts on the ground. The first building was a series of one story garages boarded up and covered with graffiti. The garages were almost fifty feet deep and through holes in the doors and walls, some could be seen to be filled with trash and car parts. "Yes, that is one of the places. We did some there, but Jamal did not like it because it was too close to the road. The milk plant is just around the curve," Afif pointed ahead.

Jamal was fast asleep. The pills were building their effect on him and just two more knocked him out. He never stirred when the dark blue van turned around at the end of the big parking lot and went back out onto Passyunk.

Afif pointed out two more buildings farther down toward the airport and then they drove back north to the police station where South Detectives was housed.

The desk man eyed them suspiciously. "Yeah, you can wait out here. Nobody from the DA's Office is here yet," he gruffly told Sam. Sam decided not to pick a fight. He sat Afif down and tried not to look pissed.

"They'll be here shortly," Sam told Afif. He noticed a man wrapped in a blanket sitting at one of the guest chairs at a detective's desk just behind where the desk man sat. He looked like he was naked under the blanket. Another detective was sitting at a computer terminal tapping his foot anxiously. Finally he slammed his fist onto the top of the monitor and said, "Piece of shit! Hey, Charlie you got the book so I can find the freakin' sector number for the parking area in Cobbs Creek Park below Pine Street?" Sam's ears were injured, but he heard that and walked over to the counter to ask an obvious question.

"That the guy who's car was stolen by Jerome Yancey?" Sam asked flatly. Both detectives looked at him and then at each other. "He have any idea where Yancey might be now?" Sam nodded his head toward the naked man.

The detective sitting at the computer asked, "Just who are you, pal?"

Sam grinned, "Why, don't you know? I'm from the government and I'm here to help you."

Afif interrupted, "Corporal Deland, why is Yusef's picture up on the board there?" Afif pointed to the wanted bulletins and a composite picture of a dark featured young man with collar length hair.

Sam turned back to the detectives, "Looks like your clearance rate just went up," Sam pointed to the Wanted for Rape poster. "I'll take that one, too."

Frank Dugan came through the door, followed by Don and the other detectives and troopers. The small lobby filled with the noise of the men talking and portable radios rudely interrupting. Afif looked lost in the crowd. Ozzie made it a point to stand next to him and tell him who everyone was.

The lieutenant was one of the nicest men Sam had ever met. Just something about him made it easy to like him. Joe Calderone was tanned from his recent trip to Myrtle Beach and his shiny bald head glistened in the overhead lights. "We've got a room in the back we cleaned out for you folks to set up in. The ADA is on the way and the tech guys from the Narcotics Unit are ready to help get your source wired up. Come on back and get comfortable," Lt. Calderone wore a crisp white shirt and sharply creased olive slacks. He pulled a small ring of keys from his pants pocket and opened the door to a room fifteen feet by fifteen feet with two tables and several folding chairs. "This is normally our meeting room for the community groups. The captain likes to bring them into the office for visits. Helps them get to know us a little better," he smiled a gleaming, perfect toothed smile.

Sam looked the room over and said, "Your help is really appreciated. We're going to clear up a lot of business today if we get lucky."

"Well, from what I understand, one of your men damn near died from these creeps. Anything we can do to help is not enough. Make yourselves at home, and good hunting." Lt. Calderone shook everyone's hand and went down the hall to his office.

"The DA's here," said Don. Sam guided Afif into the room and motioned for everyone else to leave. The young woman in a navy blue suit and carrying a briefcase introduced herself as Assistant District Attorney Ann Hoffman and closed the door behind her.

"Sam Deland and this is Afif Ahmed. Afif is here to help us catch Jerome Yancey, also known as Jamal and Yusef Naji, Afif's cousin. Naji and Yancey are suspects in three murders outside the city, numerous car thefts and the operation of a stolen U.S. military weapons ring. Nice fellows.

We'd like to put a transmitter on Afif, with his consent, and have him go back to the house in the project where he stayed, until late last week, while he participated in the stolen car and gun operation." She was listening closely.

Sam gave her the verbal version of his affidavit, "When Afif became the victim of Yancey's physical assaults and became suspicious of the possibility that Yancey and Naji murdered people, he left and tried to get to his home in Allentown. He saw a newspaper there and recognized the name of Patrick McFadden, another partner of Yancey and Naji in the stolen car and stolen automatic weapons and anti-tank rockets conspiracy. Patrick and his wife Ginny were murdered last Saturday in Lehigh County. One of the guns used was the same gun used by Yancey to shoot Trooper Calvin Livingston last night in West Philly. That gun was also used in the murder of a young man in Lancaster County a few days before. I have a lot more, but that covers the high points. Afif turned himself in to me this morning and has agreed to try to engage Yancey, Naji or others in conversation that will be of an evidentiary nature concerning these specific crimes and other crimes that these people may have committed or are planning to commit," Sam took a breath. "Yancey is known, by Afif and through our investigation, to frequent the house in the project and the area surrounding it. A car Yancey stole at gunpoint last night while fleeing from the shooting of Trooper Livingston, was found less than ten blocks from the house today. I have prepared a request for the intercept and a court order to be signed by a judge authorizing the intercept in a residence. Once you obtain Afif's formal consent and authorize the intercept, I'll go to the judge at the Criminal Justice Center and have the order signed."

She stood there for a bit digesting the information and said, "Let me see the affidavit and the order." Sam handed her the documents. Among them was her formal consent inquiry of Afif. She looked them over and began asking Afif a series of questions designed to insure he was actually allowing the taping of his conversations voluntarily. "You understand the state police and the Philadelphia Police Department and the District Attorney's Office are making you no promises for your cooperation?"

"Yes, I have asked for none. I will do this because it is the right thing to do. What happens after is in God's hands," he quietly said.

"Corporal, the U.S. Attorney and the FBI are going to have jurisdiction on the military thefts. They may not appreciate Mr. Ahmed's cooperation as much as the state does. Mr. Ahmed, do you understand you may also face federal charges for your involvement in these matters?" she asked Afif.

"It does not matter. I will take whatever punishment is necessary, I still wish to help you. I will not change my mind," Afif told them.

"We've been working with a chief warrant officer from Army CID. He's been briefed on the latest we have through the police in Lancaster County where the third murder took place. He can deal with our federal brothers," Sam told her.

She finished her questioning of Afif and signed the forms. She was there less than twenty minutes.

Sam turned Afif over to Don and Frank to get him wired by the narcs. Ozzie took the keys for the black Crown Vic from Don and he and Sam hustled out the door to see the judge.

Afif sat and listened to the young narcotics detective explain how the transmitter worked, "I'll strap it to the small of your back and run the microphone up over your shoulder under your shirt. It's only about the size of a deck of cards," he showed the small rectangular device to Afif. "Even if they pat you down they would have to reach all the way around you to find it. If that happens, don't panic, just announce that they found it and to come on in and we will. No secret codes to remember. Say what you have to, to get them to talk about the killings. Don't worry about the cars and guns. It's more important to get them to admit they did the murders. Put yourself in their position. What would someone say to you that would get you to talk about it. The most important thing is to let them talk. Don't interrupt and don't talk over them. It's too hard to make out all the voices on the tape. Call them by name if you can. Don't make it sound obvious. And try to be calm. Speak normally, don't shout or sound like you're reading something. Any questions?"

"You don't have to worry. I will get what we need," Afif said confidently. The detective tested the equipment and began hooking Afif up.

Ozzie flew up Broad Street catching most of the lights green. At City Hall, he swung wide to the right and parked where several police cars were just across the street from the Criminal Justice Building. "Stay with the car so it doesn't get towed, I shouldn't be too long," Sam said to Ozzie.

Sam made his way past the line waiting at the metal detectors by badging the sheriff's deputy and found an elevator ready to go up.

The judge was a personal friend of Frank Dugan's. No one was supposed to know that. He cleared his afternoon to accommodate the urgent request from his old friend. Sam found him funny and charming. The whole process only took eight minutes.

Afif bent over and tested the lightweight strap holding the transmitter. The antenna was taped inside cocktail straws and ran up his spine over his t-shirt. He kept his long sleeved shirt off until it was time to go. The narc had to put in the battery at the last minute to insure it lasted. Once the battery was in, the transmitter was on.

Ozzie kept looking at the pizza and sandwich shops as they wove in and out of traffic. "What's the matter, Ozzie, hungry?" asked Sam.

"I can't believe I've only had a doughnut, well, two and coffee today," grumbled Ozzie.

"This won't take long. If Yancey's there and Yusef won't or can't come, it'll be over quick. We'll have steak to celebrate while Jerome cools in the holding cell," assured Sam.

Frank organized the cover teams. He put an older detective in the car that would appear broken down on the expressway. He had a good set of binoculars and a fresh battery in his radio. The younger, faster men were in the chase cars at either end of the project. Plainclothes troopers partnered with the Philly detectives and two marked units with two uniformed officers, each were to be a block farther away to stop any vehicles leaving. A wagon, which is a marked police van, was standing by with one of the marked cars to go in for prisoners. Frank and Don would be in the surveillance van to tape the transmissions and relay them to Sam and the others. Sam and Ozzie were the roam car. They went where they were needed.

Everyone turned when Sam and Ozzie came into the room. Frank took a copy of the paperwork for the van and gave a quick, final briefing to everyone. "Last piss call, drop 'em and drain 'em, boys," Frank told them. Everyone did.

Sam spoke quietly with Afif for a few minutes. He tried to give him confidence and told him he would be just fine. "Don't even think about the transmitter. Try to remember everything that's said. Don't rely on the tape. We'll be real close if you need us."

The narc put the fresh battery in the transmitter and read a brief statement onto the tape recorder running in the van, giving the date, time, his name and asking Afif if this was being done with his consent. "Yes, it is," answered Afif. Afif slipped his worn backpack over his shoulders and walked out the door and up the street. The cover teams moved into place and watched him as he turned into the project.

Don parked the van at the end of the street the house was on, among several other cars and trucks. The older detective pulled to the side of the road on the busy expressway and got out to raise the hood. He put on his flashers and sat back in the car watching Afif walk up to the front door.

He didn't knock. Like when he stayed there before, he just walked in. The children looked at him and went back to their super hero show on the television. Two of the women were on the couch and the big woman was in the kitchen. She said, "You go on vacation? Jamal been lookin' fo you."

"I had family business. I'm back now," said Afif. He went through the living room and into the bedroom where he'd slept before and sat on the bed.

She followed him in, "You got them real mad. But they got work fo you. Somethin' 'bout the auction."

"Well, I'm back if they want me to work, I'll need a ride," Afif tried to sound as normal as he could. She left and went back to the kitchen. She was allowed to use the phone in the house to call Yusef. It didn't go to Yusef anyway, but to his neighbor who would put him on the phone.

When the call came in, the neighbor was sitting with Yusef on the steps in front of his house watching the ever changing show of people around the markets. He answered on his cordless phone. "Yeah, he's sitting right here. It's for you," the neighbor handed the phone to Yusef.

"Oh, he is? Good, keep him there. I don't care, bake him a fucking pie, just keep him there. I'm getting Harold to pick me up and we'll come over. Where's...ahh, never mind. I'm on my way," Yusef cut the call and dialed another number. "My cousin's back. At the women's house. Pick me up, we'll go talk to him. I don't know where Jamal is, I thought he was with you."

Frank could hear Afif rustling what sounded like a magazine. When the woman told Afif she was making him something to eat, Frank figured one of the bad guys was on the way. Jerome didn't seem to be there right now. Everyone settled in and watched the cars coming into the project.

"Damn, he's not there," Sam said after Frank gave a quick update over the radio. Ozzie's stomach rumbled.

"Red Ford, four door turning onto your street," one of the chase cars reported.

"Going by, not stopping," the expressway lookout filled in.

It went that way for the next half hour or forty minutes. Frank heard the television, the kids and Afif's magazine. Afif whispered into the tiny microphone taped to his shoulder, "Jamal's not here, but I think they called him," when he was sure no one was around him.

"Blue Ford van turning, black male driver, white male passenger," the chase car reported.

Sam picked up the Philly portable he was carrying and said, "Heads up, everyone, this sounds like the van from last night."

"Stopping in front, white male carrying a black bag and a black male entering the house," the expressway car reported.

"Fuckin' Yusef, with the Uzi, I'll bet," said Ozzie.

Frank heard over Afif's transmitter, "You little fucking rat!" then the sound of a struggle and groans. He was almost ready to call in the cavalry when it all went quiet.

Afif heard Yusef coming through the living room screaming at him. Yusef dropped his bag and grabbed Afif by the hair and threw him onto the floor. He jumped down on top of him and pounded his fists into Afif's head and sides. He hit hard and Afif thought briefly about calling for the police to come in and help. Just as quickly, Yusef stopped and hauled Afif back up onto the bed. Yusef slapped Afif sharply across the face and spit into his eyes.

"So, little cousin. You got the message I left with your mother. You have come back to us. You little coward. I told Jamal you would be back without me dragging you. Did she tell you how much she enjoyed my company? How she cried for me to stop? How she begged me not to hurt her anymore? She is an old fool and you are a young one."

"The police were going to arrest my father. She had to go to the hospital," Afif ducked as Yusef hit him again.

"Bitch, fucking old bitch. What did she tell them? What?" Yusef choked Afif and demanded an answer.

"That she fell. The police did not believe her and thought my father did it," Afif spit blood and tried to wipe his mouth. "She did not tell them it was you that hurt her so badly."

"If she ever does, I'll go back and finish the job, and your filthy whore sister, too. I only let her live to tell you, you little shit," Yusef laughed.

"He's been shot," Harold said through the open door. "Jamal been shot, last night by the po-lice up to Nancy's. Woman says he at the milk plant waitin' for dark. I have to pick him up there. Gonna go to South Carolina. Got an aunt or somethin' down there."

Yusef stood staring at Harold, "Shot? How bad?" Yusef asked.

"In the foot, but it's infectin' on him. Gotta get him to a doc down there, fix it up," Harold said. "Says you two 'sposed to get Ricky and do some cars at the auction. Send the money down. They's some of the guns in the attic up there. They pay me the money once they on the boat. Be dark pretty soon, gonna get somethin' to eat."

"What do you want to do, Sam?" asked Frank.

Sam was standing next to the van listening on a small earphone through the window. "He's got to stay in there and get something on the murders. They're all going to be waiting around, he'll get them to talk. I'll take Ozzie and one of the uniform cars over to start a perimeter of the milk plant. Once we get set up we'll call in the Stake Out Unit and grab Jerome.

Sam and Ozzie drove to the marked unit at the south end of the project and told them to follow. They drove quickly down Passyunk and Sam tried to get the helicopter into the air to help watch the building. "Too close to the airport, Corporal," the pilot said over the radio from Belmont. "I can orbit where they tell me, but can't maneuver freely that close to the landing patterns."

"Get airborne and do what you can. Once they set you up, let me know where you are," Sam told him.

Ozzie drove the Crown Vic into the small road and slowed at the curve. Sam motioned for him to stop there. "He can see us coming in. Let's get closer on foot and try for a blind spot," the uniformed officers weren't thrilled about clomping through the mud and trash to circle around to the back, but did what Sam asked them to do. Sam tucked the two portable radios into his back pockets and led Ozzie into the tall weeds.

"Too late today to go to the auction, but we can go up tomorrow and look at the cars for the Thursday one. Pick out some good ones," Yusef said.

"The dude will call me later to let me know what he got to offer. Steal anything we want if he don't have it," Harold said between bites of turkey sandwich.

Afif took a chance, "Are you getting SUVs and vans again?"

Yusef just looked at him.

"I mean the last time there was still space to put more of the rifles and rockets in. The vans have a cargo area under the mat, too," Afif looked down at the table.

"We still waitin' on some more of that stuff from the Army Spanish dude. Kinda reorganizin' that end of it. We send what's here," Harold said.

"Little greaser better come through. Jamal will be pissed after he made the deal. Dude should be dead. Jamal could'a whacked him right there in the car," Yusef was getting warmed up now.

"Why, is there a problem? I thought Jamal had a steady supply of the military stuff?" it was reaching, but Afif thought it was still okay.

Yusef was feeling the edges of the power now with Jamal on the run. Someone had to make all this happen. It was between him and Harold; Yusef flexed his strength. "Fuck, that went dead with old Patrick. Cheatin' old prick try to get off on Jamal. Playin' to those Latin dudes tryin' to wring more out of us. We ended that," Yusef said. "Old man talked down to us. He thought he was better than us. That bitch wife, yellin' and wouldn't shut up. She chattered the whole time about what wasn't any of her business. Old Patrick just stood there and watched her jump and jiggle. He didn't even try to get his own gun out. Didn't believe what he was seeing. Made her jiggle," Yusef looked pleased with the thought.

"What did Jamal do then?" asked Afif.

Yusef thought a moment. "Well, I guess the talk was over by then. It didn't matter once they wouldn't come off their stupid rip off price. They had to die. Set a bad example of how to do business if we didn't. Jamal was so cool, bam, bam, bam. His .45 came out so smooth and he put it away almost before old Patrick hit the floor. Real smooth," Yusef stared off again.

The light was beginning to change to that shade of yellow just before sunset. It cast a golden tone over the brown grasses whipping at their coats and pants. Sam tried to keep some cover as they approached the ruined building. They had the sun behind them and found a small ditch running to the corner of the south wall. It provided some disguise and they eased up to the brick and stopped to look and listen. The loading dock had six big doors. All were spray painted in hideous patterns and multi colors. Plywood covered holes and what used to be windows. The side of the building had several windows that were boarded on the first floor, but were just broken glass on the second. Sam figured the uniformed officers were at the rear now and he looked for the best place to set up to watch the exterior.

"Gun!" Sam and Ozzie heard the officer shout from behind the building. Pop! Pop! Poom! Poom! Poom! *Jeez, gunshots.*

Sam followed Ozzie down the side of the building. Both were holding their Glocks in both hands out in front ready to defend themselves.

Poom! The heavy sound had to be the .45 Jamal carried. Someone was in real trouble. Sam didn't think about the radio, he needed to get to the officers, fast.

Ozzie got to the end of the wall and dropped down close to the ground. He looked back up at Sam and then took a quick peek around the corner. He pulled back and turned to Sam and shook his head, no. Ozzie moved up to a kneeling position and took another look. Still nothing. Ozzie looked at Sam who shrugged and they both stepped out and sprinted, guns in front, toward where the shots came from.

"That's it, I'm calling it. Everyone move in, set up in your assigned positions." The signal for Afif was that Frank would knock on the door three then two. Afif was to come and open the door and step out quickly. Open door, come on in. Simple and quick. It worked. When the knock came, Afif got up and before anyone could say or do anything, the room was filled with policemen and guns. Yusef's bag was still in the bedroom. He screamed like a child when Don Mitchell grabbed him out of the kitchen chair and dropped him to the ground. Harold put up his hands and didn't resist at all. He'd been through this before. The women tried to cause a verbal disturbance, but shut up quickly once they were in handcuffs.

Sam heard the "in custody" report on the Philly portable. At least something is going right. Sam pulled the portable and keyed the transmit button.

The shuffling feet were just silencing when Dugan's radio sounded. "We need help at the milk plant. Gunshots," it was Sam.

Poom! Sam dropped the radio and put both hands back on the Glock. Pop! Pop! Pop! That had to be one of the Philly 9 millimeters. They were still fifteen feet away from the steps up to the indentation in the wall where the shots were coming from. One more sprint and they stumbled into the sweat stained back of one of the officers. He was shaking so bad his gun was wobbling in circles as he pointed into the door opening.

"We're here. Where's your partner?" Sam demanded. He got no answer. Ozzie eased past and pushed the officer's gun back and held on to his hands.

"Easy, take it easy. Where's the other officer?" Poom! Ozzie ducked and pieces of brick splattered all three of them.

"Hostage," the officer croaked. "The Black guy got Teddy. Took him inside."

"Back off, I'll kill this blue motherfucker!" it was Yancey.

"Owwww!" that was the cop, thought Sam.

"He's gonna die, get the fuck outta here!" Yancey screamed.

"Help me!"

"We saw something and I guess we got too close," the sweating officer told Ozzie.

"Ohhhh!"

"Shit he's gonna kill him, Sam," Ozzie said and moved inside.

"Ozzie, no!" Sam said too late. Poom! Tinkle, tinkle. Sam could hear the shell casing bouncing off the floor inside.

He took one breath and followed Ozzie. Inside the door was a landing that then turned hard right into a hallway with doors on either side. Offices. Ozzie was in the hall crouched next to the first door. "Bad odds, Ozzie. We should wait for the cavalry," whispered Sam. Ozzie shook his head, no.

"Give it up, Yancey. No way out, don't be stupid, throw out the gun and let the officer go!" shouted Sam. Sam motioned to Ozzie that he was crossing to the other side. They had to clear each room. "Look, I know you need a doctor for your foot. Don't make this...," Poom! The wall above Ozzie's head exploded into dust. They both hit the floor.

Sam thought a minute and figured he probably wasn't in the room closest to them. He would have put something between him and them. *Most likely one of the last rooms and on the left.* The angle for the shot over Ozzie's head made that figure. *But which one?* Sam began to slowly crawl down to the first door on the left and Ozzie matched him on the right. They got to the door frames and did a silent three count and cleared both rooms at once. So far the theory held.

Don left the prisoners with Frank and the others and scrambled for the van. Frank was on the Philly radio trying to get the idiot in the radio room to shut up so Frank could broadcast the location of the assist. The dispatcher didn't have the slightest idea where the milk plant was. He never heard of it. Finally the 1st District sergeant on the air stepped in and started directing his radio cars in that direction. Cars from the 12th District also were responding.

Sam and Ozzie were now down to the last four rooms on either side. Sam knew they had to be slow and quiet to pull this off. The officer could already be dead. Yancey certainly didn't hesitate to kill people. They had to end this quickly. Sam put his finger to his lips to urge Ozzie to be silent. Sam froze.

He signaled Ozzie just across from him and pointed at Ozzie's cell phone. Ozzie got the hint and reached to silence it. Sam signaled, no and pointed to the rooms. He pulled his cell phone from his jacket pocket and mimicked as if he was dialing. He then mimicked that he could hear something. Ozzie gave him a big grin. While Sam pocketed his phone and covered Ozzie, Ozzie quickly called Dugan and whispered, "Call Yancey's cell," Frank looked puzzled, but caught on quickly and grabbed Harold and spun him around.

"Phone!" Dugan yelped. Harold couldn't stop before he tilted his head down to his right. Dugan grabbed Harold's pocket and felt for the cell phone. He plucked it from Harold's pocket and punched the 'contacts' icon. Dugan quickly scrolled down to "Jamal" and dialed.

It took less than 15 seconds for the signal to be transmitted and reach Yancey. Sam and Ozzie were up in crouched positions and heard the sharp tone from the last room on the left. They moved at the first sound, Ozzie going low and Sam high. They hit the door and when they swung to the opening. Sam was just in front of Ozzie and entered first. He saw the officer on the ground and Yancey desperately pawing at his hip to silence the loud little box. The blood stain under the cop was spreading out from his side, but his eyes instantly told Sam he was alive and desperate. Sam pushed the .45 out in front and saw Yancey glance back up toward him and raise the Colt in his direction. Sam pulled at his trigger and kept pulling. He felt the blast from Ozzie's gun beside him and the room echoed with the final sounds of the journey Jerome had taken them all on. Sam heard the tinkle again. His and Ozzie's shell casings bouncing off the hard floor as Yancey slumped and dropped his gun. Sam and Ozzie didn't move. The officer rolled onto his side and away from Jerome's body.

Ozzie stepped forward and kicked the gun away from Yancey's hand and across the floor. Sam put his gun away and knelt by the wounded officer as Ozzie flipped Jerome over on his stomach, wrenched his arms behind him and put on handcuffs. Ozzie looked over to Sam and nodded. It was over.

Sam didn't know what he was feeling. He was so scared just a moment ago and now felt safe again. Tired, worn out. The chase to stop what was now the lifeless form of Jerome Yancey pinned underneath Ozzie was indeed over. Sirens and the whump whump of a helicopter could be heard coming closer. Sam suddenly thought of his dream, the rocks coming up at him, no place to land. He knew that Jerome was the one who landed in those rocks. Misjudged his descent. Didn't figure the sink rate right at all.

About the Author

After writing professional documents for many years, Mike has finally devoted time to his true passion, writing fiction where the story and characters come alive in the reader's mind. While his days were filled with authoring hundreds of detailed crime reports, arrest affidavits, search warrants and grand jury presentments, he took some of his own time and devoured books by the dozens. Reading not only was a rewarding diversion, it provided him with the added education he needed to function at a high level in his profession. Mike writes with the real life experience that many years of law enforcement shaped and influenced. The stories may be fiction but are based on how things happen in the real world. His books are honest and captivating novels written with a unique voice that will both chill and charm. Mike is a veteran police detective. He did it all from rookie patrolman to Senior Special Agent. His life has been enriched by a wonderful marriage, parenting, work, flying, sailing and good books. Mike is a lifelong outdoorsman, an experienced tactical firearms instructor, champion sailplane pilot and the captain of his own sailboat. All of these skills have made his novels vivid, exciting and real. Now retired after a career with three law enforcement agencies, Mike enjoys winters writing in Naples, Florida and summers sailing, writing and researching the next novel at his rural Pennsylvania home.

Visit Mike at his website to catch up on the latest about his books: mikefullerauthor.com

Coming March 2016
by
Mike Fuller

Rope Break
Sam Deland Crime Novel Book Two

He's worried about being due in Federal Court tomorrow and trying to enjoy his day off when it turns ugly once again. Corporal Sam Deland is drawn into another mystery double murder in his usually quiet suburban community and Sam's team of state police investigators have to dig deep into the gang and drug underground to find the shooters. The Oz, Calvin and Johnny are as different as could be but these tough, smart state troopers meld together their talents to work through the twisting trail of leads on this bloody case with Sam. But just as Sam sees the mystery starting to come together he is slammed in the face with his own family tragedy when Sam's 18 year old son and his son's beautiful Cuban-American girlfriend turn up missing and in danger over a thousand miles away.

Chapter One

Any moment now, coming in from the right on an angle, the sound of wings dragging on the ground grew a little clearer and louder. Still no movement in that direction, but he was there; they knew it. Sam willed his eyes to move ever so slowly in that direction and then let his head swivel a bit to center up his vision on the hemlock cluster at the edge of the field. He emptied his hands of the slate and striker and kept them still. To his left he could hear the rustle of his partner's clothing and knew Ken was rising up for a sight picture.

"Putt, putt," almost a whisper, Sam used the mouth call to bring the gobbler out to them.

"Gobble, gobble, gobble!" the roar of the close in bird startled Sam and he jumped just a bit.

The small trees and low bushes were just sprouting a tad of green and the air was still cold and crisp this first week of May. At this altitude, the morning chill wouldn't leave the woods until later on. Even with the now rising bright spring sun, Sam had to control his breathing to keep the steam of his breath from giving away their position. Just past the evergreens the first bit of blue head peeked around and was followed by the black and brown feathers of the tom. His tail was fanned wide and he scraped his down turned wings in the leaves and grass, stirring them with hollow scratching noises. The gobbler stepped deliberately out in to the meadow, tilting his head side to side, seeking the location of the hen that had been calling him to her for the last forty minutes. His cautious approach had been slow and the wait required all the patience these two humans could muster. Two more steps and the sun broke through a space in his spread tail and glistened off his back.

Click clack. The bird startled at the sound and looked right at Sam. Click clack, click clack, click clack. With that series of sounds, the gobbler exploded into movement, noise and feathers launching the fat bird into the air and away from the threat. Click clack, click clack, click clack, click clack. Grass and dirt flew up into the air to mark the spot of the shot.

"Absolutely beautiful!" Ken shouted and stumbled to his feet from the tree trunk where he had been sitting just in front, and to the left of, Sam. Ken reached over and gave his father a slap on the shoulder. He pulled down his camouflaged face mask and grinned a big toothy smile. "Gonna be great pictures. The sunbeam came right through his tail in that little space. Wow!"

"So what's the verdict?" Sam nodded at the camera Ken was holding in his gloved hands. "The extra noise of the SLR worth it?"

"Oh yeah," Ken said, turning the Nikon digital over in his hand. "No question. I never could have gotten the shots of his scramble without it. I'm going to have to get used to all the manual features. I did him on auto. Felt more comfortable with that."

Sam got up and stretched. He put the slate call in his pocket and pulled out a plastic bottle for a long swig of sport drink. They had been sitting still trying to coax the turkey up out of the little valley and Sam was cramped from the cold air.

"Here, finish this off." Sam handed the bottle to his eighteen year old and only son. Sam looked out over the field at the beautiful sight of the valley. Woodlots of gray, brown and black spattered with light green sprouts, scattered evergreens and plowed fields spread out in a panorama showing that spring was beginning to take a hold on the middle part of Penn's Woods.

"You ready to buy me breakfast, Dad?" Ken asked. "This is going to be the day. I can see the start of a few cloud streets already," he pointed out to the southeast and Sam could feel the breeze come into his back from the opposite direction. "Might be the only meal I get until tonight at the Airport Diner."

"Let's go then, genius." Sam gathered up his seat cushion from the ground and untied the blaze orange streamer from the tree trunk above his head. Ken slipped his new Nikon camera inside of his camo jacket and together they started back through the woods to the logging trail that brought them up the mountain from the parking area at the edge of Black Moshannon State Forest.

Sam followed behind Ken and watched him glide through the woods. Sam knew that if he stopped for just a minute he would lose sight of Ken and his son made so little noise that even hearing him in the leaves and underbrush would be impossible. They picked their way down and crossed several small streams bringing the spring waters down from the tops of the hills toward Bald Eagle Creek. In twenty minutes they hit the dirt jeep trail and made their way out to where Sam's Pathfinder was parked.

"Thanks again for the camera, Dad. It's a great graduation present. I won't get to use it a lot this summer, but by Christmas things will loosen up a bit and I can get some winter mountain shots," Ken said as they crossed the small field to the edge of the parking area. Ken was reporting for his plebe year at the Air Force Academy in Colorado this summer and knew that new cadets didn't get any free time for photography. "I'll try it out on the palm trees and saltwater birds when I get down to Sarasota. Grace is going to take us out on her sailboat to shoot the shoreline lights over the water."

"What time does her flight get in on Tuesday?" Sam asked.

"It's in the afternoon. I have the numbers written down at home," Ken replied. "Eileen's okay with Grace staying with her?"

"Oh, she can't wait to see her. Eileen has a million questions for Grace. Our ears will be burning all during graduation week," Sam laughed. Ken's long distance romance with flight attendant, Grace Echaverria, was about to be tested with their first face to face meeting since New Year's. The black haired twenty two year old beauty was finally getting a break in her schedule and was flying into Philadelphia to attend Ken's graduation at Varnum Military Academy out on the Main Line on Wednesday. Sam arranged for her to stay with Sam's most recent lady friend, Eileen Matthews. The men had plenty of room at their house, but Sam thought it was a better idea to keep some distance, especially at night, between the youngsters.

The meeting last fall of these two had sprouted a telephone and online courtship that somehow lasted over the long winter. This in spite of their age difference, her new job and his final semester of preparation to go to Colorado Springs. The couple managed a brief visit in Miami over the New Year's holiday and since had planned her visit to Pennsylvania and Ken's trip back with her to meet Grace's mom in Sarasota for a few days before Grace had to go back to work at the airline. Grace was still a rookie and didn't get much say about her own schedule. A few of her fellow stews swapped days and flights to give her the several days off she needed to string together so she could be with Ken.

At the sound of an approaching vehicle, both Sam and Ken looked up and saw a black pick-up truck come around the curve and skid into the parking lot stopping next to Sam's burgundy Pathfinder.

"Heck of a hurry," Sam muttered. They took the last few yards up the bank and as they stepped into the lot, a small, fair haired man wearing a denim jacket over a flannel shirt and jeans jumped out of the black pick-up and walked quickly over to them.

"Game Commission. Hold it right there," the man ordered. Both Sam and Ken stopped, looked at each other and then back to the other man. "Doin' a little Sunday huntin' are ya'? Let me see your licenses right now." He held out his hand waiting for them to comply.

Sam smiled and shook his head. "Who put you up to this? Did Jack Conner set this up; very funny." Their host for the weekend was old, but he was notorious for pulling a leg here and there. "Old Jack thinks he's real funny."

"I said the licenses," the man pulled his hand back and slid his jacket aside to show Sam and Ken the .357 Smith and Wesson revolver he had in a holster on his right side.

Sam said, "Whoa, friend. You need to show me some ID. No need for any guns here," Sam held his hands up to show he was unarmed. Ken stood beside his dad and tried to figure if this guy was for real or not.

The man went into his jacket pocket and came out with a black leather case which he opened and showed Sam a badge and identity card that said he was a Deputy Wildlife Conservation Officer. Sam recognized the credentials as genuine.

"Deputy...Souder," Sam said, picking up the name from the ID card. Sam and Ken stood stunned for a moment then first Sam then Ken complied and got out their hunting licenses. Ken kept his eyes on the bulge at the deputy's belt and handed his to Sam. Sam handed the two licenses to the deputy.

"Look, Souder. We're not shooting any birds, just out with a camera taking pictures," Sam said. Ken held up his graduation present to show the officer.

"Yeah, right. Give me your car keys and stay here. I'm going to search your vehicle and check the woods over there for your shotguns and any poached turkeys you've taken," Souder held out his hand again for the keys.

Sam thought a minute and said, "No, I don't think that you're going to do any of that. We haven't been hunting with anything but a camera. Far as I know, that's still legal here in Pennsylvania, even on a Sunday. You have no probable cause to search anything. You can look in the woods all you want, you're not going to find anything."

"Now listen here, pal! You shut the fuck up and give me those keys. Else I'll smash a window if I have to and haul you two off to the magistrate for resisting!" the deputy shouted and turned into a defensive stance.

Sam replied in a calm voice, "You don't get it do you? You're out of line here. I don't think you want to pick this fight. I think you'd better cool down and try to listen to what I'm telling you."

The deputy looked at Sam and then at Ken deciding if he was going to take the next step. "You going to give me those keys?" he asked, a little less loud this time.

Sam slowly reached into his hip pocket and came out with his own black leather case and handed it to the deputy. "My ID, deputy. Take a look. We can go as far with this as you want. Right down to Elmerton Avenue in Harrisburg if need be. My son and I are not going to be pushed around by some rabbit cop." State Police Headquarters was just down the road from the Game Commission's.

After he opened the case Sam handed him, the deputy said. "Shit. Look, you know I'm just trying to do my job..." Souder didn't get to finish.

"Your job? It's Sunday, deputy. You're not even on duty now are you?" Sam flashed a little anger.

"Well, I, I..." Souder stuttered.

Sam snatched back the case from the man's hand and pulled out a business card. He handed the card to Souder and took back the hunting licenses. "You find anything in the woods, come look me up down in Lehigh County at the Straus Valley State Police Barracks."

The deputy said, "I'm sorry, Corporal Deland. We work with the state police all the time. I didn't mean anything by this. I saw the truck parked here and assumed it might be poachers..."

"Then you know you should have called in and had a full time game protector come out or you should have called the state police to handle this. Off duty and out of uniform is the wrong time to start acting like some cowboy out here. If we had been poachers, you'd have been outnumbered and outgunned. Think about it. You don't get paid enough for that," Sam lectured. "Any further business here or can I take my son to breakfast now? He's mighty hungry."

The deputy just shook his head, walked back to his truck and left.

"Man, I thought he was going to go nuts on us," Ken said, almost out of breath.

"Part time volunteer cop wanna be's. Thought he would roust us and buff up his ego. Makes me sick. These deputies have a bad enough reputation. The few really good ones have to suffer for all the jokers like him. Come on, I'm not letting Barney Fife spoil the day," Sam tossed the keys to Ken. "Drive us to Mabel's, genius." In twenty minutes they were laughing and drinking hot chocolate at the small family restaurant next to the gliderport on Route 220.

~ * ~

The room smelled like stale cigarettes and cat piss. His arm was around her shoulder and her hair was frizzled and dirty. She didn't move in the bed when he rolled over to sit up and let his head settle down. He was pretty sure her name was Kathy or Kate or something that started with a K or a C. It was hard to remember. Two big black flies waddled one after the other on the torn screen at the bedroom window and buzzed as they flew up and over him to the other window on the opposite side of the small, desperately dirty and cluttered room.

Toby needed to piss and get another hit of crank going to start the day. He fumbled at his dirty jeans on the floor at the side of the bed and found the bag in the side pocket. He held it up and cringed at the small amount of the crystal that remained inside. "Fuckin' greedy bitch," he muttered and reached behind him and slugged the sleeping girl hard between the shoulder blades.

"Get up, you cunt. Get out! Steal my shit!" She winced, but didn't move fast enough. Toby dropped his jeans and got up on his knees over her. His penis flapped back and forth between his bare legs as he hit the girl four or five more times in the back. She screamed and tried to shuttle off the side of the bed away from him. He went after her and grabbed her hair from behind.

"No, stop. That hurts, you maniac!" she screamed and swung on him, scratching at his face. When she missed, he kicked her between her legs and she went to the floor. He kicked her again in the face and heard bone crunch.

"Fuckin' cunt! How much did you take last night? Didn't leave me shit. Get out!" He threw clothes at her as she scrambled to her feet and ran naked out of the room and then out the front door of the trailer.

Toby was breathing hard and had to lean against the door frame to stop the room from spinning. He staggered back over to the bed, retrieved the bag and took it into the bathroom to shoot up. The girl was in the front yard trying to put on her shorts and called back toward the trailer, "Okay, Toby. I'm sorry. I'll call you later, sweetie." He couldn't answer, he had a shoelace in his mouth trying to shut off the blood flow to his left arm to produce a visible vein.

~ * ~

If you were some distance away, the two would sound an awful lot alike. In the hills and valleys around State College, the drumming of the male ruffed grouse's wings against a log to attract his mate and the thud, thud, thud of the John Deere tractor moving down the grass taxi strip of the gliderport were very similar. Jack Conner sat on his prize 1940s tricycle tractor, slowly pulling the Schweizer 2-33 two seat glider from the tie down area to the end of the runway near the small office. His almost ninety year old eyes scanned the sky and he smiled a wrinkled grin at the whiffs of white cumulus beginning to take shape out of the northwest. If this kept up, the ridge would be working and boomer thermals would be popping before noon.

Jack lied about his age to join the army air corps in 1942 and then survived the hedgerows of Normandy in 1944 and earned a Purple Heart and a Silver Star for the heavy fighting he took part in after safely landing his glider full of infantry in a flooded field. A real tough kid who had to grow up quickly. He returned home after the war and had a few different jobs that paid the bills so he could teach the subtle art of flying sailplanes to several generations of eager students.

Forty five years ago, he bought the land and carved out his small airport to take advantage of the almost solid ridge that ran from near Williamsport to the northeast all the way southwest into Tennessee. Flights of several hundred miles in a glider were possible from his little airstrip if the wind hit the ridge at the proper angle and forced an updraft of air over the mountain that could keep a sailplane riding the crest. He moved past the line of power planes and gliders resting at their straps and waved at the father and son getting their small sailplane ready for the day's flight.

Sam watched his old friend on the green tractor pull the trainer past and wrung the wetness out of the cloth he was using to wipe the wings of his and Ken's shiny 1-26.

"That tractor sounds like it's still new," Ken said to his dad. Ken was bent over in the cockpit slipping in a fresh battery for the aircraft radio. The bubble canopy sat on a mat on the ground next to Ken and glistened as the rising sun reflected off the clean Plexiglas.

"I put in an extra bottle of water and a couple packs of cheese crackers to hold me over." Ken at eighteen, was an experienced pilot. He'd been flying, actually hands on, with his dad since he was six. His last year at General Varnum Military Academy had been in the preparatory program for the Air Force Academy and he had been flying twice a week, weather permitting, at school and every chance he got with his dad on weekends and holidays.

"These cloud streets line up the way I think they're going to, you'll be sitting in the Airport Diner in about five hours after takeoff. Or, I could be digging you out of a field somewhere in the mountains. What do you think, hot shot?" Sam smiled at his son. They had been looking for this weather set up since mid-April. Each spring they brought their single seat glider from its fall and winter quarters on the ridge to the farm field surrounded airport at Kutztown, one hundred and twenty air miles to the southeast.

"I think we launch in an hour, hour and a half. I want the thermals cooking good for the first half of the trip," Ken said. Landable fields were few and scattered in the mountainous area southeast of Jack's airport. Ken needed lots of uprising air in the thermals generated by the sun warming the ground to give him distance and options. Once released from the tow plane, he would have to find and circle in the rising columns of air to regain the altitude he would lose when flying straight ahead.

"Go on in and call Flight Service again for the latest weather, Ken. I'll finish up and pre-flight the Citabria," Sam said. The day before, Ken had earned enough 'credit' with Jack by flying tow plane to finish paying for most of the hanger fees for the 1-26. Sam added to that by flying backseat in the 2-33, giving rides and instruction to Jack's customers and today would fly the Citabria tow plane up until he had to leave to follow underneath Ken with the Pathfinder and trailer.

If Ken didn't make it all the way to Kutztown and had to land in a pasture somewhere, Sam would be close by to help take the wings off the glider and put it on the trailer for the rest of the trip. The 1-26 was ready to go and Sam slipped the canopy back on its hinge and stowed the cleaning gear in the bag behind the seat. One last visual of the cockpit assured Sam that Ken had everything he needed for the flight. All Ken needed to do before launch was release the ropes holding the wings to the ground and pull the ship to the starting line.

Sam walked past several other privately owned sailplanes in the tie down area and made his way to the end of the line where Jack kept the little tail dragger used for towing. The two seat Citabria was a climber and did an excellent job pulling the gliders up to two thousand feet above the ground where they would release and either catch the ridge lift, a thermal, or make their way back to the field and enter the landing pattern. There was no tower at this field and both glider and power pilots used the glider frequency at 123.3 megacycles on the aircraft band to announce their takeoff and landing intentions.

Sam found the routine of the pre-flight to be reassuring. Since his Naval R.O.T.C. training at Villanova and navy aircraft carrier qualifications and flight operations, he had learned a lot about pilots and airplanes. He was patient and paid attention to all the little things that kept him and the aircraft safe. Pre-flight was how he made sure everything that could be done to make the flight routine, was taken care of.

Other owners and glider crews were arriving and setting up for the day. Jack didn't fly by himself anymore and depended on Sam and a few other good friends and customers to help him around the place. There was always a fresh supply of eager glider nuts from Penn State University up the mountain that would work to earn tow fees and rental time. In the busiest times of spring and fall when the cold fronts brought strong northwesterly winds and cooked the ridge into a glider highway, Jack would break down and actually pay a tow pilot and back seat glider instructor to fly the trainer and sell rides and lessons. Broke his heart, though.

It had always been tough to earn a living running a small airport. Anything that had the word 'aircraft' in it just plain cost more and was harder to find. Insurance and taxes bit in to the rest. Jack didn't grumble too much anymore, though. His partner for the last ten years was only in her early sixties and still made his eyes glitter. He hooked up with her at some resort he got talked in to going to on a rare vacation and she moved in two years later. She had a heart of gold, loved Jack, and could keep a set of books well enough to fend off the IRS and the County Tax Collector.

June Bea was known to everyone as just Bea. She was from Baton Rouge, Louisiana and retired from nursing. Jack parked the 2-33 and wheeled the John Deere around back of the wooden office building. Bea stepped out onto the covered porch and plopped down on one of the eight big rocking chairs overlooking the grass runways. She sipped on a cup of apple cinnamon tea and counted six glider owners and crews prepping to run the ridge. She could see Sam under the cowl of the Citabria checking the oil and inspecting the engine.

The first student for the 2-33 was due any time now and one of her regular instructors was just pulling into the parking lot. Sam and Ken were part of her family here. She knew all the names of the customers' kids and grandkids and most of their dogs, too.

"Gonna miss me, Bea?" she heard the young voice say just behind her. "I won't get back here until next year." She turned to see Ken standing next to her.

"Oh, my yes, Kenny. Your dad better not be a stranger, though. When will you take the 1-26 out to Colorado?" Bea asked.

"Not until my second year, if then. No way a plebe can get off campus for personal flying for the first year. Dad says we'll put oxygen in it and fly the wave. I'm gonna miss it around here. Once I graduate, they'll ship me all over." Ken knelt down next to Bea and put his arm around her. "You and Jack have been real special to Dad and me. I want you both to know how grateful I am for all that you've taught me." He kissed her on her tanned cheek.

"Hey, two timer. Sneakin' 'round with the young bucks again," Jack caught them as he stepped up onto the porch from the side steps, wiping tractor grease from his well weathered hands. "Only gonna' be left with this old fart when the young one here runs off to college on ya."

She turned to him and said, "He's not the only one I got runnin'. Whole college full of them up the hill. You just be thankful I can still bat my eyes and bring them in. You old crust." They all laughed and Jack plopped down beside her in the next rocker.

Sam clipped the cowl closed and began his walk around the tow plane. He watched the young glider instructor walk up to the office from the parking lot and knew he would be towing the first flight of the day within the half hour. Bea had another tow pilot lined up to take Sam's place after he left to chase Ken.

Sam inspected each control surface and the pins holding them in place. Jack kept the Citabria immaculate and in all the tows Sam had run in it, it never even coughed. He reached the rear of the plane and connected the 200 foot tow rope to the release under the tail. The rope was new as of yesterday. Ken had handled the situation without any trouble.

Ken was in the tow plane towing a heavy fiberglass high performance sailplane the owner had weighted down with water in the wing tanks. At about 700 feet above the ground, the glider bumped into a strong thermal and strained the tow rope beyond its capacity. The few seconds that followed the rope break caused much concern among the glider pilot's crew on the ground, but no one got hurt and the surprised pilot followed his training by dropping his nose for a turn into the wind and did a 180 back to the field. It was quite a sight to witness the low level return of the long winged white bird dumping water from its wings and dashing for the end of the runway.

Ken maintained his climb after the rope break and allowed the glider to make the emergency landing before he entered the pattern and touched down. The glider owner refilled his wings with a little less ballast and got back in line for, hopefully, a less exciting tow.

Sam remembered his first rope break. When he returned from the navy to raise Ken after Ken's mother was killed in a wreck on the turnpike, Sam got several civilian ratings, including his glider and later his glider instructor ticket. The last ride with a glider instructor before solo is the test of all the safety training the student has been exposed to. After the tow plane pulls the trainer out over the end of the runway at about 300 feet, the instructor in the back seat pulls the tow rope release to simulate a low altitude rope break. The surprised student is expected to turn quickly back to the airport to land.

Sam was smart enough to realize he would be put to the test and wasn't really surprised when his turn came. It still was a bit of a shock when he felt the pop of the release. The noise triggered his reaction and at the sudden loss of speed, Sam dropped the nose of the trainer and built up his airspeed before turning back toward the runway for the landing. He soloed on the next flight and had built up hundreds of hours since.

When he finished preparing the Citabria, Sam walked over to the office and sat next to Bea. "I can give you about two hours this morning, sweetie. You going to be okay after that?" he asked.

"Yep. Tommy is coming in from Harrisburg. Should be here about the time Ken launches," Bea said. A college age boy and girl walked in from the parking lot and said hello to everyone on the porch. The girl had her blue covered log book in her hand and then walked over to the 2-33 to start her pre-flight with the instructor. "Time to get to work, hot shot. Give her a good thermal, Sam. She's almost ready to solo."

~ * ~

"Okay, I'll be there." Toby ended the call and sat back to feel the speed rip through his system. He reached to his left and opened the drawer in the battered end table next to the couch he was stretched out on. The black revolver lying in the drawer was worn and the silver metal showed through around the cylinder and at the end of the barrel. Toby didn't like the semi-automatics they used on TV. Too many parts to get broken. Too many buttons to remember. The old .38 was his grandfather's and worked every time he needed it to. Besides, it was too old to be registered and could never be traced back to him if he had to dump it. Once he stood up, he stuck the gun into the back of his jeans and pulled his black Harley t-shirt out over it. Between the meth and the gun, he felt like he could take on almost anything. He bounced out the door of the trailer and stumbled down the metal steps, crashing face first to the ground in a cloud of dust. Not a good start for his adventure today.

He was broke again. He had fifteen dollars and change in his pocket and needed gas for his Chevy pick-up. The old truck ate gas and he wouldn't get far, what with prices these days. Well, if everything went as he had brilliantly planned, he would have plenty of money by the end of the day. He brushed the grit from his shirt and pants and climbed into the truck for his ride south.

~ * ~

"Ozzie, would you cook chicken on the grill for us, please?" Marie asked.

"Yeah, Dad. You make the best chicken!" the twins chimed in unison. They crinkled their noses at the thought of saying something at the same time. They couldn't help it, though. No matter how much they tried to be different.

"Please, Daddy, good chicken, yum, yum," chirped little Katie.

Ozzie was really Walter. He didn't let anybody call him Walter, though. Only his beautiful wife, Marie. But she usually called him Ozzie, too. Except when she got mad. Then she used Stanislaus, his middle name. Ozzie came from Ozliewski. Big and blonde and Polish on both sides, mother and father. Marie was dark haired and Italian on both sides. The six kids were a mixture. The new baby, Vinny, came out blonde like his older brother, Walter Junior.

Trooper Ozliewski was off duty and driving his tribe home from nine o'clock mass. During the warm months, their traditional Sunday morning after mass brunch often turned into an early picnic on their deck with Ozzie cooking mass quantities of food on the grill.

"Just so happens old Dad stuck a bunch of wings and legs in a vat of sauce before we left for church. You guys help your mom with the baby and the salads and we'll be eatin' with our fingers afore ya knows it!" Ozzie winked over his shoulder to five year old Katie and she tittered happily at her funny dad.

Marie heard the first grumblings from Vinny's car seat behind her in the van and hoped he stayed quiet until they got home. "I'm going to feed him as soon as we get home. Connie, you and the twins peel some potatoes and make up a tossed salad. Junior, you supervise and get out the things to set the table." Connie was ten now and Junior just turned sixteen. The only thing on his mind, besides girls, was the learner's permit burning a hole in his wallet.

"Hey, Dad. After lunch can we drive over to the shopping center and practice?" Junior pleaded. The twelve year old twin girls laughed together in the back seat as the smell of the baby's diaper reached them.

Connie gagged. She and Junior straddled Vinnie's car seat between them in the van's middle seat. "Ewww! He stinks. Roll down the window Daddy, save me from the fumes."

"I got a better idea, son. I'll let you drive me over the back roads to Sam's to feed Molly. Won't be too much traffic today and you can drive slow. How's that sound?"

"Yep, that'll do, Dad!" Junior hadn't expected that.

Ozzie was real proud of his boy. Starting out to be a good driver and real careful. Ozzie couldn't wait to get the insurance bill, though. Junior would have to work that off helping with Ozzie's remodeling business he ran on the side. "Sam and Ken aren't due back until tonight. We'll let her run a bit and see if we can catch a few minnies in the creek to fish with this afternoon at the lake on the way back." Ozzie worked with Sam Deland at the barracks. They were also good friends and tomorrow they had a very important court date in Philadelphia.

~ * ~

It was hot and sticky. Even at this time of the morning the humidity slung itself across the pastures and hammocks like an invisible fog. Air so thick you felt like you were breathing water. Jimmy needed a bath. Today's sweat was running down his back over last night's dried up crust and he couldn't get the last spark plug out. The socket didn't seem to fit in between all the hoses and wires plastered all around the engine block. "Shitty little cars," muttered Jimmy. The wrench finally took hold and he skinned his knuckles twisting out the old plug.

"Wanna beer?" Russell called from the porch. "Gonna be hot agin' today."

"Fuckin' hot ever' day, big brother. Yeh, gimme 'nother cold one. I'm almost done with 'er," Jimmy called back over his dirty shoulder.

His brother, Russell, stepped back across the bowed and uneven boards that covered the porch of the small wooden house and went inside. Little or no white paint remained on the outer walls and the two windows on the front side had torn screens that didn't do much to keep out the hoards of biting insects that lived in this part of rural Florida.

This was the second house the Santees built on the family plot. The first stood fifty feet to the east and was even more run down. They had let it stand even after they had to get out of it because of the termite damage. They used it for storage now. The "new" house didn't look much better. At least the bugs hadn't eaten out the floor yet.

"Hey, get outta that beer. That's mine!" Momma yelled from her bedroom at the back of the house.

"Shut up, old woman. Me and Jimmy got work to do today. We'll bring you back some more later. Old witch." Russell grabbed two cans out of the refrigerator and walked through the living room and back out to the yard where Jimmy was working on the Mustang.

The only good things about this miserable little bit of palmetto and sand were the three big live oak trees that provided shade to this part of the yard. They spread up and out like ponderous green umbrellas to block out the scorching Florida sun. Jimmy had the car parked out under the shade. It helped a little, but he was still miserable from the bugs and the heat. Russell and Jimmy Santee were both coming off nasty divorces and had moved back in with Momma. Jimmy just recently. Momma bothered them some, so they tried to keep her in beer to shut her up.

Jimmy took the cold can from his brother and drank half of it with the first gulp, "I gotta get outta here. She's drivin' me nuts. Worse'n my ex-old lady."

"She don't mean nothin'. Ya get used to it after a bit. Specially about the third a the month when her check comes." Russell laughed a goofy hee haw like laugh and Jimmy grinned at him. Russell was a little slower than most and even though Jimmy was younger, he looked out after Russell.

Their nearest neighbor was a few hundred yards down the sandy dirt road. Their granddad settled on this piece to farm it years ago and over the years they had to sell off parts just to pay the taxes. Drank up the rest. Didn't do any farming anymore. Just a few half wild chickens. Now they hustled a bit. Sold some grass and whatever they could steal.

Jimmy wasn't satisfied any more. He wanted things. He wanted people to stop looking down at him. But with no education, no real skills and a record, it made it difficult. Lately, they figured a new one. Lots of new construction along the Gulf and it was spreading inland. Half built houses just full of copper pipes and brand new stoves and refrigerators. Most construction companies couldn't afford to hire nighttime security. That made it easy for Russell and Jimmy. All they needed now was a good truck to haul the stuff. Jimmy knew buyers in Fort Myers, Fort Lauderdale and up north in Tampa.

That was today's job. Jimmy was trying to wring some life into Russ's old Ford in case they had to make a fast exit from one of the stops they had to make later.

"Hand me them new plugs there, big brother, and go get me 'nother a them beers."

~ * ~

Ken was on the right wing and Bea was on the left dragging the 1-26 up the line behind a Nimbus and another 1-26. Ken heard the engine of the tow plane wind up and watched his dad pull the 2-33 down the runway. Ken looked up at the building lines of puffy clouds and felt a twinge of excitement inside. Flying cross country in a sailplane is an exercise in skill and faith. The success of the flight depends on the shifting air and the pilot's ability to put the glider in the right place to take advantage of the lift generated by the sun heating the ground.

Today, streets of clouds were being generated by long lines of continuous lift shaped by the northwesterly wind. If Ken could put his 1-26 in the right spot, he could ride the lines of lift under the clouds downwind in generally up rising air. That would let him cover ground at a relatively fast rate without having to stop and circle in any single thermal for too long. Heaven to a glider driver.

The 2-33 towed by Sam in the Citabria was turning downwind over them and would run a bit that way before turning back into the wind and climb to the release point upwind and 2000 feet above the ground. Then, even if the student flying the front seat didn't catch a thermal, she could easily glide back to the airport and enter the landing pattern.

Bea dropped her wing and said, "Okay, Kenny. You're set. I called Margie and Will in Florida. They'll have a 2-33 ready for you on Thursday. Good flight. See you soon I hope."

"Thanks, Bea." Ken couldn't say anything else. He felt a little choked up. He didn't think he could get back up here before he had to report to the Academy later this summer. She walked toward the office, but turned and jogged back to him for a last hug.

"You, you, just do good, Kenny. We'll miss you." Bea squeezed him and turned back to the office. She needed to get busy doing something before she cried all her eye makeup off.

~ * ~

The gas station had only one set of pumps. It had just opened and there was a teenage girl inside behind the counter. Her belly fat surged out over the top of the tight pink jammie bottoms she wore. Her hair had streaks of blue in it and needed a good brushing and her eyes were rimmed in blackness. A small silver ball was stuck in her lower lip.

Toby's Chevy lumbered up to the island and he got out. His problem was, he needed thirty dollars' worth of gas and worse, cigarettes. With only fifteen dollars in his pocket, he was stuck. He fiddled with the pump for a minute and then trudged into the station.

She was playing loud street rap on her little portable CD player stuck up on the shelf behind the register. This far upstate, she probably didn't even know anybody from the big city, but she thought it was cool. She didn't really understand what the guy, yelling against the thumping background noise, was so mad about or even most of what he was saying, she just liked the repeating beat and the sound of it. When Toby came through the door, she looked up at him and turned the stereo down just a bit.

"Damn pump ain't workin' right. I must not be hittin' the right buttons or somethin'. Ya wanna come out and get me started?" he asked.

She shrugged her shoulders and said, "Yeah, you gotta hit the little red button, I'll show you." *Dirty, skinny tough man can't work the friggin pump*, she laughed to herself.

She came out from behind the counter and Toby started to follow her out of the door. She stepped into the lot and he stopped with the open door in his hand, "Oops, forgot my keys on the counter. Be right out," he told her and swung back inside. Before she could suspect anything, he came right back out and followed her to the pump. She couldn't see the four packs of Kools and the two Slim Jims in his pants.

She smirked at him and pushed the little red button. The pump jingled and cleared to all zeros. Toby handed her his last fifteen bucks and started pumping. He thought about stealing gas from her, too, but didn't. At least he had some smokes now.

~ * ~

"You look funny, Daddy. That's Mommy's apron," Katie shook her little stubby finger at her dad. He did look funny. Over six three and two fifty five with a little strawberry covered frilly apron stretched tight around his middle, standing at the grill turning the smoking chicken pieces. Ozzie drained the beer from the bottle and wished he could have another. He could, but he wouldn't. He was the on call trooper and could be yanked out if anything big happened. It usually didn't.

Ozzie worked in the crime room, what most police agencies would call the detective squad. Pennsylvania was a little set in its ways. Ozzie was still a trooper and could be put back into uniform if the bosses ever decided to do that. He didn't think that was a great idea. Straus Valley barracks covered the area west of Allentown out to near Reading. Mostly farm country and a few small towns. The cities were moving west and east, though. Several shopping centers were already built and a new mall was in the works. All that money being spent by hard working decent folks attracted some that weren't quite so decent. Ozzie kept real busy, but if he was lucky, not today. Sunday was his family day.

Ozzie worked hard. Both at the barracks for the state and on his own, too. He and Marie had a few rental properties and Ozzie did kitchens and bathrooms for paying customers. They planned on sending their kids to college. Ozzie never got to finish at Kutztown University. A decent football player, he quit in his junior year to support his wife and new son. He never regretted it. He figured he earned the equivalent of a doctorate in the years he put in on the state police. He wanted better for his kids, though. As long as Junior didn't become a cop or a lawyer, he would be happy.

"Katie, honey. Run get me the squirter, would you? Mom keeps it on the washer." The chicken was dripping and flaring a bit. Marie came out onto the deck with a table cloth and a basket of silverware and napkins.

"How much longer, Oz? The kids'r starving. All except Vincent, he's full and asleep." Ozzie caught her pleasing profile as Marie bent over the table. She still had some pounds to lose after Vinny was born, but Ozzie didn't mind her fullness; she needed to feed the baby. Her walk was up to three miles a day now. Having the older girls to help out freed her up to burn off the calories.

"'Bout ten minutes more. Start rounding up the girls. Junior is out in the garage getting our fishing stuff ready. I'll get him in when it's done," Ozzie said.

Katie appeared with the water bottle and Ozzie saved the meat from burning up. With all the joy surrounding him, he should be happier than he was. He was worried about tomorrow. Most cops don't like going to court any more than they have to. None of them ever figure they would be going as the defendant.

~ * ~

Sam checked back over his shoulder at the big two seater behind him. He was trying to pull to the right with the tow plane just a bit to center up on a bubble that seemed to be a decent thermal. The glider was at the release point and Sam wanted to drop them in the middle of the lift. He felt the sudden release of the tow rope and visually confirmed the glider pulling up and to the right behind him. He chopped the throttle with his left hand and mashed the left rudder with his foot. The stick followed to the left and he dropped into a steep turn back toward the field. Pressure back on the stick and some right rudder and he descended through 1000 feet, leveled his wings and entered the downwind leg of the landing pattern.

"Citabria tow plane downwind, Nittany," Sam reported on the radio to let anyone in the area know he was landing. Sam could see the pilot and the line boy standing at the wings of the white fiberglass sailplane that was next in line. They remained off to the side of the runway so Sam could land before they pulled the long winged bird out to set up for the tow. Ken was next to their 1-26 and a second 1-26 was between Ken and the glass bird.

"Badger, Kestrel. It's jumping, you ready?" Sam called Ken on the radio using their call signs.

Below, Ken watched his dad start his base leg turn and reached into the cockpit of the glider and grabbed the radio microphone, "Roger, Kestrel. I'm more than ready." Ken heard two clicks of the radio and knew his dad was acknowledging the transmission.

Sam turned final and Ken could see the Citabria cock on its side as Sam side slipped the plane down as close to the end of the runway as safely as possible. Putting planes down on a precise spot was something Sam had plenty of training to do. Jets didn't side slip as deftly as the light tow plane, though. Sam greased a three point landing, straightening out just before touchdown. The tow rope dangled behind him and the tow plane slowed rapidly once on the grass strip.

The next glider was pulled out and lined up on the runway and the pilot climbed in. Sam turned left off the runway and taxied back toward Ken and the others. The young kid working the line stepped out as Sam spun across in front of the gleaming white sailplane and retrieved the tow rope. He ran back and hooked the rope to the release under the nose of the glider. Sam slowed and waited until the canopy closed and the pilot nodded to the kid now holding the glider's left wing. Sam looked left and right for any pattern traffic and, as the line boy signaled for him to take up the tow rope slack, pushed the throttle forward and rolled out onto the center of the runway. He took a quick glance at the engine instruments and then looked back at the glider for the rope to tighten and the sailplane's rudder to waggle. Another look above for approaching traffic, just to be sure. Once he got the signal, he moved the throttle full forward and started his takeoff.

Slow at first, he gained speed and felt the drag reduce when the glider cleared the ground. A few more miles per hour and he was up also. He kept the Citabria moving straight down the runway as they gained altitude and as they cleared 900 feet, started a left turn downwind. Sam knew the Nimbus pilot and appreciated his skill at keeping the big sailplane tight in behind the tow plane. Some less skilled pilots yanked and pulled the tail of the tow plane all over. Sam felt several good thermals on the downwind and judged his turn back into the wind trying to reach one as they went through 2000 feet. The Nimbus released and Sam dove back for the field. One more, then it was Ken's turn.

~ * ~

"Shoulda' done the front brakes, too, Russ. Don't jam 'em too hard. We'll take care of 'um soon as we get ahead a bit," Jimmy wiped his face with the dirty rag. "I'm gonna wash up and we'll get on down the road."

Russell didn't get up from the beach chair at the base of the oak. He nodded that he heard his brother and sipped on the warming beer. He was a might slow, but he knew they were going to move on up once they got them a truck. Jimmy had it all figured out. Just slip in to the houses and take what they wanted; sweet deal. He wondered why Jimmy insisted they keep Grandpa's Winchester in the trunk. *Just in case*, Jimmy had said. *Just in case*.

It was even hot in the shade now. The sun was full up and even the bugs wouldn't go out in it. The air conditioning didn't work in the Mustang and Russell knew it would be miserable even with the windows down. The wheel wells were starting to show a little rust here and there. This wasn't one of the real powerful older Mustangs. This one only had a six cylinder and was more like a Pinto. Good thing Florida got rid of its inspection program a few years back. Gave a clunker like Russell's extra life on the road. The brakes were worn out and the muffler was just a shell, but it got from here to there.

Jimmy shot out through the front screen door and crossed the sandy weed covered lawn. He tossed the keys to Russell and went to the passenger door to get in, "We gotta get her some brews, gettin' bitchy in there. Come on, It's almost noon."

Russell unfurled himself from the chair and made his way to the car. Jimmy usually drove, but he was suspended and on probation for driving drunk, again, and didn't want to push the issue in case the motherfucker state trooper that arrested him the last time was sitting between them and the store out on the highway. A cloud of blue smoke sputtered out of the exhaust as Russell fired up the tired six and eased them down the rutted drive to the hard road.

Also Available
At
Rogue Phoenix Press

Skylark
By
Kellie Wallace

Hollywood in 1948. World war two had ended three years ago, but crime is still growing rampant on the streets. Detective Luca Valiant returns home from war a broken man, haunted by memories of his duty. He is strong willed and passionate about his job but keeps his soldier days hidden behind a thick wall. Young women start showing up around the city shot point blank in the chest, found with stolen morphine ampoules on their person. Luca fears it might be a crime ring that ruled Hollywood in the 1930s. With his partner, Duke Williams, by his side, Luca uncovers a world of drug use, money, sex and corruption he never knew existed which truly tests his sanity. When his wife Sally is murdered by Hollywood's crime lord Don Pascoe, Luca must push his demons aside to crack the case before it consumes him.

Chapter One

Hollywood,
Los Angeles
1948

The purple kite frolicked in the air behind Karsten's head as he ran through the grass. The sun's golden rays warmed the nape of his neck and marshmallows clouds danced across the sky.

His new shoes were damp and dirtied from jumping in a puddle, but he didn't care. It was a perfect summer's day; perfect for ice cream by the lake or hiding in an alleyway stuffing his mouth with stolen goods from Mrs. Dane's bakery.

As he leapt through the field, inhaling the rich Hollywood air, something deep inside him dimmed. He wished he could share this wonderful day with someone. During the dying afternoon hours before bed, he would watch the other neighborhood children playing in the street or at the park with their siblings, wanting to be a part of their world, jealous of their kinship.

At eleven years old, he had not seen much of the world, but he knew it must revolve around Fern Rosenberg. He saw her sitting on the swing set across the park, swaying against the gentle breeze. Her head was down, nose in a book.

Ever since her family moved in next door six months ago, he couldn't understand why she never played with the other children, often sitting alone reading a book. He remembered his mother telling his father she and her family were survivors of a horrible camp in Poland. The girl barely survived, fleeing the country with her aunt and uncle to start a better life.

He never had the courage to talk to her, usually succumbing to inaudible mumbles before he walked away embarrassed.

Karsten blew out a breath of self-encouragement and arched his back. He was going to do it today. He walked across the park, his stomach rolling nervously. Fern didn't acknowledge him until his figure cast a shadow across her book. She looked up, her eyes thinning against the glare. "Hello. Can I help you?"

Karsten opened his mouth but no sound came out, his tongue turning to cement. A veil of transparency fell over Fern's eyes; she was losing interest.

"Um, my name is Karsten. I am in your math class at school."

"You sit behind me. Don't you live next door?"

"I do."

"I often see you play by yourself on the street sometimes," Fern said. "Why don't you ask other kids to join you?"

"I don't know how."

"Why?"

"I'm too scared they will say no."

"Surely that doesn't matter. You can ask me now."

Karsten looked at the kite dangling from his fingers, wondering if asking her to play was a bad idea. "You want to fly the kite with me?"

Fern's lips rose into a smile and she laughed. "I should be reading. My uncle will quiz me when I get home, but I would very much like to fly the kite with you."

Karsten watched Fern rise from the swing and gently lay her book on the grass next to her bag. She repositioned the clips in her brown hair and grabbed the kite string from his grasp. Her hands were soft. "The wind is picking up. Are you ready?"

"Yes."

The children bolted across the park, watching the kite bellow in the air. Other neighborhood children joined them, giggling at the sight of it kicking and twisting like a captured bird. Karsten and Fern spent the rest of the afternoon under the warm sun, walking home muddy and exhausted. They decided to cut through a park, crying out in delight at the sight of a mother duck waddling with her ducklings. She saw the children and scuttled away, her babies following in haste.

"Let's follow her!" Karsten cried. "Maybe she has more."

Fern followed him with the kite in her hand, chasing after him through the thick underbrush. "Slow down!"

She saw him disappear deeper into the brush, his heavy footfall breaking through the silence of the early evening. In a blink of an eye he was gone. Fern kept running. She jumped over a log, nearly running into him as he stood still staring at the ground. "Oomph! Karsten, I nearly ran into you." She pulled at his sleeve, noticing his face had gone white. "What is it?"

He pointed a shaky finger to the lush ground, his eyes wide. Fern followed his gaze and noticed white fur, speckled with blood against the twigs and other debris. She took a step closer and let out a scream.

Lying in a leafy tomb, a woman lay dead, her blonde hair messy and dusted with leaves. Her cold blue eyes frozen, her red lips open in an eternal scream.

Chapter Two

Warm blood splashed into Luca's mouth as he threw angry fists into an enemy soldier. His bloodied hands ached and bled, and within a few minutes the man's face was gone.

Someone gripped Luca's shoulder from behind and he instantly stilled. He rose to his feet, straightening his green US Army uniform and stared at the bloodied German soldier lying limp on the street. Around him he felt the stares of his fellow men burn into his back.

Luca shivered in the chill, but it was the shame on his cheeks that warmed his body. He withdrew a handkerchief from his pocket and wiped the blood splatter off his face. The steel knife at his hip winked in the sunlight.

Luca turned his back on the body, suddenly repulsed by its appearance. He heard some shouting in the crowd and saw an enemy soldier break through, a silver pistol drawn. His eyes were wide and menacing, his lips pulled back into a sneer. The gun was aimed at Luca's chest.

"You killed my men," the man snarled. The American soldier had no time to react, watching in slow motion as the German pulled the trigger. Luca watched his chest open up in an explosion of blood and bone.

As he opened his mouth to scream, Luca woke and found himself in bed, wrapped in his bed sheets. He looked to Sally's side and found it was empty. He climbed out of bed, swaying on his feet like a newborn foal.

Luca steadied himself, laying a hand on the nightstand. Once his head stopped spinning, he bent down and opened up the bottom drawer, fishing out a bottle of scotch.

After returning home from war in 1945, he came back a different man. His nights were fraught by nightmares and he feared sleep, frightened of seeing the faces of the men he killed. His police issued Colt revolver hung in its holster over the bed. He joined the police force on a whim when he returned and cemented his spot in the Los Angeles Police department.

But it was his wife Sally who was his saving grace, remaining faithful and loyal to him during his time away. As if she materialized from his thoughts, she appeared in the doorway, dressed in a pink nightgown. She held a mug of tea, ribbons of steam curling around her face. "You're up. I was hoping to get to you before you got out of bed."

He smiled as she entered; admiring how her blonde hair fell loose over her shoulders and her cheeks blushed pink. They married the night before his draft, meeting six months before at a dance. A picture of her hidden within the folds of his uniform kept him alive in France.

Sally walked up to him, her gaze dropping to the bottle of scotch in his hands. A frown settled upon her brow. "Luca, I thought you removed all the alcohol. Where did you get that one?"

"A man has his secrets."

Sally opened up her hand. "Give it to me."

Luca regrettably handed his wife the bottle.

"Now get back into bed," she ordered. "I'll stay with you until you fall asleep."

Luca obeyed, crawling into the warm sheets. She rested a hip against on the edge of the bed and looked down at him, her blue eyes stark against the dim room. "I'm worried about you, Luca. Your nightmares have gotten worse. I wish you would take some time off work and rest. You have been on your feet since getting back from France."

"We have been busy at the precinct, honey," he explained. "You know we cannot afford for me to take time off."

Her lips formed a thin line and she crossed her arms over her chest. "I don't care. I will try and make an appointment for you with Doctor Arnold this week."

Luca opened his mouth to argue but was interrupted by the vibratos call of the telephone in the hallway. Sally looked angry as her eyes fell upon the clock on the wall. "It's eleven pm. Who could that be?"

Luca flew out of bed and ran into hallway, picking up the phone in haste. "Detective Valiant."

Luca couldn't keep his eyes off the dead woman's open mouth. Her ruby stained lips were contorted into a scream. His gaze dropped to the white fur shawl wrapped around her shoulders, stained with blood. She was missing one shoe, the remaining one covered in mud, unhinged off her heel. One gunshot to her chest bled heavily through her midnight blue gown.

"Pretty one, isn't she?"

Luca turned at the sound of the voice, finding his partner Duke Williams beside him in a tan coat and hat. "Two kids found her this afternoon."

He returned his gaze to the dead woman. "Do they know who she is?"

Williams shook his head. "No one knows. I have uniforms canvasing the neighborhood, but I doubt they will find anything. Look at how she is dressed. She's not from around here."

The former soldier dropped to his haunches and withdrew a pencil from his pocket. He pulled back a lock of blonde hair from her face. She was young, her cheeks dusted with rouge she probably stole from her mother's make up.

"She had no purse on her, or identity card," Williams explained. "The coroner will be down here to conduct a thorough examination within the hour."

Luca stole a glance at the white Hollywood land sign above him, the lettering bright against the dark hills. He didn't understand why so many murders were conducted under the sign, as though the killers were trying to be symbolic. He turned away, squinting against the blinking lights of the half a dozen cop cars. Despite the time, there were a large number of spectators craning their necks to see the victim. "Has any evidence been found?" Luca asked. "A shell casing or gun?"

His partner walked up beside him. "I was waiting for you. I had a quick scan around the body but I couldn't find anything."

"Has the photographer been around yet?"

"Yeah."

"Alright, I'll take a look around. Do you have a flashlight?"

Williams nodded, pulling one out from his inner jacket. "I'll interview some of these nosy Nora's over here. See if they saw anything."

Luca walked off towards the body. This was the second girl they found in a matter of weeks, and it was always the same MO: young blonde woman, well dressed, fine clothes, gunshot to the chest. He wondered what brought someone to murder her. What did she do?

He scanned the area, the yellow light bouncing off bushes and broken twigs. She wasn't murdered here, but definitely dumped. Someone wanted her to be found. Luca turned and walked the perimeter, heading south towards the end of the park. It wasn't rare to find evidence this far from the body, particularly if the girl struggled. The moon shone above him, concealed by the lights of the city. He heard glasses clinking and music blaring from a dance club down the road. It would be hard to hear someone screaming with the loud music and drunks.

As Luca scanned the area, his light hit an obscure object lying underneath a bush. It glistened under the beam of light. He walked over and bent down, using his pencil to inspect it. It was a woman's purse. The midnight blue accessory shone like a diamond, its content spewed across the grass. Luca fished his pencil through the bag. "Hey, Williams!"

"Yeah?" his partner shouted from across the field.

"I've found something."

Williams reached him as Luca searched the newly found evidence. He pulled out a lipstick, bus ticket and a few coins.

"What did you find?"

"The girl's purse. There's just the usual stuff in here."

"What's that then?" Williams asked, bending down to point.

Luca followed his finger, noticing a morphine ampoule slip out among the woman's other belongings. He picked it up, his brow furrowed. It was the length of a matchstick, the item instantly recognizable. "What on earth is this woman doing with an US Army issued morphine ampoule?"

Williams picked up the purse and went through it. "There is not another one in here."

"It's very strange. I haven't seen one of those in years," Luca said, jotting down the contents of the purse in his notepad. "I wonder what she is doing with it."

"Do you think it's planted?"

"Doubt it."

"Maybe kept it as a memoriam for lost boyfriend or husband in the war?" Duke suggested.

Luca shrugged. "Could be, but highly unlikely. The exporting of morphine to the US troops was highly monitored, and she doesn't look like the type of girl to work in those factories."

"Was the other girl found with morphine?"

"No," Luca replied. "But somehow this seems linked."

"How did she get her hands on it then? Drug ring?" Williams asked.

"Maybe. But someone meant business," Luca said. "Look at the gunshot. It's at point blank range. Judging by the width of the wound, it could have been a Magnum revolver."

"The war affected you that much, huh?"

"What?" Luca looked up at his partner, his face obscured by the darkness.

"You know a lot about weapons," he observed.

"I fired a lot of them in the war, Duke," Luca replied, climbing to his feet. "It's something I'd rather forget."